Burning Rage

A Ced Buckley Civil War Mystery

Kelly J. O'Grady

Cover Image: "Prairie fires of the great west," Currier & Ives, c. 1872, New York. From the Library of Congress Prints and Photographs Collection, Washington, D.C., 20540.

Other books by Kelly J. O'Grady

Soldiers Just Like You

Clear the Confederate Way! The Irish in the Army of Northern Virginia

ISBN: 150528970X
ISBN-13: 978-1505289701

For Krista,

Love and Support Ever Strong

And they burnt the city with fire, and all that was therein…

--Joshua 7:24

"The Burning of Columbia, South Carolina, February 17, 1865,"
(Sketched by W. Waud), Harper's Weekly, April 8, 1865, p. 217.
From the Library of Congress Prints and Photographs Collection,
Washington, D.C. 20540

Chapter 1

Outside Columbia, South Carolina--February 17, 1865

Lieutenant Tupper Long slumped in the saddle, the long night ride near an end. South Carolina's capital writhed in General Sherman's grasp at last. Wade Hampton's cavalry had defended the Congaree River line for days, barricading roads, destroying bridges and harassing wagon trains, but the Rebel army was on the run now. The young lieutenant's mind wandered. Wasn't it ironic that the Rebels were riding north as the oncoming blue tide rolled up from the south?

The dirt lane ahead wound through swampy woods. The full moon's dull light glinted off fetid water closing in on both sides of the road. Long's heavy red beard shielded an open, fair face. His stocky frame burdened his sore-tongued war horse as only a well-fed soldier could. "This swamp stinks to high heaven," he muttered, but no one heard him. He was riding at the head of the column of two hundred splendid troopers of the 4th Ohio Cavalry, Major General John Logan's escort. The men and horses behind him snaked along the road for half a mile.

The swamp smell rose up in great yellow clouds of sulfur stink, and it was getting stronger, Long thought. Some men began to wretch uncomfortably, he noticed, turning in the saddle and looking back. Long blinked his eyes, starting to water with the cloying rank odor. He pulled his yellow kerchief up over his nose. Rounding the next bend the trooper blinked again and shook his head. "What in...God's...creation?" Long wasn't sure what he was seeing in the half light. The road straightened out for about a mile, a flat, low ribbon of sand nestled under overarching live oaks.

A hundred pinpoints of dull light lined both sides of the lane, twinkling low along the ground with reflected moonglow. The smell was intolerable now, more like rotting meat than swamp. As Long's troopers drew closer to the lights, the horses started to nicker and rear at the sight and stink. At the first of the lights, Long halted the column, holding his hand over the kerchief to seal out the rotting stench.

He nimbly dismounted and knelt down in front of the lights on the left side of the road, trying to get a better look at the phenomenon. He leaned in close but could not make out anything as a bank of clouds snuffed out the moon. The night without the moon was darker than an African field hand, Long thought. The oaks and the swamp conspired to make it so. Something splashed in the distant water, something big, an alligator perhaps, Long surmised. He felt uneasy kneeling in the darkness; a cold aloneness chilled him, even though he was surrounded by the mightiest army in South Carolina. Minutes passed and the moon stayed cloaked. The persistent blackness frustrated him.

"Orderly! Fetch a torch!" the impatient lieutenant finally ordered down the column. Presently a wide-eyed boy ran up with a dim flickering lantern. The black night swallowed the lamp's light as if it was a single firefly. Long took the lantern and returned to his investigation. Kneeling down again, he held the lamp closer, bringing his head to within a few inches of the fairy-like lights. It took a second to realize that he was staring into the eyes of a dead man. The lifeless eyes lit up again as the moon reappeared overhead. Long's screams echoed through the dark sky. "Holy Jesus! What have the bloody traitors done? The murdering sons of Satan!"

The closest troopers jumped down from their horses and ran to their leader, gathering around him, pistols drawn. They saw Long recoil, rising to his feet with the lantern held high, and they too stepped back when the light illuminated the ghoulish scene. Long's blood-curdling curses continued as he walked along the road a little further. "These are Kilpatrick's men. Mountaineers from the look of them! They have slaughtered our advance guard! That is Lieutenant Blake of the Kentuckians! The traitor blackguards have added murder and mutilation to their crimes!" Long's troopers hung back, speechless, peering after their raving lieutenant, wondering if he'd lost his mind; lost it to his hatred for the Confederates.

A minute later the sun crested the horizon and the rest of the Yankee column saw the butcher sight for themselves: a gruesome line of at least fifty severed heads along the road. All of them appeared to be Union cavalrymen, some with yellow bandannas still tied around the stumps of their necks, some wearing trooper kepis still. The heads had been carefully placed two feet apart, eyes open, screaming, snarling, contorted faces watching the road. Bayonets and picket pins, 15-inch long iron spikes used by the cavalry to hitch their horses to the ground, had been driven through the top of each skull, spiking the heads into the sand. The 4th Ohio men stood in the gloaming, mouths agape.

"Lieutenant," a sergeant called, pointing a trembling finger further along the road, "Look at that!" Up ahead, a heaping pile of headless bodies blocked the lane. A curious clutch of Ohioans who had lazily walked forward froze in horror when they saw the corpses stacked like cord wood. Some of these men began to slowly back away from the row of heads, whose expressions seemed to be mocking them, crying out or screaming in anguish. The smell of rotting human flesh overcame one man who vomited in the sand. Others followed suit though whether they were sickened with the rot or just plain fear, no one could say. Long watched his column fall apart and bellowed with rage. He knew he needed to get out of there fast. There was nothing he could do for Blake and the others now anyway. He walked swiftly back to his horse, grabbing a bull-necked subordinate along the way. "Sergeant, ride back to General Logan and report what we have found here. Tell him I have continued on to Columbia."

"Yes, Lieutenant," the burly man answered with a salute. The rough looking fellow seemed relieved that he could turn around; that he would not have to ride through the cursed place.

Long jumped into the saddle, twirled his mount in the road and yelled, "Troopers, mount up! We ride for Columbia! We shall make them pay for this!"

Chapter 2

In Columbia, later that day-General Logan's Headquarters

Brigadier General Hugh Judson Kilpatrick prodded his enormous black steed up the front steps of the mansion, ducked as he rode through the double front doors, and cantered down a wide center hall. A brown smear of dirt and droppings led from the entrance down the corridor to the ornate parlor where Logan had his headquarters office. Kilpatrick wasn't the only one who'd ridden his horse into the home of Senator John Preston, the husband of Wade Hampton's sister. The entire house reeked of horse manure, but the brash division commander of cavalry in General Sherman's 60,000 man army lived with horses and didn't notice the smell. His mind was on the murder of his scouts.

He dismounted with a thud, his heavy, knee-high boots shaking the floor boards and rattling the massive crystal chandelier overhead. He carelessly shoved open the parlor door which banged against the wall. Inside, Logan started at the disturbance and the other man in the room, perched at the oversized mahogany desk, jumped up in anger. William Tecumseh Sherman was over six feet tall in his boots, a wiry man with short tousled hair and a scruffy beard. His well-kept uniform glistened with columns of shiny brass buttons and a large constellation of gold stars orbited his bony shoulders.

"Blast all, Kilpatrick! Why do you have to slam in here like a bear in a bake shop?"

"Sorry, General Sherman, sir. I didn't know you were here, sir." Kilpatrick snapped to attention and saluted the army commander. The cavalry leader was small and thin, with bushy sidewhiskers, black eyes and, some said, an even blacker soul. At twenty-nine years old, the West Pointer from New Jersey had earned a rapacious, immoral reputation. His nickname, "Kill Cavalry," alluded to his penchant for daring attacks and foolhardy judgment. The officers who served under him thought him more beast than man.

"Apology accepted," Sherman replied more calmly. "I knew when I brought you to this army that you were a bloody fool, but I wanted just that kind of man to command my cavalry on this expedition." The army commander smiled when he said this. The line of rockinghorse teeth across his pinched face, slashing through hirsute jaws, did little to convey genuine humor however. The smile seemed more like the crazy sneer of a riled up baboon. He returned Kilpatrick's salute, sat down again and gestured to the others to sit as well.

"So what can you tell me? How goes the operation now?"

"General, the rail depots on Gervais Street and Taylor Street are set to burn. That will put the Charlotte Railroad and the South Carolina line out of business for a time. The warehouse district, what the town folk call Cotton Town, is also ready for the torch. My men likewise will destroy the tracks along Washington Street when the time is right."

"Just so. Excellent, Kilpatrick. And the public buildings in the courthouse square…the statehouse?"

"We are working on that. Yes, sir. And Colonel Poe of the engineers has secured the arsenal which is rich in shot, shell and musket balls. Also we have destroyed the newspaper presses and dismantled the Confederate mint, its foundry, with numerous dies and hand presses. The money is being gambled with by the men as if it still holds value." Kilpatrick chuckled at this and Sherman leaned back and sighed with satisfaction.

"I feel no remorse for this destruction. This city deserves it and these facilities cannot be left for the enemy to use against us when we move on. But Kilpatrick, and you too Logan, listen well. There are some parts of the city that must be left alone. For instance, this nun, Mother Lynch, who keeps hounding me about her convent school. She says she taught my girl, Minnie, back in Ohio. I suppose that's true, but her brother is the bishop of Charleston and a hard Rebel." Sherman had been raised a Catholic by his adoptive family.

He married into that devout Catholic clan, but the general was not much of a Catholic himself, even if he did have a soft spot in his heart for the faith.

Recently his wife had taken their children to South Bend, Indiana, to enroll them at the Notre Dame of the Lake school there. "Her brother's allegiance is beside the point, though. The Ursuline convent and school should be secured. They have students there and I have promised their protection." Kilpatrick and Logan nodded their understanding. "Now, enough about the city. What of the murders that Lieutenant Long encountered yesterday? Logan, what say you about that?"

John Logan was an Illinois politician before the war. He had been the commander of the Army of Tennessee until Sherman relieved him of that command. If he was unhappy about that, he didn't show it. He seemed content being back in charge of the XV Corps. At thirty-nine, his dark good looks had provided him the nickname "Black Jack." As he spoke, he twirled a drooping ebony mustache long enough to catch a fish.

"General, Lieutenant Long is here if you wish to speak with him. His initial revulsion at what he found has turned into a brooding anger now, I fear, though I can understand it. We have…ah…interviewed the few stragglers we have found in the countryside, and some townsfolk to see if a particular Rebel unit was responsible. We have nothing yet."

"What about the mayor of the city, Dr. Goodwin? Has he been any help with this at all?"

"He was helpful in that he brought us a collection of undertakers and some Negroes to help clean up the bloody mess along that road. I confess that it was difficult to watch and an infernal chore to try to match the remains, each to his own."

"Oh, I cannot imagine. And do not wish too. But God I would like to catch and punish those responsible. The bodies are being dealt with properly, then?"

"Yes, as properly as they may be under the circumstances."

"We believe the Rebs committed this horrid act to terrorize us, but it has only made us even more resolute in this campaign," Kilpatrick added.

"The troops have heard about the atrocity already and that explains the widespread looting and destruction that our provost is reporting," Logan declared.

"That sort of horseplay does not concern me," Sherman countered. "A certain amount of that behavior is not only expected, but can be useful in breaking the spirit of the enemy, while bolstering the spirit of our own soldiers. On the other hand, we sit here in Wade Hampton's family palace. We will use it for our purposes. We may treat it roughly, but we will not destroy it out of sheer vandalism. Senator Preston's house has no military purpose. Sure Preston married into this boastful family, but he'll not suffer for that reason alone. It is Wade Hampton who fancies himself a special champion of South Carolina, not his sister and he is on the run now."

"They say his grandfather was the wealthiest man in the country in his day," Kilpatrick said. "My troopers have already set upon the other Hampton estates, Woodlands, Millwood and General Hampton's own Diamond Hill. They'll no longer be producing food or cotton for the enemy." Sherman shook his head, resigned to the fact that the Hampton family legacy would be irreparably damaged by the war.

"Very well," he sighed, drawing himself up in his chair. "Now, to the reason for my visit here. Logan, bring in young Long and let us get the horrible particulars from him."

Logan left to fetch his cavalryman, but when he returned, he had in tow not only Long, but a white-wimpled nun of about thirty years and a one-legged young man in a gray hooded robe who walked with a hand-carved blackthorn cane. "General Sherman, General Kilpatrick, I give you Mother Baptista Lynch, the superior of the Ursuline Convent, and Brother Cedric Buckley."

Chapter 3

Mother Lynch was all of five feet tall, with a sweet round face and blue eyes that could burn a hole through armor plate. She didn't wait for Sherman or the others to speak but charged across the room as if she owned the house. "General Sherman. What a pleasure to finally meet you."

"Yes, I feel I already know you from the three missives you've sent me since yesterday," Sherman retorted sarcastically. The army commander clearly had no time for the woman. She plowed on though, bobbing her head as she spoke, the large, white, boat-like cornette that topped her habit tossing about like a ship in a storm. Buckley hung back, letting the energetic woman take the lead.

"General, you must realize that your reputation precedes you. And I am charged with the safety of my school. I only wish to know that you will refrain from burning it and this city, no matter how wicked, to the ground." Mother Lynch seemed hardly like a mother at all. Still youthful, she spoke with a cultured Southern accent with just a hint of the brogue given her by her Irish immigrant parents back in her hometown of Cheraw. Sherman waved his hands as if to dismiss all her fears.

"Sister."

"Mother," she retorted pointedly.

"*Mother* Lynch, as I have told you through my subordinates, I have no wish to destroy your school, your convent or the city as a whole."

"But your subordinates, sir, have not the high ideals that you obviously hold. I have seen hundreds of them in fits of rage and drinking. They take what they want, destroy what they don't and your officers seem unable or unwilling to stop them."

"And have these soldiers harmed a bit of your Ursuline School?"

"Not yet, but Brother Buckley here tells me that your soldiers are building bonfires just down Main Street. Like fervent Apocalypsians, we await the final conflagration." Sherman stifled a smile at the nun's dramatic assertion. He looked over at Buckley, a lad of perhaps eighteen, rangy at six feet tall, but lanky like a horse run wet for months at a time. His clear green eyes and boyish attitude hid the fact that he had been a Confederate soldier defending Charleston only a year ago. He wore a simple rough gray tunic that came down to mid thigh. An oversized hand-carved chestnut wood rosary dangled from his waist. Sherman noticed his missing leg, cut off just below the knee, and supported by a sturdy length of blackthorn. Remnants of homespun gray trousers fell to a well-worn boot and stopped just short of the remarkable, spiked, dark-wood peg-leg.

"And does Brother Buckley know anything of military affairs?" the general countered condescendingly, beginning to anger at this unwanted intrusion. He did not wait for an answer, but blustered on. "I tell you, Mother Lynch, your school will be spared. I will double the guard I have already provided for you and I wish you to leave this house now and refrain from interfering with military business!" Sherman stood up as if the interview was over. Kilpatrick rose, as did Logan, who moved to show the religious out, but the mother superior was not finished.

She did not budge and seemed to dare the darkly menacing general to make her. Logan had opened the door expecting the visitors to leave, but when they didn't, he awkwardly stood there like he was a servant rather than a major general. Lieutenant Long knew enough to keep his mouth shut. Buckley held his ground with Mother Lynch, tapping his blackthorn stick on the floor nervously and clutching his crucifix with the long thin fingers of his right hand. But he did not speak. Mother Lynch crossed her arms resolutely and looked over at the young brother with a tilted head.

"In fact, General, Brother Buckley was indeed in the army just last year, so he does know something of military affairs," she answered, more calmly now. "And the Brother is something of a detective as well."

"A detective?" Sherman said incredulously. "A detective of crime, do you mean?"

"Exactly, General, and he has been looking into the crime perpetrated along the road into the city yesterday."

"Just so!" Sherman exclaimed. He eyed the boy closely, appraising him seriously for the first time. "Tell me, Brother. What battle did this to you?" He stabbed a finger at Buckley's ravaged limb. Buckley seemed as calm as the sea on a warm summer day, looking the imposing general straight in the eye. He answered quietly.

"It was last July, sir. On James Island. I was with Colquitt's raid on General Slocum's expedition along the Stono." Buckley tapped the floor rapidly again and finished the jumpy drumroll with a tympanic rap on his blackthorn leg. He clomped over to a red silk parlor chair embroidered in gold lace and sat down uninvited. Sherman followed him with squinting eyes and a bewildered look.

"That was when the 54th Massachusetts stood and fought, wasn't it?" Kilpatrick interjected.

"Indeed it was," Buckley replied enthusiastically, pleased that someone here remembered the regiment of black soldiers. "You may recall they were captured later in an assault on Battery Wagner. At least some of them were."

"Yes, Battery Wagner, an infernal fight for nothing, if I remember the reports," Sherman said.

"Truly it *was* for nothing, General. The fort was held, but today it is like the Mayan ziggurats or the Egyptian obelisks. A monument to a lost empire. As a child I loved to build sandcastles on Folly Beach. It was the happiest time of my life. Wagner is just another castle of sand, another collapsed sand castle. When I was a little sand-caked boy, no one ever told me that the ultimate destiny of every sand castle ever built is total destruction." Buckley nonchalantly threw his false leg across the other like he was sitting down to a camp card game. Sherman stood in the middle of the room, pondering the disarming, philosophical young man. The commander began to feel like a visitor in his own office, but he sat down too and continued,

"Yes, I remember reading about the imprisonment of the 54th,the trial and acquittal. They were charged with being rebellious slaves and were to be re-enslaved or even summarily executed. The trial reinstated their lawful status as Union prisoners of war."

"I testified in that trial, sir."

"Now, what can you have known about all that?"

"You see, my Union friend, by the grace of God, I was rescued by the very same black men who were on trial—on trial for their lives. They found me half dead near Grimball's Landing. They saved me from a brushfire, and gave me water…and hope…hope that I could survive. I testified about all of that in the trial and made a vow that I would take a vocation because I lived."

"Just so! A one-legged priest. Aren't you something then?" Sherman's face stretched into a smile that crinkled his eyes.

"I'm not a priest, General, I'm a Benedictine brother. But I do have some information about the murder of your men."

"Tell me then. And Logan and Kilpatrick here."

"Yes, it was Kilpatrick's men they were after."

"What? What do you mean?"

"You see, sir, these murders resulted from what happened last year; when I was still that humble soldier. Last February, around Richmond. With General Kilpatrick here."

"What are you talking about, boy?" Kilpatrick asked balefully.

"How do you know all this anyway?" Sherman wanted to know.

"The men who did this, who killed the Union troopers and mutilated the bodies. They were fighting in Virginia last year…when Kilpatrick raided around Richmond. One man who knew the story found himself incarcerated by the Columbia city police for a time. I heard him confess these things--the whole tale-- before he went to meet his maker." Sherman stood up, swiveled his head around and clamped incredulous eyes on Kilpatrick.

Kilpatrick stared open mouthed at the young religious, then slowly turned to the others, first looking at Sherman, then Logan, then Mother Lynch. He swallowed hard and shook his head. "I...I don't understand," he stammered. "Partisans, deserters, criminals did this." Brother Buckley still reclined in his appropriated chair, his long limbs spread apart. He leaned forward on his cane with both hands and seemed to be a much older man suddenly—a professor lecturing his students.

"Perhaps, sir. The men who are involved in this are invisible to you, General. They fight an invisible war. They die, but their deaths are not noticed. Their blood is unseen, their loss is not grieved, their lives are dishonored. The man who died in Columbia's jail; the soldier who confessed. He saw them; he told me all that he had seen."

"This is a fantastic story that gets more interesting every second," Mother Lynch interjected, a self-satisfied smile on her cherubic face. Sherman's eyes lingered indignantly on the woman even as he spoke to Brother Buckley.

"I fail to see how all of this is related." A clearly intrigued Sherman looked over at Kilpatrick again, who had broken into a nervous sweat. The army commander sat down at the desk again, ready to get to the bottom of things. "Start at the beginning and tell the whole story, Brother." He waved his arm at the others. "Gentlemen, Mother, please be seated. We all should hear this." Lieutenant Long remained standing at the door, as if on guard. Brother Buckley settled back in the comfortable red chair and looked up at the coffered ceiling as if seeking inspiration from the almost royal appointments of the mansion's parlor. Mother Lynch sat opposite the boy detective in a matching chair, while the others crowded together on a green damask sofa facing them.

"As I said, my investigations have revealed that this is not the first atrocity concerning those dead troopers in the swamp. I can show that all of this began last February on the outskirts of Richmond… and it is not over yet. What General Kilpatrick has set in motion may well end in tragedy for us all."

Chapter 4

One year earlier-February 1864, Ely's Ford, Virginia.

Primeval, that's what it seemed. Long-haired, bearded men crouched close around a blazing campfire, trying to survive a cold night, struggling to avoid the wet ground, hoping to frighten away hungry predators. The scene could have been from ten thousand years ago; a group of hunters plotting an attack, stalking an unsuspecting prey. But the cluster of Union officers in the clearing on a bluff above the roaring Rapidan River had not returned from the primordial past. They were very much modern men in the midst of the most efficient killing machine the world had ever known: the Union force of 130,000 men known as the Army of the Potomac.

A winter rain had swept through the Blue Ridge Mountain foothills two nights earlier and its downpour had swollen the river west of Fredericksburg. Judson Kilpatrick had just arrived back from a secret meeting with President Lincoln and Secretary of War Edwin Stanton. The fire in his dark eyes told Colonel Ulric Dahlgren all he needed to know. The plan was approved. Dahlgren rested on a cracker box amidst the others, the officers who had both legs still. At twenty-two, the handsome, blonde-headed son of Sweden knew his life was all but over. Gettysburg had taken his leg, but he would not quit. It was partially his fault. He was the one who had wanted out of the safe staff jobs his famous father, Admiral John Dahlgren, inventor of the Dahlgren gun, had finagled for him. But his loss was not completely his fault, no. He would not quit until the Rebels were made to pay for his pain, for his lost youth, his lost looks, his ruined life.

Judson Kilpatrick snapped him out of his self-pity for a moment. "Alright Dahlgren, our plans are perfect. We will raid the cursed Rebel capital!" The cavalry general treated the younger man like a little brother. At times too familiar, often too controlling, always condescending. This was something that rubbed the grandson of a Swedish aristocrat the wrong way from the start. Kilpatrick outranked him in the army, but he was not his social equal. The senior man unrolled a map of Virginia and stabbed at key locations as he talked. "Custer is heading to Charlottesville as a diversion. We will drive off Hampton's guard at the ford and ride for Spotsylvania Court House. There we will split up. You will take five hundred men and ride east of Goochland Court House, cross over the James River and recross to come into Richmond from the south. The blackguards will never think we'd try that. I will take the remaining three thousand troopers and head down the Telegraph Road right into the city. They shall be trapped in our pincers!"

"And what if Hampton follows? Shall we engage him or outrun him?"

"He will not be able to stay with us for long. We have fresher horses, and he will not leave Lee's army to follow us cross country." Dahlgren did not seem convinced of this, but did not object to Kilpatrick's conclusion. "Dividing our force will make him choose anyway. Whoever the rich old devil tails must lose him before we meet up again."

"And where will we meet?" Dahlgren loathed having to ask Kilpatrick anything, much less listen to "Kill Cavalry" explain his plans to him, but if it led to revenge against the Rebels, so be it.

"Here," the general pointed at the map lit only by the campfire. "Hungary Station. It is a central meeting place for both of us with arteries directly into Richmond."

"And we are sure the city is held by little more than three thousand militia?"

"That is what Mrs. Van Lew had told our operatives. Stanton believes the information."

"Do they not call her Crazy Bet?"

"The Rebels do. She affects an eccentric public demeanor.

We believe it is an act she puts on so that Richmond authorities do not see her as a threat. As you must know, she is a staunch Unionist living in the heart of the Confederate capital and no one takes her seriously."

"Except us," Dahlgren said sarcastically. He did not think Kilpatrick even caught his smart remark; the buffoon.

"It is a calculated risk, I suppose. It will be well worth it if we can free those in the rank prisons in that wicked city. Belle Isle, Libby Hill, and Castles Thunder and Lightning."

"Indeed," Dahlgren agreed with little enthusiasm. He stood up with a grunting effort, hopping up and down to catch his balance over the prosthetic leg fashioned out of hard oak and leather harnesses. The heavy replacement made Dahlgren feel trussed up like the horse he would ride this night. Kilpatrick made a show of pulling a silver pocketwatch from his waistcoat. He turned the watch face toward the fire.

"It's 11 o'clock now. We have little time to waste…Major Wolfe!"

"Sir!"

"Give the order to mount up."

Chapter 5

A driving rain was turning to sleet as Kilpatrick's troopers picked up the pace near Yellow Tavern. "That's the Brook Hill up ahead. Richmond's outer defenses. We are but five miles from the belly of the beast," Kilpatrick yelled to his staff.

"Hampton has given up, General," Lieutenant-Colonel Fielder Jones hollered back. He led the 8th Indiana, a new unit with little battle experience. "Richmond is ours!"

They were on the Telegraph Road north of Richmond. The rumble of over three thousand horses, with a train of six artillery pieces, and several caissons and ambulances, moved steadily through the sparsely populated countryside. It seemed a fair sail into the Rebel city unopposed. The Union force had left Hampton's pursuers, about three hundred horse troops, miles behind. They'd had a free-for-all at Beaverdam Station, destroying the Virginia Central Railroad, cutting the telegraph lines, and burning the station buildings. And they had seen no one on the road since the South Anna River crossing at Ground Squirrel Bridge.

The sun was just beginning to illuminate the horizon; it cast a dull, dark light cloaked by rain and ice. The rolling farm land stretching out on both sides of the road seemed a rich prize in itself, a powerful part of creation that gave back five-fold what an honest farmer put into it before the war. Kilpatrick and Jones rode at the head of the column, crossed a rickety wooden bridge over Brook Run, a little creek swollen with rain, and started up the next rise toward the capital city. Fog was rising off the rushing water, filling the natural ravine with a dense white shroud. No one saw the line of six guns at the top of the hill until it was too late.

With Dahlgren-Near Goochland Courthouse

Ice pellets stung Colonel Dahlgren's tender pale face like blasted sand on a porcelain teacup. He patted his black horse, Valkyrie, named after the handmaidens of Odin, the Norse war god. Dahlgren's troop of horse soldiers had been unopposed all night, slipping away from Kilpatrick's main force at Spotsylvania with little notice. The Confederates, Hampton or anyone else, had not even bothered to pursue them. That was good, Dahlgren thought to himself. Isolation in enemy territory meant a free hand to do whatever he pleased.

At Frederick Hall Station, he cut the Virginia Central Railroad and as he passed through the deserted crossroads village at Crozier, he didn't see a living soul. The cold rain kept spying eyes inside and closed shut in cozy slumber. The ride had taken most of the night with two stops to water and feed the horses. The James would part before them soon. Galloping down the final plunge of the river valley, Dahlgren's troop burst out of the tree line and the young colonel watched the sky open over treacherously swollen water. Just then the morning dawned through heavy gray clouds.

"Column, ho!" Major Wolfe called when he saw the impassable river, fifty yards across, rushing over it normal banks. Wolfe was a monster of a man, over six and a half feet tall with a back as wide as a sixteen hand stallion. His bear-like arms terminated in hands that resembled good-sized hams when balled up into fists. And Wolfe did use his fists. Thirty years old now, he had been the foreman in a lumber mill back in Louisville—a boss no man, black or white, dared cross on the job. A beastly countenance made him even more intimidating. Mangy brown hair slithered down around his bull neck, while dark heavy eyebrows shadowed cruel brown eyes. His facial hair was sparse and unkempt, swirling in long tendrils where it grew, but leaving patches of pale skin where it didn't. The effect lent his face the unfortunate look of an old possum. In the gray light, Wolfe's 2nd Kentucky, hard-bitten mountain men, stopped abruptly. Some of the horses neighed and reared with the rough treatment. A detachment from the 2nd New York under Captain John F. B. Mitchell brought up the rear. Dahlgren peered impatiently across the muddy James.

"Blast this wretched weather!" He had to yell to be heard above the crashing torrent. "Wolfe, we need a local guide who can help us ford this river. There must be a better place to cross." The cavalry leader pointed uphill toward a fine farmhouse perched on a knoll less than a mile upstream. "Roust those people and see about that."

"Yes, sir," Wolfe replied dutifully. He picked five men and sent the squad to inquire about a guide. The column stood at ease while Dahlgren and Wolfe rode under some trees trying to get out of the steady falling sleet. Though the sun was rising, it did little to warm them. Dahlgren clapped his gloved hand on his wooden leg and motioned for the Kentuckian to move in closer.

"Wolfe," he almost whispered. "Now is the time to split up our force as we planned. The condition of the river gives us the excuse. Captain Mitchell is not part of this as you know. The 2nd New York usually rides with Sheridan, not Kilpatrick. I shall send them along the north shore of the James River canal with orders to disable the locks and burn any mills, stores and boats he finds. I shall tell him to plan to meet up with Kilpatrick at Hungary Station. That will take him and his New Yorkers out of the picture as we head to Belle Isle and our ultimate target." Wolfe thought about the risks inherent in such a mission and worried about splitting an already meager force. He wanted as many Union men as he could muster once they entered the Confederate city.

"Will the prisoners in Richmond join us in our mission, do you expect, Colonel?"

"Major, from what I've heard about prison conditions there, our men, once freed, will jump at the chance to take revenge on the Rebel leaders who have punished them so. Yes, they will scream for it, as shall I." Dahlgren shivered with rage as he spoke, thinking of the moment of triumph. Wolfe bared his teeth, pondering the opportunity to torch the traitor city and take what treasure he would find there. "Fetch Captain Mitchell now," the colonel growled at Wolfe. As the Kentuckian rode off, the squad sent to find a guide cantered up with a young colored man of about fourteen years riding behind one of the cavalrymen. A sergeant saluted.

"Colonel, this boy is called Martin Hill. He says he knows a river ford we can use."

"Greetings, Martin," Dahlgren purred. "There is a Yankee dollar in it for you if we find this ford quickly."

"Yes, suh. Go upstream just heah," the boy said pointing. He was light-skinned, with close cut brown hair. He did not make eye contact with the colonel which gave Dahlgren an uneasy feeling about the local boy.

"Is there a ford to the east? That is the direction we mean to head."

"Oh, no suh. The closest ford is just two miles west. A good, hard-bottom crossing, no matter the weather."

"As you say. Lead on, then," Dahlgren answered.

Chapter 6

With Kilpatrick-On the Telegraph Road

BOOM! BOOM! BOOM! The Confederate guns perched on Brook Hill blasted fire out of the gray gloom. On the road below, Kilpatrick's horse careened in a circle while the general tried to control his mount and figure out what was going on up ahead at the same time. The enemy guns were well-entrenched behind ten foot walls of dirt and logs and covered by the fog. The general looked about and saw that no one in his troop had been hit.

"The bloody green blackguards have fired over our heads!" Kilpatrick yelled. "Column! Dismount and take cover!" The Federal troopers quickly evolved into a battle line. The force dismounted and sought cover in the bushes on either side of the open highway. They sent their horses to the rear. A few seconds later another volley of artillery missed again, landing fifty yards in front of their position. Kilpatrick spied a line of Confederate riflemen at the base of the hill and resolved to push them aside. He ordered a rifle volley of his own directed at the defenders.

"Fire at those rifles there," he ordered, "And bring up our guns quickly!"

Confederate Defenses-Atop Brook Hill

Colonel Walter Stevens was a New Yorker, a graduate of the United States Military Academy and… a Rebel, in charge of the fortifications around Richmond. He had but five hundred men on

Brook Hill, mostly factory workers from Tredegar Iron Works, to oppose Kilpatrick's fearsome cavalry division. He had known for some time that most of the city's defenders weren't really soldiers and he'd tried his best to train them for battle, but when the first volley missed completely he fully realized what trouble Richmond was in.

When word had come yesterday by telegraph that a large Yankee force was barreling toward the city from Spotsylvania, General Lee's son, George Washington Custis Lee, had taken the bulk of Richmond's defense forces west of the city. Acting on reports that Union cavalry was raiding down the Virginia Central line, Lee gambled that an attack would approach from that direction. But the main striking force, probably led by Kilpatrick himself, was here on the main road and Stevens' little detachment was all that stood between it and the Confederate capital.

The New Yorker knew he had to stand and fight, and get word to his superiors at headquarters that he needed help. Stevens turned to a young lieutenant just as a volley of rifles roared across from the Yankee side. The subordinate flinched, though the fire had no chance of reaching Brook Hill's crest. The commander let out an anguished groaned when another volley from his own green batteries missed again.

"Lieutenant, send word to General Elzey that Kilpatrick is here in force, a division with train, and that reinforcements are needed."

"Yes, sir. Right away, sir," the junior officer answered. Stevens couldn't help but notice that the boy's salute was offered with a trembling hand. The youth might have been eighteen, and was probably tapped for rank because he'd been a V.M.I. cadet a few months before.

When Stevens turned back around he saw his picket line running toward him, retreating from the base of the hill.

With Dahlgren-On the James River

Wolfe backed away unsatisfied. He had beaten Martin Hill with practiced brutality. But a few crushing punches to the boy's face and a body blow that drove him to his knees were not enough. Even so, Dahlgren had ended the punishment. The colonel loomed over his captive, his yellow gauntlets in his free hand, a horse whip in the other. A 6-pounder field gun and limber sat precariously in the fast moving water, sunk to the hubs. Martin knelt on the ground, heaving for breath, his hands bound behind him. The boy's cream-coffee face ran with thin blood watered by the rain melting on his hot skin. His upraised eyes focused on the noose dangling from the big oak tree standing just by the shore.

"You have lied to us, boy, but you have not fooled us," the blonde colonel thundered from astride his stallion. Martin tried to explain; if he could not convince these men that he had made an honest mistake, he sensed that they would kill him.

"No, suh. I thought this was the crossing. It has been raining for days. I have never seen the river this high. I swear it, sir."

"You work for our enemies, your masters. How can you betray yourself so, betray your own people so?" The boy looked defiant suddenly. He glared directly at a disgusted and sneering Dahlgren.

"My people are from Virginia, suh. I would not betray them. My master is my father anyway." Dahlgren exploded, realizing now how this boy had intentionally wasted so much of his time. He angrily threw the whip at Wolfe, who raised it high over his head and brought it down hard across the boy's light brown face. The leather cut deeply, leaving a slash of oozing bright blood that spouted from the top of his forehead and ran across his nose to the side of his neck. Martin grunted in pain and fell backwards on the sleet encrusted ground. Wolfe stepped forward and kicked the boy into the river, a certain death sentence in the cold, rushing water.

"Now, now Major, that is no way to treat our Southern host," Dahlgren cooed sarcastically. "Fish him out so we can hang him properly." Martin was flailing around like a hooked trout, arching his back, trying to keep his face above water. Two soldiers roughly grabbed his feet and dragged the boy out of the river. He lay there, bleeding and shivering in the cold.

"Martin Hill," the sadistic colonel announced sternly, dropping the simpering voice he'd used a moment before. "I find you guilty of the sabotage of a United States Army detachment and hereby sentence you to death by hanging." The boy began to cry, and then he screamed in pain as his muscles started to cramp from the cold. Dahlgren looked over at Wolfe and smiled.

"Thus always to… traitors? Kill him now, Major."

Chapter 7

On Brook Hill

Colonel Stevens stepped forward, sword raised high, as the pickets crested the hill running straight down the middle of the road. The fleeing men had the wide eyes of frightened children, but when they saw the old engineer standing there calmly, they stopped in their tracks. Stevens used that moment to enlist them into his rally. "Battalion! Form up here behind these brave men, two ranks now!"

"Colonel," the breathless sergeant of the pickets called. "I've never seen so many Yankee troopers before. It must be Kilpatrick's entire division down there." The panicked soldier was sixteen at the most.

"Yes, Sergeant, I know, and we must hold them to save the city." Stevens said this in a matter-of-fact, steady voice as if he'd just calculated the square footage of a new warehouse.

"Yes, sir. We must," the boy replied sheepishly. But the young man straightened his back and set his jaw. Moments before, the sergeant had planned to run all the way back to Broad Street. That was all he could imagine doing in the face of such a Federal army. But here was the old man, Stevens was forty, determined to fight on this ground, and so must he.

"Bring the Napoleons into the road and fire again!" Stevens commanded. He would get some fire on those people if it was the last thing he did. And chances were very good that it would be.

With Dahlgren

The black boy's bleeding body swayed in the cold wind coming off the water; then it dropped again, the force of the fall driving him to his knees. The rough-roped noose cut into Martin's neck making it hard to breath, but with wide eyes the boy gazed up into the tree where the rope was secured. He had pondered the arrangement for several minutes now. At first he had prayed the rope would somehow break or come loose when the moment came. Now, alone with the sadist Wolfe, he begged his maker for a swift end to it all. A quick death is all he could hope for.

The minutes seemed like months. Dahlgren and his force had moved from the river bank awhile ago, but Martin's torture continued. Wolfe smiled as he wound the death-tether tighter around the pommel of his saddle. The half-breed liar should linger, he thought, as he edged the horse forward inch by deadly inch and slowly lifted the traitor farther off the cold ground. The horse's advance pulled Martin up from his knees as the rope tightened. Once on his feet the prisoner instinctively tried to run; a pitiful, desperate attempt to escape his execution. But Wolfe merely spurred the horse farther forward and pulled the boy off his feet again. Martin's legs spidered around as he fought the tension around his neck. But rather than finish the job, the major reared the horse back again and let the boy drop back to the hard dirt.

The Union major's maniacal laugh drowned out Martin's helpless sobs. The boy lay on the frozen earth, trying to breathe and cry with the same precious air. And then strangled choking sounds filled the wintry sky as the prisoner rose off the ground again, slowly up, up, up until the weight of his body stretched his neck into unconsciousness. "I'll wager he's not dead yet," Wolfe said to himself, backing up his horse again, driving his mount like an exacting farmer carefully plowing a field.

Then he whipped the steed hard and the animal bolted forward with such force that Martin's limp body shot into the air, his neck snapping like a dry twig in winter. Wolfe nodded with satisfaction when he heard the bones crack. A job well done, he thought to himself. "That's what I get paid for," he muttered. He tied the rope off to the nearest branch with workmanlike precision and left the beaten, broken, dead boy hanging there—a warning to other traitors.

A steady bitter blast bore in the winter storm from the west as Wolfe joined the other Union troopers down river and the detachment thundered away. With so much time lost, Dahlgren had decided to forget his plan to cross the river and enter the city from the south. Like the freezing weather, he would ride in from the west. "Wolfe, we must avoid Mitchell as we work our way closer in." They were on the River Road about ten miles from the capital. The two men rode side by side, near the middle of the column.

"Mitchell should be working along the canal, not this far up, Colonel."

"Good, I pray he is well south of here. Our plans still can be salvaged, but not with the New Yorkers along."

"Yes, sir. It seems odd that we have to watch for our own men as well as the enemy."

"No matter. I make us about eight miles out now. We must pick up the pace and strike quickly."

Just then a rider came up and saluted. "Colonel, sir. Captain Mitchell's detachment is coming up from behind, sir."

Dahlgren looked horrified, but saluted and dismissed the messenger. "Bloody Hades," he muttered. "Wolfe, halt the column. We have to come up with an alternate plan now.

Chapter 8

On the Telegraph Road

Kilpatrick took a bold decision after the second volley missed his advance guard.

The key to decisive cavalry action was speed and maneuver, he knew… and surprise. Having seen the missed volleys, he believed now that the defenders in his front must be green as an August apple or at least soldiers unprepared to fight a battle. He decided to attack. "Lieutenant Jones! Mount up your Indianans and take that hill!" Jones eagerly jumped at the chance.

"Yes, sir! Inn-diii-annaaah! Mount up!" The Indiana regiment, almost five hundred troopers, took to their horses, formed into two ranks, and lined up perpendicular to the road. A thickening fog disguised the rows of horse soldiers arrayed across the rolling fields facing Brook Hill. Here and there, some horses in the lines bucked and reared in anticipation of the grand charge. The animals knew what was coming as much as the men did. The regiment held its position as officers dressed the lines one last time. Sporadic rifle fire cracked in the distance, but the road seemed open before them now. Fog still hid the top of the hill; the enemy as invisible behind their works as actors behind a curtain.

Jones stood in his stirrups and called, "Battalion! Draw sabers! Charge!"

On Brook Hill

Colonel Stevens' timing could not have been better. "Fire!" he ordered, getting off a volley just to prove that his soldiers could do it the right way. Young gunners needed to find a rhythm to be effective, he believed. Stevens had rallied the artillery for another try without regard to the enemy. He could not see where they were concentrating anyway. He had even personally sighted a battery of guns this time, aiming only for the bottom of the valley below. It was sheer luck that the Indiana regiment had formed in the open at the precise moment when six 12-pounder Napoleons went off as one. Exploding case shot reached the Indiana regiment just as its men kicked horses and crouched forward to begin the charge up hill. The first rank of soldiers went flying and dozens of horses fell as hot shot exploded in the dirt along the width of the road. Though the center of his line was decimated, Colonel Jones sent the rest of his regiment forward anyway. "They must reload!" he yelled. "Close up and charge!"

The remaining mounted troops closed the breach and climbed the hill into the teeth of the defenses. The cavalry charge surged forward, a near perfect line of men and mounts in irresistible motion. The fog cleared for an instant, revealing the darkly clad troopers outlined against the dull white atmosphere of a February morning. While the Napoleons reloaded, much larger 30-pounder Parrot rifles in the Brook Hill works opened on the closing Indianans. The colossal Parrott shells blasted the Hoosiers mercilessly, but their colonel would not give up the charge.

"Guide on the road and ride down their works!" Jones implored. The regiment caught glimpses of the defensive positions, now. They could make out the St. Andrew's cross of a Confederate battle flag rippling defiantly behind the smoke from the cannon fire. The remnants of the attacking regiment also could see the line of muskets they would face if they survived the deathly gauntlet of cannons; but stubbornly they rode on.

Atop Brook Hill

With the artillery holding its own, Colonel Stevens turned his attention to his rifle line. "Make this one count, men!" he called out from his new post beside the factory workers now dug in along the road. The officer noticed that many of them held their muskets awkwardly, like young fathers hold a newborn baby. They were used to holding tools, implements of creation, not weapons of destruction. "Aim low and you'll hit your mark!" he encouraged them. It seemed ludicrous that he was still teaching basic techniques with a division of cavalry bearing down on him and the capital city.

"Steady, steady. Wait for it, wait for my order." the colonel begged. He needed his men to be patient while he watched for the right moment to unleash the volley. He knew timing was everything in an encounter like this. Let the enemy get close enough for the fire to do the maximum damage, but not close enough that the charge might carry the position. And the mid-Westerners were getting closer now.

A hundred horsemen galloped along, hunched low, sabers glinting in the gray daylight like the bloody Light Brigade in the Crimea. Stevens held his own saber high and watched through the smoke and the fog. And then he saw a lone Yankee trooper dash beyond his line, waving the colors, exhorting the Hoosiers to finish the job, a mere fifty yards away. Stevens slashed his sword down and bellowed.

"Clear the way! Fire now, boys! Fire now!" And his citizen soldiers responded splendidly. The cloud of death blew a hole through the charge, men falling and mounts collapsing; and the beautiful horses still standing, reared and spun around in chaos and fear. Seconds later another punishing volley from the Confederate artillery scattered the survivors and convinced the rest of the Union attackers to return to their valley of death as quickly as they could.

With Dahlgren-On the River Road west of Richmond

"Colonel Dahlgren, my mission went off better than even I anticipated. We were unopposed, except for a few pickets of Custis Lee's City Battalion." Captain Mitchell stood next to his horse, looking up at the young colonel still mounted. He held his hand over his eyes to shield them from a pelting cold rain. Wolfe hunched in his saddle, half listening to the report, while he thought of a way to detach the New Yorkers again. "We rode along the canal as ordered and destroyed six grist mills, a saw mill, six canal boats loaded with grain, the coal works at Manakin's Bend and one of the canal locks."

"Excellent work, Captain," Dahlgren answered. He tried to sound sincere, but the fact of the matter was that Captain Mitchell was his biggest problem right now. He had to get rid of him. He looked over at Wolfe, hoping he had come up with an idea.

"I also ordered the firing of a very nice barn that a local darky told me belonged to no one less than the Reb Secretary of War James Seddon." Mitchell chuckled at this and grinned like a cartoon cat who'd caught the biggest mouse in the kitchen. Dahlgren, with more sinister plans than burning a traitor politician's barn, was not impressed.

"That's wonderful, Mitchell." The colonel stifled a yawn. But just then booming cannon fire caught his attention. It was distant, but intense.

Chapter 9

At the Brook Hill Battle

"They are running! Look at them run!" Colonel Stevens slapped a heavy gloved hand across the sizzling muzzle of one of his field pieces as he watched the Indianans heading the other way. Behind Union lines, Kilpatrick kicked one of *his* cannons in disgust.

"They have found their mark finally, the bloody devils. And they have a strong position on that hill." The general was not about to give up yet, though. He turned to his command sergeant with a staccato set of new orders. "Sergeant-Major! Assemble a line of three more regiments. Have the artillery pound that hill, now!"

"Yes, sir!" The grizzled old soldier stepped off with a stiff salute while Kilpatrick considered the strategic situation.

"Where is news of Dahlgren, dang it?" the general muttered to himself. "Where can the Swede be?" The boy colonel should have sent word by now, by way of Captain Mitchell's detachment. It was too early to assume Dahlgren was in trouble, but the lack of a report troubled the mission commander and now the Confederates in his front posed an even greater problem. The enemy was not supposed to be this strong.

Presently the Union guns commenced firing, drowning out his thoughts as the thunder echoed across the shallow valley leading up to the Confederate entrenchments. The Rebels returned the fire as an artillery duel ensued. Twenty minutes later Kilpatrick ordered his big guns quiet as a force of over one thousand horsemen prepared to challenge the hill fort again.

With Dahlgren

"Those guns you hear are Kilpatrick's. He is forcing his way into the city," Dahlgren told Mitchell and his assembled officers. With the detachment together again, and Kilpatrick providing a demonstration to the north, the opportunity he'd hoped for presented itself. The time had come to execute his daring plan. Dahlgren and his subordinates sat astride their mounts clustered at the head of the column. They were less than five miles from the capital along the River Road leading in from the west. Dahlgren moved to put the New Yorkers behind him for good this time. "Mitchell, you will take the rearguard as we ride in. If you meet no opposition, post a guard along the road and keep our avenue of escape open."

Hopefully that will put him well behind us, Dahlgren thought to himself. With luck the Rebels will attack him and really keep the New Yorkers busy. Was that too much to ask? Dahlgren hurriedly exchanged salutes with Mitchell. "Dismissed and good luck."

"Yes, sir. Understood, sir." the New Yorker answered as he turned his horse and rode off. Dahlgren lowered his head like a predator ready to strike. He sidled his mount up to Wolfe so that only the major could hear him. The colonel's steely blue eyes still watched Mitchell as he trotted off into the distance but he was hissing his next order already.

"Major, you and I shall ride at speed. We will leave Mitchell far behind. It will be dark in a few hours; no better time to do our work. Night will aid us in our mission. You have a street map and the list of cabinet members and addresses?

"Right here," the major snarled, tapping his topcoat's breast pocket.

"Good. But remember the traitor Davis and his mansion. They are mine. Now is the time."

The column fell in and cantered off along the road, which wound its way over rolling fields punctuated by weathered white frame farm houses and clusters of outbuildings. The well-maintained byway more or less paralleled the flow of the James into the heart of the city.

Five minutes later Dahlgren loosed the reins and goaded

Valkyrie into a fast gallop. He leaned forward clutching the cords of leather in a death grip, straining to keep his mount with only one leg. His long blonde hair tossed in the breeze, his eyes shining like a Norse hero riding to Valhalla. The other horses in the column began to strain to keep up. Suddenly puffs of smoke appeared along a ridge fronting the road. Custis Lee's Confederates were firing on the exposed column. At first, Dahlgren didn't hear the guns as he entered a small valley dominated by long ridges of high ground on either side of the highway. Moments later case shot whistled in, causing the column to pull up abruptly.

"We are exposed here," Wolfe yelled. "Take cover behind those hills," he offered, pointing back about two hundred yards where the valley opened.

"No! We stop for nothing," Dahlgren countered. "We ride around this ridge and continue to the capital!" Just then another volley rained down on the road, throwing a man off his horse.

Dahlgren gritted his teeth as Valkyrie reared, but he held on. "Follow me!" The boy colonel led the column back to an intersection and followed a highway to the north. This route connected to the Manakin Road that ran east-west, several miles away. Turning again to head into the city, Dahlgren raised his hand to halt the column when he spied a line of Rebel pickets up ahead. He was about to order a saber charge when he saw the men run to their horses and ride toward their own lines.

"These people know we are here," Dahlgren hissed. "We have lost the element of surprise on this front."

"What shall we do, then?" Wolfe asked.

"We will ride further north toward Kilpatrick. Then we'll probe for a better way in and reset our trap."

On the Telegraph Road

"Troopers, draw sabers!" Kilpatrick issued the command as if he was ordering a new saddle, but his calm demeanor belied a blood thirsty determination to clear the road into Richmond. He realized he had underestimated the Confederate defenses on Brook Hill when he ordered the first attack. Now in this assault he would use an overwhelming force to carry the position. The Indianans and their ambitious colonel would be the tip of the spear. "Major Jones, when I see our flag on top of the hill, I will send in the rest of this division.

Plant the flag and prepare for victory! When you are ready, go forward."

Atop Brook Hill

Colonel Stevens saw the new assault forming. "They are coming for us!" he announced in a loud voice. "Get those men into line to the right of the road and have them lay down a flanking fire." Another two hundred men had just arrived from Custis Lee. City Battalion troops, most of whom had seen real battle during the Seven Days Campaign in 1862. They were falling into line now with two more guns and clean rifles. "Remember, we fight for our homes here. Don't let those devils get past us."

The Union Line

"Deee---tach—mennnt! Chaaarrge!" Kilpatrick's assault commenced with the speed of the featured stake race on a Saturday night. One thousand horsemen took off, sabers waving overhead. Atop the hill, Stevens watched the long looping line of storming horses swarming towards him. When his eight guns went off this time, the first line of attackers had just reached the center of the valley. The horse soldiers were perfectly exposed, and this time the gunners had measured the distance well.

"That's what happens when you bring a saber to a cannon fight," Stevens smirked when he saw the huge holes blasted through the long blue line. But the survivors closed ranks and continued riding forward. Still a formidable force, they began the rise up the hill. That's when the City Battalion men laid down a flanking fire that sliced into the left side of the advance. The remnants of the Indianans rode on the Union left and already battle shy from the first assault, they began to falter. First, the harried regiment shifted to the center of the attack, pulling up so that it could fall in behind the first rank. Soon the middle of the line became a tangle of rearing horses and circling riders, just waiting to be picked off by Confederate rifles or blasted by well-aimed artillery.

"My left is crumbling." Kilpatrick said to his staff. He watched the action through his field glasses from the hill across the Brook Run valley. "I believe that fort has reinforcements now. The Rebel capital is not as weak as we have been led to believe." In minutes, the Union attack stalled completely and then it was in full retreat under withering Confederate fire from two directions. Nothing was more demoralizing to a soldier in battle than to have fire coming at him from two sides.

Kilpatrick watched what was happening. The mass of Union horsemen looked like milling beeves, trailing back down into the valley. The general kicked the dirt in exasperation. But he quickly moved to another plan.

"Sergeant-Major, blow a retreat. It is getting dark now. We are leaving this field and will move as quickly as possible to the railhead at Atlee."

Chapter 10

With Dahlgren at Short Pump

Night was coming on and Dahlgren's group had passed through a little crossroads called Short Pump, less than ten miles west of the city center. He was circling northeast around Richmond, trying to shield his movements from more Confederate pickets and at the same time look for Kilpatrick. He already had learned from his own scouts that Kilpatrick was not at Hungary Spring as planned. The general's main force likely then had moved further east. Luckily Dahlgren had captured one of Custis Lee's pickets, a talkative, boastful man who told him that Kilpatrick had been thwarted in his attempt to take Richmond by the Brook Road. Wolfe had been unable to get any more information out of the man no matter how much he had beaten the traitor.

"Likely the poor boy simply didn't know anything more," Dahlgren laughed. Valkyrie walked along the dirt lane, the leisurely clop, clop, clop of his hooves providing what passed for a military cadence for the cavalry group.

"When his ignorance became apparent, I took it upon myself to end his suffering," Wolfe replied, slicing his hand across his neck. He smiled a little smile as he cut his eyes over at Dahlgren.

The colonel ignored his subordinate's murderous admission and went on.

"I tell you, we can still do this…tonight. We can't find Kilpatrick tonight, anyway. I say, let's take some picked men and head into town."

"Your wish is my command, Colonel," the burly killer answered. Twenty minutes later, Dahlgren and Wolfe, with about one hundred men, were riding east again, into the city under cover of darkness.

With Kilpatrick at Atlee Station

"Where is he? Where is Dahlgren?" Kilpatrick was in a quandary about what to do about his missing detachment. He was encamped in the broad fields surrounding Atlee Station a few miles from the Brook Hill battlefield. The temperature had dropped near freezing, though the mix of snow and sleet had mercifully stopped for awhile. He planned to decamp in the morning and move toward Williamsburg, where he could join Benjamin Butler's Army of the James which controlled Virginia's peninsula between the James and the York Rivers.

"I cannot believe the colonel has sent no courier to me with a progress report," the general continued.

"Perhaps he has dispatched runners who have been captured," Major Jones replied. Kilpatrick ignored the Indianan and continued his thought process. He twirled a shaggy black sideburn around a blunt, bony index finger.

"And I have had no news of any raids on the prisons in Richmond. Surely if he had succeeded, the entire countryside would be up in arms. No, either he is captured, killed or is still making his way here. That is my conclusion, Major."

Just then the night air cracked with rifle fire from a tree line on the other side of the station.

"We are under attack, from the north!" a voice cried out in the darkness. Kilpatrick immediately assumed the fire came from Hampton's cavalry.

"Mount up and form a line!" he ordered without even thinking. "Hampton took his time but he never gave up the chase, I suppose," the general said to his assembled staff.

He was right that it was Wade Hampton, with a large force. Earlier, the South Carolinian's small cavalry detachment had rendezvoused with a troop of Marylanders under General Bradley T. Johnson, a Princeton educated lawyer and Democratic politician from Frederick. The combined force of about two thousand men also included a local defense company called the North Anna Guards and eight guns detached from Jubal Early's infantry division. The Confederates had continued their pursuit south from Hanover Court House into the evening. Finding Kilpatrick at Atlee Station was a stroke of luck that Hampton did not plan to squander.

With Hampton

"We must press them, now!" Hampton cried, punching a gauntleted fist into his other hand. He knew a night attack was risky, but the element of surprise was everything in a cavalry fight.

At forty-six, Major General Wade Hampton was the closest thing America had to an aristocrat. He was physically imposing, tall, muscular and athletic. With his broad, strong face framed by a full beard he resembled Zeus, the Greek king of Olympus, ruler of the Olympians, the god of thunder and sky, a hurler of lightning bolts. But Wade Hampton seemed more powerful than Zeus. Wealthy beyond imagination, he not only commanded a division of cavalry, he controlled a plantation empire with roots in South Carolina and branches intertwining large swaths of rich land in Mississippi. "We have them on the ground. It will take them time to mount up and fight. Now is the instant to drive them from the field or destroy them." The thirty-five year old Johnson, red-faced and gruff looking, seemed ready to burst with the excitement of battle.

"General, the guns are concentrating on the right. My Maryland men are ready to charge at your order." Johnson had been with Stonewall Jackson at the First Battle of Manassas, so he was no stranger to hot contests. Hampton strutted back and forth like a peacock in a yard full of hens. He could not believe his luck this night.

"Have the artillery commence and fire at will. Then we will send in your Marylanders to finish the job."

Kilpatrick's Camp

When the first artillery volley thundered into Kilpatrick's bivouac, confusion turned to chaos. Thousands of half-dressed men and their horses began to panic. Kilpatrick decided to retreat.

"They have us, men!" Kilpatrick said disconsolately, turning to his brigade commanders. "Colonel Murray, get your brigade in line and cover our retreat. The rest of the division will retire to the east by column. We will aim to assemble at Mechanicsville."

Chapter 11

With Dahlgren

Near midnight, Dahlgren's guerillas approached the outskirts of Richmond. They had ridden to the northeast, avoiding picket posts on several occasions. They slipped between the layers of carefully engineered defensive earthworks that guarded the capital by traversing rocky ravines and taking deer trails through stands of scrub pines and brambles. Twice they had encountered mighty star forts guarding the intermediate line that ringed the city, which they easily sidestepped. Finally the clandestine troop turned due south and discovered a small forest that shielded their movement almost all the way into Richmond's northside.

Soon Dahlgren had ordered a bivouac in the woods below the bluffs of Shockoe Hill. He left most of his detachment and their horses concealed in a deep ravine overgrown with briars and sumac. In the early hours of the morning, Dahlgren prodded Valkyrie up the steep slope to the top of the hill with Wolfe and eighteen of his Kentuckians. The sleeping city unfolded before them. The men had discarded their blue top coats and exchanged them for a variety of tan and gray short jackets. Some of the men shivered in the night air.

"Nothing has gone right thus far, Wolfe, but now we have a chance to fulfill at least part of the mission." Dahlgren and his second in command rode side by side as they emerged from the valley onto level land. The weather had cleared and the moon provided occasional light as it peaked around rushing banks of smoky clouds. "So, you say the speech I prepared for the men is unnecessary now?"

"Oh, these men need no speeches, sir. They understand their aim is to burn this hateful city and not allow the Rebel leader Davis and his traitorous crew to escape," the major replied.

Ten minutes later, Dahlgren and Wolfe lay prone on the crest of a hill overlooking a quiet cobbled street and a neat collection of stately brick homes. Dahlgren consulted a map lit by the snub of a candle he carried in his pocket. The flickering light rested on a tall granite stone rounded at the top, one of dozens that surrounded the guerilla band. Wolfe lit up a short cigar letting the white smoke waft up over a stone Star of David crowning the grave of a rich Richmond merchant, 'Died 1842.'

"We are in the Hebrew Burial Ground, here on Shockoe Hill." The colonel pointed out the location to Wolfe with his right hand and whiffed the cigar smoke away with his left. "Now let's go over what we know of the whereabouts of our targets. The executive mansion is less than twelve blocks to the southeast, at 12th and Clay Street. I will take two men to attend to Davis there." The young colonel's eyes burned with revenge as he saw the fruition of his plans laid out before him. "You take two men with you as well, Major. Otherwise we will attack in two-man teams. You will kill Alexander Stephens who will be found on the northwest corner of 12th and Clay. The vice-president has two rooms in the Lancaster House, upstairs. Two men should be sent to kill Colonel Smith at the Governor's Mansion on Capitol Square. Secretaries Seddon, Trenholm and Postmaster General John Reagan are close together, here, at these homes on Franklin." Dahlgren slashed at the neighborhood farther to the south as he eyed Wolfe to see if he was following along. "Two more men will find Navy Secretary Mallory on Main Street, the red brick house in the middle of the block between 3rd and 4th. Do all of the men have copies of this map, Major?"

"Yes, sir. And I have already designated the teams and their targets."

"Good. I would expect no less. Now, their new attorney general is a man named Keyes. He is staying at the Spottswood Hotel, Room 236, by our latest intelligence from Mr. Lohman. So there you have it, the president and his cabinet as well as Governor

Smith."

"What of the Jew? Benjamin?"

"Of course, how could I have forgotten him? And here in the midst of the chosen people in this God-forsaken cemetery? The secretary of state last had a suite of rooms on the top floor of the Powhatan Hotel at 11th and Capitol Square." Dahlgren stood and brushed off his pants, removed his dark officer's coat and hat and pulled himself atop Valkyrie. "Ah, my Valkyrie," he purred, stroking the horse's silky mane. "Like the handmaidens of Odin, you shall hover over this battlefield and mete out death to our enemies…or bear our heroes off to Valhalla." The blonde warrior ended his reverie and turned to Wolfe. "Nine targets and nine teams. We will assemble back here at this stone, blow up the powder magazine just across the way there, up from Hospital Street, and then ride like the devil across the valley and out of town by way of the Mechanicsville Turnpike."

Dahlgren's horse was champing to get going, but not as much as Wolfe and his assassins were. They had been planning, training for, and thinking about striking this blow against the traitorous government for months now. By the morning, the world would wake up to a new country. Dahlgren and his death troop would go down in history.

Wolfe saluted with his right hand while he held the remnants of his cigar away from his body with a wide left-handed gesture. "Understood, Colonel. And may God have mercy on the traitors' souls. They are as good as dead already."

Chapter 12

With Hampton

"We must stay on their tails, Johnson. We must drive them to the river east of here and destroy them." General Hampton was pleased with the continuous reports he was getting that Kilpatrick was running. The two men stood over a map of the region, studying their options.

"Pin them against the Chickahominy or Pamunkey and we could cut them to pieces, yes sir," the Marylander replied, pointing at the two major rivers on either side of them. "If only we could get ahead of them and set a trap. Then we could do some damage." Hampton crossed his arms imperiously and gazed off toward the eastern sky, thinking.

"Yes, Colonel. I believe they are heading for Mechanicsville. There are heights there to defend and a major road to their supply base at Tunstall Station. For now the main force shall merely pursue. But let's send a battalion here along the Meadow Bridge Road to try to slow them down abit." Hampton stabbed at a parallel route that linked Atlee with Mechanicsville. "Their rearguard fights well, but we must harry them at every turn."

With Kilpatrick

Kilpatrick's main force had filed away from Atlee Station and found the Shady Grove Road, heading for a better defensive position astride the turnpike that led further east.

"A dispatch, sir!" a voice echoed out of the darkness, followed by the knock-knocking cadence of a fast moving horse. "Dispatch for General Kilpatrick!" A courier rode up alongside the division commander as the column made its way at a brisk trot. He saluted and handed him a carefully rolled foolscap sheet held by a cigar's paper band. Kilpatrick slowed his horse and snapped the roll open with one hand.

"Scouts report that Rebel troopers have arrived at the intersection with the Meadow Bridge Road and they are digging in there," the general read out loud. He smoothed his frazzled sideburns. "We must punch through there. It is the only way away from here." One of Kilpatrick's brigade leaders, Colonel William Lowe, pulled a map from his coat pocket and reconnoitered the situation.

"We can punch through and turn east again, taking the Meadow Bridge all the way to the turnpike further on," he offered.

With Captain Mitchell's New Yorkers

"Dee-tachment! Halt!" Captain Mitchell pulled his horse out of line and stopped what was left of Dahlgren's force. The New Yorker had lost contact with Dahlgren almost an hour ago. Down the road he glimpsed his scout, returning with a report. A young sergeant galloped up, horse and courier steaming in the cold air.

"Captain, there is no sign of them, just enemy pickets up ahead, blocking the road," the rider said. Mitchell was frustrated. He had not been kept abreast of anything Dahlgren and Wolfe had planned on this raid. Now the New Yorker felt abandoned by the expedition's leader. The whole thing was odd. Mitchell thought of his men, isolated in enemy country; he pondered his responsibility to them, and the young captain came to the simplest decision.

"We will ride north then and try to find Kilpatrick as planned. That surely is where the colonel is heading if the road in front is blocked." He turned a sore and tired body in the saddle and waved the column forward, toward the base at Tunstall Station. Mitchell was happy to put Richmond and the whole useless campaign behind him.

Chapter 13

With Dahlgren's Raiders, in Richmond

The assassins fanned out, seeming to stroll out of the Hebrew Cemetery like Sabbath School had just let out. The straggling group, with Dahlgren astride his horse, crossed a deserted Hospital Street and entered the eerie Shockoe Hill Burial Ground, heading for the silent neighborhood. A thousand stones and monuments cast heavy shadows even darker than the night. An Egyptian obelisk loomed along the central path while Classical columns framed a crypt adorned with a Greek Cross. It was near two a.m. The frosty air, with close hanging clouds, was deathly quiet when it was quiet, but the slightest sound echoed like thunder off every hard surface. The men lumbered along, alert to every snap and cough. The icy ground crunched beneath their feet as they wound their way through the cemetery toward the city proper which began with Jackson Street.

"Well sure that's mighty fine tobaccah I smell!" The high-pitched, sing-song voice was so unexpected that the Union men stopped breathless as if they'd been punched in the testicles. A man with long black hair and a scruffy full beard just going gray literally rolled from his seat behind a red marble facsimile of Bonaparte's sarcophagus in Paris. The monument rested upon an opulent pedestal supported by triangular piles of cannon balls.

Not a Union man spoke, unable to recover their wits for several seconds. The interloper, obviously sleeping off a drunk, stood and stared at the strange band. He moved toward Wolfe, who still sucked on his stogie. "And sure, where did a good Southern man get such a fine smoke?" The rummy leaned in. "Do you have anymore?" he whispered, a sly smile on his face. Finally, Wolfe found his voice. He tried to ward off the interruption with a smile of his own and some small talk.

"Why, you speak with an Irish brogue don't you, old man?"

"Indeed. I came here from Cark, in '52. Been in Richmond ever since." The Irishman pulled his old head back a little, realizing suddenly that something about these men wasn't right. There were about twenty of them, out in the middle of the night. Young men, but not in military kit, not exactly. And they talked with the wrong sound.

"And you don't seem like you're from around here, ye-self, eh mate?" the Irishman asked, a tinge of instinctual fear in his voice now. Wolfe moved forward, still smiling while his hammy left hand reached inside his short coat for a long knife. The others closed around Napoleon's tomb, but did not make any sudden moves. They waited for Wolfe to act.

"No, we are from Tennessee," Wolfe lied.

"Aye, Give General Archer my kindest regards." In Robert E. Lee's army, General James Archer led the brigade that included troops from Tennessee, the Irishman knew. Wolfe did *not* know this fact. In the darkness, Wolfe could not see the old man's eyes cut away, looking for the best direction to run. He did not see his face fall when he heard the killer's reply.

"General Archer?" Wolfe asked. He realized his mistake almost immediately. The Irishman turned to run, but tripped over a cement border, falling with a grunt on the hard ground. Wolfe was over him in a flash. Without a thought he plunged an eight-inch blade into the old man's gut. He held the man by the throat with his right hand and twisted the knife with his left. "Alright, Paddy. We're not from Tennessee and General Archer can go to Hades," he hissed.

"You're here to kill old men, then? Is that how the Narrth fights a war?" the dying man panted.

Wolfe laughed, his bare white teeth and his hoary breath the only things the Irishman could really make out in the darkness. "Oh, yes, we are here to kill some old men alright. That's exactly what we are here for."

"The president, you mean. You are assassins, then."

"You're one smart Paddy, aren't you, old man?" Wolfe

laughed again. "Yes, your president, as you call the bloody rotter, and whatever partners in crime we may find in this fine little city of Richmond." The Corkman was failing now, his eyes flickering, blood oozing from the corners of his mouth. He coughed as he squirmed there on the cold earth, still held by Wolfe's murderous hands.

"God help you, soldier," he whispered. "You may murder the government in its bed, sure. But remember, what you do to us, we will do to you. Our people will repay this to your people."

"Hmph! We'll see about that," Wolfe scoffed, but the man was already dead. The Union major pulled him up again and threw the limp body on the ground, wiped his knife on the man's coat and with a hand gesture moved the group forward. A few second later a shaking fellow emerged from below Napoleon's crypt. He scrambled over to his friend and confirmed his worst fear. Crouching over the body, he snapped his head back and forth frantically. Looking after the assassins who had picked up the pace toward Jackson Street, he clenched his fists and ran for the powder magazine and its guard post.

Chapter 14

With Kilpatrick at Cold Harbor

"Colonel Lowe, that was some fine fighting at the Meadow Bridge." Kilpatrick roughly slapped his brigade leader on the back as the two men rode side by side through Old Cold Harbor. They had put the last running battle ten miles behind them near Mechanicsville. The entire column and its artillery train were across the swamps that feed the Chickahominy. They headed northeast toward the Union supply base at White House on the Pamunkey.

"The column moved fast enough to bring the force we needed to take the intersection, General. The laurels go to those troops and their captains."

"True enough and very generously said. But it's not over yet. It is that rat Bradley Johnson who is harassing us still. Because of the continued pursuit we will push on through to White House and then on to Williamsburg. This campaign is over."

"And what of Colonel Dahlgren, sir?"

"I have not heard from him even now. I have however heard from Captain Mitchell, who is in charge of most of the detachment. He does not know where Dahlgren is either. He lost contact with the head of the column several hours ago and is to meet us with about two hundred fifty troopers at Tunstall."

"I fear the worst has befallen the young colonel," the brigade leader mused as his tired horse barely trotted through heavy woodland. "In retrospect, his plan to ride into the heart of the city and release what may be ten thousand prisoners was more than bold, perhaps it was foolhardy."

"It was a daring raid. But that is what the cavalry is about, is it not, Lowe?" Kilpatrick chuckled. "This is the same country where J.E.B. Stuart rode around McClelland in '62. I say if Old Beauty can do it, so can we, blast it!"

With Dahlgren's Raiders

"Colonel, do you think we should attempt to release at least some of the prisoners from Libby Prison if time permits?" Dahlgren's delicate features contorted with disgust at the thought. Though dark, he recognized the voice of Lieutenant Mortimer Blake, one of Wolfe's Kentuckians, a skinny lickspittle of a man

"To the infernal regions with them, Blake. What we are doing is bigger than a few men given meals and lodging by the enemy. Besides, it taxes the Rebels to have to feed so many of our soldiers. I say our prisoners here are doing their part merely by imposing on this drab little city."

The guerillas neared the intersection of Jackson and Clay, the point where the teams would divide up and find the appointed addresses. The neighborhood featured gray cobblestone streets lined with fine three-story red brick and brownstone townhomes. Black wrought iron gates and fences secured each mansion's street-side garden. The raiders paid no heed to their rich surroundings, but moved stealthily along, sticking to the darkest shadows.

"I just thought that if something goes wrong tonight, say some of us are captured. At least we would have a noble excuse for being here," Blake sniveled. Dahlgren kept moving, but sought to put off the lieutenant with excuses.

"The prison is quite abit farther afield than our targets. It is down in the bottom, closer to the river; harder to make our escape from once the mission is done. Besides, nothing will go wrong for us tonight, not here, not this night." He goaded Valkyrie to a faster tempo as a way to signal an end to the conversation. The other men on foot struggled to keep up with the new pace, but all of them suddenly stopped dead in their tracks.

BONG BONG BONG, BONG BONG BONG! It was the Capitol Square bell tower, sounding an alarm. Three bells, three bells, the call to battle. The insurgents watched paralyzed like bank robbers caught red-handed as the city awoke. The streets flooded with men wielding all kinds of household weapons, broomsticks, hammers, firetongs and brickbats. Some residents held arquebuses that hadn't seen dry powder since the British burned Washington. Dahlgren's horse reared as a group of young black men ran toward them. They carried pikes as they rushed from the city hospital toward the Capitol Building.

"Hell-fire, what is this, what is this?" the colonel cried.

"Come along, massa," one of the black men called to Dahlgren who was turning his horse back toward the Hebrew Cemetery. The Yankee assassins had drawn pistols and knives, the implements they had planned to use to kill the top level of the Confederate government. The black men, six of them, stood in his way. The leader of the pikemen, seeing the armed group's hesitation and thinking them confused Richmonders, answered Dahlgren's shrill question. "It is the Yankees. They is attacking the city. Ride to the Cap'tol and rally around the statuh of General Washington!"

"General Washington and the Yankees indeed!" Dahlgren screamed. He was filled with rage that somehow he had been found out. The black men stood there, pikes in hand, mouths open when they realized that the whites before them were the very Yankees they were searching for. The Negro who had spoken to Dahlgren was the first to fall, a round ball leaving a neat hole in his forehead. Bone and blood exploded into the cold night, sending off a puff of frosty steam that hung in the air long after the dark body hit the ground. The men with pikes charged, but Wolfe and his killers put several bullets into each black man before they had taken two steps; all but one. The last pikeman realized he was alone, dropped his weapon and ran back down the street. Dahlgren kicked Valkyrie into action and chased after the remaining defender. In seconds, the war horse easily knocked his prey down and trampled him unconscious. Dahlgren pulled up his mount, spun around, drew his army revolver and plugged the man three times in the chest. Without hesitation he called to the others.

"To horse, men! We ride out of here!"

Chapter 15

Valkyrie reared on hind legs as Dahlgren whipped the black steed around and spurred him back down Jackson Street. Entering the burial ground, the raiders broke into a run, and followed the Union leader across Hospital Street and into the Hebrew Cemetery. A small band of citizens, white and black, ran after them. But after watching how efficiently the raiders had murdered the pikemen, the civilians with makeshift weapons didn't run very fast.

Reaching the edge of the ravine, Valkyrie balked and Dahlgren catapulted over the horse's neck, slamming to the ground with a curse. He fell headfirst down the slope, rolling and sliding all the way to the bottom. He sat up in a muddy stream just as Wolfe and the others caught up with him.

"Come along, Colonel. They are on our tail still," Wolfe yelled. He and another soldier grabbed Dahlgren by the arms and hoisted him to his feet. His wooden leg was twisted sideways, making it difficult for him to find his balance. Bruised and cut from the fall, Dahlgren was furious at the turn of events. He limped over to a river birch, leaning on it to catch his breath.

"Find Valkyrie, quickly. I need my mount, blast it!" The alarm continued to sound across the city and just then a cluster of dim lights appeared at the top of the ravine. Shots rang out, the city's ersatz defenders firing blindly into the deep ditch below the cemetery. Bullets whistled around them as another soldier brought up the colonel's horse which had wandered down the slope at its own pace. In moments, all of the troopers were riding northeast toward

Mechanicsville.

Almost an hour later the column slipped past the Ellerson depot and riding hard, took the Meadow Bridge Road. They did not know it, but they were following Kilpatrick's retreat route now. "We head for Tunstall Station. It is only another hour ride. There we should be safe," Dahlgren yelled to Wolfe and his company commanders. But as the riders approached Pole Green, about fifteen miles from the city, a regiment of Confederate cavalry stood in their path. Dahlgren could not know that the northeastern roads leading out of Richmond were swarming with Rebel troopers returning from the chase of Kilpatrick.

It was nearly five in the morning now and the boy colonel knew that daylight would bring even more scrutiny from civilians as well as enemy soldiers. There was no time to stop, no time to fight, so without knowing where it led, he turned the column down a side road to the north to avoid the enemy unit. Eventually the road took him through a little crossroads called Haw's Shop.

In a stand of trees near an old church, Dahlgren paused long enough to light a candle and peruse his map. He was sweating, though it was very cold in the saddle. The hard ride had done little to quiet his anger over the failure of the mission. And as he tried to concentrate on getting back to Union lines, he realized that his body was aching from the hard fall he'd taken. Wolfe did not know how badly his colonel was injured and did not understand that his leader was not thinking straight.

"We must cross at Hanovertown, two miles this way," Dahlgren decided. "This must be a ford through a branch of the Chickahominy. There is a fine road to the east from there." With no time to waste, Dahlgren stuffed the map in his breast pocket and moved the column forward again. But the commander was mistaken. He was farther north than he believed. At Hanovertown he would cross the *Pamunkey*, putting the river between him and his intended destination.

Twenty minutes later, the Union troopers rode into a Confederate guard post at the Hanovertown ford. The broad, flat plain leading to the river crossing gave Dahlgren time to see how small the force holding the ford was and he prepared to fight his way through. But the Confederates, about half a dozen men, jumped in the saddle and rode off. The Union force continued across the river at speed, not thinking the crossing guards would cause them any more problems. But the Confederate riders weren't just running from a fight, they were going for help.

With Dahlgren-One Hour Later

The Union raiders had been riding on a good road in open country with no sign of trouble for some time now. At this point Dahlgren started to relax, but at Manquin, he began to realize that the countryside did not match his understanding of the map. Injured and exhausted, Dahlgren had lost all conception of time and distance.

A few miles further along, the colonel's disorientation was the least of his problems when a company of the 9th Virginia Cavalry, part of Fitzhugh Lee's Division, appeared behind them. The company had been alerted by the guards at Hanovertown. Led by a twenty-four year old lieutenant named James Pollard, the Confederate force bore down on the tired Union men and their exhausted horses. Although Dahlgren was as good as dead in the saddle, Wolfe was not about to give up yet. Just ahead, the major saw a fine wooden bridge crossing a substantial river, the Mattaponi, near Aylett. He drove his horse up next to Dahlgren's and yelled out a plan.

"Colonel, cross that bridge and burn it, I say. That river can't be easily forded. Those bloody Rebs will have to let us go. From that side, we can make our way southeast again." Dahlgren did not even answer, but simply saluted his approval and leaned into his saddle. Crossing that bridge to safety was his only thought.

Chapter 16

With Lieutenant Pollard

"The blackguards must be crossing at Dunkirk Bridge," the bright-eyed young officer surmised as his cavalry troop trotted along the turnpike to Aylett. James Pollard was a local boy, from a long line of Virginia farmers. His short blonde hair framed a fair-skinned face reddened by the cold and roughened even at his young age from long days in the sun and in the saddle. He pulled up at a crossroads close to the Mattaponi.

The turnpike would follow the Union raiders to Dunkirk Bridge across the Mattaponi River. The lane to the right, the King William Road, led southeast to another river crossing at a village named Walkerton, or Walker's Town, as the old timer's called it. Pollard had a strategic decision to make. Chase the fox or try to head him off. The young lieutenant knew the roads and the river here. That much he could trust. But would the Yankees turn to the east once across the river? He had to gamble that they would certainly try to return to their own lines. But why had they run so far beyond their base on the Pamunkey. It didn't make any sense, but he decided to play the odds. Lieutenant Pollard turned to a soldier even younger than he was, a boy of eighteen in a black slouch hat who leaned over a sleek gray pony. Pollard spoke quickly. "Sergeant, you have the fastest horse in the company."

The boy swelled with pride at this. In another world the horse would have been a racer. The boy sergeant trained horses and rode for money in that other life. He spit on the ground as he smiled and arrogantly said, "Yes, sir, Lieutenant, he is the fastest." Pollard simply snorted at the boy's answer and continued.

"Ride ahead and tell Captain Fox we are heading across the river at Walkerton. I believe the raiders will turn down the King and Queen Trail. Tell the captain I reckon we can ambush the devils if we are quick about it. I shall look for him at the bridge if he will join me. Now ride!"

With Dahlgren-On the Mattaponi River

The sun was rising as the wooden deck of the Dunkirk Bridge shuddered at the clop, clop, clopping of a hundred horses. The Union column filed over the single span high above the water. Absent the bridge, a crossing here, down a steep ravine and through the deep, wide Mattaponi, would be near impossible. Wolfe and five others jumped down and began to build a fire. It was slow work and they believed the Confederate troopers behind them were minutes away. A small crossroads village and its general store stood beside the bridge and Wolfe sent a man to look for any combustibles, lantern or cooking oil or coal tar, anything to hasten the flames. In the meantime, he put a match to brush and kindling gathered from the roadside.

The cold and damp made the tiny flames sputter and Wolfe began to worry that he couldn't destroy the span in time. He kept one eye across the river looking for any sign of the enemy, and another on the soldier at the store. The man smashed a shop front window with his rifle, after fumbling with the door lock for awhile. He soon emerged from the shop with three cans of lantern oil. People in the village were peeking out of their windows by this time, awakened not just by the bright sun, the first sunny day in a week, but by the invasion force. The whites stayed in their houses, but several blacks appeared out of nowhere and fell in behind the soldier as he left the store. By the time he got back to the bridge, perhaps a dozen black people were with him.

Wolfe eyed them suspiciously. "Here now, off with you all! This is Federal army business."

"You gonna burn our bridge, General?" one old black man asked in a shaky voice. Wolfe ignored the question and the gathering crowd, but ordered his detachment to prepare to set the fire.

"Here, dump that oil across the planks there."

"We are Mr. Robinson's slaves," the old man persisted. Wolfe ignored the remark as he had the question. He looked across the bridge again, searching for the Confederates. "My name is Henry, sir," the slave continued. "We want our freedom. We want you to take us away from here." Wolfe turned to the man at this. Henry's gray head sparkled in the daylight. He carried himself with a permanent stoop from a lifetime of working the fields, but his eyes held a quiet dignity. The people around him were silent, so afraid of the Yankee men they didn't dare speak a word. They held their collective breath, hoping the blue clad soldiers would lead them to freedom.

Though powerless before the law, Henry possessed an inner strength that the other slaves looked up to. He had labored for most of his seventy-five years on John Robinson's rich land between the Pamunkey and Mattaponi. And while he'd never left the peninsula between the rivers, Henry understood how the world worked and strove to make it better. Over the years, Henry had often convinced Robinson, the veritable prince of the largest plantation in central Virginia, that he should improve the lives of his workers. Even John Robinson respected the old slave. That's why every Robinson slave saw Henry as their leader. He alone spoke for over one thousand men, women and children spread out over three counties.

"Old man, we are being pursued by the enemy. We have no time or room for you." Henry ignored the substance of the officer's reply. The very fact that he finally had gotten the officer's attention actually emboldened the old slave.

"My name is Henry. Henry Clay Robinson," the old man replied with a gentlemanly bow. "But I thought that's what ya'll is fighting for. To free us slaves?"

"Old man," Wolfe repeated, not willing to use his name. "I fear that if we don't break this bridge in the next few minutes, *you* will still be slaves and *we* will be dead! Now off with you!" Just then Colonel Dahlgren sauntered up and saw that the flames were beginning to rise now, the bridge timbers snapping under the yellow heat. He had heard some of Wolfe's exchange with Henry and was interested in the old man's claim.

"Yes, Wolfe, let us take these people with us. It doesn't appear the Rebels who were chasing us will catch us now. We are heading east from here and will be at White House in a matter of hours." Wolfe, still in panic mode, tried to voice his opposition, but could only sputter a reply.

"These....people will only hamper our ability to escape this country, Colonel."

"Major, this entire raid has been a failure. The least we can do is rescue a few of our brethren from the misery of slavery." Wolfe turned away to hide his disgust with the colonel's decision, but he said nothing more about it.

"Thank you, Colonel. God bless you and thank you," the old man said. He all but knelt on the ground before Valkyrie. At the same time, he turned to another slave and whispered. "Tell the whole village we is leaving. Now!"

"Bring up a wagon and have the troopers double up their horses if needed," Dahlgren ordered. He seemed to have regained some of his energy and presence of mind. The bridge was in full flames now and as the raiding party set off, they took a total of forty-two slaves with them. Every able-bodied slave in the village.

Chapter 17

With Pollard at Walkerton

Pollard breathed a sigh of relief when he saw Captain Edward Fox and his company from the 5th Virginia Cavalry rumble into Walkerton. He'd already consolidated a small number of men from King and Queen County into his unit. The combined force of one hundred fifty troopers crossed the river as the first rays of the sun played over the dark-watered Mattaponi. They turned southeast immediately and galloped toward the county courthouse village.

One of Fox's sergeants, a Mattaponi Indian scout named Little Turtle Custalow, rode next to the company commander on his own black and white pony. Heading southeast, the Indian led the Confederates along a narrow path through the woods; an old trail his tribe used when they fished the river for shad in the spring, he explained. The head of the column stopped where the path intersected with a broad, sandy road running north-south, linking the King and Queen Road with the river. The copper-skinned Custalow had a long black silk of hair hanging below his kepi. His Indian features contrasted sharply with his bright blue eyes, evidence of some recessive gene from over two hundred years of interaction with whites. The intersection was heavily wooded on every side and the road leading south to the Mattaponi cut through a tall thick tunnel of trees.

"My people farther up the river tell me the Yankees have

turned off the King and Queen Road and are making for the Mattaponi now. They will be here in less than an hour."

"Good, Sergeant Custalow," Pollard answered. "A perfect little spot for an ambush, just like you told us it would be." The lieutenant turned to Fox. The captain as the senior officer should have been giving the orders, but Pollard seemed to have the whole operation worked out in his mind, so Fox led him take the reins. "Captain, I propose we fan out on both sides of the road here and lay in wait for the bloody dogs to walk into our trap."

"As you wish, Lieutenant. This is your operation."

"The King and Queen Guards will block the road to their village. If you will take your company into the field opposite, I will post my men along the road on this side. Custalow here will lead half of my men up river on this fishing path to circle back behind the invading force. We should have them on every side with that."

"Fine work, Pollard. God be with you and your men." Fox tipped his hat as he spurred his horse and waved his company across the road and over into a tree line bordering a field of cut corn. The local guardsmen galloped down the road nearly three hundred yards to the crest of a hill and formed a line meant to stall the Union advance. While Custalow's detachment started upstream, Pollard had his men back into the woods on the river side of the road. The ground dropped off after about fifty yards, the first incline of the valley sweeping down to the Mattaponi.

"Now we wait for the blackguards," Pollard said to no one in particular. "It took awhile catching up but we have them now. We will punish them for invading our land. We will show no mercy. That we leave to God."

With Dahlgren at Walkerton

The young boy sat on the porch of a weather beaten frame house at a crossroads that led down to the Walkerton Landing. He spit on the ground as he watched the Federal soldiers walk their horses through what passed as a town. The column stopped to rest their mounts and water them. Dahlgren eyed the boy closely but decided he posed no threat to his men. He took in the urchin's loosely fitting homespun clothes and worn out boots with distain. Obviously of a rustic white family little better than the slaves he had in tow. But I won't be leading you to freedom, will I boy? There will be no redemption for you, he thought to himself. The colonel coughed when he tried to laugh.

A thick wad of phlegm welled up in Dahlgren's throat, choking him like a hand around his gullet. When he finally caught his breath, he continued to eye the boy he had passed. About twelve or thirteen, the child stared back at him but didn't say a word. A half-hour later, Dahlgren still watched the boy as the troop left the village. Wolfe cantered along beside his colonel at the head of the column and looked back to see what had captured Dahlgren's attention. "Has the boy caused some disturbance, sir?" the major enquired. Dahlgren cleared his throat and replied in a strangled voice.

"I want more scouts before us as well as behind. I feel we are being watched." Wolfe spun his head around at the boy and quickly looked along both sides of the road.

"Surely that little scamp is not a spy?"

"I don't know what role he may play," the Swede replied sharply. "But I don't think we can be too safe." Dahlgren coughed again, uncontrollably this time, no doubt a sign of a sickness brought on by the cold damp weather and the long ride. Wolfe showed little concern for him though as he turned out of line. "One more thing, Major." Dahlgren stopped him before he rode off to find more eyes and ears for the fleeing force.

"Yes, sir?"

"Have the slaves brought to the front of the column. We will let them lead the way to the Promised Land," Dahlgren said with a smile. Wolfe managed a wicked sneer in reply.

"They will sweep the country before us, then?"

"Indeed. If there are enemies down this road, they will destroy their own property before they kill us." Minutes later the troop had left the crossroads well behind them, but the boy had chased ahead of them along the Indian trail.

Chapter 18

The Union column with four dozen slaves in front moved along slowly. They had been riding for some time and had passed through the country peacefully even without the cloak of darkness. Dahlgren had relaxed abit as the afternoon wore on and now fading rays of sunlight danced along the broad open fields bordering both sides of the road. Rounding a curve, the farm fields ended and overarching oaks and poplars, growing close on both sides, cloaked the road in dark shadows.

Swamps and switchback creeks flanked the lane, which had been built up with earth and planked in sections. The sound of hooves echoed along the shadowy tunnel giving an eerie quality to the journey. Dahlgren's hacking cough was the only hint that humans inhabited the place. At the far end of the tunnel of trees, a circle of brighter light promised an end to the dark passage.

"Uncle Henry, this is a bad place," an old slave woman croaked as they walked along the ghostly road. "I have a bad feelin' about our way here." The other blacks heard this warning coming from a woman they knew to have a sixth sense about the future. The group stopped walking and gathered around her. One woman moaned in fear, a long, low wail that was repeated by many of the others. Some of the children started to cry and Henry picked one child up and hugged it.

"Helen, every road has rough spots along the way. We must keep on." He patted the child's head as he spoke and touched the old woman's face tenderly. She turned her head away brusquely.

"Unh, Unh, Henry. I have a powerful feelin' about this. I think we should turn around and head back to Robinson's before it is too late." Dahlgren had seen the slaves stop in the road and he cantered up quickly just then.

"What is going on here, Henry?" he called with some exasperation. At that moment the woman seemed to go into a trance. She looked up at the sky and held up both hands. Her eyes were closed and her lips began to move even before the words were audible. Before Henry could answer Dahlgren's question, Helen began to speak.

"I see men, lots of men, in gray suits. They hide in the shadows. They are angry with hate. And they have death in their hearts. We must leave out of this place and return to safety at Robinson's farm." As she spoke the others in the group shivered with fear and their growing wails and moans rang off the tree tunnel walls. The mounted troop had closed up around the gathering and some of the horses began to toss and nicker at the commotion.

"Holy Christ," Wolfe snorted with distain.

"Here now," Dahlgren yelled, trying to gain control of the situation. "We must move on, quickly!" He waved his arms around like he was shooing children. "Henry, get your people going! Now, old boy!" But Henry had fallen under Helen's spell and didn't move immediately to comply with the order. Dahlgren exploded in fury and rose up in his saddle. "Major Wolfe, have the troop push these ignorant people down the road! We must move now!"

"Yes, sir. Right away, sir!" Wolfe answered. "Company E! Form a line and push these darkies along." Twenty-five mounted soldiers lined up along the road and began to advance slowly into the crowd, which found itself carried forward by a wave of horse flesh. Thousands of pounds of irresistible force pushed the people along, knocking some down, but allowing them to rise before herding them forward again like cattle. The slaves finally began walking on their own again, fast enough to keep from being bumped or trampled. Henry put an encouraging arm around Helen's slim, shivering shoulders and led her to the front of the group. She wept at her helplessness. Henry spoke to her in soothing tones, trying to calm her. Ten minutes later, the dark tunnel ended and the contingent burst into the bright sunshine again. Dahlgren rode in the center of the line just behind the slave walkers. He allowed himself a paternal smile, thinking still about the superstitious beliefs of his black charges.

CRACK, CRACK, CRACK, CRACK-CRACK-CRACK! The change from dark to light had blinded him, but there was no mistaking the rifle fire that came from the woods. They were under attack from the right. Dahlgren rose up to order a charge, but at that moment, the slaves in his front fell to the ground in fear, blocking the road. He hesitated for only a moment; more rifle fire galvanized the colonel into action.

"Charge! Trample these people and charge!" The Union cavalrymen, evolving into a hasty battle line, drew pistols and kicked their mounts forward. Screams filled the air when the slaves saw the horses coming at them. The weakest among them never stood a chance. A metal-shoed hoof crushed the head of a little boy with one pounding stroke. Helen heard her leg bones snap as another rider bounded across her prostrate body.

Dahlgren rode to the front as Valkyrie jumped over one clutch of teenage girls who cowered in the sand, shielding their heads with thin brown arms. But Valkyrie was not quick enough to avoid Henry, who had tried to stand up again to drag Helen out of the road. The black horse left its feet, spurred into open air, and clipped Henry in the chest on the way down. The collision upset Valkyrie's balance and the heavy steed fell sideways, landing on top of the old man. Henry felt the breath punch out of his chest as he fell backwards. The two-thousand pound horse landed full on top of him, cracking every rib and crushing the man's body cavity with a grinding crunch like the snapping of a tree limb. Dahlgren had held tight to his saddle's pommel and tried to goad Valkyrie to his feet again, but just then the boy colonel's chest erupted in blood. A well-aimed bullet killed him instantly.

Chapter 19

Logan's Headquarters, Columbia, 1865

The tap-tap-tapping from Buckley's blackthorn stick reverberated off the walls of the otherwise hushed salon. The monk's narrative describing Dahlgren's death had astounded the gathering into shocked silence. The staccato rapping filled the void, ticking frantically like an over-wound timepiece.

Buckley lowered his head to pray and no one spoke until he stilled the blackthorn to bless himself and raised doleful eyes to General Sherman. "An extraordinary story, Brother," the commander said quietly.

"And a sad one, my Northern friend," Buckley answered. He struggled to his feet to stretch his rangy frame and looked at Kilpatrick. "As you see, my information does not link you to Dahlgren's sinister intentions, though you commanded the military operation at that time."

"Indeed, I knew nothing of the man's plan to assassinate anyone," Kilpatrick replied with hooded eyes, umbrage in his voice. He squared his face on Sherman. "I had no inkling he had such maniacal ideas."

Sherman reared back, suspiciously eyeing his cavalry leader. "You say what you did *not* know, General. Now tell me what you did know *exactly* about Dahlgren's intention in this raid." Kilpatrick shifted uncomfortably, beads of sweat forming on his high pale forehead.

"It was just as Brother Buckley here has said. We planned a two-pronged operation on Richmond, with the chief objective to release our men held in that city's prisons. Nothing more."

An awkward standoff oppressed the room while Sherman considered his subordinate's answer. On its face it seemed rather forthright if not fully forthcoming. Just then, an aide peeked past the doorway where Long stood guard and beckoned silently to General Logan. Sherman saw the junior officer.

"Come along, young man. You have something for your general, bring it in," the army commander called to the aide. "This is your headquarters after all, Logan. Do your business." Logan nodded at his commander's accommodating attitude and waited for his aide to speak.

"We have a lead on the newspaperman Timrod, sir. He's been seen at a dry goods store, seeking food for his baby. The provost guard is searching the precincts near the store and hopes to have him soon."

"Fine, Captain. I should very much like to speak with him when he is taken. Bring him to me."

"Yes, sir, certainly, sir," the aide replied, saluting as he left the room.

As soon as the door clicked shut, Mother Lynch rose quickly. "Gentlemen, I really must see about my students," she said breezily. She stopped short of the door as Long opened it for her. "And General Sherman," the nun said, turning to look pointedly at the man seated at the fine desk across the room. "I'll thank you again for your assured protection of the school and convent, sir. And I'll pray for you," she added more gently.

"Certainly, Mother Lynch," the general answered wearily. The men stood as the mother superior bustled out, seemingly sucking the room's oxygen out with her.

When all were settled again, Sherman immediately shifted his attention to Buckley. "So, we all are aware of the firestorm created by Colonel Dahlgren's raid, even before we learned of the salacious details you have brought to us; the murder of civilians, an assassination plot, the trampling of freedmen." The general ticked off the allegations one by one on stubby fingers. "Even if I accept all *that* as fact, Brother, Dahlgren is dead now. What does the raid have to do with our murders here?"

"Well, I'll tell you, my martial friend," Buckley began with a slow breath. "Dahlgren's raid last year is perhaps the most infamous example of the secret war being fought by both the Union and the Confederacy; an ugly kind of war that has incited countless acts of hatred and revenge that the people hear about from time to time. And more to our case, Dahlgren's operation is what lured the monster Wolfe out of his beastly lair back in Kentucky."

"Ah, Wolfe. The man who murdered the mulatto near Goochland in your account of the raid."

"The very same, sir."

"But how did this man end up here in Columbia? What is *his* part in this atrocity?"

"A very good question, my blue-clad friend," Buckley replied, with a fire kindling in his green eyes. "That is a story that begins on the high seas. It is a very old story; one that involves one of the deadly sins, the root of all evil, they say. It is a story of greed. For our Major Wolfe was not only a murderer, but a thief. It was greed that brought the beast to Columbia, General Sherman, it was gold."

Chapter 20

March 1864-Aboard *C.S.S. Alabama* off Capetown, South Africa

Captain Raphael Semmes still marveled at the speed of his ship. Whether under sail or steam, the *Alabama* could hunt down any ocean-going craft afloat. Downwind with a full head of steam behind her twin three hundred-horsepower engines, the British built barkentine could make fifteen knots. She carried three hundred-fifty tons of coal to keep the engines cranking. But if coal reserves ran low, an ingenious lifting device that hauled the enormous screw propeller out of the water reduced drag enough to make the *Alabama* swift under sail alone. At two hundred-twenty feet she was big enough to threaten almost any warship. But the *Alabama* preferred to target civilian ships, Union-owned merchantmen, and she had the guns to bully them with impunity. The Confederate privateer carried six 32-pounder smoothbores, a 100-pounder Blakely rifle on her bow and a 68-pounder pivoting smoothbore abaft the mainmast. In his own words, Semmes considered a merchant ship a panting breathless fawn to *Alabama*'s inexorable staghound.

But in the fourth year of the war, Semmes was exhausted and so was his ship. At fifty-five, he still looked boyish, with a full head of blonde hair and a waxed mustache that stood straight out from his cheeks, stiff as a fresh midshipman's salute. A sharp goatee funneled attention straight at his cold black eyes. But now those eyes often labored over a captain's log with a narrative nearing its end. At sea for almost two years, Semmes had captured over fifty ships and threatened or boarded almost five hundred. From Singapore to the

Gulf of Mexico, no merchantman was safe from the Confederate raider and its ruthless skipper. By some estimates she had cost the Union at least five million dollars in goods and vessels. Sometimes Semmes merely boarded a ship and robbed it, allowing it to continue its voyage and bidding the crew tell the world about the terrible predations of the *Alabama*. Sometimes he destroyed his victim, sinking the smoldering hulk and setting the crew free on the closest shore. Occasionally, Semmes deemed a vessel sound enough to capture and refit as another Confederate privateer.

Semmes had been the terror of the seas for a good long run, but he could see now that his luck was running out. The *Alabama* was being hunted. Union warships patrolled the world looking for her in earnest. That fact didn't worry Semmes though as much as what he should do with a particular cargo he carried at the moment.

"Lieutenant Kell. Do you remember when this all began, in the Azores? When we outfitted what the Brits then called *Ship 290*?" Semmes sat in a round-back, leather chair in his cabin. The well-appointed room gently rolled in the gusty winds of Table Bay, a broad harbor tucked inside a hook of land crowned by 3,600-foot Table Mountain. Lieutenant John McIntosh Kell stood across the cabin dressed in a gray vest and white drill trousers. He held his peaked cap in his hand. The executive officer was a hard man, tall and athletic, with a sweeping dark mustache and clean chin. He had the grit to control the crew, a crusty collection of men from all over the world. And he could be brutal if need be, but he was perhaps the only man on board whom Semmes could confide in.

"I do, sir. Them was heady days."

"The whole world was our bathtub then, but the water has grown cold for me." Semmes had come a long way since, at age sixteen, he'd first gone to sea as a midshipman in the United States Navy. His latest conquest was the capture of the *Conrad*, a bark that he armed and crewed and sent off to pirate on its own. Aboard the *Conrad*, Semmes had found recent American newspapers that reported defeats for the South on almost every front, including the fall of Vicksburg and Lee's retreat from Gettysburg. Now he was looking at the next challenge with a jaundiced eye. "Here now, Kell. You should know that I have decided to head back across the Atlantic for one last campaign."

"Rest assured that I will be at your side, whatever happens,

Captain." Kell stood at ease, but still seemed as stiff as a boarding plank.

"Yes, I appreciate your loyalty and service, Kell. But I am bone tired. The past months have laid the load of a dozen years across my back. I feel our days are numbered and I know we must do something with the gold before it's too late." The gold. Part of what worried Semmes was what to do with the gold. It was a secret cargo he wished he wasn't responsible for. It was worth close to one million dollars. The exact origins of the treasure were unknown, but Thomas Conolly, the grandson of the Speaker of the defunct Irish Parliament, the lord of Castletown House, the largest great house in Ireland, had entrusted him with it while in port in Cadiz. Conolly, an Irish supporter of the South and a member of the British Parliament, had appeared out of the blue, asked to speak with Semmes in private, and announced that friends of the Southern cause wished to help the Confederate war effort. They wanted anonymity of course, but Semmes soon understood that the money came from elements of the wealthy British cotton industry, businessmen who counted heavily on the American South's important crop. Semmes seemed the perfect channel back to America, Conolly said.

The captain could always claim the gold came from the *Alabama*'s depredations if questions arose. It had been an arms-length transaction with Semmes swearing that he would get the gold to Richmond somehow. The heavy treasure slowed down the *Alabama* in battle, but it weighed on Semmes even more than that. Kell could see the gold problem was eating a whole in his captain and the lieutenant's mind searched for the simplest solution.

"Might we find a sympathetic Southern ship in Simonstown or Capetown? Someone we can trust to take the gold back for us?"

"The only man I would trust to do that is someone bound by the legalities of the army or navy. Do you think we can find a Confederate soldier or sailor here? In Africa?" Semmes snorted at the idea without thinking. He looked up and glimpsed the crestfallen look on Kell's blunt face and caught himself immediately. He hadn't meant to deride Kell's earnest suggestion.

"I'm sorry, Captain. I only meant to help," Kell murmured.

"No, no, no, Kell. I am the sorry one. I didn't mean to push aside your idea. Perhaps there *is* someone on the Cape whom we can trust with the treasure."

"We will go ashore then, first thing in the morning," Kell replied brightly. "This is the center of the South African government. There are British agents here sympathetic to our cause. As strange as it may seem, there may be Confederate contacts as well, even at this far end of the dark continent." Semmes fiddled with a briarwood pipe on his desk and nodded his head while he pondered that.

"Indeed, Lieutenant. I envy you your optimism. For my part, I long to be back in Mobile, living in peace." Semmes stood up and waved Kell over to the captain's excellent liquor cabinet. A mahogany side table provided a stable bar though the ship rocked high and low on building swells. The captain deftly poured two glasses of Napoleon brandy, handed one to his first officer and raised his own in a toast. "Kell, you said you will be with me no matter what happens. Well, I will tell you that no matter what happens in Capetown or on our next voyage, I see shadows of a sorrowful future for the South, a million in gold or not." Kell shook his head as if to put that thought out of his mind. He smiled as he accepted the draught of brandy, which tilted to one side of the glass when the cabin floor listed with a swell.

"To your health, sir. To your health."

Chapter 21

The launch that brought Semmes and Kell to shore tied up at a dock filled with ships from every point on the globe. That was no surprise. Cape Town, one of the world's great maritime centers, commands the Cape of Good Hope, linking the Atlantic with the Indian Ocean, the New World with the Far East. The winds of the Roaring Forties notwithstanding, the South African provincial capital boasts a harbor that mariners can track for miles using the coastline's landmark two-thousand foot Lion's Head peak.

The British controlled the Cape Province, but it had been settled in 1652 by Dutchman Jan Van Riebeeck of the East India Company, who built a fort there. Cape Town had been a rest station for the world's most intrepid seafaring vessels rounding the cape thirty miles further south ever since. The port city's sturdy if simple stone buildings clung to the bowl of land beside the sea while rocky Table Mountain, shrouded in the mist, soared in the background.

As the Confederate pair walked toward Buitengracht Street, heading for the Malay Quarter, gangs of heaving stevedores babbled in Xosa, Afrikaans and oddly accented English. Semmes and his first officer walked in the shadow of Signal Hill, a 1,000-foot mountain landmark at the center of the city. The American men weren't in uniform. Kell's vest and service whites were nondescript. He carried his cap in hand, its only Confederate insignia, a black fouled anchor. Semmes was in summer rig, a white straw boater, white drill trousers and a gray frock coat that billowed in the steady winds howling in off the bay. Three gold stripes on his sleeve were the only military telltales. A warm, summer breeze still lingered, even as the season shifted into South African autumn.

They had just entered the city proper. A broad avenue stretching out before them revealed Van Riebeeck's 17th Century star fort called the castle. A small Dutch Colonial inspired city hall stood in the central square, which also included a bronze statue of the founder and the relatively new Groot Kirk or Great Church, the cathedral of the town's Dutch Reform burghers. The British had installed an updated Cape Town train station and a burgeoning mercantile neighborhood clustered around the government complex. Radiating out from the city square, modest, flat-roofed houses, built of gray stone, swept up to and along the ridges of Signal Hill. Semmes took all of this in, trying to remember landmarks from his last visit, when a clear voice welled up behind them like a soft bay breeze.

"Good morning, gentlemen. And where might you hail from?" Semmes glanced back before he realized it, but tried to ignore the salutation. However the South African seemed familiar to him. The man was young, maybe twenty-six or seven, and he spoke English with the dull vowel sounds peculiar to the African Dutch.

"Do I know you, my good man?" the captain answered, stopping short and turning to face the stranger. Kell almost tripped as he tried to halt as quickly as his skipper.

"No, I don't believe so, but I know who, or shall I say, *what* you are." The man smiled slowly. He was tall and thin, with ginger hair and a mustache and pointed goatee that made him look like a 15th Century Dutch master. Semmes was put out by the man's coyness.

"Come, now. Explain yourself. I have no time for riddles."

"Of course. Allow me to introduce myself. I am Franz Coetzee. And you are from the United States if I am not mistaken?" The South African twirled his mustache as if he was sizing up what he should pay for a basket of fruit. Semmes did not offer his own name in return.

"Mr. Coetzee, the States are not so united anymore, I am afraid. They are at war. Luckily I am from Maryland. A border state. I have no allegiance to either side." Now it was Semmes's turn to be coy. The Afrikaner nodded as if he accepted what he knew to be a lie.

"Ah, yes. I have heard of this war. I am a journalist and have traveled widely. Most recently to London, working for my paper, *The Times*."

"A newspaperman. Of course!" Semmes brightened. "The newspaperman is always the youngest chap in the room. I have read *The Times* whenever I can get it. In my travels."

"And you do travel, don't you, Captain?" The South African swept his eyes away, looking east toward the sharp peak of Lion's Head.

"Now, see here. I feel you have the advantage of me, Coetzee. Have I met you before?"

"Indeed, no you have not, but I know of you, Captain Semmes." Coetzee stared directly at the raider as if he was accusing him of some crime. The Confederate gritted his teeth at the mention of his name. To think that a stranger on the street thousands of miles from home knew who he was, hunted as he was by Union authorities! A thousand possibilities raced through his mind as he considered the implications of that. His eyes darted around, looking for agents who might be ready to pounce. But the people around them continued to brush past in the bustling square. Semmes turned his eyes back to the red-headed journalist, who while not smiling, could barely suppress an amused expression.

"Not to worry, Captain. Your secret is safe with me."

"How do you know me, then?" Semmes demanded, whispering now.

"I saw you from afar when you were on Sao Miguel."

"The Azores?"

"As strange as it seems, I watched the *Agrippina* sail into Pont Delgada. I saw you direct the arming of Mr. Bulloch's *Enrica* there and I saw you sail the *Alabama*, newly christened with Stars and Bars flying, out of that Portuguese port. This world, it is a small place."

"Indeed it seems it is." Semmes expelled a breath that released the tension of the last few moments. Coetzee saw him relax, looked furtively from side to side, and pressed him.

"And what brings you to South Africa, Captain?"

"The business of war, of course." He motioned to Kell that they should move on and the Afrikaner fell in beside them.

"You are the second American…ah businessman I have met in Capetown this week."

"Oh?" Semmes seemed uninterested but politely followed the man's conversation as he headed for a public house he had frequented before.

Coetzee continued, "An American ship captain who frequents this side of the Atlantic perhaps more than he should." Semmes filed that in the back of his mind. He needed an American ship with a man he could trust. He was here after all to get Conolly's gold back to Richmond. The trio continued to walk into the Malay Quarter, an enclave of Chinese merchants and related service businesses. A jumble of storefronts displayed a variety of wares. Almost every business touted storefront dragon designs with bright gold and reds punctuated by the bold black letters of Chinese calligraphy.

"In normal times, I would welcome the mention of any American in this exotic place, but I must ask. Is this ship captain of the North or the South?"

"He is from Maryland like you. But I do not know his allegiance. Though I would suspect, based on the nature of his cargo, that he prefers the slave states."

"He traffics in slaves?" Semmes stopped and looked at his interlocutor again. So Kell's optimism had been well-placed. Capetown did harbor a man from Semmes' own state who seemed to sympathize with the Confederacy. Coetzee caught the spark in the Rebel captain's eye.

"He has just returned from Havana where I believe he delivered close to seven hundred men, women and children to the Cuban slave pens." Semmes sensed a trick and staked out an unassailable position.

"Surely you know that it is against both American and British law to traffic in slaves. It is constitutionally forbidden North and South." Semmes had certainly seen slavers in his depredations on merchant ships, but they were few and far between, especially since the hanging of a Yankee slaver in New York City in 1862. The group entered a small courtyard, the entrance to a watering hole that touted European food and drink. A sign in English pictured a dark bottle of liquor. It read: American Style Whiskey. Semmes waved Kell and Coetzee to a corner table as a Chinese family in loose fitting white pajama-like suits scampered across the room. A young Oriental man bowed perfunctorily and bid them welcome in perfect Afrikaans. Coetzee answered with an order for three glasses and local beer before turning back to the others.

"Evidently the reward is worth the risk. Even as we speak he is refitting his ship, the *Salem*, down at the Alfred docks, so that he may pack even more black contraband into his hold next voyage." Semmes sat stiffly as he keenly listened to the Afrikaner. His mind ran a mile a minute considering the possibilities of using the *Salem* and its captain for a gold run.

"Where does he take these slaves from? Certainly not from the British territories here?"

"No. He sails to the mouth of the Congo River where tribal leaders or Mohammedan henchmen round up the losers in tribal wars and pen them until the next slave ship comes a calling. Then it's off to market in Cuba or Rio."

"The Triangle Trade still lives," Semmes replied dispassionately. The Rebel raider knew well that the commerce of slaving still boomed around the world. More to the point, he was intrigued that the slave ship's captain had the audacity to flaunt strict anti-slavery laws; that he possessed the skill to elude both British and Union ships sent to stop the slave trade. He made a decision. "Listen, Coetzee. I would like to meet this man. What is his name and where can I find him?"

Chapter 22

The sea air seeped through gaps in the warehouse's weather-grayed boards. Coetzee had led Semmes and Kell back to the docklands where he reckoned the *Salem*'s captain spent most of his time overseeing the work on his ship. They entered the large ramshackle building, sagging with age, but still sound enough for the varied pursuits of the men who built and repaired ships. A crooked sign hung above oversized double carriage house doors.

JEDIDIAH ARMSTRONG & SONS
SHIPWRIGHTS SINCE 1742

A cavernous open room, big enough to contain a two hundred-foot vessel, echoed with carpenters hammering and the steady rhythmic clanging of a busy blacksmith. Long oak timbers lined one wall, the precious wood having been brought in from Europe. Another part of the space harbored a group of sail makers, unrolling a heavy piece of canvas across the floor. Coetzee, Semmes and Kell paused at the head of the open warehouse, while Semmes inspected the scene with an expert's eye.

"Like any good shipwright, this place buzzes with work," the captain mused. He tugged on his dark wood pipe and beamed as a carpentry crew climbed over the bones of a newly-laid hull. Coetzee nodded his head at Semmes' observation.

"Armstrong's is Capetown's best. Captain Tilghman spares no expense. He can afford the best and he knows his trade." The

South African stood on his toes, peering down the long broad expanse that faced the water. The enormous doors there were open and blocked by a giant marine railway harness that lifted ships out of the water and used a twelve-horse team to haul them into the shelter of the warehouse. "Ah, there is the man; with the smith." The group made their way across the floor, deftly avoiding a gang of men coiling three-inch hemp rope. A sizeable ship would use it for dock lines. The South African reached out to shake the slaver's hand and gathered Semmes in with his left arm.

"Captain Nathaniel Tilghman, I give you Captain Raphael Semmes of the *C.S.S. Alabama*."

Tilghman cast a dark eye toward Semmes and then Kell, but also eyed Coetzee with a cruel look. A moment later he flashed a gold tooth when he smiled at the men, realizing who Semmes was. The presence of an infamous celebrity amused the seaman.

"Well, well. It is the devil himself," he mewed. He still held onto Coetzee's hand with a controlling grip, holding him as an ominous warning: *this man you've brought here better not cause me trouble.* The reporter pulled back but couldn't get loose until the captain finally released him. "At least you are the devil according to the Northern papers I read." Semmes ignored the comments and poker-faced, resorted to formalities. He turned to Kell.

"Captain Tilghman. This is my first officer, Lieutenant Kell. I wish to speak with you privately about a business proposition." Tilghman nodded toward Kell as his smile faded. He looked again at Semmes.

"Of course. I am always open to making money." He turned and directed the group to a small, glass-windowed office in one corner of the warehouse.

They found seats around a heavy, rough-hewn table situated in the middle of the room. The enclosure's windows allowed the business's proprietors to work at the table or an adjacent roll-top desk while keeping a keen eye on the floor. Kell noticed the walls did not extend much beyond seven feet high, so the office barely muffled the industrious noises of the shop. However, thanks to the walls, the men on the shop floor could not hear conversations in the office. Semmes drew himself up to the table and sized up his new acquaintance.

The slave ship captain was a big man, over six feet tall. A hard face glistening with an oily complexion hid behind a wide bushy black beard. Greasy long hair snaked from under a soiled bowler hat. A black double-breasted frock coat flowed down around salt-crusted raw leather boots. Semmes cringed at the grimy green tarnish on the coat's column of brass buttons. He shrugged off the offense to his military sensibilities and began with small talk.

"Tilghman is an old Maryland name, is it not?"

"As a Maryland man, yerself, you danged well know that every time you leave Baltimore or Annapolis, you sail past my beloved Tilghman Island shore." The slaver bobbed his head as he spoke, an aggressive attitude clearly part of his personality. Semmes tried to mask his revulsion at the man's crude appearance and rough language.

"Ah, yes, the island where the Choptank opens onto the bay. You are a man of the sea and that is what I need right now."

"Captain Semmes. Let's not wrestle with each other. I know you are a murderous pirate and you know I am a villain as well. What is it you need exactly?"

"Very well, Tilghman. A man of few words." A bone shaking clang ripped across the shop floor, causing Semmes to pause. He checked the bank of windows before he leaned in and spoke in low tones. "I do not know where your American sympathies lie, but my government needs an important shipment delivered to Confederate authorities. Where are you heading when you leave here, if I may ask?"

"Well, that's none of your business. But if you must know, I am heading for the Namib and then Cabinda where the Congo meets the sea. From there, if all goes well. I'm off to Havana or if need be, Rio. I suppose I could alter that route if it's worth my while though."

"I will pay you ten thousand dollars in gold if you can get this shipment safely into Baltimore Harbor." Tilghman cocked his head as if he had heard wrong, but then he exploded.

"Baltimore Harbor! Curse all! Baltimore is heavily patrolled. I would have to enter as if I belonged there. There's no sneaking into that port, because of the war." Semmes pulled back at the slaver's stark reaction, but he had expected some reservations from the man. He continued calmly.

"But yours is not a *Confederate* ship. I'm not asking you to run the blockade. I have thought this through. Hear me out. I would not expect the *Salem* could run the blockade off the Southern states any more than my *Alabama* could. But in Maryland waters, I would not expect the Union authorities could stop you for any legitimate reason. I reckon your knowledge of the Chesapeake and your Maryland pedigree would make Baltimore the best landfall for you."

"But I am a slaver, Captain. It will be hard to disguise that fact, even with empty holds. Even now, the smiths here are fitting more shackles below decks and I wouldn't like to tell you why."

"That is something I do wonder about. How many Negroes do you…ah..take on a voyage?" It was Kell, speaking for the first time. He felt like the wording of his question made it seem like he was asking about livestock instead of human beings. The young lieutenant loathed slavery even though he sailed for the South.

"Last voyage I brung in four hundred fifty. It's not that I am making room for more. But it was six weeks past when I came upon a sight, one I hope to never see again, not even in my worst nightmares." Kell squinted at the oily sea captain who gritted his teeth at the memory. He noticed that besides the big gold tooth in the center of his mouth, the slaver's other teeth were black with rot. Kell leaned in for more information.

"And what was that? What did you see?"

"It was off the coast of Bermuda, I saw a ship floating free, sails struck, no flag. A ghost ship, she was. We boarded her and found she was a slaver like us, or used to be. Of Portuguese registry, the *Corvo*." Tilghman shivered at the picture in his mind. Seeing this reaction from a thug like Tilghman made the hair on Kell's neck stand on end and even Semmes shifted uncomfortably in his chair. The slaver's dark eyes bugged out as he stared at each of them in turn. Neither Confederate interrupted.

"There was no one left, gentlemen. The slaves were gone, though it was clear from the smell of human waste and Negro misery that it had contained hundreds."

"You mean they had abandoned ship?" Kell prodded.

"Well, the Negroes certainly had. All the whaleboats were gone. But the crew, they…was…all…still…there." He said this staring at nothing in particular as if he was seeing the scene all over again.

"But you said no one was left." Semmes corrected him.

"They was all dead, all the crew. But they was still there, what was left of them. You see, gentlemen, the savages took their time dealing with their captors. They must have escaped the hold and then in a revolt taken the crew, near a hundred Portugee, hostage. But it didn't end there." Kell gulped and Semmes, with some idea of what had happened, looked over at his young lieutenant, regretting that he'd opened the line of conversation.

"They cut them up, they did. All of the whites. The decks ran red with blood, gallons of it. They cut each arm off, and each leg, and each hand, and every foot…and all the heads. It must have taken some hours with the few good cutlasses the ship's officers had carried. A sailor's knife wouldn't do the job we saw."

Kell had turned pale with the thought of the mutilations and Semmes actually put his hand on the younger man's shoulder to steady him. "Then, what do you think they did with two hundred arms and two hundred legs and four hundred hands and feet and a hundred torsos and a hundred staring skulls?" The officers shook their heads, unblinking, unbelieving, as the slaver glared from man to man before he continued. "They laid them out in a pattern on the main deck. Some kind of African design, I suppose. A rectangle of limbs, around a circle of torsos, around a square of hands and feet, with the heads spiked in the center facing out, staring at the bloody scene."

"How ghastly!" Semmes exclaimed as the pattern framed itself in his mind.

"I tell you, Semmes. It was from another world. Like a new-fangled novelist's worst hallucination, it was. That, gentlemen, is why I am here at Armstrong's. This will not happen to the *Salem*. I am refitting with more shackles, some cages, to make sure my…ah…passengers stay below decks and don't get access to the ship's cutlery. The shipwrights are almost finished and the beauty part is the Armstrongs ask no questions of men like me."

"More shackles is one solution, I suppose." Kell had recovered and felt the anger building over what he had heard. He wasn't so angry about what the slaves had done to the Portuguese. He was angry at how terrible the conditions aboard the *Corvo* must have been to drive them to such savagery. "I might consider ending my slaving career if I had seen that." Tilghman's head snapped around at the young lieutenant. His voice turned to a frightening hiss.

"You don't approve, I know, Kell. Neither does the rest of

the world. I don't care. I provide a service and people pay me well for it. That is all that matters to me." Kell opened his mouth to reply, but Semmes cut him off.

"Yes, Tilghman, we understand what motivates you. Now, *I* need your services. Certainly you would need to keep the authorities from inspecting your hold, but this is not an insurmountable problem. Now, what is your answer? Can you deliver the goods? And will you?" The slaver sat back and the air went out of him.

"What are the goods, exactly, Captain? It can't be worse than slaves. Kell here wouldn't have it." He smiled mockingly at the first officer, who simply met his sneer with his own steady glare.

"It is gold. Bound for the government in Richmond."

"And you trust me with your gold? I'm no Confederate, you know."

"Trust you? No. I don't have to trust you. You must know, Captain Tilghman, that if you cross me, I have the means and the will to track you down and destroy your ship. What the slaves did to the Portuguese will seem a child's game compared to what I would do to you." Tilghman's head bobbed uncontrollably again as he stared at the Confederate pirate whose reputation for plunder exceeded his own. His decision took a few seconds, but ten thousand smackers in gold was too much treasure to turn down. The big sea captain slapped his hands on the table.

"We have a deal, Semmes." He stood and offered his hand to shake on the contract. Semmes examined the meaty ham of a hand as if he might see fresh blood on it. But standing, he took it and firmly shook. "What is the next step?" Tilghman seemed eager to get underway.

"As soon as you are ready to sail, we shall rendezvous in Table Bay and shift the cargo. I will give you the particulars of your contact in Baltimore at that time."

"I should be ready to shove off on the tide tomorrow evening. Tell me, Semmes. How much gold are we talking about?"

"Near a million dollars worth." The Confederate didn't blink at the enormous amount, but Tilghman's eyes bulged with excitement.

"By the gods! A million dollars! That must weigh at least a ton!"

"Two thousand, two hundred and forty-seven pounds,

actually," Kell interjected. A broad grin painted the slaver's rough face, his open mouth flashing gold shadowed by black. He looked from man to man beaming.

"I'm glad I met you, Semmes." The slaver turned to the Afrikaner fixer for the first time since the group met. "Coetzee, I owe you a whiskey. Huzzah, I'll even buy *you* one, Kell," he laughed, winking at the American sailor. Kell did not find the man's offer amusing, but Nathaniel Tilghman continued to roll with laughter, louder now, his gold tooth shining for all to see. A sober looking Semmes could only hope the slaver would be closemouthed when it came to the Confederate gold.

Chapter 23

The sun sat becalmed in the western sky, to the naked eye unmoving as if it was a more distant star. Puffy, maritime clouds raced past it, making the yellow orb seem even more static. Lieutenant Kell knew *all* the stars moved, of course, but to his impatient eye, this one hadn't budged one wit. Had time stopped, he mused?

The *Alabama* lay at anchor seven miles off Capetown, waggling in the strong, steady westerlies that constantly batter the cape. The executive officer had seen the tide change almost two hours ago and he was beginning to pace, wondering what was taking the *Salem* and its unsavory skipper so long. Just down the rail, Semmes smoked a fresh bowl of Virginia leaf while loitering on deck looking off toward land. He could make out the shore's vague outline but little detail was visible in the mist. Even Capetown's towering mountains were imperceptible. Semmes smiled at his fidgety first officer.

"Relax your bones, ol' Kell. The slave ship must not have been built for speed; she was built for misery." The lieutenant scowled.

"It is a miserable business, slaving. And I have a bad feeling about Tilghman. He is outlined in black in my mind. Sinister he is."

"I do not trust him either, but the threat and the reward will keep him in check, I reckon."

About four o'clock, a set of gaff-rigged masts emerged from

the ocean's misty shroud. Tilghman's two-masted, one hundred fifty-six foot schooner made straight for the *Alabama* at speed. The *Salem* was a black-hulled Baltimore clipper, modified with steam-powered sidewheels. At one hundred-seventy tons, the ship *was* fast and maneuverable for a miserable slaver.

"Ship dead ahead!" the watch called out to the deck warden. "She flies the flag of the United States. Send for the captain, Mr. Laycock!" Five minutes later, Semmes and Kell emerged from below, eager to get the exchange done and underway. They watched the slave ship maneuver into the wind, preparing to draw up alongside the rolling *Alabama*. The gap between the ships closed quickly as Tilghman expertly eased his craft to within ten feet. Several deckhands were arrayed along the port gunwale ready to tie the ships together. Experienced at gauging swells and distance, men on both vessels exchanged lines and the seamen heaved the ships tight together before cleating them off.

"Stand down!" Kell ordered once the ships were tied fast. Now the two vessels, of almost equal length, rose and fell as one as the ocean rolled in four foot seas. Twenty-four nondescript wooden crates sat on the *Alabama*'s deck. A stenciled number and a simple merchant's seal identified each crate. Tilghman leaped aboard uninvited, his heavy boots pounding the deck when the big man landed. He walked over to the crates and slapped a hand on one as he read the seal.

Naysmith & Tansley

Steam Hammer Co., Edinburgh

Semmes and Kell, further down the deck, began to walk forward to meet the slaver. The Confederates made eye contact. Tilghman's lack of boarding protocol disgusted them, but they didn't say anything. As they arrived, the slaver turned to them, still resting a covetous hand on the hefty box. He smiled in his now familiar sly way.

"Good evening, gentlemen. Naysmith and Tansley? Do I know this company?"

"A complete fiction, though I believe steam hammers are manufactured in Scotland," Semmes answered, all the while looking across the gunwales, sizing up Tilghman's crew. What kind of seadog works on a slave ship these days, he wondered?

"Steam hammers are heavy equipment. Heavy like gold. A good choice for the seal." Tilghman rubbed his eyes and stretched his arms. "Shall I have my men begin moving?"

"Yes, Kell here and six sailors will assist. Let us retire to my cabin to speak of details."

The captains left the deck, while Kell asked to see where the crates would be stored. Aboard the *Salem*, the slave ship's boatswain took Kell below and led him forward beyond the crew's quarters. Kell was pleased when he learned that the crates would not be kept in the hold. The boatswain hinted at a better arrangement. The smell of the *Salem* and its deepest regions disgusted him, he thought to himself as he made his way through a series of passageways and hatches. Slave ships reeked of human rot and no amount of cleaning could expunge that wretched stink. He had come across it before, he remembered.

He recalled another sea voyage, when he'd made a slaver from near two miles away. It was the smell of the thing, he told his mates. When the passing ship closed to within one hundred yards, the whole crew could see that it was indeed a slave ship, with a hundred shackled Africans crowded on the deck. But it was the name of the reeking vessel that most sickened Kell. *Yankee Freedom*. How wickedly ironic!

Finally they arrived at the space the boatswain had described. When Kell saw that Tilghman would store the gold in a secret cabin concealed behind a false bulkhead, he realized that the slave captain was an old hand at smuggling. Captain Semmes would be happy that the gold was hidden away like any good treasure should be.

Back in the *Alabama*'s captain's cabin, Semmes lit his pipe while Tilghman settled into a comfortable chair behind a scratched and scarred compact desk.

"So, Tilghman, this is what I want from you. I understand you are going to the Namib and Cabinda, and then on to Rio?"

"I won't go to Cabinda if I can fill my hold in the Namib. *Then* I go on to Rio."

"I see. It is good that you have a varied itinerary. It will keep whoever may be watching you on their heels." Semmes referred to some notes as he continued. "I know what cargo you take to Rio, of course. But what will you have once you leave Rio, bound for Baltimore?"

"A cargo of bananas, corn and perhaps corned beef. The slaves of Brazil are a very productive group."

"Indeed, Brazil is the largest slave-holding country in the world. It is no surprise that the mutilated seamen on the *Corvo* were Portuguese. Perhaps the black men of Brazil have every right to annihilate their brown masters there."

"You are not the first to express that thought." Semmes nodded his head as if he knew this, then continued.

"The people of Baltimore will rejoice at the Brazilian bounty you bring them. Once there you will find a Mr. Kane at this address." He handed the slaver a slip of paper. "It is the Catholic cathedral. St. Mary's. You know it?"

"I know it by its reputation, certainly. But I've never darkened its door." Semmes pursed his lips in understanding.

"Hmm, just so. Mr. Kane, who is the former marshal of police in the city, can be found in the first pew before the statue of Mary every morning at eight. He is a devout Catholic and prays the rosary each day. He prays for peace…through Confederate victory, of course. He will arrange to meet the *Salem* out in the harbor. Off load the gold at his direction. Then it will be his charge."

"And my payment, Captain? Should all this come to pass?"

"Should it *not* come to pass, I expect you to contact me or Marshal Kane or some other Confederate authority to make new arrangements."

"And what if the gold is taken, or lost, what then, Captain?" The question lit a fire under the Confederate raider.

"I expect you to guard this gold with your life, Tilghman," Semmes hissed through clenched teeth. "That is why I am paying you so well. As to your payment, your gold is in crate Number twenty-four. I have instructed Mr. Kell to place it in your cabin. It is a measure of trust that I tell you that. The shipment though must not be *taken*, as you put it; and it better not get *lost* as you say. I shall have no tricks from you and there will be no other problems that you can't solve. Do you understand?"

"Very well," Tilghman answered with a shrug. "I shall do my best. But I think the price for such a mission is low. I wonder if we could not renegotiate my payment?" Tilghman smiled slyly as he tried to shake more gold out of the Rebel captain whom he thought must be desperate at this point. Semmes glared at the smiling pirate. If he *was* desperate, he did not let it calm his anger.

"Alright, Tilghman," the raider growled. "You want a new deal. Well, here is the new deal." Semmes snatched the pipe from his lips and leaned across the well-worn desk with both hands stretched apart. "I will pay you the ten thousand dollars in crate twenty-four and…I. Shall. Let. You. Live. If I hear no more about this!" Tilghman's smile slowly faded to a scowl. Semmes reared up and strode to the other side of the cramped cabin, his hand on his navy revolver in case he needed it. But Tilghman wisely reconsidered raising his fee. He sighed disappointedly.

"Very well, Semmes. We keep the deal as is." His last few words were drowned out by a heavy knock and a panicked cry from the passage outside the captain's cabin.

"Ship ahoy, Captain! A warship! She flies the Stars and Stripes!"

Chapter 24

Semmes bolted from his cabin, rushing for the bridge like a flushed-out rabbit. Tilghman pressed himself against the bulkhead to let the Confederate by and then followed. When Semmes hit the spar deck he started calling out orders. A boy ensign manned the helm in the absence of Kell.

"Ensign, hoist our own Union banner. That will buy us time." Semmes often used a U.S. flag when he encountered another ship at sea. European ships, especially the British, kept clear of Union vessels. American ships often let down their guard when they spied the familiar flag. Semmes was not above the subterfuge. Tilghman lumbered up behind the *Alabama*'s master a few seconds later. Semmes ignored him.

"Fire up the boilers. Tell the engineer we'll need full power."

"Already done, sir," the ensign answered.

"Has Kell completed the transfer?"

"I sent a seaman to get him. He should be returning shortly."

"As soon as he is aboard, weigh anchor and cast off from the *Salem*."

"Sir."

"And stand by to get the bloody gollywobblers up." He turned to the slaver then. "Tilghman, it's hard to say who they are after, you or me. You have the gold now. Godspeed and good luck."

"Same to you, Semmes. If we split up, they'll have to choose. If I never see you again, I wish you a fair breeze and a good fight." The slaver swept his hat low, stalked off the bridge and made for his own ship. He passed Kell on the way, but neither man spoke.

Semmes plucked his field glasses from the nearest cutlass rack. He'd had them since the Mexican War, where he'd served with Winfield Scott. Those days seemed so distant now; but the thrill of battle he'd first felt at Chapultepec had never left him. He sized up the Union craft bearing down less than three miles away. "It is the sloop of war *New Haven.*" The three hundred-foot ship carried sixteen nine-inch Dahlgren smoothbores, eight of them in broadside batteries on each side. There were 30-pounder rifles on swivels fore and aft, and several Howitzers for close in fighting. Semmes noted that she was heading down wind coming in from the west.

'Sir, the mizzentop watch says they have sanded the deck and hoisted the deck nets already. They clearly plan to fight if need be." The ensign held a speaking tube that connected with the man atop the mizzenmast who had a clear view of the battle preparations aboard the *New Haven*. Kell ran up the steps to the spar deck two at a time and reported to his captain.

"The gold is secure aboard the *Salem*, in a hidden chamber."

"Very well. Now let's ease away from the slave ship. Keep the sails furled. Just steam right now. I don't want to make it obvious that we are trying to flee, though we will run when the time is right." They could hear men calling out orders on the *Salem* as both ships slowly turned away from each other. Their steam engines strained and both funnels coughed up black smoke. Semmes ordered a course due north, a favorable broad reach for the *Alabama* once she hoisted sails. The *Salem* took longer to get underway, but turned south as its sails unfurled one mast at a time.

The sound of alarm rattles carried across the water just as the ensign announced, "Captain, the watch says the sloop is going to battle stations. The crew is running around like cats with their tails on fire." Then BOOM! A shot fired from the 30-pounder on the *New Haven*'s foredeck splashed in front of the *Alabama*, a warning shot meant to stop its progress.

"Maintain course." Semmes ordered calmly. Another shot followed immediately, this one across the *Salem*'s beam. The slave ship was still hoisting sails, and its steam engine, though fired, made slow progress compared to the *Alabama*. But Semmes wasn't ready to dash away yet. He waited for the warship to make a choice. The thump-thump-thumping of the *Alabama*'s twin engines seemed to count down the seconds. Minutes later the *New Haven* edged toward the slave ship and Semmes took the opportunity. "They are turning for the *Salem*. Hoist the sails, Kell. Chart a course for the Canaries." Semmes kept his eye on the other two ships as he sailed off unmolested.

Chapter 25

Aboard *Salem*

"Give us full power! The cursed blackguards are coming for us!" Tilghman on his bridge leaned into the wind as if his momentum could hasten the acceleration of the overburdened slave ship. The sails were filling now and the *Salem* lurched ahead when the hard west wind ballooned into them. "Semmes, you lucky devil," Tilghman muttered to himself. Looking north, he could see the *Alabama* shrinking in the distance. The slaver tore his envious eyes away from the Confederate pirate and focused on the Union ship bearing down on him, sails flying and smoke pouring from the centrally located coal stack. The warship fired a round that fell starboard of the *Salem*; a second warning that Tilghman ignored.

"They are making time on us, Captain," the first officer yelled. He had carefully eyed both ships and estimated that the *New Haven* was coming on fast. "They must be making fifteen knots in this wind." Tilghman calculated his odds for escape.

"We can best that. He is fast downwind, but we are faster on this reach. Make sure the stokers are working as hard as they can." Tilghman looked up and noticed that his smokestack offered but a few weak puffs of white smoke. "Get down below now and find out why our fire is lagging." Just then another round from the warship fell just abaft, but then another and another ball dotted the water beside the slave ship. A fourth shot landed before the bow, near enough to douse the foredeck with water. It splashed so close that Tilghman ran across the open deck to see if the shot had hit the bowsprit. Although he carried four carronades and a howitzer, he realized he could not fight the three thousand ton sloop of war if it caught him. It was within a mile now and still gaining. As he considered his next move, a seaman ran up, red-faced.

"Sir, the engine's slipped its shaft. The engineer says he cannot fix it without a calm sea and two hours." Tilghman gritted his rotten teeth at the news.

"Blast it! Helmsman, heave to, turn into the wind! Ensign, Run up a white flag! I shall have to talk my way out of this."

Twenty minutes later a launch carrying a *New Haven* officer, accompanied by a detachment of eight marines, tied up to the *Salem*. They wasted no time boarding. Tilghman, hat in hand, stood athwartships next to an open gate in the starboard bulwark. He noted the marines carried Springfield rifles, sidearms and cutlasses. He could see they meant business. A clean-shaven young midshipman jumped aboard, cutlass drawn and began speaking almost before he hit the deck.

"I board this vessel in the name of the United States Navy. I am Lieutenant Gordon Strong of the U.S.S. *New Haven*. You are in my custody, sir." Tilghman looked the eager, well-scrubbed boy officer up and down, smiling obsequiously. He spread his long heavy arms, feigning supplication.

"Certainly, Lieutenant. As you wish. But what does the navy want of a poor American merchant ship?"

"Why did not a poor American merchantman heave to at the first warning shot, Captain?" The navy man spoke quickly, in clipped staccato measure; a New Englander by the sound of it. He was angry and suspicious, it was clear. Tilghman answered slowly and in a sweetly calming voice.

"I simply did not hear a warning shot. You were downwind, I suppose."

"No, we were upwind of you. What was that other ship, the one that ran at our approach?"

"Ah, my sister ship what also is a merchantman. Is there something wrong with trying to make a living, even in the midst of our war against the Rebels?" Tilghman looked at the navy man with innocent cow-eyes. The sailor tightened his ruddy face peevishly.

"I would see your papers of registry and your bills of lading, Captain," he barked. "Where are you based?"

"Of course, Lieutenant." Tilghman motioned to his second in command, sending him off to his cabin to retrieve the ship's papers. He turned back to the naval officer, talking quietly, moving slowly. "Baltimore is homeport, though this ship has a long history that stretches back to its building in New England." Strong was not impressed by Tilghman's allusion to his native region.

"And what is your cargo? What is your business here, off the coast of Africa?" the young man spit out impatiently. His eyes darted around the ship looking for anything amiss. Tilghman tried to follow what the officer was looking at without seeming obvious. The slaver affected a pleasant, helpful look on his face.

"I have no cargo at the moment. I have just been refitted in Capetown." Tilghman knew that if the naval scrub or his marines went below, they would see the hardware installed to contain slaves. He must not let the inspection get that far or the fight would be for survival. His eyes swept toward the *New Haven*, its sails struck, its heavy guns bristling from open gun ports. He tried to hide the desperation in his eyes. The navy officer had relaxed a touch now, but he crossed his arms and sighed in exasperation, waiting for the slaver to give him more specific information. Tilghman spluttered convincingly before he continued obtusely.

"We usually carry finished goods which we exchange for agricultural products on this side of the Atlantic," he lied. The ship's second in command had returned by then and the Union lieutenant accepted the papers handed to him by the first officer and began perusing them. Two minutes later, he handed the papers back to Tilghman.

"Your papers are in order, Captain. But this is a very suspicious vessel as was the one that got away." The naval officer turned to the marines, but kept his eyes on Tilghman as if to see his reaction. "Sergeant, take four men and inspect the holds." Tilghman stared at the Union man, praying he would not have to kill him. His voice remained calm and matter of fact.

"Lieutenant, you are welcome to inspect the entire ship if you wish. But I should tell you that we've had a run of Yellow Fever in the last month. I wouldn't want you or your men to contract that dread disease." The marine sergeant heard this as he led his inspectors toward the hatch leading below decks, and he looked to the lieutenant to see what he would do next. The officer raised his hand to stop them. He fixed Tilghman with a perturbed stare once again.

"That's very considerate of you, Captain. I would have hoped you'd have warned us of that before we came aboard."

"But you jumped aboard so quickly, Lieutenant, like the marines storming bloody Tripoli. I had no time to warn you off." Strong nodded at Tilghman sourly, the navy officer's head snapping about as his face reddened in frustration. Then he spoke quickly.

"We shall take the chance and check below decks, anyway." He beckoned for the marines to continue as he kept talking. "The world is a dangerous place these days. Pirates, Rebels, slavers. We take chances everyday out here on the wild sea. Yellow Fever does not hold much threat to the United States fleet."

Tilghman made eye contact with his first officer who quietly slipped away to gather the crew to fight. It would be a bloody mess but there was no way to avoid it now. A few minutes passed. The marines must have discovered what the *Salem* was about by now, but they had not returned. The lieutenant and his remaining contingent waited as did the slaver, but not a word passed between them. Then Tilghman jumped at what he saw across the waves. It was behind the boarding party, so the lieutenant didn't notice, but the slave captain suddenly realized the time for words was over now.

Chapter 26

BOOM, BOOM, BOOM! The *Salem*'s bridge deck rocked with thundering concussions, staggering the men collected there. It took Lieutenant Strong a moment to realize the slave ship had not been hit. He spun around on rubbery legs and looked off toward the *New Haven*. The warship's funnel had fallen across the deck, a mast was gone and a fire burned along the stern where the rudder should be. The *Alabama* had returned, sneaking up on the Union craft and tucking into it before the Yankees knew what hit them. Tilghman recovered his sea legs quickly and floored the still gawping Strong with a blind-side blow to his head. The ship's crew quickly overpowered the marines and threw them and their lieutenant overboard.

"Get this ship underway!" Tilghman ordered. The remaining marines, the ones still below, would have to wait. Semmes had circled around and observed the other two ships. The Confederate raider had decided his gold was in jeopardy when he saw that the *Salem* had heaved to and had been boarded. Now he had disabled the *New Haven* with his first three shots, giving the slaver a chance to get away. The destroyed funnel had turned the warship into a smoking wreck, making it difficult for the gunners to see their targets. And the rudder's destruction made it nearly impossible for the sloop to fight back. With no steering, The *New Haven* could not turn in the wind or the waves, and could not bring its guns to bear on a maneuvering target.

On his own bridge, Semmes tugged on his pipe, his free hand behind his back, mulling over his next decision; destroy the Union vessel or leave it to the pirates. He decided to press a decision on the *New Haven*'s captain.

"Raise the Stars and Bars," he ordered. "Let the blackguard know what he's up against." The *Alabama*'s skipper watched the other vessels patiently, more concerned with his gold aboard the *Salem* than the wounded Union ship. The rising Confederate banner had an immediate effect. The *New Haven* steamed off at speed. By a stroke of luck, its damaged rudder steered her on a course perpendicular to the Confederate ship. Although heading into the wind, the Yankee ship seemed to be running away. Meanwhile, the slaver still lingered, trying to restart its faulty engine, its sails luffing with the breeze. "Come on, Tilghman," Semmes muttered nervously, as he watched the idle ship. "Get yourself to safety, get my gold away from here." His attention on the *Salem*, the Confederate raider didn't notice the *New Haven*'s next move.

"They're hoisting the headsails and coming about," Kell cried, pointing at the Union warship. Using a staysail to catch the steady westerly, the ship swung back toward the *Alabama*, and in mid-turn unleashed a volley from its broadside of Dahlgrens. BOOM BOOM BOOM BOOM BOOM BOOM BOOM BOOM. The shots echoed across the water like closely synchronized bass drums. Most of the shells exploded harmlessly off the chain armor protecting the ship's wooden hull. But two shots struck the bow of the charging *Alabama*, dismounting the 100-pounder Blakely rifle on its foredeck.

Semmes and his staff fell to the deck, rocked by the blast. Rolling with the blow, the captain jumped up again and began barking orders. "Signal they must surrender now or there will be no quarter given!" Despite the *New Haven*'s stinging broadside this was not an idle threat. Both captains realized the Union sloop was mortally wounded. Semmes fumed at his mistake. He should have known a powerful ship like the *New Haven*, though damaged, could still be dangerous. And Semmes knew now that the Yankee skipper would not surrender. He would fight to the last. That's what Semmes himself would do. He also understood that the *New Haven* had meant to fight all along.

"That glorious Yankee steamed upwind, maneuvering for a fighting position," Semmes muttered admiringly. "I should have seen it," he chastised himself. "Drop the chains, sand the decks! Come about! If it's a fight the devils want, we'll give it to 'em!" The *Alabama* nimbly turned back toward the *Salem* on an easterly heading, keeping itself between the Yankee guns and the gold-bearing ship. "Have the gun crews fire at will. Kell, prepare the starboard 32-pounders for a volley."

"Sir!" came the reply.

The Confederate raider sailed off, gaining some distance for maneuver. Leaving the clumsy *New Haven* sailing on the *Alabama*'s stern, Semmes gave his ship a slim profile, a difficult target to sight.

"Helmsman, on my mark, come hard about." While Semmes raised his hand and waited to signal, the *New Haven's* bow-mounted 30-pounder opened on the *Alabama* with no result; then fired a defiant round at the *Salem*, the shot carrying beyond the slave ship harmlessly.

"Now!' Semmes ordered. "Helm, come about behind the sorry blackguard!" The *Alabama* started a wide turn away and around the Yankee ship. Semmes turned to Kell and sized up his enemy. "He has more guts than brains…and he shall pay for that." The Confederate captain set his square jaw and squinted his eyes. He realized he would have to execute the enemy ship like he would a wounded animal; too dangerous to let her live. It would not be a fair fight or a pleasant task.

Almost in unison both ships let loose broadside volleys as they came abreast of each other at two hundred yards. The Union shells went wide or struck the *Alabama*'s chain armored hull. But aboard the *New Haven*, the upper deck bulwark exploded into wooden shrapnel. Agonized cries mixed with the thunder of the guns and a dozen sailors went down. When the breechings of a smoldering Dahlgren broke loose, the mighty gun jumped its rails and crushed a powder boy between its cascabel and the bulwark. A second explosion cut down two gunners like a scythe cuts through wheat. Pools of blood welled up on the sanded deck where they fell. A nearby gun crew watched the life pulse out of both sailors who lay on the deck with long sharp splinters of wood sprouting from their chests. Others gunners flinched when the *Salem* joined in with a volley from its carronades. The small cannons the slave ship carried made a lot of noise, but they were too short-sighted to reach the Union sloop.

The warships had passed now and the *Alabama* closed in on its prey. Rudderless, the *New Haven* could not come about for another broadside; she could only run. By steaming in behind the Yankee vessel, Semmes would cross the T. The classic naval maneuver would bring the full force of his broadside volley to bear on the warship's stern while taking the *New Haven's* powerful Dahlgrens out of the fight.

In the meantime, on the *Alabama*'s spar deck, six men on the 68-pounder pivot gun worked like the well-crafted parts of a fine timepiece. Three men sponged, loaded and primed the gun. One man dropped the hinged bulwark, the ten foot wide door revealing the giant smoothbore to the open sea. Another man used a system of overlapping rails or racers to train the gun at the enemy and an elevation screw to adjust the aim. The gun captain, using glasses, marked the distance and gripped the lanyard.

"Elevate to two hundred yards downrange."

"Marked at two hundred yards. Ready, sir."

"Fire!" Seconds later the sixty-eight pound projectile exploded into the rigging of the hapless *New Haven*. Grapeshot exploded above the heads of the deck crews, showering them with a deadly iron rain. Gunners aboard both ships ran through this routine a hundred times in the next few minutes. The *Alabama*'s pivoting gun allowed the maneuvering raider to fire on the run without a direct angle that a broadside needed. Both ships fired over and over, shot and shell coming down like a storm, but most of the blasts missed the mark, finding only water. But the running battle would not decide a victor.

The *New Haven* realized she could not let the *Alabama* move in behind her, and the Yankee vessel tried turning away. But the foresail turn she had made into the wind was not working now that she was heading downwind. A gang of sailors valiantly tried to hand-sheet the sail hoping to scoop up enough air to move the ship off its course.

The *Salem* continued to harry these men with carronade shots that got closer and closer to hitting the bow of the approaching ship. Another group of two dozen sailors and marines used an improvised rudder, fashioned from a long, heavy spar shoved in the water abaft the stern. They were not having much luck, the spar whipsawing back and forth but not really changing the heavy ship's course.

The *Alabama* finished its half circle maneuver and prepared to open on the Union vessel. Semmes simply shook his head when he saw what was about to happen. He was close enough now to see the Union seamen working at the stern, the most exposed part of the ship now that the Confederate raider had crossed the T. "Fire when ready!" Semmes commanded. "And may God have mercy on their gallant souls," he murmured under his breath.

The broadside blew the Yankee sloop's stern completely away and the Confederate gunners cheered when they saw dozens of sailors fly into the sky and then fall the forty feet down again into the cold, roiling water. A second blast swept the bridge deck, killing every man who stood there. In seconds the ship listed dangerously, its bow pointing crazily up in the air. Minutes later the *New Haven* disappeared beneath the waves with all hands aboard.

Semmes ordered that they circle around and look for survivors. On the return lap, Kell counted thirty-six floating bodies, but saw no one alive. Semmes looked to the east and spied the *Salem* heading north under full sail. Beyond, he could make out a whaleboat carrying the midshipman and his marines from the boarding party. Tilghman had spared all of them. They were rowing toward where their ship had been moments before. Perhaps they would find survivors, but no one aboard the *Alabama* thought they would.

"Signal to *Salem*, we are heading off," Semmes said. He was not happy about what he'd had to do. He was not optimistic about his next voyage either. "Kell, set a course for the North Sea. We need to repair this tired old killer of a ship."

Chapter 27

Logan's Headquarters, Columbia, 1865

Sherman's lean, hard face showed the strain of the long campaign as he struggled with the facts of Buckley's narrative.

"So this gold, English or Irish gold, is on its way to Baltimore at this point, aided by the infamous Semmes and this slaver?"

"Yes, my friend," Buckley answered with a half-smile, amused by the general's puzzled demeanor.

"I must say this tale is beginning to verge on the preposterous, Brother. How does European lucre, smuggled from Africa, intertwine with the Kentucky cavalry and murder and plots of murder?"

"I understand your consternation, General. The gold draws it all together, doesn't it? You see, my Federal friend, your murders here are but part of the secret war being fought, a war in hiding, and there are agents fighting this secret war on both sides."

"You keep calling me friend, Brother Buckley. Are you so sure I am your friend?" Sherman asked.

"You'll excuse my presumption, sir. It's merely a peculiar affectation of mine, a way of speaking. You see, General, I have been a soldier. I have seen war. I have been shot in battle. I want everyone I meet to be my friend."

At that moment, a voice like a shrill siren sounded in the mansion's center hall, halting Buckley's explanation. Long cracked the parlor's door to see what the matter was. A sharp rap on the door near his head startled him. And then he saw Mother Lynch. Through the narrow opening, Long glimpsed the white dreadnought atop her head, bobbing and quaking as she gave Logan's aide an earful. The man was trying to reason with her, though the confrontation had escalated when she must have reached around him to knock on the door. When Long opened the door fully, the little nun jigged from side to side, trying to push past the young officer. The aide blocked the way by stepping to and fro like a boy learning his first waltz. "Here now, Mother, you can't just barge into the general's office. Madam, please!"

"I'm sure it's no imposition on the general, my child. He'll see me now or he'll see me in the Everlasting Fire!" The determined woman finally outflanked the nonplussed captain and lunged through the doorway. Long deftly yielded to her, stepped back and bowed her in with a theatrical flourish. The little nun swept in like a summer storm, still puffing from her fracas with the aide. The captain followed her in and collapsed against the doorframe out of breath. Sherman stiffened at the sight of her, but turned his attention to the hapless aide.

"Outflanked by a nun? Eh, Captain?" Sherman chuckled. "Your good father did this army a favor when he procured this staff job for you, I see." The general dismissed the mortified man with an imperial wave of his hand. Then he turned grudgingly to the red-faced woman before him. "Mother Lynch, is there a problem?" he said politely. Still breathing hard, the little nun took a deep breath before she began. She chuffed like a locomotive getting its steam up before it left the station.

"General Sherman, I mean to tell you there is a problem! The fires are spreading, sir, and a large wall of flame is only blocks from the school now. I pray you will send more men to contend with the conflagration. St. Peter's is threatened now too! Are you to allow your army to burn the Catholics out of Columbia?"

"My, my, Mother, that is certainly not my intention and it cuts me to the quick to have you think it so. You must understand, my dear woman. There are fires everywhere in the city, and fires are hard things, madam. I have ordered destroyed certain stores and munitions, but these raging fires are not technically my army's responsibility. Even so, I am assured that my men are doing their best to protect what the Rebels left of Columbia. But I must admit there is only so much they *can* do."

"But no matter who is responsible, you said the school and convent would get your personal attention, sir. Surely there is *more* you can do?"

"Well, I'll concede that my attention has been diverted by your Brother Buckley here, but I shall send my personal emissary to see what they might help with. Logan, may I ask you to see to that?" Logan left the room with a nod and Mother Lynch seemed assuaged by the new effort.

"Thank you, General. I shall gratefully instruct the girls to say a novena for you at Vespers. May God bless you, sir," the woman added. She curtsied and retreated toward Long's position at the back of the room.

The battle over, Sherman turned back to Brother Buckley without a word. The general's long-suffering look was all the monk needed to resume his narrative.

"As I was saying, the secret war has men and women from both sides working behind a murderous curtain."

"Spies, you mean," Sherman tried to clarify.

"Spies, some sanctioned and some not. Agents of every stripe; murderers, thieves, saboteurs, and I dare say there are such men in hiding right here in Columbia though you control the city now." Mother Lynch coughed nervously upon hearing this, prompting a chortle from Sherman.

"Some provocateurs may even be disguised as priests or nuns, eh Mother Lynch?"

"Yes, perhaps," she smiled good-naturedly. Buckley continued before another word passed between the two antagonists.

"And there are Union spies in Richmond, as we'll see, and there are Rebel agents in Washington City, a most grave threat."

And our Major Wolfe of Dahlgren's raid is at the center of it all?"

"Ah, well, Wolfe is but a waterspout in a continental whirlwind, but the raid on Richmond certainly was the first ill-wind of our storm. But even a small waterspout can do a lot of damage.

Chapter 28

Spottswood Hotel, Richmond, March 1864

The headline in the *Richmond Enquirer* captured the city's outrage.

Murderous Plot!

Young Dahlgren Dead

Had Plans to Assassinate

President Davis, Cabinet

Wade Hampton shook the paper angrily. "I tell you Johnson, no matter what Washington says, this raid had to be sanctioned by the tyrant himself and his circle of black Republican courtiers. Stanton, Seward, Chase, all rascals quite willing to win at any cost."

Bradley Johnson didn't answer, but languished on a red brocade chair in the finest suite of rooms the hotel had to offer. Hampton had footed the bill and it was a good thing considering the cost. Snow blanketed the city and the hotel room provided the pair a warm, dry refuge. Indeed the Spottswood was the perfect blend of modern accommodation and classic appointments. The five-story ironfront faced Main Street at 8th, the center of town, the best hotel in the city. Hampton had taken rooms there when he returned from the cavalry romp that finally caught up with Dahlgren's raiders. Johnson was not far behind. It had been two weeks since the encounter. Hampton paced the floor, his imposing frame and regal posture dominating the hotel room like an actor on the stage.

"Grant has been promoted to what they call General-in-Chief, a third star marks the rank," he muttered as he perused the news headlines. "Listen to this," Hampton read:

Word has come to us since our publication of the now infamous "Dahlgren Papers" that no one less than General Lee himself has written to General George C. Meade, the latest in a long line of commanders of the Army of the Potomac. General Lee asked point blank if the Yankee government had devised or sanctioned the violence proposed in the captured letters. Meade of course has disavowed any and all knowledge of Dahlgren's plot; though he did not claim that the papers were forged and planted on the boy colonel as some of our Northern friends have written. Our own brave General Wade Hampton has told us that he himself took the papers from the innocent hand of the boy who found them, young William Littlepage of King and Queen County, a schoolboy, a farm boy who claimed he watched the Yankee column rumble through his village, at Walkerton, just before the ambush that took Dahlgren's life. The Yankee rake, General Judson Kilpatrick, who was Dahlgren's most direct commander, has contended that neither he nor any of his subordinates had plans to burn Richmond or kill our civilian leaders. He said Dahlgren was to try to free Union prisoners on Belle Isle or at Libby Prison, and he expressed sadness that this plan had failed.

"Sadness indeed," Johnson huffed. "How did he fathom he could ever enter Richmond with one hundred riders and free thousands of prisoners?" The two Confederate generals hovered close around an enormous mahogany table laid out with finger sandwiches, fruits and farm cheese and a local brew of German style beer. Hampton set the paper to the side and reached for a small black cigar, a Havana *pequenos,* and a box of matches. He offered one of the smokes to Johnson who declined.

"They were to sneak in at night, cross Mayo Bridge and use the freed prisoners to fight their way out of the city. A bold plan. He could not have known that most of the prisoners were sick from the long, cold winter with little food. They would not have been much help to him. The lucky ones had already escaped with Colonel Rose in early February. The desperate rascals and their tunnel. I have to credit them for their audacity."

"And what of the prisoners we took at Walkerton? Are they at Libby now?" Johnson asked. He helped himself to a ham sandwich.

"Their officers have been added to the rabble there. The accommodation is too good for them. I eyeballed them myself. They were murderers more than soldiers. They would be more at home with the river rats in Rockett's." The ambush in King and Queen had lasted all of ten minutes. When Dahlgren went down, the rest of the raiders surrendered almost immediately. Ninety-two soldiers and thirty-eight slaves.

Hampton continued his report. "They were led, after Dahlgren's death, by one Major Wolfe, a surly man whose hatred for us bled from every pore. He languishes with his officers at Libby. The Negroes were returned to a grateful Mr. Robinson."

"And what did Wolfe say about Dahlgren's plans for the raid?"

"He was completely uncooperative. I'm not the sort of man to beat a prisoner, even under interrogation, but I came within a rabbit's hair of punishing that arrogant mongrel. I tell you, Johnson, his heart was dark. I have no doubt that he meant to kill the president and any other civilian leader he may have found. His eyes reflected his murderous nature. He wanted revenge of us for killing his precious Dahlgren. The gall! But see here, Johnson. Let us not cloud the issue, I know the truth of the so-called Dahlgren Papers. The boy Littlepage told me himself that he rummaged the papers from Dahlgren's overcoat. While the colonel lay dead on the ground still. He told me he saw an old colored man crushed by Dahlgren's horse and his body lay just beside the colonel's. A liar does not make up such peculiar details."

"More to the point, the custody chain of the papers proves beyond any doubt that they are genuine," Johnson, the lawyer, agreed.

"The boy is a simple child. He could not have manufactured all this evidence. And I believe Meade in his heart knows the depths of Dahlgren's conspiracy."

"Again, I agree. The question is, my dear Hampton, what will we do about it?" Johnson picked at his sandwich and downed a hefty swallow of beer. He peered beyond the long gold and green drapes that flanked tall windows looking out on Main Street. The wide thoroughfare was covered in a wet, late-March snow.

"The government will protest the violation of the laws of war, and then nothing more will come of it, I'm afraid. The lily-livers will prevail."

"No, no. That is not what I meant. I meant what will *we* do about it? You and I?"

"Men of action, not of words, you mean," Hampton laughed. "Tell me, Johnson. What do you propose?"

"I have thought about such things for some time. Dahlgren's indiscretion gives me the excuse to follow through on my musings."

"Yes?" Hampton leaned in across the table, lighting another *pequenos* from his rich, private collection.

"Tit for tat. A raid for a raid. Something to put the fear of God into Lincoln himself."

"But that would make us as bad as our unworthy opponents. Men like Dahlgren."

"I don't propose murder, but merely detention, perhaps ransom, perhaps even a peace settlement."

"Mmmm. Tell me more, tell me how."

"Lincoln often takes a summer hiatus just outside Washington City. His summer retreat at the Soldier's Home on the north side suburb would provide an opportunity for the right force to nab him; away from the relative security of the executive mansion." Hampton looked at his companion with hooded eyes, contemplating the greater ramifications of a kidnapping.

"I like this idea. But we must plan for it, down to the last detail. And wait for the right opportunity." Johnson lowered his eyes, pleased that his wealthy patron accepted the premise, and knowing that Hampton had the connections, the power and the wealth to make it happen. He raised his glass, smiling.

"Let's toast the idea then, General." Hampton took up his beer in one quick motion.

"Thus always to tyrants, Johnson."

Chapter 29

Libby Prison was a warehouse, never meant to be a prison at all. And it seemed it would not be a prison much longer. The bold block letters painted on the three-story, brick pile gave a hint to the origins of the building.

L. Libby & Son, Ship Chandlers

When John Winder, Richmond's Provost Marshal, commandeered the warehouse, Luther Libby had meekly protested. But Libby was a Yankee, a native of Scarborough, Maine. His protests fell on deaf ears. Even so, Winder assured him the confiscation was just a temporary measure and that he would soon get his building back unscathed.

That was after the Battle of Manassas…in 1861. Since then Libby Prison had become infamous in the North. The terrible conditions there were a symbol of the barbarity of the Rebels and Libby's name was forever attached to that symbol. In fact, though he had fled the city, a *Union* cavalry force had recently captured him and his family and imprisoned them at Fortress Monroe in Hampton, the central command post of Benjamin Butler's Army of the James. Libby was a man without a country and a man likely never to see his warehouse again.

But Libby's property was never meant to be a prison. The tin-roofed building was anything but secure. The prison only housed officers while enlisted men languished in tents on a muddy island in the middle of the James River. The cavernous structure at 20th and

Cary Street backed up to the Kanawha Canal and the James, and countless windows allowed easy avenues of escape. Over a hundred Union men broke out in February after digging a sixty-foot tunnel in the frozen earth. The daring getaway and repeated attempted raids by Butler's cavalry and Kilpatrick's horseman called for changes. First, the prisoners were moved upstairs, held in big open rooms on the top two floors. The first floor and its windows were off-limits now. The rest of the structure's windows were nailed shut and veiled by iron bars. In addition, gunpowder had been packed into a tall, six-foot square on the ground floor, ready to be lit if another cavalry attack made it to the prison. That would spell the end for the officers and destroy Luther Libby's warehouse once and for all.

While these changes were drastic, they were not as drastic as the most recent decision. The Confederate government planned to move the thousand or so officers held at Libby to Macon, Georgia soon. The news of the impending departure had filtered down to the prisoners quickly.

Major Wolfe sat in a corner near a window on the third floor, surrounded by four roughneck Kentuckians. A hardbitten, red-headed lieutenant lounged nearby. The corner perch provided scant privacy on the open warehouse floor packed with a milling, restless mob.

"They are moving us to Macon because they know our people are coming for us, Wolfe stated." He looked beyond his clutch of men when two New York officers started yelling. They fell onto each other fighting over something. It was a common occurrence in the overcrowded room. Wolfe idly stuck a sharp dagger into the window frame as he talked. "I tell you, Kilpatrick will not rest until he succeeds where Dahlgren failed. Now we hear that Grant is the army commander. He will certainly attack Richmond like he did Vicksburg. Sheridan's cavalry presses on one side and Butler to the south."

"Doesn't all this mean our days are numbered here, one way or the other?" It was Wolfe's young toady Blake. He wore a black slouch hat. The skinny, blonde-haired man had a broad, flat face, dull gray eyes and the uneven sprouts of a boy's patchy beard.

"It means, Lieutenant Blake, that we can't wait for them to

blow us up or take us to Georgia. We need to bust out of here as soon as the weather breaks." The other men almost as one looked around furtively to see if anyone had heard this. Wolfe caught himself and lowered his voice as the group leaned closer to hear the major's plan.

"Just like Colonel Rose, we'll use the eastern side to escape. It is the least watched." He looked out the window on the scene below. He could see the next cross street was 21st, which led away from the water, through mainly open lots for two blocks up to Franklin Street. He didn't know what he'd find on Franklin, but he knew it was only four blocks further east to a cross street to Grace. Once on Grace it was just another block to a safe haven. Wolfe paused to glance around for eavesdroppers and then eyeballed his small group again.

"The guard tent is out front. We know when the patrols come through." They had been using their spot on the third floor, and its high windows, as a watchtower over the streets below. "We will try to go down one floor, just before lights out. We'll use this rabble here as a diversion if need be," he said, waving a meaty hand at the room full of unruly prisoners. "We'll have to work the nail locks and the iron bars from one of the windows beforehand, so it'll open easy when we need it to. From the second floor, we can lower our feet as close to the ground as possible, before dropping the fifteen feet to the ground."

"Simple enough," Lieutenant Blake commented. He nodded his assent as did the others. "But what to do once we're outside?" The major crooked his slab of a head toward the lieutenant nearby.

"One of the officers they recaptured from Colonel Rose's escape will lead us to the Van Lew house. The woman is a Union sympathizer living right under the Rebels' noses. She hides runaway slaves and she will help us escape too." Blake peered at the outsider warily, nodded to the man, before he turned back to Wolfe.

"Can we trust him?"

"We have to," Wolfe hissed impatiently. "We don't know this city. And once outside these walls, we can't afford to get lost. Red has escaped once and has seen the woman's house. He seems a stout man; from Ohio. Captured at Mine Run. Hang fire, Blake I've had to trust you blasted lieutenants with my life for this entire war. I reckon I can trust one more." Blake accepted this logic with a sigh and a hanging head.

"Well I reckon the only question left is when. And who else will go with us?" another man asked.

"No one goes but us Kentuckians and Ohio Red," Wolfe whispered. "A small group is the safest way. Tell no one about our plans."

"You will not tell the colonel then?"

"I know I am legally bound to tell the senior prisoner of any escape plan, and get his blessing. But not this time. I fear he will say no."

"And it's better to ask for forgiveness later, if we are caught and brought back." Wolfe glared at the boy with murderous eyes. Then he slowly shook his head.

"I don't plan to get caught, Lieutenant. I don't plan to be brought back either. We escape or die trying." Blake shuddered and the others shifted uncomfortably. Wolfe was disgusted by his show of weakness. "Blake, I want you to wander downstairs tonight and work on that window. The major then addressed the others. He shook his finger at each man, one at a time. "All of you, fill your bellies if you can. Rest up, prepare yourselves. The snow is melting already. Tomorrow night, we run."

Chapter 30

Libby Prison hummed. Wolfe thought the snoring of hundreds of men asleep on the floor seemed like the steady beat of machinery. A human carpet covered the block long room on the third floor. From his window corner, he sat up and looked around.

The scene reminded him of a weekend whiskey binge back in Kentucky. In 1861, his entire company had passed out on the ground and slept like babies. But were these prisoners sleeping soundly? Pale, dim moonlight filtered through the windows. Wolfe waited several minutes to see if any others stirred, but at two in the morning, no one moved. He signaled to his men and the Buckeye officer that they should creep toward the stairway to the second floor. The raiders weaved their way around a snoring cluster, walking quickly, but on tip-toes.

They all gathered at the head of the stairs where Wolfe tapped a thick index finger across his lips. The rickety wooden staircase squeaked with his weight. He froze at the noise, but behind him each man's step creaked as they descended too. There was nothing they could do about it so they continued quickly. Wolfe heard a cough right next to his ear as his head descended below the floor. He realized there was a man lying up against the railing, his face not a foot away. Alright, asleep.

Down below, the second floor scene looked much like the third. The same hum, sometimes punctuated by the snorts and whistles of sound sleep. The small group clustered together and made their way toward the window they would use for the escape. Near the center of the room, a Union guard posted by the senior ranking prisoner to police his own soldiers was fast asleep on the job. Good thing for him, Wolfe thought. He would not hesitate to kill anyone who stood in his way.

Blake raised the window and fresh, cold air flooded in, the smell of freedom. The lieutenant went first, removing a loose section of rusty, iron bars and quickly thrusting his legs out the opening. He sat on the sill, turned around and lowered himself and let go. He grunted when he hit the ground. He looked around once outside and called up in a whisper, "Clear!" Wolfe went next while one of his men kept an eye on the room. In less than five minutes all six men crouched behind an old wooden boat, rotting on its blocks.

"We stick together," Wolfe said. "If we get separated, Van Lew's is in the middle of 23rd and 24th street. We go to the back door. Kill for your freedom. No one lives if he sees you."

They ran up 21st street, the ground rising steadily up to Franklin which climbed the ridge of Church Hill off to the east. They passed through a tidy neighborhood of two- and three-story brick and clapboard homes, dormer windows peering down on the escapees with menace. But no one was out this time of the morning. The damp cold air bit into their faces, their frosty breath the only sign of life on the deserted street. Minutes later they turned up a cross street that should bring them to Grace.

The narrow lane was unlike other city streets; it had been cobbled and ran steeply up the hill. Wolfe stumbled on the uneven surface, fell, and cursed when he skinned his knees. The commotion roused a dog in someone's back yard. The dog snarled at first, but then started barking. "Keep moving, boys," Wolfe ordered. But then they heard the steady clickety, clickety, click of a charging canine, his heavy paws tapping the cobblestone pavement. A shadowy mongrel ran up barking, stopped just behind the group and yapped like he'd tree'd a coon. The relentless barking echoed off the stone houses lining the street, a hoarse, guttural siren.

"Shhh, shhh, boy. It's alright," Blake whispered, trying to calm the animal, but the dog jumped to and fro, lifting right off the ground with the force of his alarm.

"That's it, get his attention, Blake," Wolfe urged, as he circled around behind the dog. The other men jerked their heads around looking up the street for signs of human activity. A dim light appeared at the house next to them, in the front doorway.

"Now, now. Who's there?" a woman's voice called. Just then

Wolfe fell on the dog from behind, his left arm grabbing the animal's still barking muzzle, then shifting into a choke hold. Silver flashed in the moonlight as his knife sliced the dog's neck so deeply that the head almost came off. A muffled yelp marked the end. The major, kneeling on the pavement, dropped the body, the head flopping off to one side.

"Was that Joe Hooker? What have you done to my dog?" the woman called out again, angry this time. She had walked out into the street, holding a lantern up above her head, trying to make out the shadowy figures in front of her. The soldiers saw she was an old black matron, in plain white housecoat, with a brown kerchief wrapped around a graying head. Wolfe had regained his feet and he lunged at the woman, driving his knife into her heart. She was dead before she realized what had happened. In one motion, he picked her up and carted her toward the house. Blake stifled a nervous laugh, but the other men stood frozen, staring at the surreal scene. Wolfe glared at the group impatiently.

"Get the mangy dog and bring him inside too," he hissed. Blake retrieved the dead hound and the men quickly ducked into the little ramshackle house. They gracelessly dumped the bodies on the floor of a dingy parlor. No one else seemed to inhabit the place. Wolfe looked out the window. The street was still empty, quiet again. Within minutes, blood from the old Negro woman had formed a pool on the bare wood floor. The red liquid welled up and circled the now headless dog. The furry body seemed to float on a crimson lake. The canine's head rested where it had been tossed, cradled in the woman's lap. The dog named Joe Hooker stared up at them, its long tongue lolling from one side of his muzzle like he was laughing. Wolfe waited with the door cracked open a few minutes to make sure the street was clear.

"Let's go. We're almost there," the major ordered, and the escapees took off.

Chapter 31

The Federal-style estate occupied an entire city block, its white Doric columns standing sentinel for Richmond's most prominent abolitionist. At forty-six, Elizabeth Van Lew was unnaturally thin, which only accentuated a stern, angular face and a disproportionately large head. She had never married; didn't like men and hated slavery even more. She kept her long, dark hair plastered flat across her tight-skinned forehead and often wore mannish black clothes. Her Richmond neighbors called her Crazy Bet, not only because of her unfortunate looks, but because of her Union sympathies and rude, unorthodox behavior.

She wasn't crazy at all of course, but she *was* a Union spy. Confederate authorities kept a curious eye on her house much of the time. But they had neglected her for most of the winter and she had helped orchestrate the escape from Libby Prison earlier in February. They had watched her house for awhile after that, but things had died down again. What could the eccentric daughter of a wealthy hardware merchant really do to harm the mighty Confederacy after all?

They had no inkling that she had infiltrated President Davis's household with one of her agents, a housekeeper who relayed information back to her. They could not imagine that she had organized an extensive network of operatives who passed information, escaped slaves and other contraband through the Confederate defenses and into Union lines. When fire broke out at the Confederate executive mansion, nothing tied the attempted arson to her, though she had initiated the idea to burn Davis out. Crazy Bet was crazy like the proverbial fox, and a very dangerous one.

It was after three in the morning, and she was awake, planning her next project. She heard boots clomping on the back porch and immediately feared a visit by the Confederate provost guard. She moved like a ghost in the rambling house, stealing to a floor-to-ceiling window and peeking out from behind the blue toile drapery. Six men huddled next to a column, one of them seemingly giving instructions to the others. Their uniforms were nondescript; they definitely were not Rebel marshals. She was used to intrigues in the middle of the night. But she must be cautious. She cracked open the sash and whispered.

"Who are you and what do you want?" The leader turned and squinted in the darkness.

"We come from Libby Prison, looking for your help." No answer. The window slammed shut. Seconds later, one of the home's double doors creaked open and the men glided over to the entrance. "Quickly, come in!" Van Lew's voice squawked from behind the door. The men bustled through and found themselves in a marble-tiled round room, a foyer that included a spiral staircase up to the next level. Wall sconces lit the space dimly, but the men could see a black man on the landing above them, a six-shot revolving carbine in hand. Van Lew dashed nimbly to the stairs and moved half way up. She kept her eyes on her visitors, but addressed her guard.

"Now, Walter, you've got a ball for each man here. Just hold them right there while I talk to them." She turned to the raiders.

"Tell me, quickly, what is your unit?"

"2nd Kentucky. We were with Dahlgren when he was killed," Wolfe replied. Ohio Red hadn't been with them then, of course, but Wolfe didn't complicate matters with further explanation.

"Who is the warden of Libby Prison?"

"Major Thomas Turner, when we were taken there."

"How did you escape?"

"Jumped from a second floor window."

"And what is your name, soldier?"

"Major Simon Wolfe, Miss Van Lew." He smiled and watched her exhale. He knew this willful woman must be the one he had heard so much about.

"Aim your carbine away from our guests, Walter." Van Lew came back downstairs and went to the far wall where she pushed a panel revealing a hidden door. "Go below, Major Wolfe. I will be with you shortly." The men filed into the narrow opening and descended a rough set of steps that led into the darkness, a secret room in the mansion's basement. Van Lew closed the door and turned to her guard, still standing on the steps.

"Fetch the Union army lists and look for the officers of the 2nd Kentucky. Verify Major Wolfe's membership in that organization." The man nodded and turned for the landing to the first floor of the house. Van Lew climbed the steps and followed.

Wolfe and the raiders waited in the secret chamber for over an hour. The room was long and narrow, about five feet wide and twenty feet long. The space had been carved out of a storage larder in the cellar, a false wall creating the hidden chamber. Some cots, spare wooden chairs and a small table with two lanterns were its only appointments. But in one corner sat a pine coffin, smelling of green wood. It was simply constructed and unadorned. Light flooded the room when another door opened in the wall opposite where they had entered. Walter bid the men follow him. They went upstairs again, this time into a drawing room in the front of the house. Van Lew presided at a large mahogany desk, inherited from her father.

"Gentlemen, I have checked your story and believe you are who you say you are."

"Yes, ma'am, Miss Van Lew," Wolfe answered quietly.

"Call me, Miss Lizzy. That's what my friends would call me if I had any friends," she murmured wryly. "Now, I am a very busy woman with several projects underway right now. The fact that you rode with Dahlgren makes me inclined to help you get out of the city. And I have just the way to achieve that."

"Whatever you wish, ma'am. We are the men to do it."

"I have been working on a plan for some time now. It is a two-fold scheme and now your escape makes it even more complex, even more dangerous."

"Just say the word, we are dangerous men." Van Lew eyed Wolfe closely, turning her head slightly as she considered this statement.

"Yes, Major, I believe that is true. Here is my plan. There are usually slaves in my secret room waiting to be spirited to Union lines. *They* are easy to pass through Confederate checkpoints, but not so white men of a certain age. Your age. You would raise suspicions. Why are you not in the army, they would ask? They will be looking for men like you. Especially when the alarm of your escape is raised, probably within the hour now." She looked over at a mantel clock about to strike five.

"We want to get out as quickly as possible, ma'am. If you can help us."

"Yes, of course, Major. But it may take some few days. And there is something you can help *me* with. You see, I have Dahlgren's body." She blurted this out with a sneering half-smile, knowing the news would raise the hackles of ordinary men. She was not disappointed. Blake's beady eyes bugged out in horror while the others seemed paralyzed by the eerie fact. Even the thuggish Wolfe seemed surprised by the woman's cool blood.

"Lord, no, Miss Lizzy. You have…How did you come by it?" the major asked.

"I drove out to Oakwood Cemetery where our hero had been buried by the Rebels," she answered matter-of-factly. But then her reedy voice took on an angry tone. "After they mutilated the body, I might add. They took his leg and shaved his head before they buried him. So I reckoned I would rescue the dear boy, a very pretty boy." Van Lew drifted into creepy reverie as she remembered the exhumation. "I had him dug up, watched Walter take up his beautiful body like Joseph of Arimathea holding the crucified figure of the Savior." And then she seemed to pull herself back to reality. "You see, Major Wolfe, I want to bury Colonel Dahlgren in a secret grave until this war is over."

Ohio Red swallowed a mouthful of bile that had welled up from his throat while he listened to the macabre plan. Blake though rubbed his skinny hands together and giggled with maniacal glee, while Wolfe simply gritted his teeth, angry that the memory of his commander had been desecrated by the Rebels in this way. They all realized now what the coffin in the basement contained. "What will you have us do?" Wolfe asked through clenched jaws.

"I will have Walter take his body to the old Hebrew Cemetery. For burial there without a stone. You, Major Wolfe, and perhaps this man," she pointed at Blake, "will dress in livery and ride with Walter. I may ride along behind the coffin, as the darkly-veiled, grieving woman folk of this old Jew. We will call him Mr. Thalhimer.

Once there, you'll bury the man. Along the way, pass yourself off to anyone you meet that you are undertakers sent from Alabama to inter and catalogue dead men from your state.

On another day you and the rest of your men will travel to Chimborazo Hospital and once again pass yourselves off as undertakers from Alabama, looking for men from Mobile. I will have papers for you, and clothes. Once your identities are established, I will send you out to Oakwood which is on the most direct route out of town. You will be heading east toward Butler's lines. With any luck you can just keep riding until you see a Union picket post."

"An intriguing plan, Miss..ah, Miss Lizzy. The kind of plan that proves your reputation as a brilliant secret agent."

"Very well, Major," Van Lew replied with a wary eye. She was unfazed by the flattery. "For now though, you must return to the cellar room. I've no doubt the Rebels will come calling when news of your escape gets out. We will lay for cover for now. But be ready. The time will come."

Chapter 32

Wade Hampton seethed over the latest Libby Prison escape. He was angry, but he was not surprised. With winter receding, the spring campaign would open soon, so his thoughts should have been in the field. He'd been wrestling for days with the quartermaster, trying to find more horses and better food for his troopers. And now this news that the blackguard Major Wolfe had escaped. The provost marshal had swept the city, especially paying a visit to Mrs. Van Lew's mansion, but they'd found nothing. Hampton's steward was packing the rich general's personal items as he prepared to vacate the Spottswood Hotel suite. Bradley Johnson was also packing up for the new campaign.

"Where must the Kentuckians have gone?" Johnson asked the South Carolinian.

"They couldn't have left the city so quickly, so easily. I reckon they are somewhere in hiding. Perhaps close by."

"They may be plotting again. I assume the president is well protected."

"He has doubled the guard at his mansion until more is learned about the escape."

"And what of *our* plot? You've talked to Captain Conroe, I hear." Thomas Nelson Conroe, a twenty-seven year old school teacher, had taught in Georgetown before the war. He'd served in the 3rd Virginia Cavalry for a time, but now he was a clandestine operative for the Confederate government. He knew Washington well. And Hampton kept in contact with him.

"I have. The Secret Service, as he calls it, has been watching

Lincoln's routine around Washington city. Conroe says the security around him is surprisingly lax."

"How have they been able to watch the enemy leader in his lair, as it were?"

"Conroe says he has himself sat on a street bench in a park near the executive house, marking down the dates and times of Lincoln's comings and goings. He has noticed a pattern."

"A weakness that can be exploited?"

"I believe so, Johnson, but the president, President Davis that is, vetoed any plan to kidnap his Union counterpart."

"I see. Even though the Dahlgren plot came to light? Even though the other side was trying to kill *him* and burn his capital!"

"He still will have no part in a plan to capture or kill Lincoln." Johnson just shrugged.

"But that does not mean that we cannot use Conroe's intelligence to plan our own operation." Hampton smiled. "And we shall. Perhaps during this campaign."

The undertaker's wagon groaned under the weight of an oversized coffin as Wolfe drove it down 25th Street. He wore a black suit and black top hat, the disguise he'd worn for most of a month now. He'd established himself in the city as Hieronymous Lumsden, an Alabama undertaker from Mobile. With a black-suited Lieutenant Blake by his side, he was finally leaving Richmond. Ohio Red sat in the back of the open wagon, dressed as a mud-spattered grave digger. The hefty casket in the wagon contained the other three men. Ostensibly they were headed for Oakwood Cemetery. But with any luck they would not stop there or for any other reason until they found the Union army. A light rain was falling, water just beginning to moisten the wagon ruts in the street.

"I won't miss this miserable city," Wolfe grumbled as he pulled his coat collar tight against his neck to ward off the chilling drizzle. "The devil himself would not abide here, even if he had only Hades to return to." Blake simply smirked at the remark. The wagon creaked as the city street narrowed to a rutted lane. They moved snail-like along the New Bridge Road so as not to attract any undue attention. It was an agonizingly slow escape. Stands of scrubby pines and brambles began to dot a flat landscape as the escapees made their way east of Richmond.

They had passed Oakwood Cemetery a ways back, so it would not be easy to use their cover story if they were questioned. Fewer and fewer houses lined the road. Here and there small farmsteads began to replace the disappearing city lots. Blake wondered if they should pick up the pace. They hadn't met another traveler yet, maybe because of the rain, but the young lieutenant was worried they would be caught if they didn't get farther away from the city. He almost impulsively spanked the horse Miss Lizzy had given them into a trot.

"Maybe we should forget the act and ride on out of here now, Major."

"Well, now, running won't work with that patrol coming," Wolfe answered, pointing a quarter mile up the straight, flat road. "These men will want to speak with us," he said calmly.

Wolfe looked over at his startled passenger, and saw Blake's pinched face blanch with fear. "Let me do the talking, boy, and we'll be fine." The younger man only nodded his agreement, too afraid to answer.

Three Confederate riders pulled up shortly, one dark-mustachioed sergeant raising his hand to stop the wagon.

"Good morning to you, gentlemen," Wolfe called out, pulling up the wagon's horse. "I am Hieronymus Lumsden, of Mobile, Alabama, and this is my assistant Mr. Blake."

"Sergeant John Nolte of the Richmond City Guards, Mr. Lumsden." The sergeant tipped his cap. "What is your business here, this cold, soft day?"

"I am taking the remains of this Alabama soldier to his final resting place at Oakwood." The top-hatted man jabbed his thumb at the pine board coffin in the back of the wagon. At the same time, he clutched a Colt revolver inside his suit coat. Sergeant Nolte peered at the box, spit on the ground and caught the eye of the Confederate trooper to his right.

"Oakwood is a good mile behind you, sir. Did you not see it on your way from the city?"

"I did not, I do not believe so. But I am not that familiar with the vicinity. Most of my burials have been at Shockoe Cemetery in the city." Wolfe smiled sheepishly and spread his hands as if to say he was at a loss to explain.

"Of course, I understand entirely." Nolte looked over the

casket carefully. "That's a mighty big burying box. Who is the deceased, may I ask?"

"A soldier like yourself, from the 6th Alabama, died of his wounds from Gettysburg." Wolfe was ready with the story. Nolte looked skeptical though.

"Mr., ah, Lumsden, we've had a problem of late with contraband entering and leaving the city, and, you must admit, parts of your story don't tally. Mind if I have a look at the..remains?" Wolfe reared back indignantly and snatched off his hat solemnly. Blake simply stared straight down at the ground, trying to hide his nerves. In the back, Red sat quietly, nonchalantly chewing on a bit of straw.

"As a man entrusted with the care of a martyr for our cause, I must object to the desecration of his earthly body."

"There'll be no desecration, and if the box checks out, you'll soon be on your way," Nolte answered quietly. He nodded to his men, who dismounted and climbed in the back of the wagon. Red, playing his part as a lowly grave digger, tipped his grubby cap to the Rebels and jumped down without a word. One man took a bayonet to pry the top off. He shoved the blade under the boards at one corner of the box while the other man held the opposite side of the coffin. If they heard the cocking of the .45 caliber pistols inside, they didn't have time to register what the sounds meant. BOOM! BOOM! Flames flickered out of air holes on each side of the box. The staggered explosion knocked both men down instantly, their dead bodies falling off the wagon and hitting the muddy ground. A third shot fired by Wolfe at point blank range caught Sergeant Nolte between the eyes before he could react to the death of his men.

"Move quickly!" Wolfe yelled, making sure with a swiveling head that the stretch of lonely road was still clear of witnesses. Get these bodies in the wagon so we can leave this place." The men in the coffin pushed off its lid, climbed out and jumped to the ground. They carried Nolte around to the back of the wagon, collected the other two Confederates from the muddy road and heaved the dead bodies into the box on top of each other. Next they tied the troopers' horses to the wagon before moving on. Minutes later, the entourage turned south along the Darbytown Road where they presently came upon a little white farm house with peeling clapboards and a cedar shake roof.

Wolfe, pistol in hand, kicked in the front door, and Blake checked the house, finding no one home. The men wandered into the kitchen looking for food. A German language Bible rested on the counter before a picture portraying the Sacred Heart of Jesus. The sight caused the marauders to leave the house unmolested. Meanwhile the major had gone to the wood shed and found a well-used, but sharp, heavy ax. The six escapees gathered in back of the house where a wild-eyed Wolfe told them what was next.

"We can't leave a trail for them to follow. They'll be looking for these men soon, and I don't want them to find them…just yet. But when they do, I want them to know what we have unleashed on the Southland. Carry these traitors into the dining room," he ordered, pointing at the box full of bloody bodies. Wolfe carried only the ax. Inside he carefully removed his top hat and long black coat before he began his work. A large rectangular chestnut table took the ax blows with little complaint. The dead Confederate soldiers did not complain either.

A half an hour later, Wolfe left the abattoir he had created. Blake and the others did not dare even look at the major when he came outside and washed up at the stone cistern in back of the house. Ohio Red and the Kentucky men had casually walked into the surrounding fields when the hacking began in the little farmhouse. Now, as they gathered again near the wagon, no one spoke, including the gore flecked Wolfe.

The men who had hidden in the coffin rode the horses out of the farmyard, happy to have some fresh air to breathe. Blake, Red and Wolfe remained in the wagon, but the pace was much quicker than before. Ten miles later they met the vedettes of Benjamin Butler's Army of the James.

Chapter 33

Logan's Headquarters, Columbia

Buckley stared straight ahead, his soothing baritone voice trailing off. He had moved little while relating the story so far. Mother Lynch had left to see to her convent school, while Logan and Kilpatrick paced the floor at the far end of the room. Kilpatrick's eyes rarely left the floor's wide boards. Often during the narrative Logan had been seen shaking his head in disbelief, cutting his eyes from Buckley to Sherman to Kilpatrick. Tupper Long stood at ease, still manning the door.

"This Wolfe was a wicked, wicked creature." Logan offered absently, finding a seat along a far wall.

"This war has made many soldiers wicked, angry men…wretched animals," Buckley replied. He caught Long's eye, but the lieutenant quickly averted his gaze. Sherman pushed away from his desk and leaned back in his chair uneasily.

"That is why I have tried to end the conflict as quickly as possible, by any lawful means." The general looked into the distance as he talked, not sure if even he believed his last remark. Kilpatrick smirked, sat down next to Logan, but did not speak. Buckley tapped the floor as was his way, adjusting himself in the parlor chair he had held for over an hour now.

"Laws mean little when men are so inured to killing," the monk offered. Sherman nodded in agreement.

"There is killing in war, but there is a line beyond which a soldier must not go. Killing can be justifiable, while murder--cold-blooded, merciless murder and mutilation--is never justified. It seems to me this Wolfe, and others, crossed that line and I have heard enough to call for a Court of Inquiry about the whole matter." Sherman stood up and stretched in an effort to end what had become a lengthy intrusion on his morning. Logan rose quickly, hoping he would regain his headquarters office now. Kilpatrick leaned forward in his chair, hoping against hope that he would be dismissed without further delay.

Buckley though didn't budge and his blackthorn leg, seeming to have a life all its own, tap, tap, tapped the floor as if it was calling the room to order. The tapping had seemed but a mildly curious habit at first, but Sherman had come to loathe it now. It visibly unnerved the irascible Union general, who was not sure if Buckley's leg tapped from a nervous twitch, or if Buckley's spasm was a conscious effort to annoy him. Still he did not mention it to the wounded veteran.

"General, a Court of Inquiry is undoubtedly needed, but there is more I can tell you now…"

Sherman gruffly cut him off in midsentence. "Yes, yes, boy, ah, Brother, but I have a war here to run." Tap, tap, tap. The sound echoed up to the fourteen foot ceiling. Buckley was not cowed by the officer's interruption. His soft, guileless face did not reveal one wit of fear or concern as he looked up at the powerful Yankee looming over him. His voice was calm when he spoke.

"And who is your war's commander-in-chief?"

"You know bloody well who he is. And what on God's green earth has that to do with anything?"

"That man is in danger because of all this and I know the nature of the threat." Kilpatrick, who had never stood to leave like the other two generals, dropped his enormous head and buried his face in rough raw hands. Logan simply stared at the scene, his mouth agape. The bluster left Sherman like the air whooshing from a popped balloon. A heavy gulp issued from pursed lips.

"Tell me then," he said resignedly, sitting back down, throwing his heavy booted feet onto the desk. He wrapped his arms across his chest. "Tell me everything you know."

Chapter 34

Washington, the District of Columbia, June 1864

The young man was eating his lunch; a crusty roll, an apple and a thick wedge of yellow cheese. The food was lined up on an ersatz lunch counter, a stack of old books laid across his knees. The bespectacled fellow loved old books. The sun was shining brightly and beams of blinding light bounced off the white sandstone walls of the executive mansion across Pennsylvania Avenue. The man used the blade of a dangerously long knife to shuffle another slice of cheese into a mouth concealed by heavy brown mustaches. Between bites, he jotted down a message on a small sheet of paper weighted down by the apple. A sharp breeze made the sheet flap around the edges.

The bookworm appeared to be just another government clerk who inhabited Washington these days; a worker like many others taking his mid-day meal out in the sunshine on a warm day. But he was not that at all. Thomas Nelson Conroe was an agent of the Confederate secret service, stalking the Union's president. His bookish appearance was an act. The knife he deftly held was the first clue to his true occupation. He handled it with a practiced touch. He had a slender, athletic frame, a physicality and swagger that an average bookworm did not possess. His pale, soft-skinned complexion belied the determination of a blue-eyed killer.

The operative plucked a brass pocket watch from his waistcoat and shielded the machine's face from the flashing sun.

Almost one o'clock. He had to be in front of the Blair house in ten minutes, with the note. He hastily finished writing it and folded the paper tightly before securing the missive in a slit in his lunch roll. Wrapping the cheese in a cloth, he folded the knife and put it and the apple in his coat pocket. Lunch would have to wait.

Across the avenue, Conroe could see two army guards on the north lawn, near the portico in the distance. There were always two and the doorman, Thomas Burns. The spy stood up, holding the roll in one hand and his books in the other, and walked toward his assignation a short stroll away. His eyes swept the circular drive that led from the street up to the arched portico. He saw three groups of people on the road, coming and going like the world was on fire and because the man who lived there was the only one who could douse the flames. He could just make out Old Edward, Lincoln's steward coming outside. But where was Conroe's mark? The steward's presence might mean Lincoln himself was on the move. A beggar in filthy tattered Union uniform ambled up at that point, leaning on the hitching post in front of the buff limestone mansion where Conroe was to pass his note.

"Hail, young fellow, have you a penny for a veteran of the Peninsula?" The man fairly croaked at Conroe, who wretched at the smell of him.

"Go away, you blackguard. There are agencies for the likes of you, if you really want help." But the unsavory man did not go away; he leaned in and whispered dramatically.

"Help? This Union has been no help to me! And the man in that house across there has been a curse, a curse to me and my country." The man stuck a dirty finger towards the executive mansion and then in a different voice continued, "Now see here, young man, have you not even a crust of bread for a man who's given everything for the Union?" Conroe smiled.

"If you put it that way, soldier, I do. Take my lunch roll and take care with every bite." A couple strolled by, delaying the conversation for a moment, but as soon as the sidewalk cleared again Conroe whispered. "Good show, my friend. There's a job in acting for you when this war's over. Now look, Old Edward is on the drive. The man himself may be leaving now." Not awaiting a reply, the agent walked off toward the stable where his horse awaited him. Keeping up the charade and proud that he fooled the great Thomas

Conroe, the beggar called after him.

"Bless you, son. May tomorrow find you as well as our beloved president!... President Davis," he whispered. He looked over at the big white house, looking for Old Edward. Yes, there he was, talking to the guards. No sign of Lincoln though. Taking up a seat on the ground against a stone wall, he bit into the bread like a starving man and deftly concealed the note in his hands while he read it:

N. lawn gate-every day at 2. Dest.-Soldiers Home cottage. 2 guards, Beware Burns look-alike.

Yes, Burns did resemble Lincoln and could have easily been mistaken for him from a distance. The Soldier already knew the doorman might fool a casual observer, but Burns was not nearly as tall as the six-foot-five president. The differences were much more apparent up close, and The Soldier had been close to Lincoln before, on a trial run; a test of how he might accomplish his mission.

No, Burns had nothing to fear. If The Soldier got that close again, he'd see the difference in Lincoln's grotesque face too. He'd see the face of a tyrant as he realized he was dying. The Soldier looked up at the house again, this time with a disinterested sideward glance. He continued to chomp on the bread. An open carriage, drawn by two black horses, pulled up from the side, the steward approaching its driver with instructions. He was likely telling him the route to take to the Soldiers' Home three miles north, where Lincoln and his family escaped the heat of the city in the summer. They tried to vary the route.

Just then the guards, two of them as it said in the note, cantered up on great black war horses and took up positions in front of and beside the carriage. Impressive, but not insurmountable security. A crippled Union veteran might get close enough to do the job. He would be just another well-wisher now that word had come from Baltimore that the Republicans had nominated the president to run for another term. No doubt Grant's progress through Central Virginia this spring had convinced the delegates to the party convention that the war could be won. But could the North vanquish the Confederacy if its great leader was taken from them?

The Soldier tried not to jump when he saw the Union president quickly exit the mansion doors, acknowledge the guards and leap into the waiting carriage. Traffic had picked up along Pennsylvania Avenue since Conroe left. Delivery wagons had resumed their routes after lunch and official Washington was returning to work as well. The Soldier stood up slowly and began walking along the sandy road toward the driveway entrance. He carried his weapon of choice, a bone-handled, hard-steel dagger. A silent killer that he hoped to slip between the tyrant's ribs. A quiet thrust into the heart and the deed would be done before anyone knew the president was even in danger. A two-shot riverboat derringer nestled in his uniform jacket if needed.

The Soldier moved closer to where he knew the carriage would exit onto the street. He would try to attract the president's attention when he was away from the house and its security, but not too far away. Which way would the carriage turn? A direct route would take it to the right, toward 14th Street, where it would turn due north toward Rhode Island Avenue. Or the driver might elect to turn left and double back through the Federal city before heading north to Lincoln's two story house at the Soldiers' Home along Rock Creek Church Road. Either way, The Soldier would try to amble along with the carriage, waiting for it to slow or stop for traffic or pedestrians.

Though The Soldier appeared old and handicapped by his wounds, he was in fact a young, athletic man with catlike reflexes and stone cold intentions. It wouldn't take much to approach the open carriage carrying Lincoln, elude or kill the guards, and pull off a point blank attack. A quick thrust or a well-placed bullet to the head would take mere seconds. Anyone who witnessed the whole thing would be amazed when the crippled old soldier ran off into Lafayette Park like a hound chasing a rabbit. There, at the statue of the Marquis De Lafayette, Conroe held a fresh pony that would take him into the Maryland countryside. It seemed too simple; and perhaps it was.

The driver turned right out of the gate, The Soldier less than one hundred yards behind it. The president's stovepipe hat jerked left and right with the motion of the heavy black carriage. A direct route today and the driver was pushing the horses to move briskly up Pennsylvania Avenue. The snap of the whip echoed off the fine stone houses on the opposite side of the street. At this rate, The Soldier might not catch up before the carriage turned left onto 14th Street. But an assassin needed to be patient, he knew. The president's conveyance reached the intersection, the presidential guard's horses trotting ahead and blocking traffic while their charge's carriage practically careened around the corner. "Hold up, there!" one of the guards yelled. He held up a buff colored gauntleted hand to stop an approaching wagon-load of corn and tomatoes.

The Soldier lost sight of the president after that. The street traffic collected quickly, blocking his view. Even after the assassin got to the corner he could not see the presidential entourage for the line of horses and wagons lined up on 14th. The president had gotten away this time. But then he realized that the backup was because the president's carriage itself had stopped. The Soldier quickened his pace. This might be the opportunity he needed. Half a block down, he could see the president standing in the carriage, hat in hand, speaking to a crowd of at least fifty people of all stripes, an impromptu speech to a gaggle of admirers. This was officially the election season now after all.

Well let's see if Lincoln would press the flesh with one more potential voter. The Soldier smirked as he talked to himself. I don't think the old croaker can resist a Union beggar or the chance to secure one more vote. The killer slowed again, checking himself, measuring his lameness, remembering his character. He reached for his dagger, one arm tucked in his coat as if it was withered. The thrust would be swift and then he would run. All he needed was proximity and a few seconds and it looked like he would get that now, here. He was but fifty yards away.

A man in a fine cotton suit of clothes called out, "We support you and the Union, Mr. President!" Cheers and applause punctuated the man's statement. Lincoln waved his hat, smiling, and began what seemed a prepared stump speech.

"Never before have our armies had such an opportunity to win this thing," the executive was saying. "General Grant has brought his mighty force to the very gates of the Rebel city. He commands legions of the finest soldiers this world has ever seen, the gallant sons of our great coun___."

"Here, here! The Union forever!" a coarse, loud voice interrupted. With a purse-lipped face, the president looked out over the crowd and stared at the man who'd cut him off. Everyone followed Lincoln's eyes and turned to see the dirty Union soldier, shining a half-witted smile.

"Yes, thank you for that show of support, soldier," Lincoln

answered good-naturedly. He winked at the crowd as if to say, *Now that's a strange one*. He tried to resume. "Now you have all heard by now that I am the Republican candidate for another term…"

"Mr. Lincoln!" The Soldier loudly interrupted again. He moved toward the president, pushing through the closest knot of onlookers. He was a few feet away now. He clutched the dagger in anticipation. It would happen quickly. He smiled as he advanced. As the civilians parted, a guard spurred his big black horse forward interposing the beast between the unruly man and the president. The blocking maneuver shoved The Soldier back forcefully as the warhorse shifted on unsteady legs.

The Soldier bellowed indignantly. "Whoa, my good man! Would you deny a comrade-in-arms a handshake from his commander-in-chief?" With a raised withered arm, The Soldier peered up at the guard who did not answer, but glared down at the beggar with suspicion and contempt.

"Now, now, Sergeant," Lincoln admonished the guard, "Let the man pass so that I may speak with him." The Soldier renewed his smile as the horse moved back. Under his coat, he held his right hand close to his body and tightened his grip on the dagger. He stepped around the equine's muzzle, only three feet away now, and reached out his left hand to touch Lincoln's outstretched arm. The president leaned down from his perch in the carriage.

Just then a uniformed rider turned the corner at Pennsylvania and 14th and dashed at speed straight for the president. The out of control horse fought the violent tug at its bit as the rider clumsily tried to pull up next to Lincoln. The foaming animal snorted mightily. And then he reared and pulled away, knocking The Soldier on his behind. Thinking he had been found out somehow, the killer jumped up and ran toward the far side of the park. Lincoln's jaw dropped when he saw the crippled veteran take off. A murmur sputtered through the crowd at the sight.

The rider, oblivious to the havoc he'd caused, announced, "Mr. President, Secretary Hay has received a telegram, and thought you should have it urgently." He handed over a slip of paper.

"Thank you, my good man." Lincoln bowed slightly to the crowd, asking for their indulgence. He fiddled for his glasses with one hand and snapped the paper open with the other.

John Hay's cursive flowed across the page.

Mr. President:

We have word that the Alabama has been defeated and sunk off Cherbourg, France. Semmes has escaped and is on the run somewhere on the continent.

J.H.

Lincoln raised his eyes and smiled. Another victory he could run on. Why not share it with the crowd?

The Soldier limped into the park, back in character. No one was following, but he was not sure what had happened back there. He had been so close and then an inexplicable complication. One of the intangibles of war. The Soldier reached the French marquis in minutes. He spied Conroe, lounging as the horse grazed on a clump of overgrown fescue. When their eyes met, The Soldier merely shook his head.

Chapter 35

Mindelo City, Sao Vicente, Cape Verde Islands

The hulking black-bearded man peered over a copy of the *London Times*, several days old. All around him, people talked, using the Portuguese language that was little more than background noise to the tall, menacing seafarer. He was respected here as a slaver, one of the remote places left in the world where the trade was still legal. The outdoor café looked out across Porto Grande, a broad circular harbor sitting astride the Atlantic shipping lanes off the West African coast. The morning sun had already cut through an overnight fog. The view was good but the food was wretched; some kind of creole stew with beans and hominy and very little meat.

Bland *cachupa* was not the only thing that concerned Captain Nathaniel Tilghman. He was reconsidering his plan to sail to Rio before he made for Baltimore. He wanted to get his heaviest cargo to the Maryland city as soon as possible. The captain still hadn't worked out how he was going to bluff his way into the Union-held port. But he knew if he wanted to sail straight to Baltimore, he'd have to sell his slave cargo here.

Puffy black clouds rolled across the bare brown mountains in the distance, a summer storm blowing in from the southwest. *Salem* rested beside a rough-hewn dock, one of forty or fifty ships tied to land or anchored in the busy harbor. Mindelo City was a key port for resupplying before the Atlantic crossing. Tilghman's clipper confined fifty black Africans bought at Cabinda two nights ago. This was not an unusual cargo on Sao Vicente, but *Salem* surely was the only vessel in the Cape Verdes ballasted with crates of gold. Even so, almost all of the ships in Porto Grande were of questionable registry; running slaves to Brazil, supplying the Confederates with guns, running contraband of every kind to ports across the world. Should one of these dodgy ships forgo its planned run to Brazil and expedite its gold delivery to Baltimore? Tilghman needed to make a decision soon. The slave auction started in less than thirty minutes.

The slave captain's eyes wandered as he pondered his options. Down on the quay, a young white couple stood out like sore nipples on a sow pig, he noticed. They were respectably dressed, the man in a mid-thigh black sack coat and gray moleskin trousers. A black slouch hat covered a full head of brown hair. He had dark good looks, blue-gray eyes and a lean, strong face adorned with a cinnamon-brown beard, cropped close. The woman was darker still, a Mediterranean beauty with shiny black hair parted in the middle and tied in a bun under a lavender poke bonnet. A deep blue traveling cape covered a brown jacket and matching ankle length skirt. A simple white cotton chemisette contrasted with her dusky olive skin. But Slim John Sweeney and his wife Carmen, while comfortably dressed, were not rich. They clutched everything they owned in four cloth satchels.

Slim John set his bags down and waved as the gray schooner that had brought them across the sea swept its bow about and headed out again. Their new friends, Captain Sam Barbee and his crew Junius and Apollo Moxley, had made the passage in good time. For the price of one thousand U.S. dollars, the newly freed slaves and their ship, the *Sable Eagle*, had run the blockade out of Charleston. Now Sweeney, a Confederate deserter and his new wife, a dark-haired beauty with a heart of gold and an iron will, had to find a way down the African coast. The tall, hard-bodied ex-soldier turned to Carmen, cocking his weight to one leg the way an athlete does to show his swagger.

"Say goodbye to our last connection to home, Carmen, my dear. Say goodbye to Charleston."

"And say hello to our dream, John," she answered optimistically. "When we find gold in The Namib, we'll go back someday. And buy the whole town." She smiled at Slim John with adoring eyes as was her way. The couple's dream not only involved getting rich in southern Africa, it also included getting as far away as possible from the Confederacy, the Union and the accursed war back in America.

"I must say I shall miss Barbee and the Moxleys. They lived up to their part of the bargain." Slim John surveyed the lay of the land and plotted a path off the busy dock as he spoke. "I wish them well in their new life as free men."

"Indeed, I pray they will prosper in their freedom," Carmen answered, while she gestured toward what seemed to be the city center on higher ground. Slim John looked where she pointed and retrieved the bags in his charge.

"Let's walk up to the town square and find something to eat." It had been a long, hard journey, with stops in Bermuda and the Canaries. But it was worth it to escape the war and the heartbreak of the last few months. It also had given them time to think about what to do next. Slim John had fought in the battles to defend Charleston from a relentless Union siege, and he had been a key witness in the trial of black Union soldiers he'd captured at the Battle of Battery Wagner. But his fervor for the Southern cause had died with the many friends he'd lost in the hopeless campaign.

The Sweeneys made their way slowly uphill away from the harbor front, wading into a large crowd of people, roaming chickens and browsing goats. The people were mostly men from across the globe from the looks of them--white men, African travelers and Arab traders. They mixed on the streets with the Portuguese and local creoles who inhabited the island. The steady stream of humanity in the market sector signaled some special event today, the couple realized, as they made their way up a cobblestone road that inclined toward the town's high street.

Chapter 36

Oko opened his haunting, bronze-almond eyes and instantly remembered where he was. Under the floor of a white man's great sailing ship. It seemed like a floating tree house pushed by the wind. He remembered how he got there too. A great man did not long forget how he became a slave. Oko's Portuguese name reflected his place in his tribe; Uma, The Number One Man. Strong, brave, murderous. Oko Uma. Since the battle where his people lost their freedom though, his standing had slipped.

All fifty of his village were on this ship and none of them showed him the respect he expected from them. He would deal with that in time. They were all that were left, forty-two babies and old ones had been slaughtered by the bushmen who defeated them. The hunting lands were gone too, left behind forever, he supposed. The light-skinned devils hunted there now.

Oko Uma stretched his battered frame and stood up. With every movement, Uma's coal black skin rippled with muscle. How did the skinny, short bush tribe defeat him? Only with overwhelming numbers. He had run through at least twenty of them before he fell. It was like swatting flies for much of the fight. Then dozens of them flew at him at once. They swarmed from every direction until their clubs knocked him unconscious. He was the great beast attacked by a herd of hyenas.

As he relived the battle, the whites of his eyes glowed in the dark of the ship's hold. The vessel's gentle rocking did little to quell his anger. He looked at the sorry lot of his people and plotted their rescue. No one spoke. Fifty people crushed into a few hundred square feet, close enough to share each others' breath, and no one dared speak. Uma only heard coughing and crying. Bodies crushed, souls crushed. Outside he recognized a familiar language, men yelling back and forth in Portuguese. He had learned the tongue as a young boy in Cabinda. The white sailors and their cop-ten didn't know that part. That he knew Portuguese, a little English; that he knew about war, and ships, and gold. They didn't see the slyness in Uma's eyes. The white cop-ten didn't realize he held the Number One Man--a man who possessed a cunning, ruthless intelligence.

Uma raised his head and surveyed the rest of the hold. His people milled about the slatted cells of iron and wood, eight shadowy little rooms that stood in rows with a central hall that ran the length of the space. The women were across the hall. The men segregated on the other side. Shackles lined the walls for slaves who resisted even the smallest order by the white men who ran the ship. Only two of the tribe found themselves restrained in this way so far. The rest of the group were housed six to a cell. Two pine buckets in each cell served the necessary functions-one for drinking water and one to catch the fluid on the other end. The buckets gave the hold its exquisitely pungent odor. And the captors expected the slaves to keep their own cells clean.

Most of his warriors then had free hands if an opportunity arose to fight or escape. The cop-ten hadn't a clue to the danger Uma's tribe posed. The white man was bold and strong, he could tell, but he underestimated his slave prisoners. He didn't know that Uma had seen his secret, his gold. The African had been emptying buckets yesterday and glimpsed the crate when the cop-ten was moving it to his cabin. He heard the white men talking about it in their language. They didn't think he knew what they were saying. He knew what a treasure it was. He even knew the Portuguese word for the secret cargo: *ouro*. The cop-ten called it the Confederate gold. *Ouro Confederado*—that's what Uma would call it if he got the chance.

Tilghman had reached a decision. As merchandise, the dark ones were not that good a lot. Twenty-four were female, never worth as much as a good male who could work the land. Most of the twenty-six males were too young to bring top dollar in the Rio slave market. And some of them were past prime age too. He would not lose much if he just unloaded them here. And that one, Oko Uma, he could be trouble on the long voyage to Brazil. He saw the anger in the dark man's eyes, even while he seemed to be docile. He would not lose much by selling that one.

And, Tilghman reasoned, he had other African goods to sell. One of *Salem*'s storerooms was well-stocked with exotic goods, rare African mahogany, ebony and rosewood, a fine selection of intricately woven baskets from the Namib, Ghana and the Zululand, a supply of beautifully polished calabash gourds, and several bolts of Malian mud cloth. This finery, sold in New York or Boston, could take the sting out of any shortfall due to the quick sale of his human cargo. Yes, he had decided to change his plans; forgo the Rio leg and get the gold to Baltimore as soon as possible.

One crate of precious metal was his after all and he wanted to get *that* back to America as well. His share would be enough to more than make up for a short sale of fifty slaves, more than enough to pay for the trip and its expenses. And then there was Semmes. He didn't want to be on that man's bad side. The slaver caught the waiter's eye, threw down a coin to cover his breakfast and loped away from the café's collection of rustic tables. He jumped across an open sewer and started down the high street toward the dock where *Salem* lay.

The slaver noticed the pretty girl first. Moving up the steep incline from the sea-level docks, she had removed her cloak, revealing a strong young body. She modestly gathered the hem of her long wasp-waisted skirt in one hand to make the climb easier and the sea captain traced her long legs down to her exposed ankles. The girl seemed confident and determined, even so far from home. She *was* far from home, the captain knew. A dark-skinned, white girl was not unheard of in Sao Vicente, but this one wasn't Portuguese. He could tell that much before he tipped his hat.

"Good day, Miss and welcome to Porto Grande." She didn't answer immediately. It wouldn't do for a lady to speak to a stranger in a strange land. The girl was so striking that he hadn't noticed her companion until the awkward silence broke the spell. Slim John wore a revolver on his narrow hip—a .36 caliber Spiller and Burr. A distinctly Confederate weapon, Tilghman knew, and a nice little gun for travel. Tilghman eyed the sidearm and the man's well-stitched white shirt and tailored trousers and knew the couple must be

Southerners even before Slim John opened his mouth.

"Good day to you, Captain. You sound like a fellow countryman. Maybe even a man of the South." Slim John set down the bags he was toting. He didn't know Tilghman was a ship captain, though his clothes and his bearing in a port city might have made it a good guess. He merely used the term as a respectful address. If Tilghman was a captain, the moniker was expected. If he wasn't, he had just been "promoted" by the greeting.

"Aye, I'm Captain Nathaniel Tilghman from Maryland, master of that clipper ship, the *Salem*." The big man swept his left arm in the ship's direction down below where they stood. He jabbed his hammy right hand at Slim John in greeting, who slapped his own strong hand into the captain's hefty grip.

"My name is John Sweeney, and this is my wife Carmen. It's good to hear a familiar voice this far from home."

"And what would be home for you, my boy?" Slim John glanced over at Carmen before he spoke. They had not discussed how they would present their past to strangers. She took over and answered vaguely.

"We are from South Carolina." She tossed long dark locks that wrestled with the sea breeze sweeping in from the west.

"Ah, the very center of God's great earth," Tilghman answered with a crooked smile.

"But beset by the Devil himself now," Slim John replied.

"I reckon it is a right hot place these days." Tilghman looked off at the gathering clouds, knowing he needed to get back to the *Salem*. "You must be pleased to be away from the war."

"Yes, we mean to start a new life, make our fortune with God's help, and wait out the war from a safe distance."

"Uh Hunh," Tilghman grunted, trying to hide his suspicious thoughts. Carmen latched on to the captain's mood and changed the subject.

"John here is a war veteran. He's done his duty and now we're free to find our way in a part of the world that's peaceful." Tilghman knew there was more to the story, but he was a slaver after all. He would not stand in judgment of this young man and his beautiful wife. He did not probe any further.

"I wish you both well then, Miz Sweeney. A finer face never graced these islands and I'm sure they miss you back home. The

South's loss is the world's gain, I say." He smiled again and Carmen returned one of her own.

Tilghman was captivated by the woman's large brown eyes. He lingered for a moment speechless before he caught himself and made to leave, speaking quickly. "Now I fear a storm is brewing and I have some business to attend to. I am bound for Baltimore with the next tide. There is a passable café at the top of the street if you're looking for something to eat." The captain bowed deeply to Carmen and shook Slim John's hand again. "If I can be of any help to you before I leave, hail my watch on the *Salem*, will you?" Slim John did not let go, but held the slaver's hand in both of his own.

"Yes, thank you, Captain. Your kindness to us in this foreign port is as precious as God's grace."

"Bless you," added Carmen.

"Just so." Tilghman backed away and turned with a flair. The couple watched their new acquaintance trudge off and John's eyes fixed on the *Salem*. He saw it flew a British flag. He spoke to Carmen in a low voice as they watched Tilghman lumber away.

"The *Salem* flies a Union Jack, but I'm betting the good captain works for himself." He suspected the Marylander could be a rough customer, though he didn't imagine that Tilghman was a slaver.

"I reckon he is concealing a part of his past too," Carmen said. Slim John didn't reply to this. She could tell that her husband was still ashamed that he had deserted his mates back in the Confederate army. That's why he had hesitated when the captain asked him where home was. He picked up their bags.

"Let's go find some warm food." The couple turned and leaned into the hill.

Chapter 37

Dozens of people milled about the docks when Tilghman got back to his ship. Africans in chains moved in long lines onto a peninsula of flood tide land adjacent to the harbor quays. This otherwise worthless ground served as the slave market for Sao Vicente. Several acres comprised an area fenced off from the rest of the mainland. One gate allowed entry and exit from the market. A sandy, open field looked onto a weather-beaten, gray wooden stage which stood in the center of the barren plot of land. The auction stage blocked the rest of the field that continued up to the point of the peninsula. Numerous thatch-roofed reed pens lined this expanse. Men and women waited in these holding pens for their march to the stage and their sale into slavery.

Tilghman dodged a line of black women all clad in thin brown dresses made from animal skins. They walked slowly toward the pens, swaying side to side, their eyes on the ground. The captain ignored the sad scene at first, then looked the women up and down comparing them to the specimens he would try to sell. Seemingly annoyed by the quality of the competition or perhaps merely upset by the tumult all around him, he yelled to his first officer who stood alone on the deck. "Bring out our women and line them up. We are to sell them here. Once they're penned, take the men out for the same purpose. We sell the dark ones here," he repeated, to emphasize to the underling that his plans had changed.

In Cabinda, Tilghman had paid an average of two hundred Reias, about one hundred twenty five dollars, for each slave. He would hope to auction them for an average of three hundred Reias here. A far cry from the five hundred he could get in Brazil, but still a profit. The auctioneers, Portuguese criminals most of them, were a cruel bunch, little more than slaves themselves, but very efficient in running a sale. They would sort the captives by age, sex, size and condition and even by skin darkness. Muscular, dark-skinned men brought the most, followed by pretty, light-skinned young women. The Portuguese auction men counted and tagged each slaver's group, then put each slave in the appropriate pen according to his characteristics.

Uma glared at the Portuguese herder. "He is a number one," Rodrigo said. The Portuguese slave trader held a slim wire whip sheathed in heavy black leather. Like his baton, Rodrigo was short and lithe and capable of inflicting searing pain. His sun-red cheeks were shiny with sweat; his black facial hair matted and greasy. He looked at Uma sideways, striking a jaunty pose, the whip resting on his hip. The African held his bound hands in front, thinking how easy it would be to rip the dry-rotted hemp strands apart and strangle the smug little man where he stood. He wanted to tell the herder that he was Number One Man, not just another number one, but Uma did not speak. He had a better idea for dealing with his jailers. With some luck, he would get his revenge and win his freedom.

As a number one, Uma was a prime piece of merchandise; dark, young and strong, potentially a good field hand whose body could bear working cotton or cane in year-round tropical heat. He towered over the swarming group of short Portuguese herders. They checked Uma more closely, one man feeling his testicles and squeezing the muscles on his arms and buttocks. Another jabbed his kidneys and stomach to test their soundness. A third eyed his feet and forced open his mouth to see Uma's teeth. After the inspection, the third herder nodded to Rodrigo, agreeing with his assessment. "As I said, take him to Pen One," Rodrigo answered smugly. One of the other Portuguese corralled the ropes around Uma's hands with a metal hook made for the purpose and roughly led him to a stockade enclosure.

In the distance, Uma heard the auctioneer call to the crowd. He peered through the gaps in the palisade fence. Today's sale would begin with the light-skinned pretties to draw in the crowd. The

Number Ones would be held for later. The buyers were mainly Arabs, North Africans and Brazilians, but there were some rogue white men like Tilghman openly flouting the laws of their own countries. There were even a few black Africans at the auction, agents for powerful warlords in sub-Saharan lands.

But Uma was concerned mainly with the Portuguese guarding his pen. He counted five of them lounging about. He saw the swaggering Rodrigo, idly slapping his baton into his free hand. Uma wanted his attention and spoke loudly in the Portuguese language. "You brown dogs bring spit to my mouth. I would eat your bloody beating hearts if we were still on the veldt." The other Portuguese keepers laughed lustily at the boast and Uma, happy he had gained a reaction, continued to yell at the herders, this time in his native tongue.

"Shut your Negro mouth!" Rodrigo snapped. He lunged at the palisade wall where Uma stood, a swipe of his whip rattling the boards

"Come in the cage and shut it yourself." Uma said quietly this time, using Portuguese again. Rodrigo drew closer, surprised the African could speak Portuguese so well. The herder flailed at the fence where Uma loomed, but the slave did not flinch. Instead Uma continued to speak quietly. "Rodrigo, listen to me. What I know will make you a rich man." Uma hissed the words conspiratorially, a tone which intrigued the jailer.

"What can a black slave know? And why would you share it with me?"

"The ship captain hides a golden treasure, *ouro, ouro Confederado*, bound for America and I know where it sits."

"And why tell *me* about it?"

"I want my freedom and you can give it."

"Keep talking," Rodrigo whispered. Then for the benefit of the other herders, "Shut your worthless black mouth!" the herder yelled again. He thrashed the fence with one, two, three more lashes. Uma smiled at the act.

"Tell them I am sick. Take me back to the ship that brought me here. Bring your men with you. Talk the crew into taking me aboard. They will be few while the auction is on. I will show you the *ouro*. We will take over the ship. You can take the *ouro* and I will make my getaway." Uma doubled over in pain and yelled out. "Master, I am ill. It is my bowels. Very sick, very sick!" He fell against the near wall of the cage. Inside the pen, the other number ones moved away from him quickly. All sickness harbored evil spirits and the evil spirits brought more sickness. Outside, Rodrigo moved in close to the wall and whispered,

"I will think about this. But if you cross me, I will feed you your own eyes and slit your throat in mid-swallow."

Chapter 38

Slim John slurped up the last of the spicy goat stew. A thick slice of rough brown bread was long gone. "A working man's lunch, cheap and hearty," Carmen remarked. She had finished hers even sooner than her husband. Slim John didn't answer, but shifted his weight on the wooden bench they had found on the market square. The district was busy with people speaking at least a half dozen different languages. During lunch, they'd realized the international gathering was due to the slave auction. Slim John's eyes perused the harbor scene below them. A growing crowd streamed along the docks and continued to gather around the auction field. He stood and grabbed the couple's bags, and gestured down the hill.

"Let's head down to the harbor office and ask about a ship."

"But let's keep away from the slaving, John. It all sickens me." They started down the path to the sea, steering around darting children, and avoiding slow, heavily loaded supply wagons.

"Yes, the auction is an ugly sight. It makes me wonder what we were thinking back home where slavery was so accepted."

"Who said about slavery, 'I tremble for my country when I reflect that God is just.'?"

"One of those Virginia…slaveowners, I think," Slim John answered, chuckling at the irony.

"I remember the nuns taught us that George Mason said slavery makes petty tyrants of us all. That I remember. That I think is very true." The couple reached sea level again and stepped up on the boardwalk leading to the harbor office fronting the row of piers where smaller, coast-hugging vessels tied up.

"Speaking of petty tyrants. Look at that cadre of Portuguese slave herders. They seem to be leading that Negro to Tilghman's ship."

A few yards away Uma, his bound hands hooked by a herder, was surrounded by a phalanx of brown men, the group moving toward the *Salem*.

On the Auction Block

"One hundred Reias!" the auctioneer cried. "We will start the bidding at one hundred Reias for this fourteen year old woman of finest quality. Fresh from the bush and docile as a well-fed cow!"

The English barker stood over six feet tall and his black stovepipe hat made him look even taller. A long salt and pepper beard covered his chest like an errant old skunk. He wielded a long wooden pointer of the kind used in a classroom. He jabbed it under the girl's chin to raise her downcast face so the crowd could see her comely eyes. They were almond shaped, of amber shades with flecks of brown and her coffee colored hair fell in wiry rings around slender bare shoulders. The Englishman whipped the pointer down and sharply tapped her arms away from her shapely torso. He deftly slid the stick up and down the curve of her hip drawing the prurient attention of the gathering bidders. The auctioneer lewdly smiled at her before beginning again.

"Let's commence with the bidding! One hundred Reias!" Eager hands began to dart above the crowd, white hands, black hands, brown hands, all vying to buy. "Do I hear one twenty-five, One-fifty? Do I hear one seventy-five? This is a fine piece of property, smooth light skin, sure to make your men happy! One seventy-five over here. One seventy-five! One seventy-five! She will work for you, in field or house. Give you *more* workers too! Two hundred! This man has two hundred. She is but fourteen, give you many years of pleasure and toil! Two twenty-five! Two twenty-five over here! I have two twenty-five. Two-fifty! Two-fifty! We're at two twenty-five, two-twenty-five once, twice, sold to Ben Ali for two hundred twenty-five Reias."

Tilghman spit on the ground and kicked sand over the wet gobbet in nervous agitation. "If that beauty went for so little, the market may be poor today," he muttered to himself. "These Arab whoresons are tight with their money." With the auction underway, Tilghman headed back to the *Salem*. It would take hours of work to ready the ship for the long voyage to Baltimore. He wanted to hurry along the resupply. The tide would begin to shift around four in the afternoon. By then he would be settled with the auctioneer and the captain wanted no delay.

Aboard the *Salem*

Rodrigo slit the first officer's throat before the sailor knew what was happening. The officer slumped to the deck outside the captain's cabin, bright red blood pumping onto the wide wood boards. Uma and two other herders stood behind the gory scene. Uma dipped his fingers into the rising red pool, twisting his bound hands toward the side of his face. He traced thick red lines down his cheek, then he did the same on the other cheek. The young white man had treated him well on the voyage from Cabinda, he remembered. He was a good seaman. Uma believed his blood would give him strength.

Rodrigo watched the African with fascination and disgust and pushed open the cabin door. "Quickly, show me the *ouro*, the *ouro Confederado*," the killer barked. Uma heard the desperation in Rodrigo's voice. He had no doubt that Rodrigo would kill him as soon as he found the gold. He'd slaughtered the first officer without a thought.

In the few minutes since he had heard about the treasure, Rodrigo had been consumed with the thought of escaping his life as a slave herder. He seized the opportunity and no one would stand in his way. It mattered little to him if he had to kill a few more people to reach his end. Already three other crewmen lay dead up on deck, their bodies stowed behind supplies and bulkheads. Five more Salem crewmen were lucky enough to have been handled by the gang's other two men. Those herders had caught them off guard below deck. They beat them unconscious, tied them up and locked them in the slave hold down below. They had reported all this to Rodrigo who told them to go back and guard the prisoners.

Once rid of the other pirates, Rodrigo had followed the African to the captain's quarters. Now Uma stepped over the first officer's body and entered the cabin. He jerked his head toward a rough wooden crate with the number twenty-four stenciled on its side. "There it is. Crate Twenty-four contains ten thousand dollars of gold just as I promised." Rodrigo grabbed at one of his gang with greedy hands, screaming with excitement.

"Carlos, open it! Open it now!"

Tilghman knew something wasn't right with the *Salem* as soon as he started up the gangway. Sacks of flour and rice, barrels of water and crates of fruit had been left on deck to bake in the sun, easy pickings for rats and thieves. "Where in tarnation is everyone?" the captain bellowed. "Who attends this bloody ship?" The yelling attracted attention along the quay. Slim John and Carmen, who were just feet away near the harbor office entrance, recognized the captain's voice.

"That's the Marylander, Tilghman," Slim John mused with a smile. He stopped and looked at the seaman who had drawn a revolver and was waving it over his head. "He's giving a snootfull to someone in his crew."

"Sounds like it's more serious than that," Carmen replied. She'd heard more in Tilghman's tone; more than just a good bawling out. The ruckus from the *Salem*'s deck continued.

"Murder, murder! Call the constable!" they heard the captain scream. Slim John's smile stiffened and disappeared.

"Wait here, Carmen," he yelled, as he ran toward the ship. He bounded up the gangway and found Tilghman behind a stack of crates looking down on a dead crewman. He looked up at Sweeney and stared at the former Confederate for an instant before he recognized him.

"It must be pirates, Sweeney. They'll be down below after my…ah, coffers. Are you handy in a fight, my boy?" Slim John deftly reached for his Spiller and Burr. He raised it to his face, pointing it straight up and closely inspecting each chamber and cap.

"Let's go show 'em out," he replied resolutely.

A faint, yellow cast fell across Rodrigo's sweat-sheened face as he gazed on rows of small gold bars in the treasure chest. The herder was on his knees, panting greedily over the vast fortune. He lifted one of the bars like a priest raising the Eucharist. It was much heavier than he expected. Runic-like assay marks noted its origin in some South American mine.

Uma did not take his eyes off the Portuguese herder, as he stole a furtive glance at the two men at his back. Rodrigo still clutched the bar with both hands and began to rise from his knees. With the quickness of a panther, Uma swung rock-hard arms at the guards behind him, first to the left and then to the right. He knocked both diminutive Portuguese down with two mighty swipes. In almost the same instant, he kicked the vulnerable Rodrigo in the face. As the gang leader fell unconscious, Uma ripped his hands apart and caught the gold bar before it dropped.

The guards regained their feet, Carlos drawing a long knife. The other raised his baton to strike Uma who side-stepped the whistling stroke and brought down the heavy gold bar on the man's temple. The blow thudded against the meaty side of his head and killed him instantly. Carlos lunged, the knife arching toward the African's chest. Uma nimbly stepped back avoiding the thrust. The herder stumbled forward off balance and Uma crashed the metal bar down on his skull. The close confines of the room amplified the hollow sound of cracking bone. Carlos fell dead, his brain short circuited before his eyes could close.

"What in bloody heaven?" Tilghman cried as he stepped inside his cabin and saw the carnage Uma had created in mere seconds. Slim John came in just behind him.

"This is bloody murder!" he shrieked. But Tilghman's mind had already moved on.

"Murder for my gold!" He raised his gun and aimed it at Uma. He would eliminate the last standing intruder.

"Hold on, Master!" the African cried. "I have killed these pirates who would take your gold!" Tilghman's jaw dropped when he heard Uma speak English. "There are two more aboard ship. And more of your crew below decks." Uma dropped the bloody gold bar back into the crate and raised his hands. Slim John stepped forward, his hand between Tilghman's revolver and Uma. He spoke to the warrior.

"If you are with us, take us below and help us free the crew."

"Yes, I help," he answered with a nod. With Uma leading the way, the trio ran out of the room toward the ladder down below.

Rodrigo's halting breath raised bubbles in the raft of thick blood streaming from the dead men. He lay face down in the dark liquid. A few unconscious minutes more and he would have drowned in the river of red. The bubbles tickled his nose enough to wake him. He gagged and spit congealing blood onto the head of one of the corpses next to him. The herder rose groggily to his hands and knees and noticed Carlos staring directly at him, stone dead. The grisly scene cleared his head and he remembered what had just happened.

The gold was in the cabin still, right there in the open crate, but without help he could not move it. He could steal what he could carry and be the richest man in Sao Vincente, but he wanted it all. The utter failure of his plan thus far focused him and anger rose in his chest. The clever African had betrayed him, but the game was not over yet. He wiped the gore from his face, left the cabin and ran along the hallway to the deck hatch.

Down below Slim John and Tilghman, guns held high, watched Uma clamber down the steep ladder into the belly of the ship. The African landed on the floor alone. The atmosphere was familiar to him. It still stunk of human waste, sweat and death. He saw the five captives, bound and gagged, sitting in a circle back to back in the darkest part of the hold. He nonchalantly crossed the room, looking for the other herders. The Portuguese men had retreated to the shadows, wary of who was coming down the ladder. Uma's sudden appearance surprised them, but did not alarm them. They showed themselves to their African confederate, who spoke quickly. "Master Rodrigo needs you on deck. The gold is heavy." The herders looked at each other for a moment. The one they called Miguel glanced at the prisoners but didn't wait any longer. He pushed Uma aside and rushed up the ladder. The other man quickly followed. Uma smiled as he watched them leave.

Miguel sensed the danger above him before his eyes could make out the burly white man back lit by the sun. He didn't have a chance to react. Tilghman leaning over the hatch unloaded his .50 caliber pistol directly into Miguel's upturned face. The ball blasted a hole where his nose had been. The man fell back, knocking the other herder down into the hold. Uma grabbed him with both hands and snapped his neck like he was a market chicken. The powerful African shoved the twitching body to the floor and with a mighty breath spit on the corpse. "Strong blood," Uma muttered, touching the dried red stripes on his cheeks, the first officer's life-blood. He took a knife off Miguel's body and walked toward the tied up crew. The captives, having watched the murder, feared he was coming for them and began to moan like dogs whose tongues had been cut out. Uma smiled as he cut the ropes and bade them stand up.

Chapter 39

From dockside, Carmen watched as Rodrigo darted down the ship's ramp and she wondered what had happened aboard. Why was the Portuguese aboard at all? She had heard a single gunshot. It was muffled but unmistakable. Panic welled up in her throat. *Where was John? I must find John.* She instinctively grabbed one of her bags and galloped toward the ship. She ran up the gangway but didn't see a soul.

The auctioneer's call echoed through the streets and the sun was reaching its daily zenith when Rodrigo tapped the fire bell to get the market crowd's attention. He perched on a buckboard wagon that had stopped to unload in front of the harbor office. "I have seen it with my own eyes, my friends. *Ouro* beyond your wildest dreams." Passersby began to gather, hoping for a diversion if not a bargain. The herder waved his baton at a group of fifteen or twenty now, and quickly pointed directly at the *Salem* in the distance. "The slaver has stolen treasure. Gold, I say, American gold, Confederate gold, *ouro Confederado."* The words affected the crowd like a narcotic drug. Many of them stood glassy eyed, staring at the ship and then back at Rodrigo who whipped them up with promises of fast riches.

"Surely a man such as the captain did not come by such a treasure by legal means. The gold is not his, and so can be had for the taking." Fifty men now crowded around the office building. The humble one story harbor office, its weather-beaten boards and tin roof, symbolized the abject poverty of Mindelo City. The mob was composed of the desperately poor of the street, most of them hard workers with little to show for a day's labor. There were few opportunities on Sao Vicente, few chances to make a better life and every man in the crowd had little hope of ever being wealthy. Except maybe this one time. "The ship is weakly guarded, most of the crew is at the auction or drinking on High Street. I tell you, follow me and I will make you rich!" The crowd cheered as Rodrigo jumped to the ground and ran toward the *Salem*.

Carmen walked out of the *Salem*'s wheelhouse where she had found no one and saw Rodrigo leading a crowd of ten rough men toward the ship. Dozens more stormed behind the raiding party. That's when she stumbled upon the dead crewman that Tilghman and Slim John had found earlier. She immediately drew a Colt Army revolver from her bag. She lifted it with both hands, and thought about how Slim John had captured the six-shot sidearm at Secessionville, a Confederate victory on James Island.

South Carolina seemed so far away, but her experience with the war there would serve her well now. Calmly she checked the gun's caps and pulled back the hammer as she made her way to the head of the gangway. She didn't know where John was or what had happened to him, but she aimed to keep the Portuguese mob off the ship. She deftly knocked over a nearby barrel, rolled it across the top of the ramp and crouched behind it.

In seconds, the mob reached the ship, yelling and pushing each other, jockeying for position. Rodrigo flashed an ugly smile when he saw the woman standing aboard, blocking the way to his fortune. The mob jostled behind him when he stopped midway up the ramp, just ten yards away from Carmen. It would be a good shot to hit him with a pistol from there.

"Get out of the way, woman. We don't want to hurt an innocent, but you are not going to stop us." Carmen squeezed the heavy gun two-handed, the way she'd been taught when the war had first started back in Charleston. You never knew when you'd have to defend your home or your virtue, her friend Ruth had told her. She'd carried a derringer when she'd worked as a nurse in Richmond back in '62. Carmen was young and beautiful, but she was no shrinking violet when the action started. These Portuguese brigands didn't understand that. That she'd seen years of war and knew how to handle herself.

"Don't come any closer or I'll fill your thieving bag of bones with lead," she yelled. Rodrigo sneered at the insolent white woman and turned to his followers. "This Americano woman thinks she can deny us what is ours by right! It is our fortune and our future she is trying to steal from us! Rush her and she will run like a leetle white rabbit!" He laughed and the men around him guffawed savagely. One of them screamed like a monkey. Rodrigo raised his arm like he was starting a road race as he settled in behind the first line of the mob.

Then he smiled again. "The first man to her can have her!" He threw down his arm and ordered, "Get her! Get the woman!" Carmen called out for them to stop when she saw the mob start toward her but no one heard what she said. She fired without hesitation and one of the toughs went down, then another, and a third, all dead as the large lead balls found their mark. The three bodies blocked the ramp and the others in the attack hesitated at first and then stopped completely. Carmen held her fire, but did not lower the gun. The men froze, waiting for the next shot. One of the brigands took a step forward and Carmen calmly gunned him down just like the others. Four shots, four men down. She had two shots more and no one moved.

"What in blazes was that?" Tilghman asked two decks below. He, Slim John, Uma and the five other crewmen were climbing out of the hold.

"Sounds like a .44 caliber sidearm," Slim John answered. He could tell the caliber of almost any weapon by its sound, one of the strange abilities gained from years on the battlefield.

"I don't know what curse has befallen this ship, but our trouble here is evidently not over yet," the captain muttered as he strained to move his bulk further up the second ladder. The group passed by mid-decks and began the final ascent out into the open. Slim John could never have imagined the scene that awaited him when he stepped on deck. He thought the danger of the robbery had passed and was in a joking mood.

"What is all the racket out here? It sounds like a half-drunk crowd at a minstrel show." And then he saw Carmen, smoking Colt in hand, holed up behind the barrel like a soldier in a shoot-out. The shock paralyzed him.

"Blast all, she's got a battle on her hands," Tilghman bellowed when he saw the situation.

Carmen half-turned, saw her friends, and relief shot through her body like a bolt of lightning. Tilghman waved his men out into the open. He pointed to a pair. "You two, man that deck gun. Train it on the mob and wait for my order." He swept an arm at the other men. "You three, set the headsails and get ready to haul anchor. I think I've had enough of beautiful Sao Vicente. We'll blast these blackguards back to Hades if we have to and be ready to run."

Slim John had recovered himself and rushed over beside Carmen. He looked at her sideways while he raised his Spiller and Burr and took aim at the cordon of Portuguese still hunkering down along the gangway.

"Well I knew that Yankee Colt would come in handy some day, but I didn't think you'd be the one plunking away at the Indians." Carmen, without dropping her aim, looked her husband up and down, making sure he wasn't hurt.

"I'm just happy you're safe, John. I saw one of them run off the ship like he'd stole the last of the potatoes and I came aboard to find you. That's when this mob showed up." She waved the steadied Colt along the group of attackers which still held its position at the foot of the gangway. Slim John looked down on the dead bodies draped along the ramp and whistled.

"Remind me not to cross you, dear wife." Tilghman joined the couple a minute later, not speaking. He looked Slim John in the eye, testing the man's mettle. He smiled admiringly at Carmen's fearless, two-handed stance. The standoff continued, but now the ship's side had more firepower.

Chapter 40

Down on the dock, Rodrigo's dream wasn't finished yet. Fuming that a woman had repulsed the attack, he hatched another idea. Did the Americans think they were the only ones with guns? A man had just handed him an Austrian made pistol fully loaded. He knew he must act quickly. He could see two men on the *Salem*'s deck loading a pivoting carronade and Rodrigo knew he would not stand a chance against a heavy weapon. He calmly told the group around him that he was going to cover the next attack. "When I start shooting at the slavers, we must rise up and rush them before they know what hit them. They'll duck for cover this time and we'll overrun them. Kill them, kill all of them, and the gold will be ours."

Rodrigo peered up at the ship and now saw three figures huddled at the top of the gangway. "Ah, the captain has joined the defense," he muttered to himself. He recognized Tilghman from the auction. He could hear men calling to each other. There were sailors working in the forward rigging. Getting the ship ready to leave. Rodrigo sensed that momentum was turning against him. He would have to move fast. "Let's go now!" He stood up and started shooting at the defenders up on deck. The mob surged forward, yelling and cursing. They closed the distance within seconds.

Tilghman and Carmen ducked at the sound of gunfire, but Slim John stood and tried to find the shooter in the Portuguese mob. There was only one man with a small arm, he could tell. He could not see him clearly, so he just calmly started shooting into the first rank of attackers. He hit one or two of the men, but the group kept coming. An instant later Carmen and Tilghman rose up and fired.

More men fell.

Rodrigo crouched behind one of the biggest attackers, pushing him along and hiding behind him at the same time. He crested the top of the gangway with three shots left. And then his human shield fell. Rodrigo dropped to a prone position behind the hulking corpse. Looking up, he saw the bearded captain ten feet away, calmly firing at the men behind him still moving en masse up the gangway. Off to the side, Slim John and Carmen were dropping back along the deck, out of bullets.

At that moment the seaman stopped for an instant and called to the crewmen manning the cannon. "Give 'em the smasher! Let 'em have it now!" The gangway was filled with attackers by that time. And Tilghman planned to end the assault once and for all. Rodrigo took advantage of the captain's distraction and fired his last two shots at the ship's leader. Tilghman groaned in pain, grabbing his leg. He gasped, sucked in a slash of air and fell to the deck.

In the same instant, the cannon fired and swept the mob off the gangway. The 30-pounder pivot gun had been double loaded with grapeshot and went off like a giant shotgun. Dozens in the mob fell, killed by a burning hail of lead balls. Many of them, reeling from the blast, tumbled into the water. Several more died where they stood. Those at the tail-end of the attack fell back and ran for their lives.

The assault was broken, but Rodrigo and three others pushed forward onto the deck. Slim John and Carmen, trying to reload, were easy targets. Sweeney handed his pistol to Carmen and dragged Tilghman away. The three of them retreated toward the bow, taking up a position behind the cannon. The gun's crew was reloading as the four intruders turned to complete the capture of the ship and its gold. Three of the men held long knives. Rodrigo dropped his empty pistol and grabbed a crankpin from the starboard windlass. He pointed the ironshod wooden lever at what was left of the ship's defenders. "Those five are all that stand between us and the gold," he growled. "Kill them and we are rich men."

Tilghman heard the Portuguese leader exhorting the others and wasn't about to give up. "Blast the thievin' mongrels, but don't destroy the ship," Tilghman hissed to his gunners through his pain. He lay on the deck, propped against the forward mast so he could see the final battle as it developed. His right leg had taken the gunshot, a small caliber ball that had fortunately missed both bone and artery.

The bleeding had stopped, but the dull throb had just begun to set in. Slim John held a knife in one hand and wrapped his other arm around Carmen. She had stood and fired with the best of the men, but she wouldn't stand a chance in a brawl.

The cannoneers worked feverishly but it didn't look like they would get a shot off before the raiders were on them. Just then, one of the crew ran down the other side of the deck for the wheelhouse as the foresail was hoisted. The ship began to move with no one at the helm. If the *Salem* pulled away now, the raiders would be trapped…or Tilghman and his crew would be.

Across the slowly moving deck, one of the raiders had turned to Rodrigo. He was lean with a jaundiced cast to his face which was dominated by heavy black circles under his eyes. A wispy black beard speckled his sunken cheeks and bony jaws. The man looked perpetually sad.

"There are four of us left. If we kill these people, we split the *ouro* in four equal shares, is that right?" he asked Rodrigo. The greedy herder had no intention of sharing the treasure with anyone, but he smiled as he lied.

"Yes, we are brothers and will take equal shares." He slammed the crankpin against an open palm and leaned forward. "But first we must take it from these white devils."

Suddenly a dark figure flashed from the shadow of the wheelhouse. Uma had Rodrigo by the neck before he knew what was happening. The sad-faced thief jumped in surprise. Rodrigo could not see his attacker, but he saw the fear in his accomplice's eyes and knew he was in a life or death struggle with the African. Uma tightened the choke hold on the greed-driven Portuguese and snatched the crankpin from his hand as Rodrigo began to lose consciousness.

The murderous African brought the heavy handspike down, smashing open Rodrigo's skull with one vicious blow. The other raiders rushed Uma, who flailed the wooden bludgeon back and forth, forcing them away in a semicircle. Just then the ship began to pull away from the quay, the gangway ripping from its mooring and crashing down the side of the ship. At the same time, Slim John and four crewmen padded down the deck and confronted the raiders alongside Uma. The Number One Man waived his club but held his position. Slim John leveled his pistol at the men.

"We have you now," Slim John called to the pirates. "Your best chance at livin' is to jump overboard as fast as your little brown legs will take you." Sweeney waved his gun toward the water as he spoke, wondering if the looters understood what he had said. The men backed toward the gunwale as the ship turned toward the open sea. Twenty, thirty yards from the docks and moving faster now.

"Let Uma kill these dogs," the African growled, his bloodthirsty eyes never wavering from the robbers.

"They're all yours if they're not off this ship presently. I don't want to waste any more bullets on the blighters." Uma took one step toward the robbers and the men turned and jumped. Slim John laughed at the sight and Uma joined in.

Chapter 41

Outside Washington City

Conroe folded his arms and leaned against a tall Celtic cross on the edge of Rock Creek Church Cemetery. A warm breeze carried the blooming honeysuckle's sweetness from the wild vines choking lichen-crusted tombstones. The vegetative vipers slithered up an ancient gnarled black locust tree shading the Confederate agent. From his hidden perch he could see the approach to Lincoln's cottage at the Old Soldiers Home. He hoped The Soldier would show up before Lincoln's carriage did. His sources told him the Union president planned to leave the executive mansion by two, putting the target's arrival here at any time now. Two fresh horses waited on the other side of St. Paul's Chapel. After the strike, the assassins would ride into southern Maryland where they would take a steamboat from Cobb Island.

Conroe saw the shadow as it darkened his face and knew immediately that The Soldier had crept up on him from behind without so much as snapping a twig. He tensed for an instant and then relaxed into an exasperated slouch. "I bid you good day, Conroe." The agent spun around and found the smiling assassin, hands on hips, dressed in his customary faded Union uniform.

"How do you do that? Each time we meet you appear before me like a wraith!"

"That's why I will be successful with our…little project over there." The Soldier tilted his head toward the buff painted, two-story cottage situated a few hundred yards down Rock Creek Church Road.

Its Queen Anne ornamented gables cast long shadows across its open yard. Conroe turned back to toward the house and surveyed the road again for a presidential caravan.

"The house guard has not changed. A platoon takes regular shifts front and back. A detachment patrols the church road. You will have to be a veritable ghost to get anywhere near the man."

"I am a patient soul. I'll take what they give me. If I can get close to the tyrant, I'll strike him. If I can't, there'll always be another chance. There always is with the political set."

"Ah, yes. They can't resist the clamor, the crowd, the adulation."

"And neither can I." The Soldier removed his slouch hat and smoothed out his long black hair. He had dusted the locks around his temples with gray powder to make himself look older. His shirt collar hung open and he'd concocted a four-day grizzle on his face. The killer raised his hand to block out the sun and angled his way into a larger patch of shade. Conroe moved away from his compatriot, but kept his eye on the road as he talked.

"You do like the limelights. I'm surprised you volunteered for this line of work, but I can see why you do well at it." The Soldier jerked his chin up, an uncontrollable tick Conroe had noticed before. Conroe thought it made The Soldier look arrogant, which he was.

"The limelights, as bright as they are, can never be brilliant enough for me," the assassin boasted.

Off to the west, the sky darkened as a bank of storm clouds rolled in. Conroe felt the cool breeze from the approaching front and shivered. The roiling black mass eclipsed the burning sun in an instant, like someone blowing out a lantern's flame. "What would we do without afternoon summer storms to cool us down?" Conroe offered out loud. The Soldier tilted his chin and barked into the howling wind.

"Why, now blow wind, swell billow, and swim bark! The storm is up, and all is on the hazard!" The impostor bowed for Conroe and said in a quieter voice, "That's from Julius Caesar, my friend." The Soldier chuckled at his performance. The agent was not impressed however and did not take his eyes off the road.

"Horses!" Conroe pointed in the distance toward the city center.

"It looks like a bloody brigade around him this time," The

Soldier exaggerated.

But he was not deterred by the enhanced guard and didn't tarry for long. He began a brisk half-drunken shamble toward the president's entourage. Half a minute later he ambled along in front of the cottage as the surry carrying Lincoln turned into the house's modest yard. The guard numbered between twenty and thirty horsemen, a strong force to defend one leader in his own nation's capital. The Soldier wandered further down the street as the dust from the horses swirled, kicked up even more by the approaching storm.

The Soldier, undaunted by the storm, the dust and the horse soldiers, cut across the property toward the Old Soldiers Home. The route took him close to the cottage. No one took notice of an old veteran walking toward the facility built for his repose. He lingered fifty yards away when the carriage stopped and Lincoln stood to exit the conveyance. The assassin could have been any onlooker taking an opportunity to see the famous president. He inched closer to the scene where the soldiers formed a protective cordon, the aisle ending at the front door of the cottage.

"Mr. President!" he called. "Have you a moment for a veteran of the Peninsula?" But storm winds were blowing now and a crack of thunder drowned out his appeal. Seconds later a cloudburst inundated the area and the president rushed to the cottage door to escape the deluge. The last thing The Soldier saw was the Union president snatching his trademark stovepipe hat from his head as he ducked into the house. The assassin muttered to himself in disappointment as he nonchalantly turned to continue a rain-soaked walk home.

"The man has begun extraordinary measures to protect himself, even in the city," The Soldier rambled, rainwater pouring down his face. "He is not Julius Caesar, is he?" the killer mused. "No, more Henry the Fourth, I think. Oh yes, the tyrant is uneasy now and I am the wet sea-boy," he chuckled, wiping the torrents from his eyes. "Now let me see," he muttered, searching for the words from Shakespeare's masterpiece. "Ah, yes.

'And in the visitation of the winds,
Who take the ruffian billows by the top,
Curling their monstrous heads and hanging them

**With deafening clamor in the slippery clouds,
That, with the hurly, death itself awakes?
Canst thou, O partial sleep, give thy repose
To the wet sea-boy in an hour so rude,
And in the calmest and most stillest night,
With all appliances and means to boot,
Deny it to a king? Then happy low, lie down!
Uneasy lies the head that wears a crown.'"**

Chapter 42

Near Hopewell, Virginia at City Point

Better mud than blood; that could have been the motto of General Benjamin Butler's Army of the James. Mud could be a tenacious enemy for an army on the march and it was no friend to a soldier in camp either, but it was better than facing death. The thirty-thousand men of the Union force south of Richmond were not marching. They were not fighting the Rebels dug in only miles away; so they had not seen the blood of battle as Grant's army had as it bore down on the Confederate capital from the north. The Army of the James had only to contend with the inconvenience of the nasty brown foe and the ennui of a hot summer. The rising sun promised another scorching day in the camps sprawling across the James River plain as far as the eye could see.

Inside a mildew-speckled canvas tent, Major Wolfe fingered a shiny brass button, dusted his britches and hiked down his waistcoat. "This army never does nothing," he groused to Lieutenant Blake, who also was dressing in new issue. Wolfe smoothed out the field coat of his fine uniform. He did not see the irony of denigrating the army which had provided it. "I'll be glad to get back with Sherman. And with Grant swiftly rolling this way, we best skedaddle as soon as the next train south can take us. I don't want to fight here in this mud bog they call Virginia."

As he strapped on his sword belt, Blake eyed his leader warily. The evening before, he, Ohio Red and the Kentuckians had witnessed another of Wolfe's pathological outbursts. As cowed by the man as he was, the lieutenant could not stop himself from saying what he said next.

"We need to skedaddle out of here before them boys report us to their white officers." Wolfe turned on him angrily, but Blake was bent over arranging his pant leg where it met his mud-crusted boot, so he did not notice the major's menacing look.

"Them boys, as you call them, deserved what they got. I warned them off, but they wouldn't leave."

"They were soldiers just like you, taking a swim in this Virginia heat," Blake retorted. "They wear the same uniform we wear, Major. And they were from Kentucky to boot." The smaller man raised up just then and stared into Wolfe's intimidating face as the hulk stood over him.

"All the more reason for them to do as I say without question." The major's words came out as a low angry growl. Blake stepped away as Wolfe continued. "When this war is over and we are back in Louisville, I don't want them thinking we are all equals." The lieutenant's bravado faltered a bit, but not enough to shut him up.

"That is true, sir, I don't really care about them boys, I jes' don't want to get in trouble for it. Their colonel may not understand what you did, why you did it, won't think it was right."

"Don't talk to me about what's right, Lieutenant!" Wolfe snapped, causing Blake to jump with fear. The major jabbed his finger into the smaller man's chest. "When did you get on your high horse about what's right?" Wolfe saw the terror in Blake's eyes and he backed off and chuckled derisively. "You scared of me, boy?"

"I am afraid…afraid of what could happen to us if they complain," the young officer answered in a whimpering voice. "And what…"

"Who's going to believe four naked niggrahs?" the major cut him off. "Who's going to care what they say?" Wolfe swung a hammy fist into his other hand and Blake flinched thinking the blow was meant for him. "When that boy croaked back at me…what did he say? 'This ain't Kentucky, Suh!' Well, I could have ripped his sweaty black face off and bleached it white in the sun!"

With that, Wolfe stormed out of the tent and Blake meekly followed. They sauntered along a slippery path and entered a proper lane that bisected the thousands of perfectly aligned army tents. Blake kept his distance, slinking behind his major. Wolfe was not finished with his subaltern though. "Like I told the niggrahs then; they were lucky I left them alive. I suppose I was feeling charitable." The bully laughed, aware of the absurdity of the idea. "Now come along and let's find the others. We have plans to make, travel plans."

It was near the end of June and General-in-Chief U.S. Grant's 120,000-man Army of the Potomac had been sidestepping the Confederates defending Richmond for most of a month. As May began, the armies had engaged in the Wilderness west of Fredericksburg for two days. The brutal battle had cost Grant's army, and Robert E. Lee's 60,000-man force, nearly 30,000 casualties. Then at Spotsylvania Court House, ten days of fighting resulted in another 28,000 men lost on both sides. Still Grant continued his drive south toward the Confederate capital. In late May, the armies jockeyed for position for four days along the North Anna River before falling to blows again in early June near Cold Harbor.

Wolfe and Blake presently found the men they'd escaped Richmond with and began discussing the situation. "News from Cold Harbor is that Grant lost six or seven-thousand men in an hour," Blake spat disgustedly. The Kentuckians, all in new uniforms now, huddled around a fire pit. They rested on their haunches to keep the mud at bay. Coffee and hardtack served as breakfast. Ohio Red had been sent to find out when the next transport south was due to leave.

"And now Grant, they call him the butcher, is headed here," Wolfe announced. After Cold Harbor, Grant had swung his force around Lee's defense of Richmond again and was making for the southeast around the Confederate flank. He was crossing the James already, joining with Butler's base camp to lay siege to Petersburg south of the capital city. "We are plumb in the middle of the final conflagration in Virginia," Wolfe continued. "Butler's army is the anvil. Grant's army is the hammer and we are fixin' to be little iron filings flying off the horseshoe if we don't get down to Sherman in Georgia."

The men nodded in agreement with the major's grim assessment. Seeing the group was with him, Wolfe stood to his full height searching the rows of white tents. Now he just needed the man he sent to find a train. "Where is that rot of a red-headed Buckeye?"

Chapter 43

Baltimore, Maryland-The Cathedral of the Assumption of the Blessed Virgin Mary

Carmen bowed her head, following the casket up Cathedral Hill from the harbor where the *Salem* was docked. Customs agents and army inspectors had warily allowed Tilghman entry into the port when they glimpsed the rich African goods his ship carried. And then there was the woman, smothered in black cloth and lace, a mourning widow, bringing her husband back from the sea, back to his native Baltimore. The authorities sympathized with the beautiful girl.

When Carmen raised her eyes and saw Baltimore's cathedral it struck her as out of place in an American city. Its twin onion-domed towers surmounting a Greek temple façade dominated the waterfront, but the gaudy building seemed like an overdressed suitor at a summer picnic.

The caisson groaned under its costly burden, with Carmen, Slim John, Tilghman and Uma walking slowly behind. A longshoreman, hired for the purpose, lumbered beside the hearse, helping twin Percheron horse-beasts struggle with the dead weight of a ton of gold secreted inside. Foot traffic on Charles Street was scarce in the middle of the day. Overcast skies too kept most people inside. Slim John grimaced when he saw the draft horses slip sideways on damp pavement. Would anyone notice how inordinately heavy this load was, he wondered? What a spectacle, he thought.

Nothing symbolized the farcical theater unfolding before

America's first Catholic cathedral more than Uma's black as night skin chafing under a stiff-collared shirt and ill-fitting cinched britches. The clothes once belonged to Miguel, the thieving Portuguese slaver. Carmen stifled her giggles as she watched her new African ally contend with the western clothing, as foreign to him as the man on the moon. She and the others had made friends with him on board ship, showing him all the intricacies of tinned food, explaining the ship's technology and accommodations, as well as introducing him to his new apparel. Uma had communicated that he wanted to help any white people who fought the Portuguese masters he had come to hate. Little did the African warrior know that the people he had thrown in with were agents of a Confederation that was fighting to preserve slavery.

Carmen dabbed at her pretty eyes as the procession reached the front steps spreading out from the columned façade facing Cathedral Street. As the group paused, she gathered the folds of the mourning clothes she'd stitched together from assorted cloth, blankets and curtains she'd found aboard the *Salem* while at sea. On cue, six black sextons dressed in white cassocks appeared and worked the casket up the steps on a four wheeled ramp mechanism used for funerals. The men didn't say a word but labored with wide eyes wondering what manner of a man could weigh so much.

Inside the church, Slim John led the others to the head of the main aisle where he genuflected before the altar like he'd been taught in boyhood. He blessed himself in the presence of the tabernacle and waited for Carmen to do the same in turn. Tilghman hesitantly followed suit, genuflecting on a leg still sore from the wound he suffered in the Cape Verdes. Uma simply mimicked the others, half smiling at the strange white man's dance. They filed into a single pew and knelt for prayer. The nave was by no means busy with supplicants, but scattered throughout the dimly-lit, quiet space, several men and women knelt in prayer or sat in quiet contemplation.

The church's workmen positioned the casket atop an oaken catafalque on wheels. The contraption rested in the apse, below the main altar, a towering white marble carving that culminated with a blue and gold statue of Mary's assumption into heaven. The intricately carved wings of a semicircular *reredos* flanking the central altarpiece portrayed the salient moments in the Blessed Virgin's life on Earth: her Immaculate Conception, the Annunciation, the

Nativity, Mary at the wedding at Cana, and the Blessed Mother at the foot of the cross.

In time, a short round man of middle age, respectably full-bearded and dressed in a fine cloth suit, ambled out of the left transept where he had been concealed by a good copy of Michelangelo's *Madonna and Child.* He went to a bank of candles to the left of the altar and lit first one, then two, then another one before genuflecting. Saint Joseph looked down on him while he prayed.

"Three candles," Tilghman whispered without lifting his prayerful head. "That's Marshal Kane. He's the one who gets the gold." A hollow wooden sound clucked off the bare stone walls when Kane dropped a handful of coins into the offertory box nearby. Then Baltimore's former marshal of police exited down a side aisle and worked his way into the foursome's pew, kneeling next to Slim John. The two kept up the pretext of prayer, their folded hands covering their mouths.

"I thought you'd never get here," the Confederative operative croaked. "The city is in chaos. Union spies are everywhere, so be on guard." Slim John answered without looking up.

"The journey was a long one, with Union ships and *other* pirates to contend with; we plowed through a storm at one stretch, but we are here now through the grace of God."

"So you are. Well, laddie, you'll find the bartenders in Baltimore are a tad friendlier than the navy's bartenders out beyond the harbor." Though the Irish politician joked, Sweeney didn't smile.

"There'll be no time for drinks. We are eager to give you our charge and get out of here. What would you have us do?" He whispered hoarsely through cupped hands, but did not look at Kane.

"Just so. Father Bates will appear shortly, say a few words over…ah, the body, and then the boys will wheel the casket into the crypt below the altar. It is a safe place for such a treasure. A secure and holy place, indeed. We only need you, the family," Kane glanced over at Uma bursting out of white shirt and collar, "and its servant, to play the role to its finale and then depart."

Seconds later, an excited priest, tall, barrel-chested, red in the face, issued from behind the altarpiece. His black robes flew around him as he rushed toward Kane and the others.

"That's Bates. What in Heaven's name?" Kane exclaimed. At

the same time the massive oak and bronze doors at the front of the cathedral swung open with a boom. A dozen Union soldiers, led by a lieutenant brandishing his saber, stormed into the narthex. The priest saw the Union men charging up the main aisle and slid along the white marble floor as he tried to change direction. In his frantic rush he nearly tripped as he neared the Confederate conspirators.

"We have been betrayed, Kane! Run for it!" the priest huffed in a loud whisper.

The cathedral stewards had run in behind Father Bates and were quickly rolling the casket toward the altar. The soldiers halted in the crossing beneath the cathedral's immense dome which illuminated them as if they were avenging angels beamed down from heaven. The lieutenant's head snapped around in all directions as he surveyed the massive space, looking for his intended quarry. Even in the distance he could make out the fleeing priest.

"Percy Bates! Stop!" he called, the order echoing in the expansive chamber. "In the name of the United States government everyone here is detained for questioning!" The officer just glimpsed the black men rolling the casket out of view behind the *reredos* and he quickly turned to his squad to give them instructions.

Slim John, Tilghman and Uma rushed into the main aisle and faced off with the Union men while Kane and the priest fled toward one side of the altar. Some of the worshippers scampered out of the transept doors, while others stood and watched. Carmen had taken cover behind the back of her pew. Sweeney yelled to the Union force, still twenty yards away. "This is God's sanctuary, Lieutenant! What business have you here among peaceful Christians?" The Yankee officer was young, with a pencil-thin, black mustache.

"That's none of your concern. Get down on your knees and prepare to be searched." Uma and Tilghman cut their eyes at Slim John to see what the next move would be, knowing a search would find the men well-armed in a city under martial law--a hanging offense.

"I've just been on my knees," Slim John answered. "Praying for the likes of you; for the repose of your Yankee souls!" The ex-Confederate meant to fight it out. He grabbed the Spiller and Burr from his waistcoat and fired at the lieutenant with no effect. Tilghman followed him with a volley of his own. Suddenly six other men in the church, Confederate operatives, moved in from all directions, firing into the Union cordon. Two soldiers fell, their rifles clattering on the hard stone floor. The Union men quickly returned fire, and shot down three of the attackers, and the other operatives fell back. The lieutenant saw their retreat and seized the opportunity.

"Charge the altar, boys!" He knew he needed to chase down the casket, which he surmised held what he was looking for. But Uma stood before the altar holding a wickedly curved spadroon.

"Holy Lord, Tilghman," Slim John muttered, pointing at the African. "It's lost on Uma that the altar is a table of sacrifice. But those Yankees are gonna understand that Christian principle shortly." The two white men could only watch with slack jaws as Uma met the advancing force and began to cut down the Union soldiers one by one. With a powerful overhand thrust, he planted his blade in the chest of the first soldier in the column. It took both of the African's powerful black hands to yank the short sword out again, but an easy uninterrupted backhand slashed across the throat of the second Yankee.

Uma's almost superhuman speed and strength dispatched the bluecoats like boys in a schoolyard. Another soldier parried Uma's attack with his rifle's bayonet, but the black warrior sidestepped the thrust and stabbed at the man's face. The knife sliced the Yankee's ear, leaving the fleshy appendage dangling by a thin fiber of the lobe. The soldier's high-pitched scream echoed against the cathedral's towering walls.

Finally the squad backed away from the tidily dressed Negro and retreated to the crossing. Sunlight suddenly breached the dome's skylights, spotlighting the Crucifix suspended above the altar. Christ's pained eyes looked down on the bloody scene and the Union soldiers stood transfixed. Uma held his ground, not even breathing hard. He advanced on the soldiers to assault another man, but heard Slim John call, "Come on, Uma! We have to get out now!" Uma turned away for a second and the remaining Union force, pressed forward by their single-minded young officer, continued up the altar steps and disappeared into the apse. Sweeney looked back to where Carmen had hidden, but she was gone. The conspirators circled around to the transept and slipped beyond the same door Kane and the priest had used to escape.

Chapter 44

The north side of the cathedral opened onto a dark alley. The gray stone edifice wedged up against a string of residences in a quiet neighborhood. Slim John, Tilghman and Uma formed a half-circle facing out, looking for the next threat. They found themselves alone and Slim John relaxed and straightened up. "Let's not look so dodgy, boys, and see if we can just walk out of here."

"You're a cheeky sort, Sweeney," Tilghman snorted. "Just walk away after killing a half dozen soldiers that caught us red-handed with a treasure in Confederate gold. All this in a bloody mackerel snapper cathedral! Just walk away, you say! We'll be lucky if The Almighty don't strike us dead as we stand here." They could hear men yelling, more soldiers or provost guards starting to cordon off the grounds.

"And what would you suggest we do, Captain?" Before the seaman could reply, Uma waved his hands to get the white men's attention.

"Where Carmen, Cop-ten?" he asked quietly. Tilghman grabbed his hat, his eyes swelling with yet another predicament, but Slim John answered,

"She's a smart woman. She'll be making for the ship as *we* should be." He looked toward the corner at Cathedral Street as more soldiers ran past toward the main doors of the church. He started for the street, which was the shortest route back to the harbor, but turned on his heel when a squad of guards rounded the corner and headed their way. Tilghman, more familiar with the neighborhood, started walking the opposite way and bid the others follow.

"Walk slowly, now gents, as Sweeney suggested. Guilty men run. This way will take us to Charles Street, and so back to the ship." At the other end of the block, more soldiers marched from Charles. Obviously the army was fanning out, surrounding the entire cathedral. The men were trapped now.

"Keep walking, we'll try to talk our way out of this," Tilghman said. He didn't sound very convincing. A soldier in the group behind them called out politely. "You men, hold up for a moment. I'd like to talk to you." Uma looked back, and instinctively started to run when he saw the armed white men too far away to catch him.

"Uma! What are you doing?" Slim John yelled. He tried to grab the African, but his hand swiped at empty space, too late. So he started running too, and with nothing else to do, Tilghman ran as well.

"We'll just barrel right through these goons," Slim John yelled, as the group of soldiers in front of them came into better view. Behind them their pursuers called out for them to halt and fired a shot in their direction. At that moment, the men coming from Charles Street formed a line and pointed rifles at the three suspicious characters running toward them. "Ready, aim!" they heard an officer order. And then suddenly, "Order arms!" And the firing line lowered their weapons for no apparent reason.

Suddenly from a garden to the left of the alley, a cluster of white cornettes seemed to float behind a hedge. Slim John realized why the Yankee officer had belayed his order.

"Bloody butterfly nuns!" he cried, laughing even while he tried to keep running. The nuns continued across the alley, and entered the cathedral, but the last one pulled back into the garden and bade the three men follow her. She led them quickly into a domed stone folly, through a door and down a steep stairway which led to a brick-lined tunnel. At the tunnel entrance, she stopped and faced them. The woman was robed in black, except for the starched white cotton wimple that formed the distinctive cornette of the Daughters of Charity of St. Vincent de Paul. Its shape resembled a child's folded paper hat or boat, or a fanciful butterfly, thus the order's nickname: butterfly nuns. This nun was young, with skin as white as alabaster, and a countenance as sweet as a cherub's. Uma stared, mesmerized by her habit as much as her beauty.

Tilghman blurted, "And what kind of angel are you? Sent by heaven. A sister of mercy?" The nun's stern expression did not soften and only then was it apparent that she was shaking with nerves, and on closer inspection, a girl in her teens. She awkwardly answered the intimidating sea captain.

"No, not a Sister of Mercy, I am a Daughter of Charity, from Emmitsburg. I am Sister Maria Anastasia. Father Bates asked me to fetch you." Her tiny voice peeped the revelation.

"And thank the Lord for that. Sister; you have saved our lives, most likely," Slim John replied. "Where does this tunnel lead?" He pointed to the dark opening.

"Into the cathedral. Our founder John Carroll had it built in complete secrecy. If the sanctuary was ever attacked or burned by nativists, the priests and the faithful could escape into the garden. We call it the Know-Nothing Tunnel now."

"But we don't want to go back into the bloody cathedral," Tilghman complained. "We have to get out of this city as soon as possible." Slim John nodded in agreement. Sister Maria did not blink, but said reassuringly,

"Be not afraid. Father Bates, Marshal Kane and the gold are safely inside. They have plans to get you out safely as well. Follow me please." She did not wait for an answer, but simply entered the tunnel. The men looked at each other puzzled and unsure. Slim John sighed. Tilghman shook his head in protest, but held his tongue and the fugitives filed after the woman. Her white cornette blazed the way in the dark passage and shortly they came into a series of brick-walled chambers divided by broad arches. Oddly inverted arches alternated through dimly lit rooms. Piles of masonry sand filled much of the space. Presently they wound through labyrinthine passages and found themselves in front of the casket full of gold. Sister Maria withdrew without a word.

"How is it that the lieutenant and his men didn't find this casket?" Slim John wondered out loud.

From the shadows a high-pitched, brogue-tinged voice said, "Don't blame the good lieutenant for not ferreting out the gold. He was admirably thorough in his search." Marshal Kane stepped from behind an archway, smiling. He bowed with exaggerated ceremony at the three visitors and continued, "But he merely searched the crypt of this cathedral—under the altar. The rest of the foundations, unfinished as they are, filled with sand as Latrobe and Carroll left them, do not appear to the outsider worthy of habitation." Father Bates also revealed himself then.

"Gentlemen, we are in the undercroft of our cathedral. The basement's basement, if you will. Few know of this place and we hope to keep it that way." Tilghman peered into the darkness around him.

"How are we going to escape this hole?" the sea captain asked with dismay.

"The Yankees have the church surrounded." Slim John added.

Kane waved his arm at a collection of crates stacked against a far wall. Stenciled on each wooden box were the words Baltimore Can Company, Tinned Beef. A smaller, empty crate, with the familiar Naysmith & Tansley label, rested nearby.

"Gents, your passage out of Baltimore," the dandy said. "We have already begun to pack the gold into these crates, which, as our story goes, are destined for Union troops in Virginia." Tilghman guffawed.

"Gold! I am done with your gold. It's delivered as agreed with Captain Semmes. The gold is yours now." Kane merely smiled.

"The gold was always destined for the government in Richmond. This is not Richmond, Captain. The men who were to take it further on, were killed or captured in the sanctuary upstairs. The Confederacy needs you, Captain. Maryland needs you."

"But, it can't have me!" Tilghman bellowed.

"The Confederacy needs you, Captain," Kane repeated forcefully. "And you need your ship and its own crate of gold. Two items that could very easily fall into the hands of the Yankee authorities if loose tongues started to wag."

"I see how it is," Tilghman replied angrily.

"Now, now, Captain, the…ah…*extension* of our contract will include added incentives."

"And what, may I ask, are those incentives?"

"I calculate the gold will only require twenty crates of tinned beef to conceal, so I am prepared to give you another ten thousand pounds of the Baltimore Can Company's finest for you to sell upon your arrival at Lambert's Point in Norfolk, Virginia, where the Union army has a base full of hungry mouths. An operative will contact you when you reach Virginia." Tilghman looked at Slim John resignedly and the ex-Confederate merely shrugged his shoulders.

"The sale of the beef would help offset the slaves you lost in Mindelo City," he noted. Tilghman had left more than six-thousand dollars on the auction block when they'd run for their lives. The master of the *Salem* turned back to Kane and gritted his teeth.

"I see. Well, I don't like it, but I see no way around the present circumstances. How will we escape this pit and this foul smelling city, then?" Kane smirked at Father Bates and drew a paper from his pocket as if he knew that Captain Tilghman and the others would agree all along.

"Here are passes issued by the provost marshal. And here is a map of the route I want you to take when you leave here. Your ship is safe and without a Union guard. It is even now being loaded with the crates of beef. From here, after dark, you will walk quickly to a public house called Mick O'Shaughnessy's, a few blocks away. Mick will give you some dinner and take you around the patrols and sentry posts in the neighborhood. High tide is at half past two in the morning. The harbormaster has been advised and customs have been paid for your departure."

"Aye, it seems you have thought of everything in a short time."

"That's what I do, Captain. That's simply what I do."

"Now there's only one more thing." Father Bates piped up.

"One more thing? One more thing? What is that, Father?" Tilghman asked wearily.

"One of you must have me hear your confession. Perhaps you, Mr. Sweeney is it?"

"What? I don't need you to hear my confession. What are you going on about?"

"Just follow my lead, young man," the priest replied. "Come with me."

The two men passed through a narrow winding passage dug through mounds of sand in the undercroft until they reached a rickety wooden stairway that led up to the crypt. Another climb left them in the sacristy behind the altar, where the priest had Slim John don a white altar server's cassock. A short jaunt took the pair into the sanctuary where Union guards stood at every entrance. They made their way to the row of carved oak confessionals next to the right hand transept, and Slim John was surprised when Father Bates silently bade him enter the confessor's side of the first private chamber in the row. A small chair was all he found in the dark cubicle. But as soon as he sat next to the screen window, he understood the holy man's intent.

"Bless me Father, for I have sinned," he heard Carmen giggle in the darkness.

Chapter 45

Canterbury Music Hall, Washington City, July 1864

Fire and blood dominated the scene. Orange and red colors flowed starkly against the white scenes of a Russian winter. The Soldier seemed transfixed by the flashing lights along a four hundred foot screen depicting the Crimean War. "Just another terrible inferno presided over by meddling governments and unchecked tyrants," he said, acknowledging the man lurking nearby in the darkness. Conroe's shoulders slumped in failure. The spy had discreetly wandered along the Stereopticon wall until he stood directly behind his agent, thinking he had crept up on The Soldier for a change. But the killer must have seen him with eyes in the back of his head. The assassin had turned briefly when he spoke, but continued his trance-like study of the bloody diorama. The Magic Lantern's lights strobed his soft, pale face, darkened only by extravagant black mustaches.

"How glorious the battle is," The Soldier finally said. His eyes did not leave the scene. It was as if he was seeing more than the theater's novel exhibit. "How glorious and how terrible death by fire is," he muttered vacantly.

"Follow me inside the hall. I feel exposed here," Conroe answered sullenly, still miffed at his failure to turn the tables on The Soldier. As they turned to leave the dark exhibit, they could hear the rise and fall of a musical show in the main ballroom. "From the sound of that, Thomas Moore is spinning in his grave," Conroe commented. "The cats in the alley behind this den of thieves make the same ghastly sound." Conroe choked and coughed when the pair ambled into the music hall. A heavy cloud of cigar smoke billowing up to the ceiling had yellowed the gaudy papered walls and cheaply made blood red and black drapery. The musical selection continued as the spies found seats near the back of the house. Even this far from the stage, Conroe winced at the high-pitched notes. A sad-faced Irish minstrel lounged on one knee keening "The Last Rose of Summer." Another man, playing the part of Lucy Long, looked away, refusing to be wooed. Catcalls filled the hall. The drunken multitude of mostly Union soldiers was impatient with the show's romantic interlude. The Soldier perused the scene with an experienced eye and added his professional appraisal.

"This group is not Dan Emmett, it's true, but they have a certain…presence. The artiste who portrays Jasper Jack fits the part, I think."

"Soldier, I tell you, I've never found these Irish buffoons at all amusing."

"Ah, but that is the true acting genius you behold here, my friend. You see, these are *Negro* minstrels in white face. The trickster Jasper Jack was the dandy Jim Crow or Zip Coon yesterday." Conroe squinted at the players on the stage but could not see it. He would never have thought they were black men if The Soldier hadn't told him. "Today, the ensemble portrays the Irish buffoon characters that have been so popular of late. Likewise, the Irish troupes at times portray, in black face, the Negro buffoons if that is what the audience calls for. That is the show; that is the business of the show." The song ended with a bang and a new revue took the stage singing "Teddy O'Neale." Two men chased a pig around the stage which had been transformed into a scene of a cutaway thatch-roof cabin full of farm animals, hay bales and whiskey barrels.

I've come to the cabin he danced his wild jigs in,
As neat a mud place as ever was seen.
And consid'ring it served to keep poultry and pigs in,
I'm sure it was always most elegant clean!

The screeching continued, as much from the audience as the singers. Men began standing in the rows, rearing back with all their might and launching wads of tobacco and spit at the bucolic stage set.

"Show some leg!" one Union captain yelled before heaving a phlegmy oyster to show his displeasure. Conroe turned in his seat to block off the unpleasant man.

"Speaking of buffoons, Soldier, the one who resides in the big white house on Pennsylvania Avenue will be on the move again."

"Just so. Then the news reports that Early is threatening the city are true? Revenge for the depredations in the Shenandoah Valley, they believe. Lincoln will remove himself from these environs before the attack; the coward." The Soldier tapped his boot to the syncopation emanating from the stage now, as Jasper Jack lured Lucy Long to his cabin. The show was building to a climax as the happy couple and then the entire ensemble cakewalked around the stage on the way to marital bliss and porcine husbandry.

"Not exactly. My source says he will visit the front today."

"Huzzah for the Union." The Soldier grimaced. "Pardon my sarcasm, my friend, but if another politician makes a show of going to the front, I'll wretch up my morning bacon. I suppose the monkey will promenade from the safety of his well-guarded cottage to nearby Fort Totten, miles away from Early's approach."

"Fort Stevens."

"Now, that *is* the front." The assassin's eyes opened wide with delight.

"Yes, my source says Fort Stevens. Tested men from the Sixth Corps are arriving now. Marching from the train depot even as we speak. Major General Wright leads them. There will be a battle and…"

"The Great Leader will be exposed to enemy fire, perhaps?" Conroe glanced at the killer next to him and shuddered at the look in his eyes. The walkaround on the stage continued, the troupe in full romp now, the crowd jeering, leering and still spitting, but The Soldier's attention was elsewhere.

"I'll leave the fire to you, then," Conroe said, standing up. A yellow wad of spittle landed on his shoulder, making him cringe. The Soldier's eyes brightened with glee at the sight.

"You've just taken a full hit, my man. Don't forget to duck next time," he laughed. He brushed away the spit. He wore white kid gloves and took his time cleaning the sticky gob. He stared into Conroe's eyes, oblivious to the noisy chaos around him, unfazed by the filth on his hands. "A messy job, but I'm just the man to do it."

The Soldier's jovial psychosis unsettled Conroe, who turned to leave. He doffed his hat politely and left without a word, pushing his way through the raucous, drunken gyre.

Chapter 46

Columbia, S.C., Logan's Headquarters, February 18, 1865

General Sherman's hand-picked judges had arrived from the field and the official Court of Inquiry began. The elegant furniture of Logan's headquarters office had been replaced with a judge's table, the jurists empanelled along one wall. Sherman as the campaign commander sat at the center of the dais, with his major generals flanking either side like apostles flanking Jesus at the Last Supper. Sherman served as presiding judge. The others on the panel were senior commanders in his force, battle-tested, serious-minded men.

Oliver Otis Howard commanded the Army of Tennessee, Sherman's right wing. The thirty-five-year-old Maine man had been a math professor at West Point before the war. He sat calmly, the right sleeve of his uniform coat neatly pinned to what was left of his arm which he had lost in 1862 at the Battle of Fair Oaks. Logan and his XV corps served under Howard.

Henry Slocum was a New York lawyer in civilian life. He led the Army of Georgia, Sherman's left wing. At thirty-eight he had an irascible demeanor and a quick temper. Like most senior leaders, he was a West Pointer and it had been said that there were few people more formidable than a West Pointer with a law degree.

The Army of Tennessee's XVII corps commander also held a degree in law. Francis P. Blair Jr., a Kentucky native, a Princeton man who practiced law in Missouri before the war. He was the fourth jurist on the panel. His brother Montgomery Blair was Lincoln's

Postmaster General. It was Blair's house on Pennsylvania Avenue where Conroe had first met with The Soldier. Generals Kilpatrick and Logan sat on the sidelines, persons of interest if not suspicion.

Surprisingly Buckley acted as the chief prosecutor for the court, though a Major Luther Stuart was the official litigator. Stuart was thin, with perfectly quaffed slicked back hair, graying in a distinguished way. He sported a neatly trimmed goatee and a fierce mustachioed I-do-not-suffer-fools face. The legal team sat at a table facing the judges and a witness chair occupied a central spot between the tables.

"Major Stuart. Are you prepared to proceed?" Sherman began.

"The court would like Brother Buckley to continue his narrative, General." The major rose in his chair just long enough to pass the baton to the clergyman. The boy monk wrestled himself to his feet, holding his trusty blackthorn. The tapping of the stick started almost immediately and continued incessantly as he began to speak. His voice was strong for a young man; the tone commanding confidence. He boldly met each judge's eye, not concerned with the hard fact that only months before he had been a mere private soldier fighting against the formidable troops commanded by the assembled war chiefs.

"I realize the court is well aware of what transpired at what is now known as the Battle of Ft. Stevens last July 12. But let me take you back to that day."

Fort Stevens stuck out like a sore thumb on a cussin' carpenter. It occupied the northern salient of the string of forts around the Union capital and as such it was the perfect target for General Jubal Early's Confederate assault on the city. On July 11, Early had reconnoitered the line there and planned to strike it again the next morning. Battle hardened Sixth Corps troops took over the front from Home Guards and Convalescent soldiers during the night and this change was enough to deter Early's planned attack. But the Virginian hung around like a four day fish.

The Soldier had assumed a cramped posture, shuffling along

7th Street Road, when a powerful horse troop noisily galloped past him. The force kicked up a tornado of road dust that nearly blocked out the morning sun. "It is the man himself," the assassin muttered, as a closed brougham carrying the Yankee leader rumbled past. The Soldier quickened his pace, thinking about the possibilities that might present themselves to him when he got to the salient fort. He was dressed in his well-worn Union uniform, affecting the persona of the wounded veteran, which had gotten him close to Lincoln before. A mile or so more, he thought. And now he could hear the sharpshooters from both sides, trying to pick off any man foolish enough to raise a mortal head above the parapets. Perhaps the tyrant himself could be got in that way. Surely he was foolish enough, bold enough, arrogant enough, to expose himself.

A few minutes more, and The Soldier neared the earthen embankments that demarcated the city's defenses, and then he saw the mud walls of Fort Massachusetts. They called it Fort Stevens now. He noticed a wooden bombproof or magazine door and saw several platforms where guns had been secured. And on the parapet to the north, a tall man in stove pipe hat, Lincoln himself! Standing on the parapet! Rifle shots ringing out! Oh God in heaven, if you exist, kill him, kill him, kill him now, and save me the trouble!

Sherman had inadvertently covered his ears with both hands, trying to dampen the annoying tapping Buckley continued to punctuate his narrative with. The monk did not notice the general's discomfort.

"But it was not to be, gentlemen. The assassin's prayers went unheeded, of course. The president shortly was led off the parapet, back to his waiting carriage, and with little fanfare, taken back to his office at his summer cottage. The man who stalked him could not get near him and thus failed in whatever nefarious plot he had planned. We know of course that it was not the first time he had stalked the president, nor will it be the last." General Slocum, the lawyer, interrupted.

"Brother Buckley. Isn't this talk all hearsay? Have you no proof? It's an interesting story certainly, but how do you know all this transpired? From the assassin's viewpoint, I mean?"

"I have a witness, who heard it from the aforementioned

Thomas Nelson Conroe himself."

"Do tell!" Slocum smirked. "I can't believe someone who associates with a Rebel spy would dare show his face here. And how, Brother, did he happen to end up in Columbia-all-Hades-broke-loose-South Carolina just in time for our proceedings?"

"Well, General," the crippled youth smiled, "A Negro man once told me, Da Lawd do work in mysterious ways. Dat He do!" Nervous laughter tittered through the room like the tick tickety tick of a dozen blue crabs running from a steam pot on a stone kitchen floor. Slocum scowled and glared down at Buckley's cane, which continued to rattle. Seriousness returned to Buckley's young face when he declared, "I call Slim John Sweeney to the stand."

Sweeney seemed even thinner than usual. He wore a clean white shirt and a fresh black kerchief. His sinewy height stretched a weathered gray waistcoat and new dark blue pants, obviously procured from the Union quartermaster. He strode into the room with his head down and went straight for the makeshift dock in front of the judges' table. He tried not to look at any of the men in blue, especially Lieutenant Long, though he couldn't help notice Sherman's reptilian head bobbing at the end of a long thin neck.

Then the bailiff, a grizzled Regular Army sergeant who served on Sherman's staff, approached the witness and shoved a King James Bible at him. Instinctively, almost like he was blocking a punch, Slim John positioned his hands as the sergeant said, "Left hand on the book; raise your right hand." Sweeney adjusted his stance while the sergeant stared at him sideways. "Do you solemnly swear to tell the whole truth to this lawful and duly convened court of the United States Army meeting in occupied Columbia, South Carolina or suffer for your lies?"

"I do."

"May God have mercy on your soul." Before the bailiff could properly withdraw, Major Stuart approached the dock, waving a corralling arm at the man.

"Sergeant, stand next to the witness, please," the prosecutor said, twisting his beard and appraising Slim John from foot to forehead. "Mr. Sweeney, my colleague, Brother Buckley, tells me you have an interesting past, a past that makes me wonder if your oath to a…*United* States Army…court is a valid one." Sweeney leaned forward, head down, resting long fingered hands on his chair's black painted armrests. He squinted up at Stuart, but did not answer. It was not a question after all. He'd been in the army long enough to know not to volunteer, even if it was only information.

"You impugn your own witness, Major?" General Sherman interjected. "The court already knows this man as the deserter who took his wife to Africa to find his fortune in The Namib."

"If the court will allow me, General, I wish only to have the witness explain his circumstances in his own words." Stuart locked eyes with Slim John and nodded encouragingly. "I reckon that a clean bill now will only strengthen his testimony down the road."

"Very well," Sherman sighed.

"So, Mr. Sweeney, tell the court about your Confederate service."

"I would only humbly say that I was a good soldier *when* I was a soldier."

"Oh, but you were much more than that, weren't you, Lieutenant?"

"Please, sir, do not call me by that title. I am no longer a soldier and I am no longer worthy of the honor."

"But did you not earn that rank, John Sweeney, when you fought with the Irish Volunteers at Battery Wagner, where you lost your beloved commander William Ryan?"

"I will only say that I was a good lieutenant *when* I was a lieutenant. I do not like to speak of those days now. I am not worthy to speak of those I left behind. Captain Ryan died defending his country and will always be remembered as a hero, a Godly man, a martyr."

"But did *you* not capture the remnants of the 54th Massachussetts Regiment, the now famous Negro soldiers?"

"Yes, I did. I would even say I had the *honor* to do so."

"Indeed, Mr. Sweeney. You think the Negroes were heroic?"

"As I said at their trial, the Negroes fought gallantly. I saw a pile of their dead thirty men deep after the battle for Fort Wagner. The heaps of slain black bodies proved their selfless bravery as far as I am concerned." Brother Buckley stood and limped over to stand beside Major Stuart.

"This trial you speak of, it fixed the status of these black soldiers as legitimate prisoners of war, as legal combatants and not slaves in rebellion as the state of South Carolina had charged. Is that correct, Mr. Sweeney?"

"Yes." Slim John squirmed uneasily, perhaps reminded of the many times he'd faced a priest in the confessional. Buckley smiled and shook his head abashedly. He had already told Sherman the story, but now he would tell his story again to the entire court.

"Less than two years ago, and yet it seems so long ago now, does it not? Like Mr. Sweeney, I was a soldier then too. A little too young to be one, and shivering with fright on a battlefield along the Stono River during that Charleston campaign." Sweeney did not answer this, and Buckley looked over at the panel of judges as he continued. "I was in the 28th Georgia, with Hagood on James Island. We fought off General Terry's force at Sol Legare, at Grimball's Landing."

"Alfred Colquitt's brigade, I believe," Slocum answered. "Hard-fighting boys." The West Point man nodded his head slowly, remembering the failed attempt to take the island. He absentmindedly smoothed his beard and pressed the pointed tip between two fingers. Buckley hopped back to his table and retrieved his cane. He began rapidly tapping the floor nervously. He remembered that terrible time better than Slocum. The terror of it gnawed at him still, especially at night when the nightmares came. Stuart seized the awkward moment and cut in.

"To get to the point," Major Stuart said, "a group of these Negroes from the 54th Massachusetts saved Brother Buckley's life that day. They saved him when they didn't have to; they saved him though he was dressed in gray; they saved him, a white boy, a helpless enemy soldier, when they could have just as easily crushed his head with a rifle stock." An impatient General Sherman interrupted,

"Good God, man! Mr. Dickens could not have devised a more compelling yarn! But what does this have to do with our proceedings here?" Mortified over his commander's outburst, the blood drained from Major Stuart's face and Buckley took over again.

"It is the Golden Rule, General! I pray that this court will understand there are good people on every side of this war. Such people treat others as they would want to be treated, even under the most despicable circumstances. But this is not always the case. There is indeed evil in the world. You will hear today some testimony about your own soldiers that you will not want to believe. You will hear a good deal of it from former soldiers of the other side. I ask that you suspend any prejudices you may have as you listen to this testimony. Suspend your uncharitable notions just as Mr. Sweeney did when he captured those soldiers of the 54th Massachusetts; just as those same sable soldiers did when they aided me. It is only in this way that we may get at the truth and stand against an evil that stalks your army and its leaders." General Blair cleared his throat. He had been sitting on the far end of the judges' panel with little to say so far. He swept his hands apart as if to calm the room and cut right to the issue at hand.

"This court had heard about your witness's ah…checkered past. For my part it's easy to see why, after Wagner, he left the Confederate army. He'd lost his captain, many of his friends had been killed; his city was doomed, he knew, and I understand he found love to replace all he had lost from his life." Blair checked the eyes of the other men at the table, taking measure of their reaction to his statement. General Howard absently tugged at his loose sleeve with his good left hand. He seconded the direction Blair had taken.

"I agree with General Blair. I can understand this witness's, shall we call it, conscription, into Captain Semmes' scheme to get the *Alabama*'s gold to Richmond. Mr. Sweeney, let me assure you, this court is not interested in pursuing any alleged culpability on your part concerning that matter. We merely want the truth of the events that led to the slaughter of the Kentuckians in the swamp." The young corps commander swept dark hair across a high forehead. "Please, just tell us your story."

Accepting these assurances, Major Stuart sat down to listen. Brother Buckley hobbled to his place, turned to face Slim John and said, "Pick up the story after you left Baltimore, Mr. Sweeney." The monk nodded for him to proceed and slouched into his chair. Sweeney took a deep breath and began.

"When we left Baltimore for what we thought would be a short voyage to Richmond and an end to the business, none of us could have foreseen the trouble we would find along the way."

Chapter 47

Hampton Roads, Virginia

The *Salem* had sailed all night, making record time down the Chesapeake. Tilghman had to scurry away from a duo of Union patrol boats standing off Smith Point at the entrance to the Potomac, but otherwise the bay's steady westerlies pushed the ship swiftly southward.

"God a'mighty! Land Ho!" called the captain. "Look at the power and wealth of the Union blighters!" Roused from below by Tilghman's excitement, Slim John, Carmen and Uma climbed topside. The ship was rounding Old Point Comfort on the starboard beam, a jot of land dominated by Fortress Monroe, engineered by Robert E. Lee in his earlier years, and now the Union lair of General Butler. To port was Willoughby Spit and then the looming guns on Norfolk's Sewell's Point, flying the Union flag since the spring of 1862 when the city was abandoned by the Confederates. But it wasn't the land that caught Slim John, Carmen and Uma's attention. It was the water.

"Look at 'em, look at 'em, look at all them ships!" Tilghman ranted, his head bobbing the way it did when he was agitated. "I ain't never seen so many floating vessels in one harbor, in one place, anywhere in the world, in all my travels."

The captain and his strange crew stood speechless at the sight of hundreds upon hundreds of Union ships. Warships, trade ships, tenders, supply ships, steamers, paddlewheelers and sidewheelers, ironclads, 40-gun frigates, barques and monitors, clippers and colliers, sloops and schooners, freighters, skiffs, ferries and shuttles. They all bobbed and puttered on the placid waters of one of the world's finest natural harbors.

Finally Slim John turned to the Marylander. "I grew up in Charleston, a pretty fair port, but like you, I've never seen anything to match this, Captain."

"They're here to strangle the South," Carmen said. "To finally end this damnable life we suffer still, this wretched war." She thought she was ambivalent about the war now, but a sad bitterness tinged her voice.

"This war! Why a country with this much where-with-all has let it go on this long; it disgusts me to think of that, it does," offered Tilghman. They all continued to stare at the tableau, talking without taking their eyes from the water. The ocean's canvas stretched to inlets and deltas in every direction. A mist hung close to the surface, flat and shiny like glass.

"A child might try to count all these boats, but he would give up," Carmen mused. Uma looked out at the mass of white wealth and technology without a word, but he looked worried.

"What do you think of all this?" Slim John asked him with a smile, sweeping his hand across the horizon. Uma locked eyes with the former Confederate and shook his head.

"I fear for my people, that these men will come for them, and take them all. And that there is nothing we can do to stop them, except die—fight them and die." Slim John put a consoling hand on Uma's shoulder.

"No, Uma, no. Understand. These ships, these men, fight to free the African. Their God, our God, tells them to do this." The African's gaze switched from Slim John's face to the harbor and back again. He nodded but did not look convinced. Tilghman scowled at the exchange and took the wheel, turning to port and heading past Sewell's Point toward the entrance to the Elizabeth River.

Before the war, the naval station here at Gosport was the largest in the country, boasting a fine granite dry dock and a shipbuilding and supply facility second to none. But Gosport was no more. It had been destroyed by the conflict and most freight and passenger traffic passed through Lambert's Point on the Norfolk side of the Elizabeth River.

"Go below, now, all of you," Tilghman ordered. "Get

yourself ready to land. I see a fine row of docks at Lambert's Point." They would land just outside the city center, but the point was served by a spur of the railhead. The plan from Lambert's Point was to board a train that could get them closer to Richmond. The group would disguise itself as Catholic clergy. Father Bates had provided simple black cassocks and zucchettos for Slim John and Uma who would claim to be a visiting priest from Senegal.

Carmen would assume the role of Sister Guadelupe, wearing a blue habit borrowed from a Sister of Charity nurse at the Baltimore Infirmary. Below decks, she struggled with the white tunic and large cornette and Slim John smiled at her efforts before he helped position the headpiece while she pinned it to her long dark hair. "I believe a good sister says a prayer as she dons each part of the habit every morning, but I must admit the nuns back in Charleston never taught us the ritual," the former soldier mused.

"I would be surprised if they did, John," she giggled. "I've forgotten how to pray these last few months," she added under her breath as she patted at the cornette, testing its stability.

"But let's try this, Sister Guadelupe. What saint's relics repose in our casket?" Slim John's query was practice for bluffing a curious provost marshal. One of the crates of beef had been altered to look like a crude reliquary.

"We venerate the relics of Saint Frumentius of Ethiopia," she answered, without skipping a beat.

"You are of what order, may I ask, blessed mother?"

"Oh dear, I'm certainly not the Blessed Mother! You may call me Sister Guadelupe, my good man. I am a Sister of Charity, from Emmitsburg, Maryland. My order was founded by Elizabeth Ann Seton. She is known as Mother Seton." She smiled with a self-satisfied glare at her command of the facts. Slim John smirked and tried a trickier test.

"And which side of our war is Mother Seton on?"

"Why she would never take sides in our war, if she were alive. She passed into her heavenly abode in 1821, surrounded by members of the order she founded and shepherded for decades." Slim John was impressed with her answers.

"Very well done, my love," he said, eyebrows raised approvingly.

Up on deck, a horn sounded and men's voices called

instructions as Tilghman brought the *Salem* about and prepared to dock. The couple left their cabin and as they stepped into the passage, Slim John gently pulled Carmen to him. He noticed then that Uma had come below. The African stood silent, his cassock barely containing his muscled torso. He wore an old pair of boots found in the cabin where he'd dressed. Slim John held up a finger to acknowledge the African and then stepped under his wife's cornette, a downy rampart that cordoned off Carmen's perfect face.

"A kiss for Father John then, before we start this charade?" Uma watched the Catholic priest passionately kissing the saintly nun, and did not see anything wrong with it.

Chapter 48

Lambert's Point, Virginia

"Captain, come ashore with manifest in hand!" a hard-looking stevedore barked. The *Salem* was still closing with the dock, but the impatient official was issuing orders already. Tilghman glanced furtively at the man, sizing him up. He wore a respectable businessman's long black coat and a bowler hat, but his ginger and gray beard looked mangy and unkempt. A quay-side gang in dirty brown suits clustered around him, presenting an organized phalanx amid the crush of busy workers crowding the docks.

Still at the wheel, the Marylander waved to acknowledge the order and smiled at the stevedore, trying to mask his immediate dislike of the man. It was hard to hide a sour face here. This close to land, the sea air carried the pungent odors of rancid fish, horse manure, pine tar and turpentine.

"Every yard's got its little Caesar and Lambert's Point is no different, I see," the skipper muttered. Slim John and Uma tossed out lines to the shore boys and in short order Tilghman loped down the gangway and presented a single sheet of paper to the longshoreman. The man snatched it up and without a glance passed the manifest to one of his group.

"Captain…"

"Simon Tilghman at your service."

"Tilghman. I am master of this port. Have been for many years under both flags." The man drew himself up on his toes, cocked back his bowler and pointed at Carmen, John and Uma, who stood at the ship's rail, all in religious disguise. The four of them had managed to sail the *Salem* to Norfolk alone. "I reckon I've seen every crew the world's oceans can spit up, but I'll be gobsmacked if I've ever seen such a crew as this!"

The harbormaster's upper lip curled as if he was in some kind of amused agony. Tilghman looked up at the unlikely trio and had to keep from laughing out loud at Carmen's enormous white cornette towering above the murderous African and Father Confederate Deserter. He choked down the guffaw rising in his belly, and replaced it with a solicitous chuckle.

"Oh, you mean the good fathers and Sister Guadelupe. Aye, 'tis a very special cargo I have." Tilghman smiled gleefully, raised his eyes to heaven and blessed himself. The master and his mob were not amused. The man with the manifest finally broke an awkward silence.

"Says he carries twelve thousand pounds of tinned beef and the bones of Saint Frumentia of Ethiopia."

"May he rest in peace and intercede for us!" Tilghman proclaimed, a bit too loudly. He blessed himself again and kissed his fingers before pointing at the sky with an exaggerated flourish. No one moved for what seemed like the millennium. Tilghman pretended to lapse into prayer, waiting out the official's next move. The harbormaster held his fire to see if the captain would let slip some suspicious babbling in the weighty silence. He had tripped up many a smuggler that way. But the Maryland man was too smart for that.

Finally the official angrily hissed, "This all seems to stink like a New York sewer!" He balled up his fists and punched them into his hips as he leaned into Tilghman's face. The captain held up opened palms in a placating gesture.

"Harbormaster, Ah…Mister…?

"My name is Higganbotham, Reginald Higganbotham."

"Mr. Higganbotham, I know this all seems….strange. But I assure you, these, ah, bones are indeed the relics of a saint, an African saint. They are destined for the Cathedral at Savannah, where certain Catholic citizens will take great solace from their presence. I have a pass from the provost marshal at Baltimore, and letters from the bishops of the respective dioceses."

Higganbotham snorted in disbelief. "The Papists do seem to hold sway North and South. Why, just last week a shipment of fine European vintages came through here stamped as Communion wine. Some of it went to Charleston, some of it went to Baltimore."

"Sweet or dry, was it?" Tilghman asked.

"It had a fruity depth that was both. Sweet at first with a dry finish," Higganbotham related, transported for a moment back to some illicit bacchanal. He caught himself too late when he realized that Tilghman's face had turned to a knowing, gold-toothed smile. Anger swept the reverie from the harbormaster's mind.

"I shall inspect these…bones!" he roared. The official turned to order his men aboard, but quick as a snake, Tilghman stepped in front of the man, his face so close to Higganbotham's that a bulging vein would have fused their noses.

"The relics must not be disturbed under any circumstances." The sudden change in the captain's friendly demeanor caught the harbormaster off guard. He locked eyes with the seaman who was suddenly defying him, but before he could say another word, a brown leather slipcase rose between the two countenances, guided by Tilghman's weathered hand. The Marylander whispered, in a voice that seemed friendly again, but also threatening.

"I have no wine to offer, but the Church prays you accept five hundred dollars in greenbacks to prevent any sacrilege here." Higganbotham's men almost as one took a moment to turn away from the captain and the harbormaster. It wasn't clear if they were searching for eavesdroppers or feigning discretion. The two men locked eyes like snakes in a standoff. Then Higganbotham quickly glanced down at the money case and snatched it like a cat swatting a mouse. A smile cracked his face, revealing yellowed teeth like you'd find on a long-pastured horse; a gray shadow of rot tinged the top row. He addressed his men loudly. "As I was saying, certainly the good saint's journey to Savannah should not be delayed, eh boys?" The dock mob, as if on cue, doffed hats and laughed heartily. Higganbotham leaned close to Tilghman's ear and hissed quietly, "A Norfolk and Petersburg train is leaving within the hour."

"There's another five hundred in it for you if my charges and their cargo are aboard before that train pulls out," Tilghman replied. "And no questions asked," he added cryptically.

"We should hurry then; you have a train to catch, Captain."

Higganbotham's men worked quickly, offloading several numbered crates labeled 'Baltimore Can Company, Tinned Beef,' and securing them on a parade of wagons drawn up on the quay. Finally the saint's black mahogany casket was lifted and muscled down the gangway with some difficulty. Eight longshoremen, none of them less than two hundred pounds, grunted with effort as they shifted the coffin ashore. John, Uma and Carmen, having tossed two meager carpet bags into one of the wagons, lined up along the dock and lowered their heads in prayer as what was left of Saint Frumentia was loaded onto its own caisson. The train depot was but a few hundred yards away and the wagons began a slow procession while Higganbotham called out for the bustling stevedores of Lambert's Point to clear a path.

At the depot, the Norfolk and Petersburg engine was getting its steam up already. A team of firemen hauled split firewood aboard the fifty-thousand pound black locomotive. Another man was hanging lanterns with red panes of glass. "Hospital train," Higganbotham noted as he stood with Tilghman, supervising the offloading of the wagons. "The truth is, Captain, this could be a dangerous passage tonight. The lanterns may keep the enemy from firing on the train, but there are other threats."

"What threats?" Tilghman asked. He noted a flatbed car carried a 13-inch mortar, with a small contingent of Union soldiers. The mortar car anchored the train consisting of three passenger cars, a freight or baggage car and a bobber caboose. The men talked while the crates were hauled aboard. Tilghman's pious travel companions stood quietly nearby.

"Swamp maroons." Higganbotham said matter-of-factly.

"Sounds like a bad cookie," the sea captain answered. "And what is a swamp maroon?"

"You'll be crossing the Great Dismal Swamp tonight. The Great Dismal is a million acres of dark wasteland. Former slave families have lived in the swamp since Colonial times. They haven't been a problem attacking trains for many years. General Mahone put this line through here back in the 1830s, a civil engineer right out of Virginia Military Institute. They had some run-ins with the maroons laying the track back then. For years the railroad had to guard the trains after some maroons realized the iron horses ran all manner of treasure through their Godforsaken precincts. Problems petered out over the years, but the war has sent many more runaways into the Great Dismal. They are desperate people, willing to get food or money any way they can."

Dozens of travelers of all sorts were boarding now. There were many Union soldiers, hoping to find a safe train back to their units in the field. Southern civilians, men and women, and their black servants, traveled for reasons as varied as the stars. Tilghman saw a line of wounded Rebels, some on stretchers, others hopping on crutches and thought they were probably paroled Confederate casualties, trying to get back home further south. This group was accompanied by a flight of nurses being herded by a doctor in charge.

Tilghman looked all this over and said, "There'll be a good many people on this train. Maroon robbers would find many full purses here." He thought of the enormous hoard of gold, some of which was his own, that he was responsible for. "I suppose I'll have to trust the Union guards to prevent that sort of attack. What else can we expect on this night ride, then?"

"Confederate raiders, working outside the bounds of lawful warfare. Understand there are Confederate and Union soldiers in the swamp, deserters, criminals who are as desperate and ruthless as any maroon."

"I see," the seaman answered gravely. Maybe more that the gold, he felt it was his responsibility to protect Slim John and Carmen and even Uma. But he did not want to give up the treasure either.

"Yes, I want you to fully understand, Captain, that crossing the Great Dismal to Suffolk is a dangerous proposition. You must pass through a lawless area where neither government holds sway."

"I will keep all this in mind, sir, and thank you for advising me of these conditions."

"You are welcome, my friend."

The engineer blew a loud shrill steam whistle, the first warning that the train was leaving within minutes. The Great Dismal Swamp Express was a tidy little train, its matching cars all painted in a pleasant forest green with red and gold trim. Large western font letters spelled out G. D. S. E. in bold black along each car and on its small caboose.

Great cottony balls of white wood-smoke belched from the

stink-pot locomotive rising into a darkening sky. The earthy smell mingled with a cool salt breeze off the river. Night was coming on, which meant the train would leave just in time to cross the Great Dismal in the swamp's black darkness. As Higganbotham's men staggered with Saint Frumentia's coffin, Tilghman and the religious trio left to procure tickets. They boarded and found a compartment in the 1st Class car in the back of the train. It was next to the freight car where the casket and supply crates were stacked for the trip. Tilghman met again with Higganbotham, who pocketed the rest of his money. The captain took a few minutes to arrange with the harbormaster for the delivery of the remaining crates of tinned beef to a supply broker in Norfolk and for the care of the *Salem* while he was away. At the close of this deal, Higganbotham shrugged knowingly and smiled cynically.

"I'm biting my tongue not to ask why that coffin is so heavy, Captain." Tilghman turned away as the train's final whistle blew, ignoring the question, saved by the station bell.

"All aboard!" the conductor called. The seaman jumped on the carriage platform, but still hung out of the coach door, a sly smile on his face. The station bells sounded, and the mighty 4-4-0 locomotive began to move. The engine's massive red drive wheels screeched and Tilghman had to yell to be heard.

"Oh, the coffin's not so heavy, my good man! It's one thousand dollars lighter than it was an hour ago, Higganbotham! Have a safe and prosperous war now! Somehow, I think you will have both!"

Chapter 49

Uma gaped wide-eyed looking out the compartment's window. A blur of people and street traffic obscured Norfolk's elegant city center as the Great Dismal Swamp Express headed southeast. Once outside Norfolk, the train turned west where it would cross the southern and western branches of the Elizabeth River. Drawbridges protected by fortified blockhouses spanned both navigable bodies of water, which slash back and forth across the flat tidal lands stretching into North Carolina. Uma settled back into a comfortable window seat once the excitement of the city began to fade.

The Norfolk and Petersburg Railroad operated under extraordinary rules allowing civilian passengers and approved freight to travel under Union and local control. This was a routine run between Norfolk and Suffolk, a small but fecund agricultural center where railroads heading west and south connected to the N. & P.

The journey took the train farther inland, through Portsmouth past the stony ruins of the old Gosport Navy Yard. The route would hug the northern edge of the Great Dismal on its way to the rail junction at Suffolk.

About halfway through the swamp, the train would stop at what was called the East Ditch, a drainage canal dug by the railroad. There the Union contingent guarding the train would disembark and return to Norfolk by handcar. A few miles farther on, at the Jericho Ditch, local railroad police guards would board and accompany the train into Suffolk's city depot. The police would remain in control of the train for its last leg to City Point, the Union supply base on the James River, which now fueled Grant's siege lines in Central Virginia.

Slim John had been able to secure a private cabin for the four reluctant smugglers. They had barely settled in when the conductor came through. "Good evenin', I'll have a look at yer tickets, please." The short, bald-faced man stuck his hand out. He spoke with an odd British accent.

"East end of London, I'll bet?" Tilghman said with a smile. He thrust the group's tickets at the black-suited official, who punched them without looking up. His shoulders appeared to be surmounted by a round black circle, the flat top of his conductor's cap.

"Aye, you'd win that wager, sir."

"And what would you be doing on the Great Dismal Swamp Express in the middle of this bloody American war?" The conductor put his punch tool away and looked at Tilghman and the others for the first time. He didn't seem curious about the odd assemblage of black and white, clergy and layman.

"'Twasn't the plan, sir, to be amidst this war. Before London, my people were Geordies."

"Geordies?" Slim John asked.

"Pitmen….from Newcastle?" The blank stares begged for further explanation. "Colliers from England's borderlands."

"Coalminers," Carmen quipped, as if she was playing at charades.

"Aye, coalminers. We use the term collier. Indeed Collier is my name. Heard tell that Norfolk would become the world's mightiest coal port in due time. The war has stymied that, for now."

"God bless you, sir." Slim John said. He wasn't just playing his part as the concerned priest. He understood the man's heartbreak at having his life's course destroyed by events he could not control. "I'm sorry our war has crushed your dreams here."

"Not to worry, Favah. I've learned this land has many opportunities for a just and hardworking man." The conductor looked over at Uma now. The African warrior stared blankly back at the Englishman, but did not speak. "Back in England if your da' was a pitman, you and your bruvahs could only be the same. Here I am already a conductor on the N&P; the folks back home laugh at the idea of a Geordie pitman making a livin' wif his head. I fink they don't believe my letters."

"Well, yes. It must be hard for the Old World to believe the opportunities which exist in America. We wish you well, and pray the war will end soon," Carmen said.

"Thank you, Sister. We all pray for that day." The man had lost the stiffness he entered the compartment with and he stepped further inside and produced a match. "Let me light the lantern for you."

It was getting darker now and the train was passing through the scattered residential precincts surrounding Portsmouth, rambling along at about fifteen miles an hour. The mournful sound of the engine's steam trumpet bellowed every few minutes as the train approached numerous road crossings along the way. "We expect to make two stops tonight. No need to be alarmed. One is at the bridge blockhouse on the western branch and another at the East Ditch where the Suffolk train police take over."

"We've heard the train can attract unfriendly attention in the swamp." Tilghman offered.

"True, but not likely," the Geordie answered. "The maroons have been well pacified, mainly with Union rations handed out *gratis*. The thieves and irregulars, deserters and the like, don't usually try the security forces we carry aboard."

"That's very reassuring, then," Carmen said.

"Yes," the conductor answered as he stepped into the corridor. "Just the same, when we stop at the East Ditch, I advise you dowse the lantern until the train is rolling again. Just to be on the safe side. Good evening, all." The door clicked shut and the group looked at each other collectively unconvinced that the trip would be uneventful.

"I was feeling at ease about our journey until Mr. Collier slipped in that last bit," Slim John said, but Tilghman had another problem to ponder.

"Agreed, but I am more on edge about meeting the man who's to take our burden from us. I didn't catch any eyes at quayside or at the depot." The black-bearded seaman lifted the lantern globe to light a pipe. Sweet thin puffs from his favorite patchouli flake wafted from the black briar bowl he carried religiously in his waistcoat pocket. He adjusted the flame a little higher to counteract the creeping blackness outside.

"We can only hope he's to meet us at Suffolk, after the local police control the train," Carmen reasoned.

"That tallies in my mind, but it seems to me that Kane told us someone would meet us when we reached Virginia. Lambert's Point qualifies."

"A vague promise, that was," Slim John offered. "And Suffolk is still a Union garrison town. I heard from some other passengers that there are over twenty-thousand Union troops posted there, though a Rebel army under Longstreet tried to free the city this spring past. Can't see a Confederate operative picking such a place for this hornswoggle."

A quiet settled over the berth as the train picked up some speed. The rhythm of the wheels and a gentle rolling of the car created a nighttime peacefulness. Tilghman was nodding off to sleep when the door rattled with a sharp knocking. The door opened quickly and in stepped a lone man dressed in black cassock, white Roman collar and the distinctive round-topped Roman hat known as a *saturno*. "God be with you," the slender mustachioed man said, bowing. Tilghman and Slim John made to rise, mumbling greetings to the stranger. The mariner instinctively laid his hand on his revolver. "Don't get up, gentlemen. I hate to disturb you at this hour." The man spoke with authority. He stood there with hips cocked in an athletic swagger, like a chap who could handle himself.

"What can we help you with, Father?" Slim John said.

"Father Thomas," the man said. "I am Father Thomas." He said this again as if to remind *himself* who he was. He quickly scanned the four sets of suspicious eyes focused on him. The group was evidently surprised by his appearance, yet another Catholic priest on a night train in the Dismal Swamp. An awkwardness ruled the little compartment and Father Thomas knew he had to dispel what was already a tense situation.

"Pleased to make your acquaintance," Slim John answered. "I am Father John and…"

"You are imposters taking a shipment of gold to the authorities in Richmond." The newcomer might as well have taken a pin to a balloon. The breath rushed out of the berth's quartet and expanded into full throated laughs. Conroe laughed along, then stated, "I'm Thomas Conroe, the man you've been looking for."

"We never doubted you, Thomas," Carmen said jokingly.

"Everything is as planned. The crates are aboard," Tilghman added.

"I deduced as much. I watched from afar, back in Norfolk. You make an interesting group of people," he said, nodding at Uma. "I'm surprised you didn't attract the attention of the Provost Marshal, but then who would suspect a group that so stupendously stood out from the ordinary?"

"You have a conniving mind, Mr. Conroe," Tilghman winked, "I like that."

The operative turned to the only non-religious in the compartment. "Captain Tilghman, is it?"

"At your service."

"Yes, well I wish I could tell you I have it all figured out, but the truth is, the remainder of the trip may well be fraught with difficulty." The seaman nodded his understanding and directed the newcomer to the others.

"This is Slim John Sweeney, his lovely bride Carmen and my man Oko Uma, or if you prefer, Father John, Sister Guadelupe, and Father Uma from Senegal." Conroe eyed each person again, committing their aliases to memory. He sidled over to Uma expecting the African to give up his seat, but Uma just sullenly stared up at the white man. Tilghman saw that Conroe took for granted that the African would show him deference. The idea made him smirk. The Confederate spy did not know the Negro was a warrior prince, a ruthless killer when called to the task.

"I wouldn't try Uma, my friend," the skipper warned him. He shifted aside and patted his own section of the bench. Conroe ignored the perceived slight and sat between Slim John and Tilghman.

"Captain, I am under direct orders from General Bradley Johnson. The plan as you know is to take this train toward Petersburg, but the rails are threatened by enemy action up and down the route."

"What *is* the war situation in Virginia?" Slim John asked.

"Not good. In the Commonwealth or elsewhere, for that matter." Conroe leaned in and spoke in a low voice. His attitude bespoke bad news. "Virginia is wriggling like a worm in the talons of two great birds of prey. Grant has laid siege to Petersburg. His campaign through central Virginia has sidestepped Richmond and assaulted the Cockade City, where he was repulsed for the time being. But the Union army sits astride the supply route to the capital like a sow pig in a favorite mud hole. I fear Grant cannot be moved against his will."

"So this train can't get to Richmond then?" Slim John asked, hoping he'd heard wrong. He knew Petersburg was between Suffolk and Richmond.

"The enemy attacked the Weldon line near Petersburg but was sent off again. As far as I know the line is still open, but under threat daily." Slim John allowed himself to relax but little at that news.

"And the other talon threatening your writhing worm?"

"Three fearful words, William Tecumseh Sherman. His army rages across Georgia. He has taken Atlanta. And you may have heard about the *Alabama*?"

"No, indeed, what of our..gold broker?" Tilghman wanted to know.

"The good ship has been sunk; off the coast of France."

"If I was truly a priest, I'd bless myself right now," Slim John sighed.

"Save your prayers. Captain Semmes and most of his crew escaped to land—near Cherbourg. By some accounts it was a hard-fought sea battle. A well-placed shot struck the Yankee ship's rudder but failed to detonate. That would have disabled the enemy vessel, but it was not to be."

"Terrible news, indeed," Carmen said.

"Yes, terrible," Tilghman added. The captain tried to hide his disappointment that the Confederate pirate had survived. He realized Semmes was still at large and could fulfill his threat to punish failure or treachery.

"All the more reason to finish our task here," Conroe said. "Semmes needs a new ship now."

"Of course," Tilghman answered disingenuously.

"On a brighter note, Jubal Early marauds in the Valley, giving Phil Sheridan a run for his money."

"You make it seem like a horse race, this war," Carmen offered.

"More deadly than a prize race, my dear," Conroe answered. "Early threatened the fortifications of the enemy capital about a fortnight ago. Then he boldly sent cavalry into Maryland and Pennsylvania."

"What can he hope to accomplish by that, I wonder?" Slim John asked.

"General Lee wants to draw the pressure away from Petersburg, I reckon. Days ago a terrible battle ensued in front of Petersburg when a Pennsylvania regiment of miners dug trenches under the siege lines and blew a hole wide enough to sail Noah's ark through. Problem was the explosion left a deep crater in the ground that trapped the helpless black soldiers the enemy sent into the breach." Uma's head snapped toward Conroe upon hearing this.

"Black troops fight for the United States?" the African asked.

"Well…yes, of course," Conroe answered sheepishly.

"But Americans from the North, Yankees you call them; they have always come for more slaves. They sail the ships. They pay the money. How can black men fight for them?"

"It's complicated, Uma," Carmen said. "The Northern armies claim now to fight to free the slaves in America."

"There are Confederate men, leaders in the army and in Richmond, who have similar ideas at this late hour," Conroe added. "But there are also people, North and South, who still own slaves or profit from the trade." Tilghman blanched at that observation. Uma's face showed the confusion he felt. He stared at the floor, trying to make sense of a white country that could fight such a great war over the lives of black men. Why did they care one way or another, he wondered? Why did they care so much; enough to slaughter each other by the thousands? This was a strange, but glorious place, he thought to himself.

"So both sides will free the slaves here?" Uma probed.

"Many feel, no matter how this war ends, that American slaves will gain freedom one way or another," Slim John said.

"This seems a great country," Uma concluded. "But I shall not trust either side until I see this freedom for myself."

"A wise course, my good man," Tilghman snorted, eager to continue talk about their chances of getting to Richmond safely. "So what of the battle of this crater?" he prodded Conroe.

"The Confederate defenders showed the trapped attackers no mercy. The attack was a total failure, a terrible slaughter. Well nigh four thousand of the enemy perished in that unholy pit. William Mahone's division cleared the crater of the enemy. The same Mahone who built this very railroad we ride tonight."

"So Lee does need to threaten Northern territory to relieve his lines here," Slim John mused.

"Matter of fact, the same day of the crater battle, General McCausland occupied Chambersburg, Pennsylvania, demanded a ransom and burned the defiant town."

"Hardly within the bounds of lawful war," Slim John said. "What is this war coming to?"

"There is no 'coming to' to it," Conroe shot back. "The despicable carnage is already here. Atrocities have been committed by both sides and both sides will continue them. We are becoming a hateful nation, I fear. A recent bomb plot at City Point narrowly missed assassinating the Yankee high command, maybe even Grant himself." Conroe didn't mention what he knew about General Johnson's plan to kidnap Lincoln or that he had run The Soldier's attempts on the Union president's life.

"It seems this war has become a burning rage of revenge and retribution," Carmen offered. "Perhaps it always was."

The train slowed. The passengers could feel the change in motion more than they could see it. The windows opening onto the dark swamp may as well have been painted black. The Express gradually lurched to a complete halt. The screech of brakes echoed off the walls of the towering cypress forest invisible in the night's blackness.

Outside, a Union sentry stepped from the square wooden blockhouse perched at the approach to a drawbridge. The soldier saluted the lieutenant in charge of the train's detachment. Returning the salute, the lieutenant barked, "Corporal Jones, inspect the bridge and report back to me here." The young inspector held an oil lamp. He jumped off the engine and holding his light low, began to closely eyeball the deck and trestles for damage or sabotage.

The other train guards stood at ready arms but with little enthusiasm for the chore they'd done a hundred times. No one noticed five Union soldiers creep out of the tall sumac along the track. They boarded the back of the train in the shadow of the flatbed mortar and entered the baggage car with the air of a routine guard inspecting the cargo. Unlike the other soldiers though, they carried no long arms.

Inside, the car was dark and unoccupied. Crates of produce and dry goods and other supplies towered to the ceiling. The cargo flanked a central aisle just wide enough for a man to walk the car from end to end. At the front of the car, a black casket occupied one side of the floor with nothing on top of it. It presented a macabre bench for the men to rest their behinds on. They stood in the darkness in single file until the second man in line struck a match and squinted around the crowded rectangle. He pointed to the black box and whispered, "Blake, you're first in line here. Drag that coffin across the door. We don't want anyone coming in here 'til we're under way."

The lieutenant leaned over and grabbed a handle at the coffin's head. He grunted with effort, but the box did not move. "Dang, Major. This stiff's heavier than a ton of bricks."

"Shhhh! Keep your voice down. Move aside, boy and let a man do it." Wolfe spit out his flame and squeezed past Blake. Laying both of his monstrous hands on the handle, he gave it a mighty heave. The force of his effort did not budge the coffin though, but pulled him forward onto the box and he fell hard onto the lid, his head crashing through the light ornamental wood. "God, almighty!" he bellowed, pushing himself up on his knees. "What manner of devil is in this coffin?" Wolfe struck another match and peered into the box. He stuck a paw into the head-sized hole like a bear looking for honey. Moments later he giggled like a child in a toy box. "It's God-blessed gold, Blake! This box is filled with God-blessed gold!"

Chapter 50

Blake dropped to his knees and sidled in toward the coffin. The others remained silent, squatting in the darkness. Blake couldn't get close enough to see. "How can this be, Major?"

"I don't know how it can be, but I know it can't be by the book. Hellfire, it might even be enemy contraband! This train is headed toward Richmond."

"What should we do? Turn it over to the provost, the train guards?" Because of the darkness Blake could not see Wolfe's face twist with derision at that suggestion.

"And let them steal it for themselves, you idiot? Heck no, it's ours, boy. And we won't have to share it with that coward Ohio Red." Wolfe was still seething over the fact that the man from Ohio had never returned from his mission to find a train to take the group of escapees south. "If I ever find that deserter I'll cut out his yellow gizzard and feed it to my horse." Wolfe was spitting with anger about it still, but smiling at the same time. "This gold is ours, and woe to the man who gets between it and my fists."

Blake, still on his knees, slinked away from Wolfe, who turned to face the group. "Now, you listen to me, all of you. We need to move quickly. In a few minutes the local train police will take control of this train. We need to get out of these uniforms. We won't be changing trains in Suffolk as planned. We're taking this one into Carolina."

"What are our plans, then, to get the gold to Richmond?"

Slim John asked Conroe. The discussion about fluid battle lines along the rails north weighed heavily on his mind now and he began to realize that he had not considered what he and Carmen would do once they arrived in the Confederate capital.

"We should not have to do anything. The train will fall under local civilian police control just outside Suffolk. We'll make a brief stop there and then turn north toward City Point. There are a few stops scheduled to take on mail and passengers. Before we arrive at the Union base, we'll transfer the cargo to wagons and make our way to Petersburg. We can only pray the enemy does not choose this night to attack the line."

"We hope and pray for the best then," Carmen offered.

"That's all we can do," Conroe answered. "It will either be an easy trip or complete disaster."

In the baggage car, Wolfe and the others had stripped down to the civilian shirts they wore under their uniforms. Their belts had no army buckles and each man had been inspected for any other military insignia or accoutrements. Wolfe wore a red shirt and a crushed pork pie hat. His workingman's disguise concealed a large, bone-handled knife tucked in muddied-up blue trousers. All five men smudged dirt from the floor onto faces wet with sweat. With ersatz costumes and makeup they would pass as railroad employees; loaders, brakemen or firemen.

Distant voices signaled the all clear on the bridge and with bell clanging, the train eased forward again. No one in the next carriage took notice when what looked to be the night shift crew exited the baggage car and routinely made its way to toward the engine. Wolfe led the way and was exiting the 3rd Class coach at the head of the train when Collier, resting on a rumble seat, raised his tired blue eyes.

"Who in bloody Heaven are you?" the Englishman asked, beginning to rise and block the aisle. But before he reached his feet, Wolfe plunged his knife between the conductor's ribs and in one motion caught the slumping body.

Nobody laughed when Wolfe cracked a mirthless smile and answered the dead man's question with, "Night crew." Wolfe's group stood paralyzed. No matter how many times they saw the officer attack someone, his brutality horrified them. And each man was too terrified to do anything about it. The major looked around at them impatiently. "Come on, now. Open that hatch there," he hissed, nodding toward a burnished oak half-door, one of the many lockers in the compact anteroom of the car. Seconds later, Wolfe hefted the limp body into the locker opening.

Blake winced when he heard the sound of the little man's bones snapping. Wolfe was stuffing the bleeding corpse into the tiny space. The killer grunted with effort as he shouldered into the heavy door until the brass clasp sealed. The major fixed Blake with a wild glare and held up a finger. "One down, three more to go," he snarled. He intended to kill the engineer and what he reckoned would be one brakeman and one fireman on the tender platform.

Blake had seen that look before—pupils staring and dilated like the big black button eyes of a dead fish. His commander always seemed gleeful when he killed. He loved to kill—to hunt men. When the war ended, as it looked like it would soon, how would Wolfe hide his crimes then? Blake wondered. He still wasn't entirely sure Wolfe hadn't killed off Ohio Red to get rid of him back at City Point. After all, the Buckeye wasn't part of Wolfe's original group of Kentuckians; and the two had had a tussle back in Virginia. Had the major murdered the young officer in a fit of rage or jealousy? A hissing sound brought Blake's attention back to the matter at hand.

"The gold is almost ours, my boy," Wolfe whispered to Blake, oblivious to his lieutenant's mutinous thoughts. Then he turned to the others. "Don't give them a chance to think. Kill 'em and throw them off the train. Everyone takes a man; all gets a share."

"The train is stopping already at the East Ditch," Conroe announced. "The Union guard will leave its mortar car on a siding and take a tank engine back to Portsmouth. For a time the G.D.S.E. will be unguarded." The train bucked and jumped, careening a hundred yards beyond the entrance to the siding. A few minutes later, after the Union sergeant of the guard unleashed some choice words at the engineer, the train inched off again.

Less than ten minutes on, the locomotive braked to a neck-snapping stop again and a contingent of train police boarded. The lawmen wore flat-top black caps and black suits appointed with shield badges. On closer inspection, the group looked to be little more than boys, but they each carried new Springfield rifles. The weapons shined like they'd never been fired and the guards looked like they'd never even half-cocked them. They filed past the gold smugglers' cabin, followed by a gray-haired officer wearing the same black uniform, a silver shield and a black bowler hat.

"Suffolk in ten minutes," Conroe told his partners in crime.

"We just stay put though?" Tilghman confirmed. Conroe had stood up as the train gained speed. He peeked out into the corridor, watching the policemen ambling into the next car, going toward the engine. He turned to nod at Tilghman as he closed the door. "That's right." The spy took his seat again and everyone sat in silence.

Chapter 51

The train steamed into the Suffolk depot about ten minutes behind schedule. Another clumsy stop shoved some standing passengers forward. The whining brakes reverberated off the hard concrete surfaces of the train platform, sounding like the screams of a rampaging swamp panther.

"I never thought I'd see heavy seas on a train," Tilghman huffed, gripping his seat's arm.

"The engineer must be hitting the hard stuff tonight," Slim John chuckled. But Conroe was not amused. Something didn't seem right to him. Trains were not operated so sloppily, especially night trains with nowhere to be. He wondered who was in control. He did not voice these concerns with the others, but rose quickly.

"I'm going forward to question the crew," the operative told the group. "See if they have any reports of the line's conditions further north."

"We pray the rails are clear," Carmen said, sounding like the nun she was supposed to be.

The idling engine chuffed, sending billows of dense steam along the dimly lit brick depot building. The Confederate spy entered the 2nd Class coach, which had already emptied and Conroe strode quickly through, grabbing seat backs with alternate hands like he was paddling upstream. He sensed an eeriness in the empty train car. Shadows flickered through the windows, the disembarked passengers filtering past the depot lamps that barely illuminated the small platform.

The 3rd Class coach was no different; empty and dark. Conroe heard the husky voice of a black porter on the platform calling for Collier, the conductor. Only a smattering of people wanted to board at this hour, but no one attended the coach doors. Conroe would have normally discounted the lapse. Efficient passenger rail service was just another casualty of the war. The British conductor was probably in the station office or using the necessary. But intuitively Conroe's level of suspicion, already simmering, began to roil.

The spy entered the steward's pantry at the head of the car and immediately eyed a glistening circle on the floor. He bent down to get a better look; blood, a pool of blood. He jerked his head up and scouted both ends of the compartment. The dark passageway showed no sign of Collier, and then Conroe saw the bloody rivulet oozing from the larder set into the wall, the dark liquid dripping onto dusty wood floor planks. Conroe straddled the bloody floor and tripped the latch on the stout oak portal. The door popped open like a jack-in-the-box, forcing Conroe back and revealing the conductor's hat still atop the dead man's pate. The Geordie's blue eyes stared out at Conroe, who realized Collier's neck was grotesquely twisted at a ninety degree angle.

Reflexively, the spy backed against the far wall and drew an Army Colt revolver. While he considered his next move, a policeman outside yelled a warning and a rifle shot boomed. "Maroons have the train!" a voice behind Conroe called. He turned to see the squad of train police board the 3rd Class stairs at the car's far end. They were coming for the engine and he stood, sidearm in hand, directly in their path.

Two young guards filed into the aisle, doused the lamp near the entrance, and went into kneeling positions behind seats on either side. They raised their long guns and pointed in Conroe's direction. The steward's hall passage doglegged around the larder cabinets, so the spy was out of view. Conroe could see the men, but he was not sure if the guards had seen him. That question was soon answered for him when their officer boarded directly behind them, a revolver in hand. He crouched for cover near the back of the car.

"There's a maroon in the car," one of the riflemen called back to the leader. "He's guarding the engine."

"The blackguards mean to steal the train and take it into Confederate territory," the other boy surmised.

The officer commanded: "You there, in the steward's mess, throw down your weapon and surrender the engine! Now! Or all hellfire will rain down on you!" Without hesitation, Conroe stepped into the aisle and raised his hands. He let the Colt dangle from his trigger finger, but at the same time called out with authority.

"I am Captain Thomas Nelson Conroe, here on the personal orders of the president. I've found the conductor murdered here. Advance and help me storm the engine." Silence followed the pronouncement as the police officer pondered the situation. The riflemen looked around at their leader, seeking a decision.

"Lieutenant, what do we do?" one of them asked meekly. Conroe called out again.

"Lieutenant, I would have shot my way out of here by now if I wasn't who I said I was. We're running out of time!"

"Jesus, Mary and Joseph," muttered the officer finally. "What in God Almighty's name has come upon little Suffolk town this night?" The man pushed himself out of his crouch as if he had to use his last ounce of energy to do it. "Follow me, boys, but stand at the ready." He stepped between the rifles and moved toward Conroe, pistol pointed straight. The guards stood up, but kept their weapons aimed at Conroe too, eyes staring down their barrel sights. Two more policemen who had lingered on the stair landing followed behind.

In seconds, the officer reached Conroe, took his handgun and eyeballed his clerically dressed captive. "Sure, you don't look like a maroon to me; you're here for the president are ye?"

"Yes, Lieutenant—."

"Hart, I'm Johnny Lee Hart of the Suffolk Train Guard." Conroe lowered his hands now. He could see that Hart was an old man, near seventy. He sported striking salt and pepper mustaches so long and drooping that they shook like puppy tails when he spoke. But his eyes reflected a shrewdness born of experience. "And which president would that be? The one you're here for?" Hart asked with a sly smile. Conroe avoided the inconvenient question.

"Lieutenant Hart, there are important envoys aboard this train. They must have safe passage north and I need your men to storm that engine immediately." As if to further deflect the policemen's suspicion, the spy's head tilted toward the door separating the car from the tender.

"It's Davis then," the police officer answered. "You're not a priest. You're here for the *Confederate* president. Can't say I'm surprised; a detective's intuition and all that. There's too many durned priests on this train." Conroe did not reply to the man's conclusion and an awkward silence filled the cramped hallway. Hart merely stared into Conroe's face while the wheels turned in his head. The old man knew he needed to secure the train no matter which side Conroe was on. "I once worked for ol' Jeff Davis myself," the policeman finally said. "Let's take back this train."

Conroe let out his breath in relief and crossed to the sturdy oak door that led to the tender's platform. He tried the heavy latch--locked tight. He rammed the portal with his shoulder and bounced off the solid door like an India rubber ball.

"Stand aside there, Captain. Let these farm boys hit it," Hart said, as he turned to the two men behind him. "Wheeler, Godwin, put your shoulders into that door." The riflemen went to port arms and crouched into a running start. Just then the train lurched forward and everyone was thrown off balance. The guards fell backwards breaking each others' fall. Conroe careened into Hart, slipping in the blood pool. He steadied himself by grabbing the door to the cupboard that held the conductor's crushed body.

Suddenly fire flashed behind them, followed by the boom of a musket. Hart's other guards positioned down the aisle were still on the floor where they fell. Conroe turned to see two men coming through the door at the other end of the car. One prone guard rose up to his knees and then fell down again dead, killed by another musket volley. The other guard lay between the benches, saved from the volley by his fall. "Reid is dead, Lieutenant!" the guard called out.

"Lay for cover, Hope!" Hart yelled back, as another shot thundered. This one blasted a hole in the tender door behind them. The volley missed Conroe and the guards, who were crouching between the bench seats. Now the car was being attacked from both ends, Conroe realized as the train picked up speed and steadily pulled away from Suffolk depot. Conroe and Hart took cover near the front of the car, across the aisle from each other. Wheeler and Godwin occupied the floor one bench away. The other guard lay prone in the middle of the car while the dead guard's body sprawled across the aisle in front of him.

"What's next, Captain?" Hart asked in a loud whisper.

"We need a way out of here, now," the spy answered

determinedly. "We need that engine too." The trapped men could see the train was turning west toward the Seaboard and Roanoke connection. Hart could feel the gradual turn as the lights of the town disappeared to their right.

"The Great Dismal Express is not headin' for City Point," the old man noted. "The bushwackers not only took the engine with ease, but knew enough to change the depot switch." Another shot came out of the darkness at the car's far end. Another round answered from the tender door, so close it made Conroe flinch.

"They are keeping us pinned down here. 'Til they get us into lawless territory," Conroe reckoned.

"But why would they want this train now? We've been sharing it right along," Hart wondered. Conroe thought he knew why, but couldn't say it out loud. How did they know about the gold? the spy asked himself. But there were other things to think about now. Another booming rifle shot shook the compartment, bringing his immediate predicament back into focus.

"What other guards do you have aboard, Lieutenant?"

"Sheeeesh, this is it, Captain. We've had no trouble like this before." Conroe had already figured that, but it was worth asking. The train was rolling full on now; obviously running away fast, steaming for Carolina and uncharted territory. There was no telling who controlled the Carolina countryside. And no matter who did, it was far from the Confederate lines of Petersburg and Richmond.

A junction with the Rebel controlled Wilmington and Weldon line was coming up fast, though. That railroad led to safety, Conroe knew. But it also would present the train with a break in gauge, just like the S. & R. did. Conroe knew the Norfolk & Petersburg was a five-foot gauge line. The Great Dismal Express could not run on other railroad company tracks, which were standard four-foot, eight-inch gauge lines. Did whoever have the train realize they were heading for a high-speed disaster?

"Hart, we have to take this thing back, no matter the cost. We're gonna have to fight our way out." The old guard did not question the desperation of their fix.

"I'll tell ye true, Captain. These boys have no battle experience. Hope back there ain't hardly fourteen." Conroe knew he meant the guard lying next to his dead compatriot.

"And what about you, Lieutenant? Ever see the elephant?"

"Chased 'em at Manassas. Shot in the guts at Williamsburg."

"That's hard work for an old man. You joined the rebellion at the jump, eh?"

"Reckoned the tussle would be over fast. Jesus, after Williamsburg, I reckoned I'd be done for soon enough too. Sent me home with a metal plate holding my gizzard in." Conroe had heard of this before. It was a common though gruesome fix for a gaping abdominal wound that would not heal. Surgeons had crafted a steel cover strapped across the old man's belly to hold his intestines in place.

"And you're still up to fighting this fight?"

"Captain, I'll tell you. I don't know who has this train, but I know I don't much like the blackguards who shot me--came down here, to my state--and shot me. When it all boils down, it's the war. I figure that's why I'm in this fix tonight. So let's fight it." Conroe chuckled at that. He knew the Suffolk Train Guard and his farm boys could not offer much help to him, but he also danged sure knew old man Hart, sore gizzard and all, was one tough son of a gun. More rifle blasts echoed down the aisle, warning the men to stay down. Nobody moved. But the time to flinch or cower was over. Conroe had a plan, desperate though it was.

"I was with Jackson at Manassas, Hart," he said with new respect for the guard. "But I am honored to fight with *you* this black night."

"Likewise, Captain. Now, what're your orders?"

"Call to your men. We'll need everyone on the same verse." Hart raised up enough to project his voice.

"Hope, Wheeler, Godwin, can you hear us up here?" The young men called back in the affirmative. "We're moving out of here. Listen to the plan and do your best now," the old man said encouragingly as if speaking to even younger boys.

"We can't get to the engine while we're flanked," Conroe stated.

"We don't know how many block the other end either," Hart offered.

"That can't concern us. That door in back is open. We need only force its defenders away." Conroe fiddled under his cassock and fished out a small brown bottle. It contained a highly flammable explosive called Greek Fire. "I have a device to blast them," the spy said. "I go first, Hart. You and these two follow and clear out anyone still standing. Your other man Hope can follow on our heels."

"Aye, Captain. On your mark."

"But first I need to get out of this disguise." Conroe flung off his black *saturno*, a nice beaver fur one he hated to give up. With some difficulty he pulled the black robes off over his head, revealing black trousers girdled by a leather holster. Hart returned Conroe's Colt revolver which he realized he still held. Conroe tucked the gun back in place and tugged down a black leather waistcoat he wore over a simple white collared shirt. He released the Roman collar that still marked him as a cleric and left the disguise in a pile on the floor. "There. That's better," he muttered. "There *are* too many durned priests on this train."

Chapter 52

Court of Inquiry, Columbia

"Stop right there, just a moment, Mr. Sweeney." General Sherman wearily gesticulated at Brother Buckley, asking him to approach the bench. The young monk looked around to confirm that the commander was waving at him. Then he popped up and shuffled to the head table wielding his cane in one hand and holding a King James Bible in the other. He stood back from the line of judges, seeming like a child at the seashore standing insignificantly before an all consuming wave, entirely oblivious to what was about to crash down upon him.

"Yes, General Sherman?" The boy cleric wobbled a little on his wooden leg.

"My good Brother Buckley," Sherman began slowly, a breath of exasperation in his voice. "Your witness means to say that a police force, duly appointed and deputized by the Union provost marshal in occupied Suffolk, acceded to aid a man they knew to be a Confederate spy? A man operating under orders from Bradley Johnson or Jeff Davis depending on which of his lies you want to believe?"

"General, the answer is yes, but..."

"And this is something in your favor; that gives your tale veracity?"

"I agree this situation seems highly irregular, but it gets more complicated than it even now seems, as you shall see." The army leader reared back in his chair and looked at his fellow jurists as if he was waiting for one of them to tell him it was all a joke.

"Am I the only one here who feels I might be losing his mind?" General Blair leaned forward then.

"Now see here, Buckley, how can this situation get any *more* complicated? Its convolutions already out twist a mad dog on a double twine rope!" Shaking heads and clicking tongues tittered all along the head table. Buckley, though, was unfazed.

"Perhaps Matthew said it best in his 10th Chapter, Verse 36." Sherman stared bug-eyed and slack-jawed at hearing this.

"Oh no, blast all," he mouthed, *sotto voce*. "Here comes the Jesus load." Buckley held up the crusty black Bible, gripping it in both hands as if he was using it as a shield. Large script letters in fading gilt read 'King James Version.' The golden words caught Sherman's eye and seemed to provide a needed distraction for the nonplussed general. "King James, Brother?" he mewled mockingly. "You're going to quote a Protestant Bible---*the* Protestant Bible?"

"These are hard times in the South, General. There's a war on, you know." The whole room jiggled with laughter. Buckley though did not even crack a smile. "The Word according to King James is better than no Word at all."

"I see," Sherman said, more serious now. "And what does King James allow us to know about Matthew's 10th Chapter?" The general's head waggled with amusement, and he sat back drumming his fingers while Buckley sheepishly fumbled through the red-edged pages, the thin foolscap sheets snap, snap, snapping with each furious turn.

"Ah, here, here it is," the novice monk finally said. "And a man's foes shall be they of his own household."

"Oh, yes, of course. It is all so clear to me now!" Sherman exclaimed sarcastically, whipping his hands through the air like a dance hall barker drumming up the crowd. The other judges rolled with uproarious laughter. Sherman's guffaws continued long after the room settled down and Buckley waited patiently while the general caught his breath. General Slocum tried to move the proceedings beyond the awkward moment.

"So you're saying, Brother, that the men who took the train were not maroons, they were Union men?" Slocum crossed his arms and reared back in the stiff-backed chair provided for the judges.

"Indeed, that *is* what I am saying."

"And that the Southerners, Conroe and the civilian police, were trying to regain the train though it was heading into Confederate territory?"

"Just so, General Slocum."

"This case is more than just complicated, then. It is as bizarre a tale ever told in a Court of Inquiry." Blair and Howard nodded their heads in silent agreement. Sherman, struggling to effect a serious mien, winked at Logan and Kilpatrick, who sat nearby sporting blank looks. They tried to evade the commanding general's attention. Logan avoided eye contact by whipping his head around to scratch a scruffy neck. Sherman gave his generals a disapproving smirk, then looked from Buckley to Sweeney and back again.

"Brother Buckley, Mr. Sweeney, please continue this unholy saga." Buckley gestured to his witness without a word and Sweeney, who had been sipping from a cup of water, hurriedly set down the battered piece of tin and continued where he left off.

Chapter 53

Aboard the Great Dismal Swamp Express

Conroe waited for another rifle blast before he made his move. The carriage was dark so the spy had to imagine the location of his target--the door at the far end of the car. He needed to lob the Greek Fire bomb in exactly the right spot. He worried he might throw the bomb clean through the opening where it would sail into the night air with no effect. He needed to smash the small bottle against a wall or the door jamb to detonate its spreading fire. Even then, he could not be sure that the bomb would hit the men firing at him.

The coach's assailants were phantoms. They still had not shown themselves or spoken a word. Conroe reckoned the train had less than an hour before its catastrophic derailment on the S. & R.'s smaller rails. If that happened, not only would the gold be lost, but lives could be lost as well. The train was at speed now, already going so fast the car rocked from side to side on the imperfect rail bed. Conroe squatted in the darkness, struggling to keep his balance, waiting to make the perfect pitch at the car's far opening. Their attackers must have eyes on that portal, and a fair toss would cause a fiery explosion in those eyes.

"Hart, I'm waiting for their next shot before I move. It could happen at any moment."

"Aye, Captain, we're ready."

Conroe struck when he saw the flash pan powder ignite, hurling the fire bomb even before the rifle boomed. Liquid flames cascaded along the far wall and he and Hart rushed down the aisle. A painful scream pierced the darkness on the landing just outside, and Conroe fired his Colt, BOOM, BOOM, BOOM, through the veil of fire and its dark outlines.

"My face, my eyes!" a voice shrieked, and as Conroe reached the door, he saw a man down on the landing. He was writhing in agony, clawing at his face, red flesh blistering up between his fingers. "Help me! Oh, God, help me!" the man pleaded. Hart came up behind Conroe, looked down at the man and suddenly realized another bushwacker behind him was scaling the ladder to the roof of the car. The other train thief had abandoned his accomplice and took off running back to the safety of the engine.

Conroe kneeled beside the suffering villain and ripped the prone man's hat off, using it to beat out stray flames flaring on his clothes; but the spy could see the Greek Fire had done its job. The man would not survive such horrific wounds. He was rolling from side to side, still holding what was left of his face, screaming and sobbing.

"You'll be fine," Conroe lied. "Who are you? Who controls the engine?" He knelt down next to the man and held him still, trying to win his confidence, trying to focus his attention.

"We are Union soldiers," the man blurted out. "Oh please get me to a doctor. Oh God, I beg you!"

"There is a doctor aboard," the spy lied again. "Who controls the engine?"

"Major Wolfe of the 2nd Kentucky." The soldier choked on the words. The Greek Fire had burned his lungs and throat.

"How many men with Major Wolfe?" Conroe pressed. He could see the man slipping away and judging from the nasty mash that was his face it was the best thing for him.

"He has four men including me." The soldier gagged again, wretching up a gusher of blood and vomit. He fought mightily to take in a breath, blue veins bulging through the raw skin on his neck. He released his face and struggled to rise, grabbing Conroe with bloody, burned hands. Conroe pushed away, seeing the poor man's dying eyes peering through the bloody gobs of charred meat that had been a face minutes before. The soldier fell back on the landing and was gone.

"This Major Wolfe has only three men now," Conroe said

quietly. He rolled the dead man over and kicked the body off the speeding platform. He turned to the others. "Hart, let's follow that other son of a gun over the top. We have even odds now." They both warily looked up at the darkness beyond the roof. It wouldn't be easy work, straddling the bucking train car speeding through the night.

Conroe climbed the ladder first and peered over the rooftop just as a canopy of pine trees gathered overhead. Wood smoke blowing from the engine's furnace choked the air. The smoke was a dirty white color, mixing with clean white puffs of steam contrasted against a wall of night shadows. The spy could not see anything across the rooftop, but he knew he was only fifty feet from the open platform that served the furnace. Just opposite that objective was the open cab where this Major Wolfe and his criminal gang were holed up.

With the gauge break approaching fast and feeling some momentum, Conroe decided to push across the top of the car. He motioned to Hart that they were moving. The train's noise and a roaring wind made it impossible to hear. The men crawled over the roof's lip and began shimmying toward the front of the car. Almost immediately a rifle shot whistled overhead.

Conroe hugged the rocking rooftop, making himself as small a target as possible. Hart though, stood up and rushed forward, leaping over the younger man. The rifleman, he reckoned, was reloading and now was the time to close the distance. He turned and commanded his men to follow, trying to make himself heard over the thundering locomotive and the blowing wind.

"Let's move, boys! He can't see us! Let's fall on the blackguard!" Wheeler tumbled up to the roof first, the others filing up the ladder behind him. Hart saw their shadows coming into the white smoke and moved halfway along the roof. But then another rifle shot boomed from the engine's direction and struck the old man down.

Conroe had risen to a crouch, but dropped down again and crawled up to Hart's motionless body. He came in close and shook him gently by the shoulders. "Hart, Hart. Are you alright?" But there was no answer. Conroe felt the man suddenly seize in what must have been a death throe. Other rifle blasts roared out of the smoky darkness. Conroe could see the fire flash from the engine's platform.

Wheeler and Godwin went prone on the rocking train car and started firing back. One man dead and a stalemate, thought Conroe. And this train's about to fly off the rails.

"Wheeler, help me get your lieutenant back inside. Let's get down from here and brace for a train wreck." Moving Hart's body off the top of a moving railcar—at night—under fire—was heavy work. Wheeler and Hope moved to retrieve the old man while Godwin kept his rifle aimed into the darkness. Conroe saw that both boys quietly wept as they slid the body over to the ladder and carefully lowered Hart down to the stair landing below. Godwin withdrew next while Conroe guarded against a full attack by the train gang.

Once all were back inside, Wheeler knelt beside Hart's body, arranging the man's uniform respectfully. "Why did this have to happen?" the boy simpered. "Train duty was supposed to be an easy ride." Godwin was bitterly staring down at the sad spectacle, watching while Wheeler continued to fuss with the old man's clothes.

"You're danged right, Wheeler. The war is about all done. He'd served his bit already and now this," the other guard lamented.

"There's no blood, though," Wheeler answered, now examining the body in the dim light of the lamp still burning in the middle of the carriage.

"What? What do ya mean?"

"I cain't find no durn blood. The lieutenant is dead and there ain't a speck of blood on him." Hart's eyes were peacefully shut as if he was taking the proverbial train guard's late night snooze. The rocking car, the clicking wheels should have been his perfect lullaby.

"Lieutenant Hart was a good man," Conroe told the boys. "But he's dead now and the bloody fools in the engine aim to kill us all at this speed. Leave him be, and get behind a bench and hold on. This train's about to reach the S. & R. and a gauge break will wreck us soon." The men sidled in behind the seats, leaving Hart lying in the aisle. They waited in the dark, listening to the rhythmic sounds of the train careening through the night.

"Captain Conroe?"

"Is that you, Hope?"

"Yes. Captain. I've been thinking. That don't sound right."

"What don't—doesn't sound right, Hope?"

"That part about the gauge break. That don't sound right to

me."

"It *ain't* right. I always said you were the smart one, Hope. It ain't right. This train's got compromise trucks. Can run on either gauge." The voice came out of the darkness as they all crouched on the floor, separated by the bench seats.

"Who said that?" Conroe barked.

"It's me, blast it! Get me off this danged filthy floor!"

"It's Lieutenant Hart!" Wheeler yelled. "He's alive!"

"Of course I'm alive," the old man grunted. "The devil shot me in the God blessed gut again. It hit my bloody steel plate, knocked the wind out of me and hurt like all get out!"

The boys laughed and rushed to his side, clomping around the train floor on their knees looking like a litter of happy puppies. "Now get me out of here. I'm *really* mad at these Yankee blackguards now."

Conroe crawled out to Hart who had sat up with a groan.

"You mean to tell me the G.D.S.E. has..."

"Wheels that fit five-foot rails *or* four-foot, eight-inch rails. The Yankees made the change thinking they could rush supplies or troops to the front once they took the Weldon Railroad." That was good news. At least one crisis was averted. "She also carries extra water; in a bunker tank under the tender car. That and the oversized saddle tank on the engine gives her a range of at least five hundred miles without a stop." This meant the train robbers could run the G. D. S. E. deep into North Carolina before she ran out of steam.

Hart was struggling for every breath. Conroe knew he needed to get him back to the relative safety of the 1st Class carriage. There he could get Carmen, the former nurse, to tend to the policeman's gut. But he wanted to attack again as soon as possible. He did not want to retreat.

As if on schedule, new rifle shots blasted through the door that led to the engine again. The gang must have heard the boys celebrating Hart's resurrection. The new attack convinced the spy to fall back, regroup and recruit Tilghman, Slim John and Uma to help take back the train.

They wrestled Hart to his feet and as the group left the car, the train's hooter, a low-pitched steam whistle, sounded a crossing. The G. D. S. E. had rolled right through the Seaboard and Roanoke junction without incident. The runaway train's wheels easily accommodated the narrower gauge tracks just like Hart said they would.

Chapter 54

Conroe and the policemen made their way back to 1st Class slowly. Conroe led the way, Colt at the ready. Godwin brought up the rear, watchful for the unpredictable gang. Wheeler and Hope, who were steadying Hart, fought against the train's downward momentum as the iron beast climbed a noticeable incline.

The express train was ascending gradually out of the swampy lowlands of southeastern Virginia onto the incipient plateau of the piedmont region. The men leaned back and reached for handholds among the seat backs as they walked. It was as if they were being pushed down a dark alley falling away into the night's blackness.

Uma and Tilghman were the first to see them when their carriage door flapped open. The African and the sea captain were in the corridor just outside their compartment door.

"We was wondering what in tarnation was going on up there. Did we hear gun fire?"

"Sure as shootin' at crows you did, Captain," Conroe quipped. "Yankee deserters control the train. They have blasted the be-Jesus out of the 3rd Class carriage."

"Do tell!" Tilghman gasped. Uma, stoic as usual, seemed to understand there was a serious problem with the train and he opened the compartment door and motioned for Slim John and Carmen to join the group. There were too many people to fit comfortably in the cabin, so they all gathered in the hallway outside the compartment's open door.

"Yankee deserters have taken the train," Tilghman told the married couple, who stared wide-eyed at the news.

"These men are the Suffolk Train Guards," Conroe informed

them, pointing to each uniformed man. "Lieutenant Hart, Wheeler, Godwin and Hope." The new acquaintances nodded to each other. Each man and Carmen had found a handhold or grab rail against the shaking, rocking ride. The three policemen with rifles had taken up positions, watching each end of the car. "We tried to retake the locomotive, but the blackguards drove us back, killed another guard, and had us pinned down in 3rd Class."

The train careened around a sharp bend, shoving everyone into a sideward lean. Tilghman was whispering to Uma in a pidgin of English and Portuguese, explaining who the policemen were and recounting what was happening aboard the smoking black monster. When the train straightened out again, Conroe continued his narrative. "We are on the Seaboard & Roanoke now with the Weldon Junction fast approaching."

The Wilmington and Weldon Railroad was one of the longest lines in America, stretching from Central Virginia all the way to Wilmington, North Carolina. The Weldon, as most people called it, also was the life line of Robert E. Lee's army, bringing supplies from the Confederate port on the Cape Fear River into Petersburg. "If we can regain the Jack, it could be an easy thing to take the Weldon back toward Confederate lines."

"So you think these robbers will head into the Carolinas, looking for Sherman's army?" Slim John asked.

"I think they'll head south, but I don't reckon they are looking for a provost marshal," Conroe answered wryly.

"They know about the gold, you mean." Carmen added, matter-of-factly.

"They most certainly know about the gold, though I can't say how," the spy countered.

"So *gold* is the reason for all this?" Hart asked with surprise.

"Yes, Hart, gold--and a lot of it," Conroe replied. Carmen realized her mistake and cupped a hand across her mouth in embarrassment. But Conroe was not concerned that she had let slip their secret. The stakes now were much higher than just the gold shipment. "So, now you know why we are here," he continued with the policeman. "There is Irish gold aboard, bound for the Confederate war effort. You can see why I couldn't take you into my confidence before."

"Of course, of course," Hart answered with an

understanding nod.

"How many are they?" Slim John wanted to know.

"There *were* five. We caught one of the blighters," Conroe said. "He told us a Major Wolfe held the engine, with four more men including him."

"So a Yankee major plus three other crooks," Hart added with some satisfaction. "Deserters, we suppose." The old man was leaning against the corridor wall, half bent and holding his belly. He chuffed raspy breaths, obviously in pain.

"The informer was killed then," Carmen concluded. She released her hold on the doorframe and lurched over to Hart and led him toward the compartment. "You need to lie down, old soul," she told him soothingly.

"Yes, thank you, Sister," the train guard mumbled, which raised a giggle from Carmen, but she didn't correct the man. Slim John watched his wife lead Hart away from the conclave, but took up the conversation again.

"So they are four; we are eight."

"We are seven," Conroe corrected. "Lieutenant Hart there has been shot." The others looked at the old policeman through the open compartment door with surprise and concern. He was gimpily trying to get comfortable across one of the nicely padded 1st Class benches.

"Didn't draw no blood. I'm as fit to fight as ever!" he yelled.

"No blood?" Tilghman asked incredulously. "Is he a man of steel?" Conroe laughed at the seaman's unwitting joke.

"He is indeed a man of steel, Captain; in more ways than one. But we don't have time to get into that now."

Chapter 55

It had taken some persuasion to convince Lieutenant Hart to stay behind, but in the end the old codger decided to stay close to Carmen's pretty face. She had revealed the truth about her nun'shabit and he looked at her in a whole new light now. With Hart and Carmen holding down the 1st Class carriage, the others left to make another assault on the engine. The team stalked single file along the dark corridors, the muffled clicking and clacking of the rails broken by an occasional heavy bump that rocked the whole train. Periodic hooter blasts warned off crossing road traffic.

Moving between cars in the darkness slowed their already wary approach. In between 2nd and 3rd Class, Tilghman stumbled and inadvertently found a handbrake wheel in the dark when he lunged for a grab rail. They were all embarrassed they hadn't thought of stopping the train using each car's handbrake sooner. If they could stop the train, an attack would be much easier to bring off. Tilghman heaved on the wheel but it would not budge. Closer inspection using a carriage lamp revealed that the screw had been mangled, effectively seizing the brake in an open position. "These brakes have been sabotaged," Hope reported, hanging down off the gangway between the cars.

"The deserters must have stolen out here during the night and disabled each device with a carefully placed pistol blast," Conroe surmised.

"It's not likely the handbrakes would have had much effect anyway at this point," Slim John added. "This train is what the papers in Charleston would call a Red Ball—an out of control, speeding locomotive. Only three ways to stop a Red Ball: crash it, let it run out of steam, or use the locomotive's Johnson bar to reverse its heavy drive wheels. The drive wheels can stop it if you have enough track to let it grind to a halt."

So the assault was still on. Conroe planned a two-pronged attack this time. He would lead the policemen, Wheeler, Godwin and Hope, across the roof while Tilghman, Uma and Slim John occupied the 3rd Class carriage and made a spirited demonstration against the tender door. Conroe assembled them all in 2nd Class to give them the final details. "Keep up a constant barrage against that door. If you hear us fighting on the tender's gangway, the door may be unguarded at that point. Try to bust it down."

"Yes, Captain," Slim John answered. "We'll do our best on this end."

"Alright then. Third time's the charm as they say." Conroe pointed at the door leading to the 3rd Class compartments. "Through that door, we split up and go." The group was filing down the aisle toward the front of the car when the door behind them slammed open.

Everyone spun around, weapons swinging up to ward off a rear attack. A shadowy figure fell into the car and disappeared in the darkness. "Take cover!" Conroe commanded, and the team scattered behind the 2nd Class rows. "Show yourself," the spy yelled again, but there was no answer. Then they heard a hoarse voice, a weak cough.

"Conroe, it's me, Hart. Help me." The men tumbled into the aisle and headed up to the old man, who lay sprawled on the floor.

"Hope, Godwin, guard the doors," Conroe ordered. He reached Hart and knelt down next to him. Wheeler did the same, and noticed a sopping blood stain that covered the policeman's coat.

"What happened to you?" the boy asked, looking horrified.

"Where's Carmen?" Slim John barked with alarm, moving toward the door to get back to her.

"They have her," the old man grunted, "but you mustn't go back there, Sweeney." Hart had been severely beaten about the face. His eyes were swollen black, and he held his gut tightly, blood caking a shivering hand. "Two men surprised me coming out of the baggage car. I'm sorry."

"They must have run back along the roof," Tilghman guessed.

"We've been flanked," Wheeler quipped.

"Outsmarted—again!" Conroe added bitterly. Slim John was checking his trusty Spiller and Burr.

"I'm going back to get her, my Carmen," Slim John announced. "Who's with me?"

"No, son," Hart croaked. "They left me alive for one reason; to tell you not to try to rescue the girl and to not stop the train. He'll kill her on the spot if he so much as hears your approach."

"Who told you that? Who?" Conroe pressed.

"This Major Wolfe. He ain't bluffing. He's a bad one. I saw it in his eyes. He's evil."

"I'm not afraid of him," Slim John stated firmly. "I've got to save Carmen. He can have the gold, but Carmen must not be harmed." The former soldier turned to Conroe, seeking agreement. "The gold and his life in exchange for Carmen—unharmed. He can take that deal or die in bloody Hades!" Conroe avoided Sweeney's angry eyes.

"Where is your steel plate?" Wheeler suddenly yelled. The young man had been nursing his beloved leader. "His plate is gone! What has become of it? What did that Yankee devil do to you?"

The old man clenched his eyes shut from the pain and answered in a quavering, hoarse whisper. "He ripped off the plate when he found it. He thought it amusing. He sunk the hoary hand of death into me. He grabbed my innards and squeezed 'til I agreed to do what he asked."

"NO!" Wheeler cried, imagining the unholy pain the old man suffered. "What kind of wretched beast would do such a thing?"

"The kind of monster who holds Carmen hostage," Hart groaned. "He is evil, I say. You mustn't test him."

Chapter 56

Hart died about an hour later. His police boys took it hard, and swore to get the men who killed their chief. But the stalemate continued. The Red Ball train made the Weldon crossing and turned south toward Raleigh. Word was out from Suffolk by now that the G.D.S.E. was a runaway. Southern authorities controlling the Seaboard & Roanoke and now the Raleigh Rail Road did not believe the telegraph reports at first. They seemed unable or unwilling to take action to stop the train even after eyewitness accounts confirmed what Union officials had been reporting.

The situation had not changed when Blake, now operating the engine alone, approached the small station at Raleigh. The sun would start its ascent within the hour and Conroe's group still hunkered down in the 2nd Class car. The young policemen kept watch on both the 3rd Class carriage and on the door that led to the 1st Class compartments. The gang held the locomotive, 1st Class and the lucrative last car on the train, the baggage car and its gold. Conroe and the others sat silently, rocking with the uneasy rhythm of the speeding train when, after hours going a mile a minute, the stink-pot began to slow.

Conroe's first thought was that authorities had blocked the track, finally taking a step to halt the renegade train. But the slowing seemed too controlled for an unexpected road block. The gang had something else planned

"We must be coming into Raleigh soon," Slim John reasoned. "But why slow down for that?"

"I'm not sure what's up their sleeves," Conroe answered. "But I think it's time we probed both ends of the train to see if they're looking to jump off. They may have packed up some of the gold and are planning an escape."

Conroe told the others to remain in place while he made a foray toward the locomotive. The pearly glow of an autumn dawn was just starting to reveal the flat open fields outside. Conroe could see the shadowy contours of mature tobacco fields hurtling past the windows on either side of the carriage as he left 2nd Class and crossed the shifting gangway to the next car. The cloying sweetness of the last honeysuckle of summer scented the air outside, but the fresh smell quickly turned sour inside the 3rd Class carriage. Collier's dead body had ripened overnight.

The train was rolling at a steady speed now, about twenty miles an hour, still fast, but a reasonable rate compared to the breakneck journey it'd made since Suffolk. Was the engineer making a quiet approach to Raleigh station before he gunned it again, hoping to catch the yard master off guard? Aside from the reduction in speed, nothing seemed to have changed at this end of the train. Conroe could see holes in the tender door made by the .58 caliber balls fired during the night. The newly born daylight shined through them. The spy crept along close to the floor waiting for another rifle blast warning him off, but as he got close to the door, no such attack came.

He was close enough now to see the unlucky conductor's blood; the jagged, sticky stain crawled along the middle of the aisle. The steward's galley stunk of death. The odor was overwhelming as Conroe inched closer to the door and he covered his nose with the gentleman's handkerchief he always carried. He stood sideways in the aisle as close to the door as he'd been last night when he'd first tried to shoulder it open. That seemed so very long ago now.

He pressed his eye against the closest hole and peered in at the engine gangway for the first time. He could see the open engineer's roost across the empty tender platform. The furnace hatch stood ajar and a large fire blazed there, throwing flickering shadows across the scene. A slightly built blonde-haired man in civilian shirt controlled the locomotive. He wore heavy, long fireman's gloves, one hand on the Johnson bar, one hand at the steam trumpet cord. There was no one else on the gangway, no fireman, no brakeman, no one in

Union blue and certainly no one in a major's uniform. One man.

Conroe was tempted to shoot him through the peephole. Too risky, though. He thought about attacking over the roof again, but how did he know a man wasn't posted there? Control of the engine and the train seemed so close. But then the spy remembered Hart's admonition about the evil Major Wolfe. He thought about what could happen to Carmen if the train stopped. He pondered what Slim John might do if Carmen was harmed because of a rash decision.

The locomotive slowed a little more. Conroe could see the man at the helm ease up on the throttle as he felt the train settle into an easier cadence. He watched the engineer yank a vertical hanging rope overhead and listened to the train's hooter horn, the sonorous whistle he'd heard all night. It was like watching a marionette show from behind the stage. The man grabbed another cord farther forward and for the first time Conroe heard a clanging yard bell signaling an arrival.

The Confederate operative backed away from his peephole and went back to the car's seating area. He angled a look out one of the wide carriage windows. He could see the tracks ahead. They were branching off into a substantial train yard. Further along, there were a dozen or more sidings and spurs feeding out in all directions. In the distance, great gray ash heaps, the waste from wood-burning locomotives, blotted out the horizon. Discarded rolling stock and long-rusted locomotives peered out of the dewy morning fog. Stacks of wood-tar creosote sleepers seemed like shadowy fortress walls lining the tracks. A round, wooden water tank stood sentinel overlooking an otherwise deserted yard.

Conroe pocketed his handkerchief while he pondered the changing situation. Wolfe was up to something here and it suddenly dawned on the spy that most of the gang had abandoned the engine and shifted to the last cars of the train. Then he heard rifle shots coming from that direction. He hoped he could get back to his team before it was too late.

Chapter 57

Conroe barged into 2nd Class, pistol drawn, ready for a fight, but no one was there. The gun fire was farther along, in 1st Class. Had Slim John finally succumbed to his need to play the hero and rescue Carmen? "Stupid man!" Conroe muttered to himself. He crossed through the empty car and could see that the doors leading to the 1st Class carriage were open. He saw Wheeler, dead on the stair landing outside. A man he didn't know, one of the gang, was dead just inside the train's last carriage. Inside 1st Class Conroe found Uma, Slim John and Tilghman holed up in one of the first compartments he came to. Hope and Godwin lay prone on the aisle floor firing at the open doorway to the baggage car. Return fire cracked from the darkened car which, Conroe reasoned, was still held by Wolfe and another man. He should have killed the engineer when he had the chance. That one had been alone on the engine, he now realized.

Tilghman, on his knees, grabbed the crouching spy and pulled him inside the compartment.

"We caught one of the blackguards coming down off the roof between cars. He killed Wheeler before Slim John shot him dead. Then the fires of the everlasting pit broke loose," the sailor reported. "Before we knew it, Wolfe was on us, firing a revolver from the 1st Class doorway. But we drove the blighter back into the baggage car and now we have this standoff."

"There must be only two of 'em in there," Conroe said, shoving his Colt toward the car carrying the gold. "There was only one man on the engine."

"But they still have Carmen," Slim John spit in frustration. "I tried to take that one I shot to trade for her, but he wasn't giving up."

"I don't believe Wolfe would have traded Carmen for one of his men anyway," Conroe said. "He wants the gold."

"Then we need to make that deal. Give him the gold if he'll give us Carmen." Conroe did not want to give up the treasure, but he was ready to talk his way out of the stalemate.

"You're right, Mr. Sweeney. Let me handle this." Conroe leaned out the compartment door. "Godwin, Hope!" he yelled down the aisle. "Stop firing!"

Silence enveloped the car for an agonizingly long minute or two. Conroe slowly moved up toward the open door, passing by the prone riflemen. The gang did not fire at him. He ducked into the doorway of the closest compartment to the baggage car and yelled.

"You in there! We know you want the gold! We're ready to talk!" A few seconds later a big, dark-haired man showed himself across the gangway at the baggage car's door. His left arm was clamped around Carmen's slender throat. The butterfly cornette was gone, her head swathed only in a white wimple. She seemed like an innocent babe wrapped in a mother's blanket. Wolfe's right hand held a long knife rammed like a spike into the soft flesh under her curving jaw.

"I got this little girl's life in my hands, gentlemen!" he roared. "I'd just as soon die killing her as not. So put down your guns, now!" He yanked Carmen's thin body from side to side, using it as a shield. He shook her like a petulant child roughly abusing a rag doll. Conroe could see the strength the man possessed and the utter helplessness of his victim. The burly criminal crushed Carmen's neck so tightly that her normally alabaster olive face glowed scarlet red.

Her eyes, usually so dark and calm, glared wide with fear. And then Conroe saw them close with a flutter like a dying flame guttering from lack of oxygen. The brute was throttling her without even realizing it. But Wolfe released the lock on her throat just enough for her to come around again, then jerked his arm tight lifting her off her feet. She passed out once more, looking like a woman going to her eternal sleep. No, the maniac *did* know what he was doing. He was choking her unconscious on purpose! Repeatedly, Conroe saw! "I'll only tell you this one more time," the Union man said, impatient with the delay. "Get those guns off me and then we'll talk."

The policemen on the floor shifted their eyes to the older man looking for direction, but did not alter their aim. Conroe looked back at the boys and motioned for them to withdraw. Then he faced the doorway again. "I've called off the rifles! We don't know who you are," he lied. "But we know you want the gold in that car! Give us the woman and you can have it all when we come into Raleigh Station!"

Slim John listened to the spy and marveled at his skills of deception. Of course Conroe didn't want Wolfe to know they knew who he was and might track him down later. And of course it would be an advantage to get Wolfe to agree to stop the train in Raleigh where Confederate and railroad officials could help apprehend him. Slim John was glad Conroe was on his and Carmen's side. Conroe had offered the kidnapper a deal bundled up in a trap, but Wolfe was having none of it. He crushed Carmen's neck again, jerking her limp body up off the floor once more.

"I've got no time for that!" the Union officer yelled back derisively. "I think I'll just take the gold now and you can have the woman now as well---if you can stop the bleeding!" The train suddenly jolted forward with a bang as if another heavy locomotive had bumped it from behind. No one noticed another man on the gangway, below where Wolfe was leading Carmen in a deadly dance. It was one of Wolfe's accomplices. He struggled with the pin that decoupled the baggage car. Then Conroe was surprised when the scruffy engineer he spied on the engine suddenly descended from the roof of the 1st Class car. The man dropped right in front of the Confederate and leaped across to the baggage car before Conroe could react.

The train had jagged to the left and was gaining speed again just as the coupling between cars reached a spur junction. The knuckle popped open and the cars began to separate, the baggage car heading off to the right on a separate track while the train continued on the main line, veering left. At that moment Wolfe roared, gritting his teeth into a grisly smile. He twisted the grip of his knife and sliced across Carmen's neck and in the same motion lifted her delicate body with his other arm and heaved her across the chasm between the cars. She landed on the 1st Class car's open platform with a hollow thud, and lay there unmoving.

The men could hear Wolfe guffawing like a maniac as the

baggage car shot away under its own momentum while the train began to speed uncontrolled again toward the Raleigh Depot.

"Blasted demon!" Slim John screamed, leaping to Carmen's side. Blood flowed freely from her once perfect neck, the bright red liquid quickly soaking the snow white wimple of the nun's habit.

Conroe realized immediately that the train's locomotive was unmanned now and under full throttle. The others were huddled around Carmen's bleeding body. She was still not moving, and Conroe did not expect she ever would again. The train was his concern now. He darted into the car, making for the engine.

Slim John and Uma picked her up and moved her into the compartment they had occupied so coolly just a few hours ago. Tilghman ripped away the tight fitting wimple, unleashing a cascade of beautiful dark tresses and revealing a bloody gash that wrapped around Carmen's silky smooth throat. He examined the wound and used the wimple's cotton fabric to stanch the blood. The girl lay unconscious, but she was still alive.

"It seems to be stopping," the captain announced. "The cut is a long one, but the carotid is not touched." He looked closer as the blood flow cleared. "Indeed the wound is bloody, but not deep—perhaps not fatal," he said, looking at Slim John. Carmen's husband had been kneeling there, eyes clamped shut, praying to God, but now he leaned down to get a better look and confirm what Tilghman was telling him. Just then Carmen's eyes fluttered open and Slim John smiled at her tenderly. She smiled back, wincing in pain. As Slim John and Carmen's eyes connected, Tilghman pulled away, beaming at the loving couple. John Sweeney kissed her softly on the forehead. "You are a lucky lady…Sister Guadelupe."

"Just another miracle, I suppose, Father John."

Chapter 58

Rolling out of Raleigh, The Great Dismal Swamp Express quickly gained speed again; the red ball's throttle full open and unmanned. The train's compromise trucks, an ingenious idea, were nevertheless a stop-gap fix, and were never designed to run safely at high speed. The wheels ran loosely on the narrow gauge tracks of the Raleigh Rail Road, making the train rock precariously from side to side. A sharp turn left or right would surely topple the cars and at fifty miles an hour or more, such a derailment would end in disaster and death.

When the rickety rocket train blasted through Raleigh, the engine took rifle fire from Confederate guards there who must have thought a Union gang still controlled it. But in the following cars, those riding the bucking bull didn't even notice when the speeding train flattened a handcar full of salt pork and tobacco that blocked the tracks.

Conroe had started for the engine thinking Carmen dead, but Uma, Hope and Godwin rushed forward to find him as soon as Carmen came to. They carried fire axes and the policemen hacked through the tender door that had proved such an obstacle before.

Out on the gangway, the group saw how the blonde bandit had jammed the throttle open using a brakeman's iron frog. The furnace had been packed with as much wood as it could hold, the fire within a conflagration in a can.

"She's a regular tea kettle!" Godwin yelled over the engine noise and the wind. He could read the Ashcroft steam gauge across the gap. The brass instrument's needle strained past the shaded part of the dial that marked the normal pressure zone. Hope pushed his way forward to get a better look. The gauge would top out at two hundred pounds. It read one-eighty already.

"She could blow any minute," Hope warned. The boy had been around trains enough to know that a steam locomotive's delicate balance of fire and water produced enormous power. Properly harnessed, that power drove a marvelous invention—the iron horse was revolutionizing America and the world. But uncontrolled, a steam boiler explosion destroyed with Biblical vengeance. The assembled men teetering on the rambling gangway were seconds away from a most unpleasant choice: being crushed to death in a high speed derailment or being immolated in a searing steam fire.

Hope rushed onto the engine platform and grabbed the firemen's gloves left by Blake before he abandoned the cockpit. The boy released the primary steam valve while Conroe removed the frog and closed the throttle. Hope then leaned on the Johnson bar and the train began to slow. The Ashcroft gauge still registered dangerous levels, but it was slowly falling now. And then on a whim, Conroe had a twinkle of an idea.

"Uma!" he called to the African. "I want you to blow the whistle!" Conroe had noticed that the black foreigner stood awestruck by the raging power of the steaming monster beneath him. He gaped open-mouthed at the blazing furnace, the intricate controls, the magical gauges, the bells and whistles. Now he stared at Conroe, not exactly sure what the white man wanted him to do. "It will release more steam," the spy told him, leading him up to the steam trumpet's cord. He made a tugging motion with his arm and smiled at the former slave. He made a whistling sound with two fingers held between his teeth as he simultaneously mimicked another tug.

Uma offered an uncharacteristic smile when he realized what the American wanted. He gazed up at the oversized balloon-style smoke stack that dominated the engine's gigantic water barrel. Radley & Hunter was etched in gold around the stack. Then Uma stepped closer to the dangling rope and tugged hard, releasing a long screaming bellow. The African warrior prince let out a deep, loud laugh, and his enchanted face beamed like a frolicking schoolboy's.

Chapter 59

Salisbury, North Carolina

"She's lost more than a modicum of her precious blood, but I can assure you she is out of danger now," the doctor said gruffly. His barrel-chested frame had been large and well-muscled when he was younger, but as he scrubbed his hands and forearms in a brown-stained porcelain sink, he looked tired, weak, beaten.

"That's a gift from God, Dr. Carter," Slim John answered quietly. "And so are you. Thank you for helping her. We feel fortunate we found you." The former soldier sat at Carmen's bedside, holding a soft weak hand, looking at her eyes, not at the ragged raw stitch line that encircled her throat like a macabre necklace. The beautiful Carmen would have a scar from the wound, but she would live. In time the ugly gash would heal and the scar would fade; perhaps more quickly than the doleful memories of the war or the violence of the terrible journey that had landed them in Salisbury.

As the train rolled along the North Carolina Rail Road, Conroe got a close look at the field pens enclosing the worst part of the Confederate prison camp in the little Tarheel village. The camp was grossly overcrowded, having expanded from the original prison established in a three-story brick cotton mill surrounded by a wooden stockade. Conroe and the others found the town overwhelmed by the fetid camp. There were five thousand, perhaps ten thousand prisoners at Salisbury now. Large dirt mounds hinted at mass graves where inmates killed by disease and malnutrition had been hastily buried.

Conroe's group had carried Carmen upwind of the camp's stench and into the town center looking for any sort of civilian doctor. They soon eyed the faded wooden sign swinging over a battered office door.

Dr. A. Carter, Medical Physician

Salisbury, North Carolina

His surgery was one of a few professional storefronts still operating on Main Street.

The doctor's office consisted of one large, rather bare room with stained wood floors and dingy yellow walls. Even so, for a medical surgery in a Southern war-torn town, it was adequately equipped. One side of the space housed a high-backed accountant's desk cluttered with piles of papers, crude surgical tools and stoppered apothecary bottles of various shapes, sizes and colors. Against the opposite wall, where the wash basin was located, a large woven basket held a neat stack of folded white towels; a second basket was piled high with bloody, soiled towels that would never be white again.

At the center of the dark room stood a shiny enamel-top table attended by a high metal stool and a cluster of large oil lamps. Jutting from the wall opposite the entrance were two low cots swathed in vaguely white sheets and roughly stitched beige wool blankets. Each makeshift bunk was accompanied by tin bedpans and unadorned tan clay pitchers and wash basins tucked away on the floor nearby. Carmen occupied one of these cots, resting comfortably under the foggy influence of a generous draught of laudanum.

The old doctor left the basin, snatched a clean towel and approached Carmen's cot, wiping dry his hands. He squinted sourly at the way the man he knew as Father John held the young nun's hand. Slim John had forgotten himself of course, distracted by the good news about his wife and he rattled on obliviously. "We noticed the horrible conditions in the prison camp on the way into town, Doc. I expect you've had your hands full with sick prisoners."

"Oh, hellfire and fudge—ah—excuse the language, Father. Fact is I helped the army out at first, but that place is riddled with disease now; dysentery, tuberculosis, take your pick. Ain't nothing an ol' country truss-fixer like me can do out there but get sick and die myself."

"Sounds horrible."

"'Tis an infernal region, really. The army just brought in another load of prisoners from Georgia. Sherman's pushing this way and the camps there are being emptied. The government should just parole Georgia's prisoners, I believe. This world wasn't meant for prison camps. Can't keep 'em clean. The bugs and lice, the water; they bring sickness and sure death. They call the perimeter of the camp the dead line, and a truer moniker was never placed on a thing. Sure the guards will make you dead if you cross the line, but you're just as likely to die if you don't. Those men need to be paroled and allowed to live. I'm done with all that now, done with the war in general."

"I see," Slim John muttered, brought back down to earth by these horrid facts. Doctor Carter's story reminded him why he had deserted the army last year. The war could not be won, he knew even then. He and Carmen had struck out to make a new life away from the Confederacy, and it was only a bizarre series of twists that had brought them back to this disastrous land.

The South, he could see, was not the South of his youth. It was to be a hard place for a long time, even when this damnable war was finally, finally over. "Well this is all very sad for you and your town, Doc. But I do want to thank you again for everything you've done here." Slim John suddenly wanted to get out of Salisbury. He wondered where the others were now. Conroe and the two police boys had returned to the depot to try to get the locomotive serviced and perhaps even turned around, if Salisbury even had a turntable. Tilghman had gone looking for a drink and had taken Uma with him. Slim John barely heard Doctor Carter speaking to him as his mind swirled with these thoughts; as he obsessed about leaving town as quickly as possible.

"She's a very lucky lady," the old doctor was saying. He was standing over the couple, rolling down his shirt sleeves, stalling for time awkwardly as if he had something more to say, but didn't know how to start.

"Yes, we feel very lucky," Slim John affirmed. Carter bent eagerly over Carmen when he saw she was waking up. Slim John could see that the doctor had a serious look on his face, a look of concern for the nun on the cot and perhaps a disapproving look for the young priest with her.

"You are going to be fine, young lady," he told Carmen in a loud voice. She merely stared up at the old tired face. "And you should know that the baby will be fine too."

"Ba—ba—baby!" Slim John stammered before freezing, paralyzed with surprise.

"Oh, blast all! Of course you didn't know! I didn't expect it either," the physician deadpanned, looking at Carmen lying there in her habit, a dreamy smile plastered on her face.

Slim John dropped Carmen's hand guiltily and jumped to his feet. "Dr. Carter, you must be thinking…"

"That you are either not what you claim to be or you are two Papists doomed to eternal damnation. Either way, it's none of my business."

"A baby, John. We're going to have a baby," Carmen gurgled. Slim John looked down at his laudanum-laced wife, recovered his wits, and drew himself up to tell the doctor the truth.

"You were right on the first count. We are…not what we seem, Doctor. My name is John Sweeney and this is my wife Carmen. We are happily married, lucky to be alive and blessed by God that we are having a child!"

"Well, I'm glad to hear it," the old man answered, relieved. He shook Slim John's hand long, high and hard. "Congratulations, boy! I would say she's near four months along."

Slim John was laughing now, with joy yes, but also with a full understanding of the humor of the whole circumstance. "Did I say thank you, Doc?" the young husband—the father to be—babbled. "I just want to say thank you!" He grabbed the stranger's hand in both of his and started galloping around the otherwise dreary room with him.

"I do believe you *did* thank me, young fella'," Carter laughed, wrestling the dancing priest to a halt. "But I want to be paid too. It's going to be twenty-five dollars Confederate." He leaned in and whispered, "Five dollars if you got greenbacks." He resumed a normal tone without missing a beat. "I'll leave you two to talk while I draw up the statement of owing." The doctor stepped over to his disaster of a desk which evidently also served as his business office. He swept an arm across the middle of the counter, clearing a writing surface, and sat down facing the wall.

Slim John had returned to Carmen's side. "You are just full of surprises, my love," he cooed. "This day, the whole journey has been full of surprises."

"All of them not good ones." Carmen murmured. She lightly fingered the line of cat gut slashing across her silken neck. She was sitting up in bed now, reclining, still groggy, but Slim John's new found love of life had lightened *her* mood, too.

"But this surprise—this baby—*is* a good one, a good surprise."

"The most wonderful surprise, my beloved husband."

"I'm sorry I've put you in such danger. I really don't know how it came to this."

"It's not your doing, John. We both know how we've been swept along on a tide of fates."

"I love you, Carmen. Thank God you will be alright."

"Sorry to interrupt." Neither Slim John nor Carmen had noticed Dr. Carter looming over them again, invoice in hand. He was smiling and shoved the sheet of foolscap between their faces where they couldn't miss it. "Hate to charge you at all," he explained feebly. "But these are difficult times for an old country doctor. Pitiful few patients I can save, even fewer horses, no cows, no pigs."

"Oh Doc, I'm happy to pay," Slim John answered amiably. "But I don't have greenbacks."

"Of course not," the doctor said dismissively. He seemed to forget he mentioned that he would accept Yankee money. "This is the South. We use Confederate money."

"Don't have Confederate either."

"Oh?" the old man's face fell. He seemed used to not getting paid, but thought this out-of-towner would have been good for it.

"All I got is this gold piece here." Slim John dug behind his clerical robe and drew out a generous chunk of gold that Tilghman had pressed into his hand when they found the surgery. It was from the captain's share of the lost shipment. Spend it if it will save Carmen, the rough sailor had told him. The physician's eyes brightened at the sight of the gleaming nugget.

"Glad I could help ya'll," he gushed. The medical man plucked the metal shard from Slim John's hand with two delicate fingers, couching the prize carefully into his pale scrubbed palm. The payment seemed to re-energize the war-weary physician. He started talking fast. He grabbed his coat and swung around looking for his hat. "Now the missus here needs bed rest for a week at least. Build up her strength. She needs to eat. Feed that baby. She's eating for two, you know. Keep that wound clean and give it time to scab over. Find a good man to remove those stitches when the sting is gone."

The Sweeneys nodded distractedly, starring bug-eyed at the physician's rapid-fire instructions. "My nurse will be in shortly to help you freshen up. She'll bring some food and fresh water. Now Father, ah…Mr. Sweeney, I wish I could recommend lodging in our little town, but there hasn't been a decent room to be had since this prison camp exploded with men. It'd be cleaner, safer on your train. I'll send a man around to help you remove there. The nurse can provide you meals while they water the train and resupply the tender with wood. The railroad won't get to that until tomorrow at least, so take your time leaving." The doctor had found his hat, a faded black bowler, which he plopped on his old gray head as he made a dash for the exit. "I'm off now. Good luck to the happy family," he called, slamming the door in his haste.

For several moments, Slim John and Carmen could only gawp in silence at Dr. Carter's whirlwind departure. Presently they looked at each other and burst into gleeful laughter.

Chapter 60

"So I'll ask you one more time. How quickly can we get the locomotive serviced and turned around?" Conroe stood before the brass screen in the depot ticket office, the police guards with rifles just behind him. He had lost patience with the yardmaster. The skinny little bald man overflowed with excuses. He had a long pointed nose that he used as a weapon. He looked down it at people like a sharpshooter sights his prey. Nothing Conroe said or offered had any effect on the official, who did not grasp the urgency of the spy's situation. He even answered too slowly for Conroe.

"I just cain't say, General," the officious clerk replied with dull eyes, tweaking the green eyeshade he wore. "I got the telegraph to run, tickets to sell, baggage to check and porter; and that's just for the regular runs we service. Your special train will have to wait."

"First of all, I'm not a general," the exasperated spy barked. He began to raise his voice in octaves chuffing higher with each passing second. "Now my good man, I thought you were the yardmaster, not a ticket clerk, not a porter, not a telegraph operator or the bloody director of railroad operations for that matter!" Conroe caught himself and his voice returned to normal as he leaned into the window. "I just need a crew and a simple turnaround service here." The clerk's dull eyes hadn't changed. *His* voice remained a flat monotone.

"I *am* the yardmaster here, sir. But these days I got to see to it all." Conroe dropped his head and sighed.

"Let me help you, then. I have some men. May I pay you for water and wood and have *them* stock the engine?"

"Well now, that's a tricky thing, sir. The railroad's got rules about who does the work."

That was it! Conroe drew his heavy Colt pistol and slammed it on the counter. "Now see here, man!" he yelled. The railroad's little dictator's glazed eyes followed the flash of the brass and blued-steel gun and he jumped back in alarm. He was unaccustomed to having anyone question his authority, much less offer to pay with lead. "I am on important government business under direct orders from the president. I shall requisition anything I need here, by force if necessary."

Conroe briefly glanced at the riflemen behind him and placed his hand on the countered gun. "Now I offered you money, labor, not to mention my patience and right good nature. Now I ain't asking, I'm telling you. This is what I want and I want it now! Service that train immediately and get it turned around north bound!" Conroe's angry bellow echoed into silence and the yardmaster's eyes widened in fear. The clerk's green eyeshade quivered ever so slightly, and below the high counter, the man's knees rattled uncontrollably. He licked his lips with a dry, sticky tongue before he stammered a reply.

"Ho-ho-holy Moses! If you say so! I'll get a man to help with the water and a wagon for the wood. I ain't got a working turntable though, through service only. If you want to head north, you'll have to back your way up to Greensboro. And I ain't got an extra crew neither. Oh, I can give you an engineer, but you'll have to work the tender and brakes for him, and hope the mechanicals don't fail." He prayed the angry man with the gun accepted what he had offered.

Conroe released the deep breath he'd been holding and simply said, "Where's your water man? Let's go."

"Yes, sir. Ask for Lem. He should be at the water tank."

"Have the engineer report to me within the hour," the spy commanded. Conroe didn't wait for an answer. He plucked the Colt from the window counter, still eyeing the clerk while he spun the cylinder. The gun deftly found its holster and without another word Conroe and his boys withdrew. He slammed the office door and stalked off toward the tracks. Back inside, the yardmaster flinched when the door crashed shut, but he did move from behind the counter. He could see the street through the glass front building and his wary eyes followed Conroe as he walked out of sight. Suddenly the little man felt brave again.

"Blast all! I knew the Yankees was heading this way, but I feel put upon already," he muttered to himself, returning to his ledger.

Slim John and Carmen ate like they'd been given their last meal. In fact the corn fritters and ham that Dr. Carter's nurse had brought them was the first meal they'd had since they left Norfolk.

"The repast ain't nothin' fancy, but it'll fill you up, sure 'nough," the young woman had told them. Her name was Lizzy, Elizabeth Dunn.

"Elizabeth Dunn," Slim John repeated out loud.

"Yes, sir? You mean me? You can jes' call me Lizzy, suh."

The tall, coffee-hued woman wore a simple printed calico dress. The garment's tiny black-shadowed rose pattern strained to cover the woman's thick bones and ample curves. A red headrag tamed long blue-black hair traced by just the faintest wave. She had yellow eyes that glowed like the eyes of a cat on a warm night. There was Indian blood in Lizzy and she was quite pretty, Slim John noticed.

"Yes, Lizzy, I know. But the world is changing. When this war ends, all kinds of opportunities will open up for a pretty, hard worker like you."

"Aw, go on," she laughed. She was tidying up the surgery, waiting to clear the dishes from the meal she'd brought. She had drawn fresh water and heated it to give Carmen a hand bath when she was done eating.

"I am being serious. Names are an important thing. Yours should be formalized. Elizabeth Dunn—a professional title for a woman on the rise." Lizzy cut unbelieving eyes at the tall white Southerner, wondering if he was losing his mind.

"Well, if you say so, suh. But I'll believe the world will change when I see it with both my eyes. One eye won't do it. And anyways, I'm more likely to see the Lord Jesus hisself when he returns to this green Earth." She giggled and kept working.

"Forgive me, Miss Dunn," Slim John chuckled back. "I didn't mean to force my opinions on you. But my wife and I are in a naming mood and yours appealed to me." The couple was finished eating now and set aside the dishes which the black nurse cleared away immediately.

"I understand, Mr. Sweeney. Doc Carter did say that Missus Sweeney expectin'. I'm happy for ya'll." Lizzy had questions for the white strangers, but didn't dare ask. How they got here, in this God-forgotten town? How had the missus got cut? Where they were headed from here? Slim John and Carmen wouldn't have had a good answer for the latter question if it had been asked. They had not had time to consider the next step. For now they just seemed content to bask in the joy of the promised baby and discuss possible names.

What to name the baby? That *was* a line of questioning the servant felt comfortable asking. "So will you name the baby after the father?" she queried Carmen. Lizzy sat down beside the cot opposite Slim John and began to carefully clean the white woman's wound.

Before Carmen could answer, Slim John said, "I'm named for my father and that's an important tradition in old families." He hesitated and Lizzy stopped working and looked directly at him. Carmen turned her neck gingerly and did the same. "My father was not a bad man. He took care of us—but he was a drinker—that's what killed him before his time. I feel he left us when he didn't have to. So I think we need to start a *new* tradition. I want to be a good father to this child, so he'll be a good father too." He gripped Carmen's hand tightly when he said this. Lizzy resumed her work and offered her thoughts.

"A good father" she mused. "For a boy, if you want him named for a good father, the Bible says Joseph was a good father, Jesus' father." Wringing out the water from a clean cloth, the nurse gently dabbed at the stitches angrily aligned across Carmen's velvet soft neck.

"Indeed he was," Carmen replied enthusiastically. "Joseph Sweeney, I like that."

"I like it as well," Slim John agreed.

"Now what if the baby's a girl?" Carmen playfully prodded with a smile.

"I'll want her to look just like you," the father-to-be quipped.

"No, a name, silly man. How about Rebekkah? The wife of Isaac in Genesis. The Hebrews associated Rebekkah with the tradition and sanctity of marriage. I've always admired the name and respected its meaning."

"I've heard all my life about Rebekkah's blessing," Lizzy added. "May your offspring inherit the gates of its foes."

Slim John smiled at the nurse in mock disapproval. He affected a stern voice. "Elizabeth Dunn, you read the Bible. *You* can read!"

"Yes, of course," the black woman whispered, careful not to be prideful of her ability.

"Elizabeth Dunn, I knew that you would go far—when the world changes."

Chapter 61

A hive of activity buzzed around the G.D.S.E.'s locomotive when Tilghman and Uma returned to the train. The unlikely duo had eaten, as had Conroe, Godwin and Hope. The locomotive's water tank had been topped off and the tender piled high with firewood; the furnace rid of its ashes. The railroad's engineer, a one-legged Confederate veteran named Silas, was directing the boys on how to fire up the boiler.

Slim John and Carmen were already aboard. She rested on a comfortable bed made up by Elizabeth Dunn in one of the 1st Class compartments. The bodies of those who died during the night's excursion had been removed. The Suffolk dead, Hart, Wheeler and Reid, were headed back to their hometown. A local mortician had sewn their bodies into gum rubber blankets and stored them in the steward's galley. The battle-drenched cars had been cleaned up as well as could be expected, but for the most part the death-rot smell remained.

Conroe had not given up on recovering the gold. The train needed to be returned to Suffolk and he would use the trip back into Virginia to retrace Wolfe's escape at the point where he absconded with the baggage car near Raleigh. The gold must be somewhere along the route, hidden in the Raleigh area, unless Wolfe was able to transfer it to a wagon or take the rails further west. Whatever had happened, that much gold was heavy and Wolfe and his henchmen could not move it far by themselves.

While Conroe waited in the train yard, the always vigilant Confederate operative noticed that a few passengers had gathered on the platform for a south bound train. They were likely headed for Charlotte, the next major depot and the last stop before the South Carolina border. From there the Columbia Rail Road connected trains to South Carolina's capital city.

"Looks like a southbound train's coming in boys! Mind the tracks!" Conroe yelled to his group working on the Great Dismal's engine. Minutes later a yard bell signaled the arrival of a passenger train coming in from Greensboro on the Richmond & Danville line. A black 4-6-0 locomotive, a mighty ten-wheeler the locals called No. 32, pulled into the station with seven dirty red cars.

The Great Dismal Swamp Express seemed little more than a toy model sitting next to the bigger, longer train. But the little engine was chuffing strongly now, its furnace raging, its boiler up and raring to ride, like a fresh pony champing at its bit. Woodsmoke and steam clouded the sky above the depot as emissions from both trains mixed. Conroe was pleased that everything seemed ready to go.

The R. & D. No. 32 held the center track of the three rails running through the station, so passengers had to cross in front of the G.D.S.E. to board. Conroe watched the hodge-podge of military and civilian travelers trundle over a ramp in front of him—the pedestrian walkway across the first track to the center platform. One of them was a priest of some sort. The spy was only a bit surprised to see yet another priest in this little North Carolina village. Uma, John and Carmen's disguises were beginning to seem very out of place, especially since they were in the countryside now where Catholics were few and far between. He was glad he had discarded his own ridiculous clerical outfit back on the train.

Conroe continued to follow the priest's progress. He walked with a cane, though he was a young man. Upon closer inspection, Conroe could see that the cleric was tapping along on a wooden leg. It spiked out just below his gray robes which were held at the waist with a leather belt; the color and style of the robes indicated the man adhered to a monastic order, but there were no monasteries here. Conroe's suspicions grew. He noticed the peg-leg did not slow him down, and he thought again how very young the monk looked. Perhaps he was not a monk at all; he could be *playing* the part like Slim John and Uma. Perhaps he was a Pinkerton.

The Union-hired operatives had a reputation for silly disguises. Spies are prone to be suspicious, Conroe mused, but what a coincidence to find another Roman cleric here. In the espionage business there is no such thing as a coincidence, a good rule to live by, he thought. But then again this boy monk would be a poor secret agent if he expected to go unnoticed as a one-legged priest in gray robes. "Too many durned priests," he muttered with a smile.

The boy priest or monk, or whatever he was, was making for the other train anyway; he was headed in the other direction. The ten-wheeler would be pulling out any time now, so the riddle of the monk in gray would go unsolved forever. With everything ready, Conroe was just waiting for the other train to clear the station and then he'd signal the engineer to begin the journey north.

He heard the conductor call, "All aboard!" and No. 32 blew a short whistle and began to inch forward, heading down to Charlotte. Bells signaled its movement and Conroe watched its red rolling stock snake out of the depot; one, two, three, four, five cars. Now the baggage car—and another baggage car. Conroe stared hard as he watched the last of the train rumble past him. Something was odd—it was a train of red cars, but the last car, the extra baggage car leaving the station, was green—it was green and the gold letters on the disappearing car read G.D.S.E.

"Engineer! Silas!" the spy yelled, running back to the boarding platform. He found the others huddled below the engine gangway. "Silas! Let's get underway! Tilghman, Uma, Godwin, Hope! Get aboard! There's been a change of plans!" The men scattered like fire ants and climbed the service ladders and crowded onto the engine. There was no time for stairs. Conroe blew the hooter himself. Then he clanged the bell and pointed at the Richmond & Danville train heading off into the distance.

"Silas, my good man! Follow that train!"

Chapter 62

It took about two hours for the No. 32 to make it to Charlotte. The smaller express train followed as fast as it could, but Silas didn't lay eyes on the red chain of cars until he entered the Charlotte depot. The Richmond and Danville train was already boarding and Conroe immediately ordered they move Carmen to the No. 32. She was on a field stretcher they'd borrowed from Dr. Carter, though she said she was feeling much stronger. She and Slim John were coming with the spy, the sea captain and the African warrior to continue their adventure. Godwin and Hope bid farewell and Silas readied the train to back it up the tracks again.

"Can't say I ever need to see the G.D.S.E. again in my lifetime," Tilghman huffed as they brought Carmen onto the platform. Just then the ten-wheeler's whistle blew. Conroe yelled over the big train's clanging bell, "We'll have to run for it. Move it boys! Get that woman on the train."

The southbound No. 32 started to creep forward and Uma and Slim John, who were toting the stretcher, broke into a jog like two soldiers carrying a wounded general off a battlefield. Tilghman had already climbed aboard the rear landing of the last passenger car, and Conroe trotted along the platform ready to jump on when the others caught up. They were only fifty feet away now, and Carmen, bouncing up and down with every canter, began yelling, "Stop, stop! Let me off and I'll run myself."

The men, who were exhausted anyway, did as she asked, stopping dead in their tracks and tilting the stretcher low to allow her to alight. When she skittered off ahead of them, they ditched the stretcher and followed at a gallop. Conroe jumped aboard first and caught the woman who lifted her habit and performed a perfect leap at five miles an hour. The jump was an easy one for the lanky Sweeney and Uma landed like a cat. They all looked at Carmen with admiration as they stood on the gangway catching their breath. The woman drew herself up with mock indignation. "I was *not* about to let a man throw me on a train like a sack of potatoes for the second time in a week," she barked.

When they'd all stopped laughing, Conroe told them of his suspicions about the gray-robed monk he saw boarding their new train when it was back in Salisbury. Of course, it was likely that Wolfe and his pirates were aboard as well. They might even try to Shanghai this iron horse, too.

"I want to check the Express baggage car first. I want to see if the gold's there. I expect it will be, but the bandits could be there as well. Carmen, Slim John, go find a seat in a forward car…"

"But I'm part of this…" Slim John objected. With a sweep of his hand, Conroe cut him off.

"You're going to be a father. Your wife is wounded," the spy answered back.

"Your *pregnant* wife is wounded," Uma interjected. "In my tribe this is very important; to protect a woman with child." This was the first time during the whole journey that Uma had offered a thought without being spoken too. Everyone blinked at the African speechless. He saw the surprised reaction from the whites and smiled with self-satisfaction.

"He's right." Conroe finally said. "Sit this one out, Lieutenant." Slim John acquiesced with a heavy sigh, took Carmen's hand, and moved toward the carriage door.

"I'll guard the whole rest of the train, while ya'll are inspecting the baggage car," he moped.

"And pay the conductor for our tickets," Tilghman ordered the younger man with a smirk. Slim John made a face and the couple started through the door. Carmen turned back at the last.

"Good luck and be careful," she told them all.

Conroe's eyes followed the couple out; then he turned to Uma and Tilghman. They were huddled on the gangway between the first baggage car—the train's regular one—and the one they wanted to inspect. No. 32 was moving at speed now, about twenty miles per hour. "We're going in guns drawn," he told them. "One way or another, this shouldn't take long."

Chapter 63

Brother Ced Buckley sat in 2nd Class talking to the only other man in the car about what he'd just witnessed at the prison camp at Salisbury. But the young cleric stopped cold when he saw Slim John and Carmen enter the same carriage. The sight of them swept him back to the previous autumn when he'd testified along with Slim John at the trial of the 54th Massachusetts Infantry.

The verdict had saved the Union prisoners' lives, but it had not saved the black soldiers from the horrors of Salisbury prison. One of Brother Buckley's saviors had already died there and the good brother had been visiting the others to let them know he hadn't forgotten their kindness.

Slim John and Carmen, who were also at the trial, did not recognize the gray-clad monk. Buckley looked nothing like the sickly, wispy-bearded boy in Confederate uniform who had been wheeled into that Charleston courtroom. The couple found seats on the cluster of benches at the far end of the car. Buckley, seeing them in Catholic regalia, realized they were traveling incognito. He decided to have some fun with them. After they settled in, he turned back to the other passenger and smiled. The man smiled back but he hadn't said much. He seemed content to listen to Buckley's chatter. He was a young man, dressed in workman's clothes. Buckley thought he could be a local farmhand perhaps or a smith or other skilled worker, going to Columbia to find steady work. He had a fine head of red hair, a heavy matching red beard. Buckley thought he carried himself like he'd served in the army.

"Now, where was I," the boy cleric continued, speaking loud

enough for Slim John and Carmen to hear him. "Oh, yes. As I was saying, the whole reason I committed to being a consecrated brother of the Order of St. Benedict is because of those men I was visiting at the prison camp. That's what I promised I would do if God saved me from death at the Battle of Grimball's Landing. And in my time of dire need, the Good Lord sent the 54th Massachusetts to help me. Blessed black angels they were. And now look at them." Buckley glanced at Slim John across the car to see if he had heard what he'd said. There was no reaction, so the Benedictine continued in a louder voice.

"St. Paul said it best when he wrote to the Corinthians: 'O Death, where is thy sting?' I tell you it is in Salisbury. 'O grave, where is thy victory?' It is heaped on the mounds of dead in the mass graves of that prison camp. Pray for peace and a speedy end to all this tragic slaughter."

"Absolutely, Father," the reticent passenger answered, thinking the monk was talking only to him.

Brother Buckley had bowed his head, but he surreptitiously peeked to see if his clamorous soliloquy had drawn the couple's attention yet. They didn't seem the least bit curious about him, so he droned on. "So I come to visit my brown brothers whenever I can. I call this train the 'Try-Weakly Line.' It can't be counted on to make its run three times a week as it promises, but it does *try*, *weak* as its effort may be." Buckley guffawed much more loudly than his joke demanded and he noticed Slim John roll his eyes at Carmen. At least he had finally gotten some kind of reaction. "I made this trip from my home in Columbia as an envoy of Abbot Boniface Wimmer, the head of St. Vincent Abbey of Latrobe, Pennsylvania." He caught Slim John looking back at him at that moment, so he addressed him directly. "Do you know the abbot, Father?"

"No, we are from Savannah, not Pennsylvania," Slim John answered coolly. Buckley smiled and continued his charade.

"Oh, the Benedictines have a mission *there* as well. St. Benedict the Moor, which serves Negro orphans."

"I have knowledge of it," Slim John lied, hoping he sounded plausible.

"Our Order has found great acceptance among the Southern people. Abbot Wimmer wishes to establish a new abbey here in North Carolina and a local family, the Caldwells, promise a five-hundred acre farm for that purpose. I am the abbot's intermediary in the matter. What brings you and the good sister to these parts, Father? If I may ask?" Slim John fell back on the group's original story.

"We bring the relics of a saint, hoping to find a church willing to venerate them."

"Oh, my! That's wondrous news!" Buckley's eyes popped at such a story, knowing it was not true. In fact he tried to imagine how the former soldier had come up with such a tale; a real belly-buster, it was. He sucked in his cheeks to keep from laughing out loud. He was about to pin his old acquaintance even tighter to the floor, just for fun, but the carriage door flew open. The trio of characters who entered looked like they could only be connected somehow to the bogus priest and nun before him. Here came yet another priest, and a Negro one at that; then there was a great beast of a man who dressed like a landlocked sea captain. The third player could have been a hard-eyed card sharp or gun-slinger. Brother Buckley felt like the Good Lord had plopped him front and center at a penny-opera stage show.

The gun-slinger bird-dogged the entire car, especially the two strangers at the front, before he sat with the others on a bench facing opposite them. Black leather, Army Colt at his hip, no hat; a bit of a dandy, that one, the Benedictine brother thought. Slim John and Carmen had turned away from the conversation with Buckley, and just as he'd suspected, the couple obviously knew the unlikely trio. They huddled close, speaking in low, conspiratorial voices.

"The gold is still in crates in the baggage car. No sign of Wolfe or the others," Conroe reported.

"That's odd. He wouldn't give up the gold that easily. He must be aboard," Slim John replied.

"He's either on the train, or has plans to meet it in Columbia," Tilghman added.

"Or he has an accomplice we don't know about." Conroe stole another glance at the young monk down the aisle. "Who're your friends up front?" the spy asked through tight lips.

"The religious says he is a representative of a Benedictine abbot looking to start a monastery near Charlotte," Carmen reported.

"He looks suspicious. He is the one I saw get on the train in Salisbury. I took him for a Pinkerton in a very poor disguise. But now

I'm not so sure he isn't in cahoots with Wolfe." Slim John nodded his understanding.

"He seems very knowledgeable about the area. He said he is from Columbia, gone to Salisbury to visit black soldiers who rescued him..." Suddenly it dawned on Slim John that only one person in the world could have told them what the boy priest told them. Ced Buckley. Sweeney jumped up and looked at Buckley more closely. It *was* him! "You're Ced Buckley! You're not a priest!" he yelled at the one-legged boy. Buckley remained calm and chuckled softly.

"Tis true, I'm not a priest. I am a Benedictine consecrated brother, not a priest, not yet a monk. But I would return the accusation to you, Slim John Sweeney. *You* are not a priest. And the prettiest evidence of that is your beautiful wife next to you, Mrs. Carmen Sweeney, who definitely is not a nun!" The Sweeneys could not help but laugh at the entire situation, but the others in the room sat there uniformly slack-jawed.

"You know this man, Sweeney?" Conroe barked, drawing his Colt.

"Put your gun away, Captain. Suffice it to say that the good brother, a soldier I knew in Charleston as Private Ced Buckley, has the goods on us and it would only bolster his argument if he knew that Sister Guadelupe here is with child."

"God bless you both!" Buckley laughed, even louder; this time with pure joy. "But tell me, please, why are you skylarking all around the Carolinas? How did we all come to this?" He pointed to the disguises, and then the humble train interior.

"It's a tedious long story as they say, but in short, we are here on a mission for the government and even now we are looking for a man who not only stands in our way, but who brutally assaulted Carmen."

"I see," was all Brother Buckley said, pondering the intriguing tale. He glanced at the red-haired stranger, not sure if anymore should be said in front of him. The others didn't seem to care who he was or what he knew.

"The blackguard's name is Wolfe, and I'll cut out his gizzard and feed it to the crows when I catch him," Tilghman gruffed. The name shot through the stranger like a bolt of blue lightening.

"What did you say his name is?" he asked with a frantic tightness in his throat.

"Wolfe. He's a Yankee major, a thief, a killer," Conroe answered.

"He's a monster," the man replied, his voice shaking.

"You know him?" Conroe asked.

"Oh, I know him alright, but I never thought I'd see him again. You are not the only ones after him. The man has many enemies. Men bent on revenge and I can't say I blame them."

"I'm not surprised at that," Slim John added. "We think he is close by, perhaps on this train. We think he may show himself once we get to Columbia."

"Let me help you find him. My name is Red—Oliver Redd," he told them.

"How do you know Wolfe, Mr. Redd?" Conroe wanted to know.

"Knew him in Virginia. He broke out of Libby Prison, killed a passel of innocent people in Richmond. Needlessly. He loves to kill." Ohio Red did not see any reason to tell this dodgy group of Southerners that he had broken out of Libby Prison too; that he was a Union soldier like Wolfe; that he was traveling in disguise like them.

"Sounds like him," the spy said. "Sounds like you want revenge on him, too."

"I want to look for him on the train, right now."

"We've already searched the baggage cars and the carriages up this far. We have reason to think he will try to claim the cargo in the last car when we reach Columbia. If you want to look for him now, we'll go with you." Conroe turned and pointed to the others. "This is Captain Tilghman of Maryland and Oko Uma is recently here from the west of Africa. My name is Conroe, Mr. Redd. Let's find our quarry if he's here to be found."

As the men left the car, Brother Buckley turned to the Sweeneys and said: "Taking relics to Savannah, indeed!" The three of them erupted into gales of laughter so loud that the guffaws carried into the next car. Uma looked back at the boisterous sounds. It riddled his mind, what white people found so funny.

Chapter 64

A cold rain pelted Columbia when the No. 32 pulled into the station on Gervais Street. Despite the weather, a military band paraded along the city's premier boulevard celebrating news that General Wade Hampton, in a daring raid, had rustled over two thousand head of cattle from Grant's stockyards in Virginia. The gold chasers shuffled off the train onto a grimy, wood-plank platform.

"Welcome to the capital of South Carolina," Brother Buckley told the others. "You'll see the largest buildings here are the lunatic asylum and the penitentiary; make of that what you will," he chuckled. The search party had found no trace of the Wolfe gang aboard the train. They gathered at the far end of the platform, using its broad, covered porch to keep dry.

"I'll say it again; he won't give up on that gold. He has to be in Columbia, somewhere nearby," Conroe reasoned, whispering to Slim John and Tilghman so Redd and Buckley couldn't hear. As he surveyed the area, he saw that the station, though it was in the heart of the city, boasted an extensive rail yard. Besides the passenger depot, there were numerous sidings, spurs, sheds and wood piles. There was a cotton mill nearby and its accompanying warehouses. The passenger station stood serenely in the middle of this maelstrom, like the eye of a swirling tropical storm. The bandits could be hiding anywhere.

"We need to spread out and look for this gang," Conroe said. The baggage car rested just down from the platform while the train idled, disgorging its passengers, its porters shifting freight and luggage. No one seemed to be interested in the orphan green car though; it obviously did not belong there and no one was claiming it. A yard crew descended on the train, waiting to service the locomotive for its next trip.

The little green baggage car had had quite a run from Norfolk to Columbia, Conroe thought. But its journey would end here if he had anything to do with it. "Slim John, May I ask you to take Carmen into the station where the two of you can watch for Wolfe if he tries to mingle with other passengers? He may be loitering in the street on the other side of the building."

"Certainly, Captain"

"I'd like to remain with my old friends," Brother Buckley offered. "I can help keep an eye on Carmen, if you'd permit me, Mr. Sweeney."

"I'd be happy to have your help, Brother," Slim John answered. Conroe turned to the others.

"Tilghman and Redd, I need you to walk back along the spurs and check through those warehouses." Conroe pointed back along the tracks they'd come in on. If the gang had jumped off the train before it entered the yard, they'd be hiding there or making their way toward the baggage car from that direction. The pair nodded and began to move off. "Uma and I will stay here and keep an eye on the car. You'll find us here if anything turns up."

Conroe and the African found a seat on the platform, trying to look like they were waiting for the next train. The spy peered in through the station window and saw Carmen sitting comfortably with Brother Buckley, who was leaning on his cane, talking to her while casually perusing the room. Slim John was not visible, having gone into the street looking for Wolfe or his men, Conroe supposed.

Conroe reached into his breast pocket and pulled out two small cigars, offering one to Uma without a word. He snapped a match into flame and lit both smokes. Uma seemed to know what to do with the tobacco and they hunkered down to wait for the next move. A few minutes later, the action began in an unexpected way.

Down the track, a tinny bell clanged, announcing the arrival of an 0-4-0 side tanker. The little porter engine eased up against the baggage car and coupled with it. A switchman released the car from the train and the little tanker skittered off like a waterbug, tugging the green car full of gold back along a side spur toward a warehouse shed. "Uma! Let's go! They're taking the car!" Conroe and the African leaped off the platform and ran down the tracks after the porter.

"So, tell me, Captain Tilghman, what's in that car that so danged important?" Ohio Red, Mr. Redd as he was known to Tilghman, tried to make the question seemed unimportant to him. The two men were paralleling a track that entered a large train shed. There was no one else around, though the tall weathered building was being used, piled to the ceiling with cotton bales. The captain didn't answer right away. They arrived at the cotton shed and Tilghman opened an entry door beside the larger portal where a train could roll inside. The men stepped indoors and found a small, dark office; the only light came from the gray-skied daylight filtering through an interior service window. They could make out another doorway leading out into the warehouse, empty of people. Through that door they could see the spur track that bisected the cavernous building.

After a brief look around, Tilghman turned to Ohio Red. "I'd prefer not to answer your question, Mr. Redd, if that is your name. Truth be told, you don't much sound like you're from Richmond."

"I didn't say I was," the red-bearded man answered with a dog-whipped face.

"Oh, I know, I know. You only said you were looking for Wolfe, too. Maybe that's because you're a Yankee like hi…"

The seaman never saw what brained him from behind. He fell to the dusty floor with a heavy thud, sending wisps of loose cotton flying. Then a familiar voice filled the room.

"*Are* you, Ohio Red? *Are* you looking for me?" Wolfe's shadow blackened the small space as he stepped from behind the interior door. The room's dark corner masked his face, but Red did not doubt who it was. A shudder of fear turned his belly. He could see the killer's bared white teeth in the blackness and remembered the hateful grimace that passed for a smile.

"I *have* been looking for you, Major," Red answered as calmly as he could. But the Buckeye's face had drained bloodless. Paralyzed, he watched as Wolfe slowly showed himself in the dim office. He held an iron bar in his slab of a hand. It was some kind of switching tool or pry bar, heavy and hard enough to divert a mighty locomotive. Ohio Red tried not to think what such a weapon could do to the human skull. Tilghman was not moving, out cold or dead. Red's eyes desperately darted around the room searching for something he could use to defend himself. He somehow knew Wolfe would murder him without delay.

"Oh, looking for me, were you? Searching the Carolinas, North and South, for little ol' me?" Wolfe purred the mocking words, glanced down at the prostrate Tilghman, and absently pounded the iron bar into his free hand. "Well funny thing is, I've been looking for you too, Lieutenant. Can't understand why you skedaddled on us at City Point?"

"Got held up by the provost; after them colored boys complained about us," the Ohioan lied.

"And now you show up again. Wouldn't have nothing to do with the gold on this here train? Would it, Red?" Wolfe nodded sideways down the track. They could hear the side tank porter clanging its bell. It was shunting the baggage car to *this* warehouse. Ohio Red tried not to look surprised. So the car contained a gold shipment, he thought to himself. No wonder Tilghman didn't want to tell him about the cargo.

"So who is your friend here?" Wolfe kicked Tilghman's limp body still crumpled on the floor. "He don't seem like he's from Ohio. No, he's not one of ours at all, is he?"

"He's part of the nest of spies chasing you still. They're coming in right behind us. They'll be here any minute," Ohio Red lied again. He knew the others were searching elsewhere.

"Oh, a nest of spies are they? Confederate spies. I figured as much." Ohio Red let out a relieved breath as the killer turned as if he was going to run. Perhaps he had believed the story enough to leave the Ohioan alone and make his escape. The yard engine was getting close now. Wolfe turned back and flexed his arms, puffed up his massive chest. His sarcastic words flowed like spilled acid.

"Well, Ohio Red, I can't tell you how enchanted I am to see you again. This has been a pleasure, but I'm afraid I must bid you farewell." Red nodded, thinking the major would walk. Wolfe looked away again, down the tracks, and Red's eyes followed. They could see the switcher engine now, chuffing along about a hundred yards away.

But the major wasn't looking at the train.

"Blake! Murphy! Come out!" Two men emerged from the recesses of the stacked cotton and slinked over to the doorway. Ohio Red recognized the henchmen of course, but did not acknowledge them. Wolfe waited for the pair to assemble behind him, then he continued his mock glad-handing tone. "Say goodbye to our old compatriot, boys. He's gone over to the Rebels and now he is leaving us again. This time for good." Wolfe drew his well-used knife and the three of them inched slowly toward Ohio Red, backing him into a corner. "Let this serve as official notice, Red. Sorry to report the Board of Directors here have voted, and we'll not be giving you a share of the gold." No one laughed at Wolfe's droll stockholders' report. They were bracing for the murderous assault they knew was coming.

Wolfe lunged at the red-head, who jumped away behind a dusty old desk. He grabbed a heavy wooden document box and fought off a vicious slash at his chest. Wolfe stepped back and lunged again, this time trying to bury the knife in the Buckeye's red-bearded face. Again the smaller man shielded the blow with the box. He was trapped in the little room though, and Wolfe, he knew, would be a relentless attacker. The combatants shifted from foot to foot, Wolfe looking for an opening, Red trying to parry another thrust.

Red looked beyond his assailant, gauging the distance to the door and survival. The other two thieves blocked it. Just then the train pulled into the shed; Red could see steam filling the air beyond the office. And then one of Wolfe's men was gone—the one called Murphy disappeared into the white mist. The steam cleared again and he saw Blake wrestling with a priest. Wolfe had turned, alarmed by a scream from Blake who was on the floor now, being brutally thrashed in the face by this priest—a Negro priest! It was Uma!

Wolfe bellowed in rage and turned to slash at the African, who leaped like a cat over Blake's bloody head. Uma came down behind Wolfe and bashed the back of his neck with a powerful two-handed fist. Blake climbed to his knees and ran from the room. Wolfe reeled forward from the blow like Goliath brained by a rock. He went down to one knee and dropped his knife. Uma came up behind him, quickly scooped up the sharp blade and in a single motion shoved it into Wolfe up to the hilt. The Union man screamed in pain. He recovered his feet and rammed his whole body into the smaller fighter, slamming him into the opposite wall. The major spun around and gaped at the bone handle of the knife sticking out of the top of his thick shoulder like a finial on a lamp post. The frightful sight further enraged him. He whirled around brandishing the pry bar with his good arm. A mighty swing brushed Ohio Red back against the desk. Another stroke caught Uma in the chest, knocking him to the floor. Wolfe saw his opening and ran from the room.

Conroe arrived in time to see Wolfe following Blake along the tracks at the other entrance of the open-ended shed. He entered the office where he found Tilghman rousing from the floor.

Ohio Red was beside the seaman helping him. "Conroe! That's one of the gold gang. Don't let him get away!" Red yelled, pointing at Murphy. The remaining henchman struggled on hands and knees groggily, trying to find his feet and escape, and Conroe pounced on him, drawing the villain's hands behind him and kneeling on his back. Uma had caught his breath and made to chase after Wolfe and Blake.

"Uma! Let them go!" Conroe ordered, watching the miscreants exit the shed more than seventy-five yards away. Wolfe was holding his shoulder, the knife still impaled there. Blake and he had left a trail of blood from where they had fallen. Uma closely eyed the two white men running away. He was upset that his knife thrust had missed the mark.

"I failed to kill the white monster," he hissed through his teeth. "I wanted his spirit."

"I don't think we'll hear from Major Wolfe again," Conroe replied, tying up the captured gang member. "And I'd guess his spirit has long been claimed by the devil himself. Right now we need to secure the baggage car. Tilghman there needs a doctor and this character," he pointed at Murphy, "needs to be locked up. Perhaps this ol' boy will lead us to Wolfe and his partner in time anyway." Uma was still shaking with unrequited adrenaline.

"Yes, Cop-ten, you may be right, but Wolfe hurt badly. In the jungle, wounded lion even more dangerous than hunting lion." Tilghman was on his feet now, holding his head, held up by Ohio Red. The man called Murphy had not said a word, and they all looked out at the engineer of the switcher who had not moved from the locomotive.

Conroe ambled over to the engine's window and calmly

said, "My good man. We've had a little dust up here, as you can see. Would you be so kind as to notify the provost or the city police that their services are required?" The man simply nodded and chugged the porter back to the depot.

Chapter 65

Court of Inquiry

"Seems like half the Union army was gallivanting up and down the Carolina rails instead of fighting the bloody Rebels," Sherman huffed. Slim John had ended his long narrative that brought Wolfe's gang, the gold it stole and the Confederative operatives who were chasing him to that cotton warehouse in the fallen city.

"The train chase does seem like a rip-roaring melodrama, General," Buckley replied, "but it truly happened that way. Of course, Wolfe and Blake high-tailed it out of Columbia after this incident and they joined your army; General Kilpatrick's command near Augusta. Seems their run-in with Oko Uma made them think the battlefield would be a safer place for them. The two were hailed as heroes for escaping Libby Prison and somehow making it through enemy territory to return to duty."

"An ironic point, I'm sure, Brother," Sherman answered sardonically. "But what of this man known as Ohio Red or Oliver Redd? What happened to him?" Buckley paused while a flash of a smile passed over his face.

"Well, this man, also a Union soldier, found *his* way back to your army as well. I have been, ah…in contact with him and it is from this man that I learned of Wolfe's atrocities around Richmond after their escape from Libby. The murder of the innocent woman who called her dog Joe Hooker; how Wolfe killed and dismembered Sergeant Nolte's guard detachment along the Darbytown Road…"

Frank Blair chimed in with another question, "And what of

the gold? Should we be searching the train sheds for this treasure even now? Did this Oliver Redd tell you what happened to the gold?"

"Well, first of all, General Blair, Oliver Redd is not his real name as you'll find out. As to the gold, well, we still don't know where it is. Remember, by the time the train got to Columbia, your force had taken Atlanta, so rail travel further west or south was unwise. Also Grant's army had cut the Weldon Railroad, so returning the gold north by rail was out of the question. I only know that Captain Conroe recovered the shipment. I believe it is still hidden somewhere in this city, though I doubt it was stored in a warehouse. Most of them have burned now anyway." Buckley added the last tidbit of information acidly, which produced a scowl from Sherman. Then General Howard took a turn with a question.

"This soldier Murphy. What became of *him*? What have we learned from him?"

"Ah, an excellent question. Murphy was thrown in the Columbia City Jail and he was eager to talk about Wolfe's crimes. This is important because he had been with Wolfe from the start."

"Did the Rebels torture the man?" Major Luther Stuart asked with a clenched jaw.

"Not at all, my lawyerly friend," Buckley chuckled. "Not unless you count confession a form of painful coercion."

"Confession?" Stuart puzzled, turning his head in consternation.

"His people were from Bardstown, Kentucky."

"An old Catholic enclave," Sherman noted. "The Kentucky diocese is as old as New York's and Boston's."

"Just so, General," Buckley answered, leveling his cane at Sherman. "The wretch Murphy fell back on his upbringing and asked to see me once he had lost all hope in his lonely cell. I went to the jail shortly after Lincoln's re-election—that was around the first week of November, I believe. There I found this pitiful little white-faced man with big brown freckles dabbed across his nose. I remember the combination reminded me of splatters of mud on faded muslin.

"This Murphy had seen it all; all of Wolfe's heinous acts. He was on Dahlgren's ride into Richmond. He tied the noose in the torture and hanging of the mulatto Martin Hill. He saw the Irishman murdered in Shockoe Cemetery. He saw the trampling of Henry and

Helen Robinson when the slaves trailed behind the Union detachment moving down the Mattaponi River. He had testified to all of this to the Confederate authorities and he wanted absolution from God for his complicity in these crimes. I have not the priestly faculties to give absolution, but I counseled him and sent for Father John from St. Peter's. Murphy died of a fever the day after Christmas."

"The day we passed in Savannah," Sherman remembered.

"This fills in many holes in our understanding of Wolfe's escapades, if we can believe what would be hearsay in a civilian court," Blair interjected.

"We do not have to cleave to the same rules of court here, General," Sherman replied. "This is not a trial. It is a proceeding seeking facts, the truth. I think we can trust what is essentially a deathbed confession."

"And Murphy's testimony is all we have anyway," General Howard added. "His is the only first person account of all this, from a bona fide Union soldier. We know Blake is dead. Lieutenant Long over there and the 4th Ohio Cav found what was left of him out in the cypress swamps south of town."

The panel of jurists all looked over at the man whose report had started all of this. Long still tended the door, a bailiff of sorts for the court proceeding. He shifted his feet uneasily, staring fixedly at the floor between his boots. Kilpatrick had dozed off until his name was mentioned in the account of Wolfe's reunion with the army. Logan was just as uninterested, preferring to read and write orders with only half an ear on the inquiry.

Frank Blair seized on the period of ennui and pressed on. "What I would like to know is what happened to Major Simon Wolfe. Do we even know?"

"We do know," Buckley said, glancing around the room, trying to mask his eyes.

"And how do we know?" the lawyer Blair asked. "Murphy did not know. Blake is dead. Was another of his gang apprehended? Interrogated?"

"The source is not one of Wolfe's henchmen, but this source did learn what became of Major Wolfe from an eyewitness who saw the Kentuckian killed in this very city."

"Well, Brother, who is this source and where is he?" Blair

pressed.

"He is here, he has been here the entire time," Buckley said, turning to face Lieutenant Long without another word. The young officer snapped to attention. The movement was instinctive.

"Hurry me to Hades!" Sherman yelled, causing the bracing Long to flinch.

"You mean Long here knew Simon Wolfe?" Blair erupted.

"How can that be?" Slocum snipped.

"Lieutenant Long is Ohio Red," General Howard deduced out loud. "And he is also the alias *I* prefer, *Oliver* Redd."

"You are correct, General Howard, *Oliver* Otis Howard," Buckley replied with a smile. "My Buckeye friend here is *the* Ohio Red who fell in with Wolfe and his rampaging Kentuckians. He knew the full import of what had happened to the Kentuckians he found in the swamp as soon as he came upon Blake's, ah, ah, head."

"Well Long, seems you have become quite the detective, eh?" Sherman cackled, leaning back and eyeing the unassuming bailiff with renewed insight. Kilpatrick sat up straight when the army commander addressed his man.

"The young lieutenant's a fine soldier, General," Kilpatrick offered. "Long's Ohio cavalry saved me from almost certain capture at Buck Head Creek near Atlanta."

Logan also took interest in the case now. "Through his own dogged determination and initiative, Long made it back to his unit after being captured at Mine Run. That's why he's in my personal escort."

"And now his testimony may put an end to this whole bloody adventure," Buckley declared.

Major Stuart rose quickly and said, "I call Lieutenant Tupper Long to the stand."

Chapter 66

Long knew from the start that Buckley would have to call him to the stand. And he knew the murder and mutilation of the Union troopers had been an act of revenge. Yes, he had had his suspicions as soon as he found Blake's spiked head on the swamp road, but he wasn't absolutely sure *who* had done the bloody deed. He also knew the Kentuckians had gotten their due and he wasn't surprised about that.

"Oh, the *scale* of the atrocity surprised me," the red-head related to the assembled jurists. "But I knew Major Wolfe would get his come-uppance when the circumstances allowed."

"And in war, in the midst of battle, when Columbia fell, the lawless chaos of it all; those circumstances presented themselves, didn't they, Lieutenant?" Buckley prodded. Long nodded his head quickly.

"Yes," he answered, tension gripping his throat. The monk tapped the floor nervously as his star witness settled in for what he knew would be a startling narrative.

"Of course you came to understand Wolfe's true nature once you were on the lam in Richmond…"

"And I stayed with the cutthroats just long enough to get back to Union lines," the young officer interrupted.

"At City Point, with the Army of the James?"

"Yes."

"Let's start there. Tell the court what happened at City Point that led to your disentanglement from Wolfe."

The moisture hung so thick in the air that summer day that taking a breath was like inhaling underwater. Wolfe said he wanted a swim to cool off. So the cavalrymen, in rolled up sleeves, traipsed along a shallow creek until they came to a pond that fed from the James River. The whole army bathed in that river that summer. This secluded pond, shaded by birches and willows, was a perfect swimming hole.

In the lead, Wolfe was the first man to see that the army's colored troops knew about the cool spot too, and he did not like that.

Four black soldiers splashed around in the placid water. They were stripped naked, their dark backs glistening with silver droplets that shimmered in the dappled sunlight. Four men, four shades of color, like coffee beans toasted to different hues of brown. Wolfe stood frozen in his tracks, grumbling to himself. The Negroes didn't notice the white interlopers until Blake called out from the shadows of the shore.

"What unit are you?" The sudden intrusion startled the swimmers and their horseplay stopped dead in the water. They stood there waist deep, mouths hanging open; somehow knowing this meeting would not end well. Finally one of them answered,

"We are the 107th U.S. Colored, soldiers from Louisville; Louisville, Kentucky."

"We're out of Kentucky too, the 2nd Cav," Blake answered nice enough. But the lieutenant felt Wolfe's menacing presence even before the major stalked up behind him. The hulking killer stood over the water from a high point of land and stared at the black men, his face contorted like he had just stepped in a pile of particularly ripe horse manure.

"These boys are in the wrong place," is all he said in low tones. Then he barked at the man who'd first answered. "No! You ain't no soldier, boy! There ain't no such thing as U.S. Colored Troops. Now, you and your little niggrah play mates get out of the water and get back to camp. The privy holes there need cleaning!" Wolfe didn't wait for an answer and started pulling off his boots and tugging his shirt tail loose to undress. The Negro leader gave his companions a reassuring glance and slowly waded onto shore. He was dressed only in loose-cut cotton bloomers. The man was tall but slender and as black and taut as a coiled snake at midnight. He stood in front of Wolfe like a soldier in formation.

Wolfe had removed his shirt but not before the black man had noted the major's star on his cuff. The white man's fleshy torso was enormous and covered in thick dark hair. He still held the heavy leather belt he'd just removed from his uniform pants as he looked at the naked swimmer. Wolfe had nothing further to say to the man; in his mind he had dismissed him back to camp. He could not imagine why the darky was still there. He gripped the belt in both hands.

"I am Sergeant Amos Clay, Major," the Negro said calmly. "We are soldiers of the United States Army, soldiers just like you, out here for a cooling swim. We don't wish to share this pond with you, sir, but we require respectful treatment as men in the same army." Sergeant Clay turned to order his companions to dress and leave, but Wolfe cut him off with a loud mocking laugh. He also mocked his calm voice.

"Massa Amos, I'd have kilt an uppity niggrah like you back in Kentucky." The black soldier turned back to look at Wolfe with opaque eyes. The white officer popped the belt in his hands, making Clay flinch a little, a motion that gave Wolfe a derisive chuckle. But the sergeant was not cowed.

"This ain't Kentucky, sir," he countered.

"No, Sergeant Clay, it sure ain't." The blow from Wolfe's belt larruped the black man to the ground before he even saw it coming. Cold-cocked and unconscious he lay there on the muddy shore like a songbird that had hit a window in full flight. Wolfe bellowed with laughter at what he had done and the other colored troops jumped through the shallows to help their leader. Wolfe caught the movement in between guffaws and slashed at them with the heavy leather thong, halting them in their tracks. "Blake!" the major yelled. "Pistols, Blake!"

The other white soldiers drew their sidearms, holding the men at gunpoint. Wolfe took a disgusted breath as if he thought it tiresome that he had to teach the Negroes a lesson. Then he very deliberately began strapping the prostrate man with heavy, full-force blows. Wolfe swung the belt like he was driving railroad spikes, landing stripes on the naked, skinny body so that it bounced off the ground with the force. Blood spattered the air, the liquid oozing in long deep lines across Clay's bare black back. Long, who had not drawn on the black soldiers, stepped into Wolfe's next overhead back swing and pinned the massive arm with his own chest.

"That's enough, Major! You've made your point!" he grunted in his ear, though he was not sure what the point was. The two men hung there, arms intertwined like wrestlers at a stalemate. Wolfe still struggled to land the blow and Long strained to hold him.

"You try my patience, Red!" he growled.

"These men will report this! You will get the provost after us all," the Ohioan reasoned. It seemed like forever, but a few seconds later Long felt Wolfe relax his arm. The major bellowed at the other colored troops.

"You all are lucky to be alive! It's not just the enemy that wants *you* dead!" He shook himself free of Long and addressed the other white men with a laughing snarl. "This boy's gonna water my horse just like back in Kentucky." He fiddled with his button fly and Wolfe's men started to giggle like school boys when they realized what he was doing. Long moved away when he saw Wolfe lean over the man's unconscious bleeding body. The major's vulgarity and his weak-minded followers disgusted him.

Wolfe loudly feigned the pleasure of relieving himself, flaring his nostrils with the effort. He forced a mean-spirited laugh. But even Blake's snickering faded into the rictus of a grin when he looked at the humiliated countenances of the other black men. Helpless, they stood with faces turned away or eyes averted. "That's gonna make those cuts burn, I'm afraid," Wolfe deadpanned. "You boys," he pointed at the three swimmers, "Come get your sergeant and high-tail it back to camp." The horrified men shot out of the water like ancient Olympian sprinters. Though the pistols were still pointed at them, they ignored the guns and instead kept their eyes on the real danger, Wolfe. Not even taking the time to dress, they gathered Clay up and ran off, their leader dripping blood and reeking of another man's urine.

Chapter 67

Court of Inquiry

"After that I couldn't stomach being around the Kentuckians any longer. I believed Wolfe was capable of any crime, no matter how perverse or despicable. I even worried that *I* could soon be one of his victims, seeing as how I had intervened to save Sergeant Clay. I have no doubt he would have killed the man had I not stayed the next blow." As he said this, Long looked down the line of generals who were listening intently, but the senior officers did not offer any comments.

"And then the provost did indeed get involved," Buckley said, moving the story along.

"Yes, the 107th reported the incident to Colonel Revere the next morning. When I found out a regimental staff officer was looking for me, I feared I would be implicated along with the others. I left camp that afternoon, discarded my uniform, found a train south and did not see Wolfe again until he cornered me in the cotton warehouse."

"So let's get to the point, then." It was General Slocum, looking put upon and out of patience as was his routine. "You told General Blair you knew what happened to Wolfe. So far, the scoundrel seems to have more lives than the proverbial fortunate feline."

"He was not found with Blake and the others," Blair reminded everyone. "The Confederates had their chances along the way, but could never seem to pin the man down like they did Blake." Sherman laughed loudly at the lawyer's unfortunate choice of words, but the others were mortified when they realized the pun that Blair had stumbled over.

Sherman though, obliviously continued the off color conceit. "The Rebs sure as shootin' pinned down the 2nd Kentucky in that swamp didn't they?" The army commander guffawed again, slapping his knee.

"That is not exactly what our investigations have found, General," Brother Buckley countered once the commander's celebration ended.

"No? Well, Brother if the bloody Rebel partisans didn't do it, who did?"

"I'll let Lieutenant Long tell the story." The Union cavalryman stretched out his legs, trying to ease his tension, and continued.

"In the ensuing months after the warehouse fight, I learned about Wolfe's return to the army. This was before I came upon the massacre in the swamp of course." Long paused, not sure how to proceed for a moment. Then he gathered his thoughts and started again. "Let me take you back to just after General Logan's force drove off the Confederates defending the bridge over Congaree Creek."

"This would have been three days ago, February 15," Buckley clarified. The lieutenant nodded agreement and continued.

"Even after he rejoined his Kentucky regiment, Wolfe never gave up his desire to get the gold back. His greed relentlessly ate at his soul, like a rat gnaws at a pinhole in a rich man's larder. The next night, when he learned that a pontoon bridge had been laid across the Saluda, he stole into the city looking to find the warehouse again."

It poured a cold rain that night as Wolfe made his way alone into Columbia. He dressed as a civilian again and moved with the shadows, the thick weather no doubt helping him evade attention. Columbia did not sleep that night. General Hampton had ordered a retreat, abandoning the city, and civil order had broken down in many precincts.

The unfinished capitol building lit up with shells coming

across the water from Union guns perched on the ruins of the Gervais Street bridge. Crowds mulled in the muddy streets, respectable people packing to leave, the disreputable ones drinking and carousing Columbia's final hours away.

Confederate soldiers had already torched the bridges and were destroying what stores and supplies they could not take with them. Once in the city proper, the tumult made it easier for Wolfe to blend in.

He had little trouble finding the warehouse, which was empty. An ancient railroad worker told him all the cotton had been shipped and as the Union army approached, no new consignments had replaced it. "First it was the quarry loads, now it's the cotton," the old man griped. "The war's shut it all down. The war's come to Columbia and shut it all down. I can understand there's no cotton, but the quarry's right here. They could still work that hole and ship it out right here."

"There's a quarry close by?" Wolfe asked.

"The bluestone granite quarry's down on the river," the man offered. He pointed across toward the Congaree. "Before the war, that hole produced enough stone to keep this railroad busy every day. Easy as Pete to haul it too. This here track is the spur down to the hole." The man waved an empty hand at a narrow gauge track that led off around Granby Hill and disappeared down toward the river. "Now we get nothing. No one to work the hole. No one to build the capitol building or cobble the streets." Wolfe ambled over to the spur that trailed off from the warehouse, eyeing its path like a dog on a scent.

"This little track only goes to the quarry then?" the major asked.

"Tain't good for nothing else. Only four and a half gauge. The big trains couldn't use it if they had to. The railroad thought about hiding some locomotives in the quarry before the Yankees got here, but the trucks don't fit."

Wolfe didn't even say goodbye. He stalked off along the spur like a bloodhound tracking a coon. Union shells fired from the crumbling bridge abutments whistled and boomed across the way. Periodic flashes of light revealed the rusty rail path descending the ridge to the river.

A few minutes later, Wolfe found the granite bowl, almost

four hundred feet deep. A bomb blast, that must have hit the Confederate Printing Plant nearby, shined across the green-tinged water which reflected stark gray walls. Wolfe descended the tracks a little farther, spiraling down to the last dig site. There he saw, nestled under a bluestone overhang, the little green baggage car of the Great Dismal Swamp Express.

Chapter 68

Court of Inquiry

"Suffering saints!" Sherman crowed. "They couldn't get the gold back to Richmond, so they hid the whole danged car in the quarry."

"We marched in the next day," Logan remembered.

"Where did Wolfe think he was going with a boxcar full of crates, and a coffin to boot, heavy with gold?" Slocum wondered out loud.

"Lieutenant Long," Howard interposed, "I have to second General Slocum's question. Your story here strains credulity. What's a lone soldier going to do with so much heavy cargo?"

"As you'll see, my Federal friend," Buckley answered, "that was the least of Major Wolfe's problems. The men of the 107th Colored would see to that." Howard leaned forward and tilted his head in confusion. "Wait a minute. That doesn't add up." The old math teacher in him got him to thinking. "The 107th is part of Terry's Corps. They left for Fort Fisher with General Schofield in December."

"*Some* of the 107th went with Terry's expedition, General," Buckley countered, "but it seems some of them remained here, attached however informally to the main force. Kind of unofficial bummers if you will."

"Can't say I'm surprised," Slocum sniffed. "Any old no account might fall in with that lot." He was not enamored with

Sherman's foragers, infamously known as bummers. He saw them as raiders who targeted civilians all too often.

Buckley looked at Sherman slantwise and saw the commander open his mouth to counter Slocum, but the monk cut him off and explained, "A small group from the 107th began a new life as swamp maroons, hiding out in the cypress forest south of Columbia. Disenchanted with Union service and resenting that nothing had been done to the white soldiers after the City Point attack, Sergeant Amos Clay convinced these men to desert. The estranged soldiers retreated to the swamp to await the end of the war. From time to time, groups of maroons snuck into town at night to steal food or other supplies. The evacuation that evening made such an expedition easier than usual. That's how they ran into Wolfe."

Amos Clay shook with rage as he watched Wolfe climb over the baggage car looking for an easy way to get inside. The former sergeant and his followers stood on a ledge a hundred feet above the basin floor. The group of black men waited until the white man emerged from the hole an hour later. Wolfe grunted with effort as he crested the ridge at the lip of the quarry.

"Going for a swim, Major?" Clay asked truculently. He and four other maroons stepped out of the shadows. The sergeant held a large fifth of whiskey, no doubt looted from a house or saloon in the city. The black men held the Springfields they'd been issued by the army, though they'd run out of cartridges for them long ago. Wolfe did not speak, but his eyes locked onto the flash of fixed bayonets pointed at him.

"Tie him up," Clay directed with the commanding voice he'd learned in the service. He pointed at a bleached white rope coiled nearby. It was attached to a rusted, wheel pulley-eye bolted into the granite wall overlooking the four hundred foot chasm. The mechanical device had been used to lift cut stones out of the hole. Wolfe, his shoulder still crippled from Uma's knifing, did not resist them; two of the deserters pushed bayonets into his throat if he had a notion to fight. A third man cinched the rope around his waist and then tied both hands behind his back.

"You don't want to do anything to me," Wolfe told Clay, staring the black man in the eye. A raw hatred glared back at him.

"You'll all hang for it."

"I'm not so confident in Yankee justice," Clay answered derisively. "Seems like a soldier can get away with horseplay 'round a swimming hole. That's what General Paine's staff man called it, back at City Point. Horseplay that got out of hand. So that's what we gonna do here now. Some horseplay." Clay took a hardy swig from the clear glass cylinder of liquor, throwing his head back so he could fill his throat with the hot liquid. He passed the bottle around, never taking his cool, dark eyes off his prisoner.

Wolfe's back faced the quarry's edge. He ignored Clay's threat, turned and looked down into the darkness, remembering how far below he'd trudged to reach the baggage car. A quaking shudder wracked his body. Then he turned back to Clay and drew himself up to his full height, straining at the ropes that held him helpless.

"I tell you, boy, ah, Sergeant, my men are coming in behind me. They are raiders riding into town from the south. They're gonna be here any minute." He knew his unit was across the river south of town, but they were not riding in like he told Clay. He thought back to how he and his troopers had raided around Richmond with Colonel Dahlgren. They could infiltrate Columbia too, he lied to himself.

"I don't reckon that's true, Major," Clay laughed. "We seen some U.S. Cavalry down along the swamp road, but we seen Confederate boys lying in ambush for them, too. Partisan rangers, these Rebs, rough looking bunch. If your Kentuckians are down that way I don't figure there's much left of them by now. And what the Rebels don't kill, we will," Clay threatened. Wolfe suddenly exploded in frustration.

"You bloody niggrahs! Blast you all to the devil!" His screams echoed down the bluestone canyon. Clay and the others snickered at his impotence. But the black leader had had enough. He paused to down another finger of whiskey, expelling a long loud rush of satisfied air after the swallow.

"Lead this horse to water," the former soldier called to the man standing by the free end of the rope. "Lead him and make him drink." The maroon hauled on the pulley line and raised Wolfe into the air so that he hung out over the open quarry. The others gathered around with their rifles and poked at the white man who dangled there like an oversized scarecrow. The fellow on the rope alternately pulled up and dropped the prisoner like he was teasing a cat.

Wolfe cursed them and screamed for help, his deep voice cascading down the solid rock walls. The echoes sounded like a hundred bellowing cows, but the continuing Union cannonade drowned out his pleas.

"I have gold!" he suddenly called to his captors. "I'll make you all rich! You can buy your master's plantation when this war's over! I swear I'll give it all to you!" The promise of riches prompted Clay to wave off the tormenters.

"Hold him still, Mose." Wolfe's head dropped to his chest from exhaustion and fear. He panted for breath. "And jes' where might I find this gold of yours, soldier?" the black sergeant drawled with arched eyebrows.

"It's in my pockets." The words slithered out of Wolfe's throat. He would not tell them about the main hoard in the baggage car below. He would only give them what he had packed into his clothes an hour or so earlier. "Let me down and I'll give it to you."

"Let. You. Down." Clay called back slowly, incredulously. "Do you think I'm that stupid, after what you did to me?" He could still feel the pink-blistered strap marks across his back. Even months later, the painful cuts prickled when he bathed or sweated. Clay had thought he wanted to inflict some pain on the sallow-skinned devil tonight, but now he just wanted Wolfe gone—gone for good. He nodded to a maroon holding his bayonet-fixed Springfield. "Run him through and put him out of his misery." The black rifleman leaned back and with a mighty thrust, lanced Wolfe in the belly. The blow clanged against steel and the thrust's momentum shoved the dangling man away from the cliffside. He spun around wildly and swung out with such force that the old rope snapped.

"Nooooooo!" roared Wolfe, who hung in the air for a split second before plummeting deep into the dark pit. The black men rushed to the edge and looked down, but they couldn't see the falling body. The white man's cries bounced off the sheer walls, "Black fools! Black fools! Black fools! Black fools!" Seconds later a faint splash punctuated the hateful refrain. The maroons saw a tiny flash of white disturb the water's surface far below.

"He had on some kind of steel armor, I think," the man who stabbed Wolfe told the others. They were all still staring down at the nothingness in the quarry bottom.

"Steel armor. A body plate? Humph," Clay muttered. "Well that and the gold he claimed he had; that'll sink his wretched body for all time."

Chapter 69

Court of Inquiry

Silence. The mute generals sat frozen. Sherman's mouth hung open, making him look like a gone-in-the-head idiot but for his triple-starred, brass-buttoned uniform. Slocum squinted uncomprehendingly like a possum caught in a coal gas spotlight. A grimace of consternation contorted Howard's usually serene face. Blair's countenance oozed a sort of self-satisfaction though. Buckley noted the rather surreal tableau and pressed on.

"The monster Wolfe had kept the plate he'd ripped from the policeman Hart, hadn't he, Lieutenant Long? He wore it like a hunting trophy, didn't he?" the monk asked.

"I think so, yes," the cavalryman answered with disgust.

"Tell the court how you know this all happened."

"Thomas Nelson Conroe related Wolfe's demise to me," the witness offered calmly. Sherman had beckoned to Logan and was whispering instructions in his ear until this revelation called his attention wholly back to the witness. Logan backed away when Sherman snapped his head toward Long.

"Lieutenant Long," the army commander said sternly, "I can understand why you fell in with the Rebel spies on your way to Columbia. But do you mean to tell the court that you've been in contact with the Confederate operative Conroe since the city fell? Remember, you're under oath here." Logan had left the room, Sherman's hoary voice ringing in his ears.

"I admit, I have." The audible tut-tut from a gimlet eyed

Sherman brought Buckley to the rescue.

"My Ohio friend has an explanation for this, General; a circumstance even more compelling than any personal gratitude he may have owed Conroe for saving his life at the hands of a murderous soldier; a soldier who was supposed to be on *his* side in this war." Sherman clenched his jaw at Buckley's sarcastic comment, ready to rebuke the younger man, but then he wearily smothered his face in pale soft hands.

"Brother Buckley, I fully realize that personal relations have made some decisions more difficult in the course of this peculiar war. Perhaps that is why it's taken so long for the politicians to allow us to win it." Sherman turned back to the witness. "Lieutenant Long, just tell us the rest of your story," he asked with a tired voice. "Tell us what Conroe reported. Indeed, tell us how he witnessed Wolfe's demise." The young lieutenant nodded and continued.

"Conroe was hiding in the quarry that night. He'd frequented the site ever since he'd hidden the car there. He was checking on the gold that evening and wondering how he might further secrete it in case the Union army ventured down into the hole. He witnessed Wolfe's plunge and later followed the men of the 107th, hoping to fall in with the Confederate troopers they had talked about. Local Irregulars could be just what he would need to help with the gold once the Union army moved on, he reasoned." Long paused a moment, interrupted by an audible sigh from Major Stuart, but he continued when the attorney did not speak.

"Conroe tailed the maroons for several miles, leaving the city, and heading south along a road that hugged the river's bluff. The ground soon flattened out and the spy found himself on the path into the cypress swamp that sprawls out from the Congaree River. It wasn't long before the maroons came upon the place of an ambuscade, just like they'd told Wolfe about. One of the deserters told Sergeant Clay that it looked like the Rebs had done the job for them, Conroe told me. Indeed dead bodies lay everywhere. But not every Kentuckian was dead…"

Luther Stuart stood up and interrupted, "Lieutenant, did, ah…your informant, if that's the word, see any insignia, banners, guide-ons or other evidence to tell us which Rebel unit committed the atrocities we found in that swamp?" The prosecutor turned to Sherman, "Surely, General, if we can ascertain the enemy unit that is responsible for the unnatural abattoir Long discovered, we should take up the matter with the so-called Confederate government?"

Before the army commander could reply, Long blurted out, "The Rebs didn't do it." Major Stuart turned on Long quick as an angry wasp.

"Whatever do you mean, Lieutenant? Of course they did. Now see here, young man, I hope you're not letting your personal feelings for the Confederates who befriended you alter your testimony. You just told the court, the maroons came upon the dead Kentuckians killed in an ambush..."

"Major Stuart, that's enough. Let him continue," Sherman barked. The lawyer sat down hard, biting his tongue and pursing his lips. Long drew himself up in his chair and began again.

"The Rebs *ambushed* the Kentuckians, but they didn't desecrate the bodies. Conroe said he found dead men everywhere, of both armies, from the battle fought there. Dead men, dead horses, pools of blood indistinguishable from the black water of the swamp. Oh, there had been a slaughter there, but the bodies were still of one piece. No heads lined up in a row, no piles of headless carcasses. And no, Major, he found no evidence of which Confederate outfit ambushed the men."

"Irregulars, according to your second hand testimony," Stuart sniffed.

"Irregulars, maybe, but Conroe did not see the heads spiked to the ground with the cavalry's own hitching pins. That is what the 4th Ohio found when I rode in there the next day. It's difficult to think anyone else was through there in the few hours that passed." The courtroom settled into silence as Stuart dropped his belligerent line of questioning, and Long paused to consider what he was about to say.

"But Conroe did witness the 107th maroons he followed bayonet several wounded Kentuckians. The deserters screamed horrible curses at the dying men, Conroe told me. Sergeant Clay and his followers laughed and taunted the white soldiers. Their catcalls mixed with pleas for mercy; angry shouts and agonized shrieks echoed through the deserted cypress barrens, he said.

"And then their taunts turned to heavy blows, Conroe reported. One man, in a wild fury, bludgeoned the head of a Kentuckian until his Springfield's stock was caked in blood and brains. Another maroon, Conroe remembered, stabbed a Union soldier in the throat as he lay there. The thrust was delivered with such force that the man's head, half-severed, tilted at ninety degrees. The maroon seemed bewitched by the sight and worked his blade into the rest of the bloody neck until he succeeded in beheading his victim completely.

"Another maroon watched the care the other had taken dismembering the corpse and came over and grabbed the grimacing head by its long black hair. He ran about with it, dangling the gruesome orb at the others, trying to thrill them with fright."

"Lieutenant Long, stop!" Stuart yelled. "General Sherman, must we listen to this disgusting tale which is hearsay, has no basis in fact and which we can never corroborate?" Sherman lowered his head and clenched his jaw.

"We knew it was second hand testimony when we started down this path, counselor. We're putting all the information we can gather on the table right now. I shall dissect the animal later, with the help of my generals here. We don't have to make much of a leap to see that men in such a frenzy and rage, and driven by drink, could have committed the abominations the 4th Ohio discovered."

"It's really the only plausible explanation for such a blood bath," Slocum added. "A crime of passion, fueled by drunkenness. It takes a powerful rage--a wild hatred--to commit such savage acts on other humans, dead or alive." Blair, who had been especially quiet during Long's narrative, had a different problem.

"But I'm still not convinced that we should trust the words of a Confederate spy in this matter. This account makes *his* troops look civilized and *our* coloreds look like rampaging animals."

"*Our* coloreds, you call them, General?" Howard interjected. "They are not ours, and they never were. And do not forget they are deserters. Their criminality trumps both their color and allegiance."

Buckley tap, tap, tapped his cane so quickly it might have been mistaken for the chatter of a distant Gatling gun. He drew the squabbling panel back into the testimony. "There is one more fact, my Buckeye friend wishes to report. It is something told him by Conroe, I believe out of personal attachment more than anything else. Something that, by its very nature, should lead the court to believe his other reports, no matter how heinous and unflattering they may be. It is something that is perhaps the most important and pressing matter to come from our entire inquiry."

"Indeed," Sherman answered with renewed interest. "You're just full of surprises, Brother."

"Lieutenant Long, if you will continue."

"Conroe told me there was a concerted plot to kill President Lincoln. A plot well conceived, based in Washington City, a plot that stalks the president at every turn."

"It's meant to distract us! To cower us! I don't buy it!" Slocum blurted out. Just then, everything halted when Logan returned to the room, clomped to the head table, and whispered into Sherman's ear while shaking his head. Murmuring among the jurists ensued, led by Slocum who continued his protests concerning Long's latest revelation. Presently Sherman hammered on the table for attention.

"Let the court hear that the warehouses around the train depot and all their contents were destroyed by the unfortunate fires last night. Furthermore, the baggage car is no longer in the quarry, if it ever was." No one in the room immediately reacted to this new bit of news, and Sherman who was consulting his pocket watch, continued, "Now, it's late. Let's adjourn for the evening and take up the good lieutenant's story tomorrow."

The other generals were on their feet before Sherman had stopped speaking. Stuart was gathering up his papers with taut, white lips, still unhappy with the proceeding's informal attention to the rules of jurisprudence. Buckley and Long locked eyes across the room, the only men in the parlor not moving. Neither could believe their warning about a plot to assassinate the President of the United States had been all but ignored.

Chapter 70

Court of Inquiry, the next day, February 19

The next morning dawned cold and damp over a smoldering city. Columbia was but a burnt offering, sacrificed on the altar of the Southern cause. What was left rested quietly, now that most of Sherman's army had passed through and gone into camp east of the capital. The city's only sentinels now were the rows of pyramidal piles of uncleared street sweepings.

The elegant parlor serving as the courtroom had absorbed the stale smoke still choking the entire region. Sherman stomped into the smelly room out of sorts. Everyone else, already seated, awaited the army commander, who had been involved in a loud exchange in the mansion's center hall.

"Mother Lynch," the general muttered, taking his seat. "So the fires reached her girls' school despite our best efforts." Sherman snapped at Logan, leaning toward his subordinate. "The most unpleasant woman has a request, Logan. We'll discuss that situation later. Remind me." Sherman said all this quietly to his lieutenant, who nodded and slapped absently at his knee-high, black boots, anxious to get the trial over with. Then Sherman spread his arms to address the whole room, and raised his tone for all to hear. "Major Stuart, Brother Buckley, I trust we shall tie this business up this morning. Where did we leave off?"

Stuart rose and called Lieutenant Long back to the stand. "If you will allow it, General, Lieutenant Long will continue his testimony of how he learned of a serious plot against President Lincoln." The cavalryman lumbered up to the dock to be sworn in again, but before he could take the stand, Sherman stopped him with a halting hand. The young officer retreated to a bare wooden chair against the wall.

"Yes, yes, the plot," Sherman answered dismissively, folding his hands on the table before him. "Major, we have discussed your witness' advisement concerning such a plot and our conclusion is that while we learn of almost daily threats against our president in Washington, this particular source is suspect and cannot be in any way confirmed. Therefore, while we appreciate the information in this matter, we don't feel it warrants any further action at this time. Now, let us proceed with the matter of the alleged improprieties of Major Wolfe, *et als.*"

Stuart frantically looked over at a reclining Brother Buckley, who seemed to be either asleep or in prayer. His bare chin rested on his chest, eyes closed. "Brother Buckley," the lawyer whispered, "they've taken the pea out of my whistle on this one." The monk did not answer or even move. Stuart tried again, speaking louder, his ears pinned back now. "Ced, they're not believing your witness. Will you protest?" Again the young monk did not answer, but he slowly blessed himself, ending a prayer; then he merely nodded at the prosecutor, and stood with the help of his ever present blackthorn cane. He began with a rather obtuse tangent.

"General Sherman, I have just now been beseeching the Almighty to bring peace to our land. I believe you and your army can be God's terrible instruments of that peace."

"That's what I dad-gum sure am trying to be," Sherman declared.

"Indeed, sir," the monk replied grimly. "This somber morning I have been pondering the first verse of Ecclesiastes, Chapter 28, and I would like to share it with the court, if you'll indulge me." He did not wait for the general to answer one way or another.

"Its theme informs what we've learned about Major Wolfe." Buckley slipped open his King James and read: "Rage and anger, these also I abhor, but a sinner has them ready at hand. Whoever acts vengefully will face the vengeance of the Lord." The monk clapped the big book shut and addressed the entire room in a different, louder voice.

"Vengeance, it is a very old word. It has been with us since Cain and Abel. Revenge is the darkest cloud in human nature. Just in this war we have abominable examples of vengeful acts on both sides. In this case, the abhorrent cruelty of Wolfe led to the vengeful attack by Sergeant Clay and the 107th Colored. By some accounts, what has been called Dahlgren's Raid targeted President Davis. Our witness here, Lieutenant Long, tells us his acquaintance, Thomas Nelson Conroe, a highly placed Confederate operative, has reported that in revenge there are people in Washington trying to kill President Lincoln. Last summer General David Hunter wantonly burned the Virginia Military Institute in the Shenandoah Valley. A month later Confederate troops led by General McCausland, who had opposed Hunter at Lexington, just as rabidly torched the unprotected town of Chambersburg, Pennsylvania. Last November, a group of Confederates tried to burn New York City with Greek Fire attacks. Their plan failed miserably, but now General Sheridan, we read in the papers, is burning civilians off their farms in the Valley of Virginia." Buckley paused, as if he needed time to summon the perfect words to continue. The judges did not bat an eye.

"Other forces in the war," he averred coyly, "have not been averse to the use of the flame in subsequent campaigns." Sherman's force by this time was notorious for burning its way through Georgia. Many in Columbia held the army commander responsible for the city's destruction. "Now, I ask the court: Is this war or is this murder? Is this lawful combat or is this simply naked terror wreaked on women and children, the aged, and the infirm?"

If Sherman or his lieutenants were offended by Buckley's remarks, they did not show it. None of the officers deigned to answer the pointed questions, but none of them interrupted either. Every eye watched as the young monk peg-legged his way across the wide, bare planks of the room. In the silence, the blackthorn limb knocked against the old floor like a loose shutter on a windy night. He finally came to rest against the fireplace mantel and waved his cane in a wide arc, making a circular motion like a sideshow magician casting a spell.

"This war has brought to our country a cycle of atrocity and retribution we have not seen before." Suddenly he pointed the cane at Sherman himself. "General Sherman, you have lived in the South. What is happening here now; this is not the South of your younger days here. I have prayed about this. What kind of South will this war give to our posterity, by my generation to the next? As I see it, this will not be a kind or merciful place. Vengeance. The darkness of revenge will descend upon this land. Yes, the South will become a hateful place. The violence and retribution of this war will make this land and its people a vile and heartless region. And I fear most of all that the venom of this vengeful serpent shall pour forth mainly on the black man and his offspring."

Buckley's baritone had risen steadily during this soliloquy, at times reaching the heights like a fire and brimstone Protestant preacher, then sinking again into mortal depths like a Catholic confessor absolving the gravest sin. And then the monk crested to a climactic moment using a noted Bible verse. "'Vengeance is mine saith the Lord, I will repay!'" he cried, as he brought his cane down, slashing the air like a cavalryman delivering a death blow. Sherman, having been set on edge by the monk's emotional argument, and snake bitten by the cane's motion, noticeably flinched when Buckley hit the monologue's crescendo.

Suddenly the room was starkly silent, the court spellbound by Buckley's fervent appeal. The commander and his generals peered at the young idealistic religious with wide, glassy stares. And then the monk continued, calm again.

"Please, I beg of you, gentlemen. See the war as I have described it. The plot against your president, the country's president, is one more example of this unholy conflict's cycle of revenge. It is a deadly serious threat. Search for the perpetrators. Save the one man who will be in a position to end the cycle of pain and hurt once this war is over! Lieutenant Long!" Buckley called, changing tack without taking a breath. He whipped his cane over to the young officer, who suddenly found himself in the eye of the storm. "What did Conroe tell you about his contact regarding this matter? Tell us."

"Only that he lives in Washington city, follows the president's public schedule closely, and is well known in society. Conroe himself only knows him as The Soldier. He is always in disguise, a master of deception." Sherman pinched the bridge of his nose wearily, and sat up to take back control of the proceeding.

"A very compelling speech, Brother Buckley. The court will certainly take your argument under advisement and hand over your concerns about President Lincoln to the Pinkertons." The general sat up straight and shuffled some papers, pretending to look busy.

"The bloody Pinkertons! Is that all?" Buckley barked incredulously. He could not believe the army commander had so little concern about the plot.

"Yes, Brother. That is all I can do with this matter." Buckley's shoulders fell and he sat down, exhausted and deflated. His face burned from Sherman's rebuke. The general moved on quickly, looking to his official court officer.

"Anything you'd like to add, Major Stuart?" Stuart did not have anything more important than the possible assassination of the president.

"Well, no. It's like my wife always tells me. Don't open your mouth if all you are doing is changing the foot that's already there."

"Fine," the general replied without humor. "The court will observe a thirty minute recess."

Chapter 71

Sherman, Slocum, Howard and Blair filed into the court room with stiffened backs and blank expressions. The army leader found his seat and when everyone else got settled he began with a heavy sigh.

"Well this has been a difficult proceeding, a load of happy horse manure." The men in the room were used to eccentric pronouncements from Sherman, but even his closest lieutenants looked perplexed by this odd opening statement. The general noticed their reticence.

"What I mean is the only one who's happy about horse manure is the horse. For the rest of us, there's not much to like; and there's not much to like about this case. Be that as it may, it's time for a conclusion if not a clear verdict." Sherman rose and walked in front of the judges' table. He held a black leather Bible in his hand.

"Firstly, the court would like to express its thanks to Major Stuart and his staff for taking on this matter at the last moment. Major Stuart, I thank you for standing in as the officer of the court. The court also thanks Brother Cedric Buckley for bringing this case to our attention. Brother, your detective work had been exemplary." Buckley slouched in his chair, twirling his walking stick absently. He still smoldered over the way Sherman had handled the news about the plot. He barely nodded his acknowledgement of the general's gratitude.

"Brother, please, if you could stand and approach the bench," Sherman continued, standing front and center still. Buckley reluctantly rose, ambled over and stood before the general like a soldier ready for inspection. "Brother, I've never been much of a Catholic, but it seems to me a deacon of the Benedictine Order should have his own *Catholic* Bible. Not to disparage the King James you've had at hand, mind you, but I want you to have this Douay-Rheims my beloved wife…ah, packed for me."

Buckley's demeanor changed like an ocean breeze on a stormy day. He eyed the tome with smiling eyes. "Well, this is unexpected, General Sherman." He hobbled a little closer to get a better look at the volume. "An unexpected gift, an honor. Thank you, General. Thank you from the bottom of my heart, sir." Sherman tilted his head to one side, considering the young man with an almost doting look.

"Again, I say, the gratitude is all on my side," he said in kindly tones. A lopsided, mercurial smile flashed across Sherman's tight face. He held the holy book close to his chest still. "Before I hand it over, I shall leave you with this." The commander paused while he donned a bent pair of round wire reading spectacles. He pried the paper sheets apart to a page he'd carefully dog-eared. "This is from Jeremias: 'Return, you rebellious children, and I will heal your rebellions. Behold we come to thee; for thou art the Lord our God.'" The bespectacled soldier looked up at Buckley, slapped the book shut and handed it to him. "I hope in some small way this thought answers what you pointed out earlier about the cycle of atrocity and retribution we've witnessed, and how the war will shape the future of the southern regions of our country. God will heal a contrite heart."

"Thank you, I understand, General. God bless you, sir." Buckley's green eyes brimmed with emotion, but he quickly composed himself, took the Bible and blessed it silently, making a humble sign of the cross against its cover. Then he opened it to a favorite passage, Matthew 5:44. "If I may, I would offer *you* a thought, this one from Saint Matthew." He didn't need to read the words, but looked into Sherman's severe eyes, saying: "Love your enemies: do good to them that hate you; and pray for them that persecute and calumniate you."

"I'll do my best, Brother," Sherman replied sincerely. The general offered his hand, which Buckley clasped with a backwards left hand since his right held both his cane and his new Bible. They regained their places in the room and the general took up a single sheet of foolscap, the findings of the court, which he read in a loud commanding voice.

"This Court of Inquiry, held at Columbia, South Carolina, 18-19 February, 1865, finds the following:

"That Major Simon Wolfe, Lieutenant Mortimer Blake, Private Robert Emmet Murphy and others unnamed of the 2nd Kentucky Cavalry did commit or conspire to commit theft, attempted theft, murder and attempted murder of the civilian populace, and assault and attempted murder of fellow soldiers of the United States Army. These men are now thought to be deceased and no further action shall be taken by this court.

"That Brevet Major General Hugh Judson Kilpatrick should have known of the actions of these men under his command and put a stop to their depredations. General Kilpatrick is hereby disciplined in this matter. He is ordered to immediately institute policies to keep better account of the whereabouts, actions, and conduct of the men under his command.

"That Major General John A. Logan is likewise disciplined in this matter for the same reasons as General Kilpatrick. He also is ordered to immediately institute policies to keep better account of the whereabouts, actions and conduct of the men under his command." Sherman paused and took a long lung-filling breath before he pushed on.

"That Lieutenant Tupper Long did conduct unauthorized fraternization with enemy operatives and effective immediately he is relieved of his command and rank and given a general discharge from the United States Army."

Buckley jumped to his pegs, gasping, grasping for words, whereupon Sherman raised a halting arm. "I know, I know, Brother Buckley. It seems a terrible injustice, but my hands are tied in this matter. I can only say that until you've sweated in my hat, you can't judge why I do some of the things I do." At that moment, a deputation from Long's own 4th Ohio entered the room ready to escort the soldier into the street. Shame, anger and disappointment flushed the redhead's face, turning it hot and ruddy.

"Mr. Long," Sherman said, "These men will accompany you to the provost marshal, who will take charge of you until your papers come through. That office will provide you with a paid train ticket to the destination of your choice. I'm sorry it's come to this, son, but a less merciful court may have had you shot or hanged. Good luck, young man." Long stood slowly, meeting Buckley's tortured eyes, and left without a word. Sherman pressed on, though his tone had lost its bluster.

"I can't say much justice has been done here, no not at all. But some things cannot be helped. Rules must be followed, and time is short."

The general rapped on the table officiously, regaining the momentum he'd begun the meeting with. "Gentlemen, this court is adjourned; the army must prepare to move again. Logan, I need to talk to you now. General Blair, cable Schofield. Tell him of this matter. Tell him to advise Terry, Paine, and Colonel Revere to confine the 107th Colored. Question each man. If any soldier has even the slightest connection to this case, try him, hang him, and may God have mercy on his soul." He dropped the document he'd read and pounded it on the table in a gesture of finality. Then Sherman looked around at his senior commanders.

"My aim, now, my Generals, is to depart this abominable place within twenty-four hours." Sherman pushed his chair out, took a deep breath and paused to think out loud.

"In this campaign, I have dealt with delinquent generals, I have defeated tenacious Confederate armies, I have taken great cities, I have managed to forage and live off the land in a hostile country. I have dealt with criminals and criminal atrocities, but right now, God help me, I must deal with Ursuline Mother Baptista Lynch, and I'd rather be chewing on an angry hornet!"

Chapter 72

Hampton-Preston Mansion in Columbia, February 20

Mother Lynch's face beamed like a celestial satellite reflecting God's own face. "General Sherman's generosity knows no earthly bounds! Bless him and thank God…and thanks be to you, Mother Angela." The nun gazed up at an oil portrait of Saint Angela Merici, the 16th century founder of the Ursuline Order. The massive painting, newly hung, dominated the center hall of the Hampton-Preston mansion. An enormous brass crucifix leaned against a far wall, waiting to take its place over the ornate high ceiling foyer. A jumble of wooden boxes, stacks of books, and school desks ascended another wall.

The middle of the room hosted a rank of church statuary, Saint Patrick, in green and gold robes; the Virgin Mary, in flowing blue and white; Christ as the Prince of Peace, a smiling child in regal crown; and Saint Joseph, the good man, the selfless husband of the Blessed Mother. School girls in modest dresses and gray bonnets rushed to and fro, bringing in more school supplies, kitchen wares, bedding and many more books.

The Sweeneys, Brother Buckley, Tupper Long and Mother Lynch supervised the shifting tumult from the foot of the house's sweeping, mahogany-railed staircase. The massive circular stairway seemed to ascend into heaven. A heavy crystal chandelier tinkled softly when something heavy fell upstairs, rattling the floor joists.

"You should have seen the sour look on that man Logan's face when General Sherman told him to clear out," the tough little nun chortled. Buckley and the others chuckled along with their host, the new mistress of the house.

"General Logan and the army are moving out in hours anyway," Buckley noted.

"It's not like there's any brandy left in the withdrawing room at this point," Slim John retorted acidly. Mother Lynch fingered the large wooden rosary that hung from her waist.

"All true, gentlemen, but I got the distinct impression when Mr. Sherman turned over this house to the school that *Monsieur* Logan did not much cotton to the notion. I got black looks from Black Jack, you might say."

"Black looks or not, it was the least General Sherman could do after his army burned down the school and convent," Carmen added with a flash of outrage.

"Or just *allowed* it to burn, Mrs. Sweeney," the school mistress corrected. "Even though he did assure me his men would protect us. Anyway, with the Preston family away and the church in such need, it seemed the perfect remedy, no matter how temporary."

"And everything right now seems very temporary," Brother Buckley said with a serious tone. His attention drifted outside where another brigade of Union soldiers, warmly cloaked in woolen greatcoats, trooped by noisily. The front double doors of the house were wide open and the group could see file after file passing the entryway's frame, the perfect lines of men looking like life-size toy soldier targets in a shooting arcade.

A thousand or more boots kicked up a cloud of dust and mud along Blanding Street in the distance. The staccato rhythm, accompanied by a steady drum pounding, resounded across the front courtyard and echoed off the mansion's imposing Classic Revival façade.

It was late afternoon. A pale setting sun cast thick shadows along the manor house's line of Doric columns which darkened the tree-lined street beyond.

"At least this army is leaving; leaving what is left of Columbia," Slim John mused, looking blankly at the seemingly endless ranks of men moving to the northeast. "And I don't reckon the other army will be back."

Buckley, never one for maudlin moods, rushed to break the sad spell that seemed to be settling over the group. "Here now, this is good news; the Yankee army is leaving and the Southern army is gone. Now that Rome is free of its legions, the war is practically over for us."

The monk hopped nervously on one foot and gathered the hands of Carmen and Mother Lynch who flanked him. "Everyone, we must thank God for what we have left, we must pray for peace, not only for ourselves and our city, but for the people and places that Sherman's blue swarm will trample next." Carmen took Slim John's hand, providing another link in the prayer circle. The former Confederate soldier stole a sideways glance at the former Union soldier who stood on his other side. Instinctively, Long had leaned away from Slim John and was staring back at his Confederate nemesis.

By then Mother Lynch has easily captured Long's strong rough left hand, and the former cavalryman found himself frozen in place, right hand unmoving. Likewise Slim John did not make the first move, but the two former lieutenants ominously locked eyes and did not speak. The others watched the awkward standoff.

Buckley did not wait for the men to make a decision, but blessed himself and bowed his head to pray. He spoke to God, but he aimed his words as much at the recalcitrant former soldiers in the circle. "Dearly beloved, as the children of God, we know we are created in your image. We know we are all equal in your eyes. And so, Dear Lord, we *all* join hands in your praise. We implore the Prince of Peace to give us the strength to offer a gesture of friendship and reconciliation to our enemies, that we may work together to forge a new land of peace and prosperity."

Those in the prayer circle all had bowed heads by then, all had eyes resting closed in prayer, and so no one noticed when each former foe simultaneously, surreptitiously, offered an open hand to the other.

Buckley continued, "Let us pray. Heavenly Father, Grant the grace of your protection to the people of both North and South. We pray that a lasting and equitable peace shall be restored to our land. Grant the victors the power of mercy and compassion and grant the vanquished the courage to accept your will. Instill in us the freedom of forgiveness and the graces of hope, charity and love. We ask this in the name of Jesus Christ, Your Son, who lives and reigns forever. Amen.

"In nomine Patris et Filii et Spiritus Sancti, Amen," Another voice loudly chimed in as those in the group blessed themselves.

"I didn't know you knew the Catholic blessing, Henry," Buckley said, acknowledging a strikingly handsome mustachioed gentleman who stood above the circle on the soaring staircase. A young mother with infant child stood on the steps above the man. The cut of their clothes revealed a well to do family. The father and husband wore a clean black suit, the woman a fashionable but modest brown dress with matching lace-fringed bonnet.

"Certainly, I do have a passing knowledge of the Latin rites. I've always found the liturgy so very poetical." The man's eyes reflected a keen intellect, but dark circles beneath them hinted at the weariness of a heavy burden.

"Everyone, this is the poet Henry Timrod of Charleston. His wife Kate and young William. He and his beautiful family are in hiding with Mother Lynch."

"For which we are grateful beyond even a poet's words," Timrod answered in a courtly baritone.

"It is the least we can do," the nun replied. "The Yankees destroyed *The South Carolinian,* Mr. Timrod's paper. Ransacked the news office, busted up the press. They are looking to capture or kill anyone with enough sense to run a Southern newspaper."

"To crush a populace, they must silence their press. They know this all too well," the journalist replied with a shrug. "The Yankees play their part, and I play mine in this tragedy."

"I commend you on your philosophical take on the war, Mr. Timrod," Carmen said.

"Philosophical, but not magnanimous, not yet," Timrod answered wryly.

"And what is your knowledge of the war as it stands now, sir?" Slim John asked.

"Well, I did have access to telegraph reports and other sources before Sherman marched in, but it seems to me that the good brother's report of a plot to kill Lincoln is the most important recent development. It is a shame it is being willfully ignored."

"Indeed," Long interjected, indignantly.

"As far as the broader war, it is terrible news all around for the South. Schofield's army has moved on from Fort Fisher and seeks to converge with Sherman's force to ravage the rest of North

Carolina. General Johnston's army is brave, but cannot stand Sherman's onslaught, I fear. At the same time, Stoneman's infamous cavalry is raiding in western Carolina and around Virginia's tip, almost wholly unopposed. And speaking of Virginia, Grant tightens his grip on Lee there while Sheridan is still rampaging in the Shenandoah Valley."

"Ah yes, I have news from the Valley of Virginia myself," Buckley interrupted. Timrod did not react immediately to the monk's comment, but went on as if he was still working on deadline. But he did not completely ignore Buckley when he addressed him directly.

"But there is some lighter news, something quite unexpected really. And I think you will be happy to hear it, Brother Buck."

"Oh, well go on then, my wordy friend."

"I know of your interest in your black saviors residing at Salisbury."

"Yeeesss?" Buckley answered with trepidation mixed with a smile.

"No one other than the inimitable Bradley Johnson took command of that dread prison camp November last."

"Oh," the monk replied crestfallen. Considering Johnson's controversial reputation, Buckley could not see how his ascension to command at Salisbury boded well for the prisoners from Massachusetts.

"You seem disappointed, Brother," Timrod said with a sly grin.

"It's just that the man always seems in the middle of the most unsavory actions. He ran down Colonel Dahlgren in that very sinister plot. And General Johnson took part in the campaign that wantonly burned Chambersburg last year. He even tried to raid a prison camp at Point Lookout, Maryland, a *Union* prison with a reputation as bad as Salisbury's. I fear he was looking for revenge when he learned of the conditions at the camp; it being in his home state."

"I know, I know, Brother. The man has the reputation of someone who bumps up against the boundaries of lawful behavior, but once at Salisbury he set about redeeming his soul. He was appalled at the conditions there and went so far as to halt a supply train headed for the Army of Northern Virginia. He had to disobey direct orders to do this for Lee's army was in dire need of provisions."

"Ha, for once the Marylander's penchant to ignore the rules provided for the good," Buckley said with a slap of his cane on the marble tile floor.

"Just so, Brother Buck. Johnson commandeered the train's food and blankets and such, and fed and clothed the enemy prisoners at the expense of the South's most important army. Then he told Governor Vance that he must parole the wretched thousands so they at least might find fresh water, some dry ground, healthy air and have a chance to live!" Timrod told this story with hands flailing, his voice soaring like a poet reciting his best verses.

"Merciful God be praised," Buckley cried, blessing himself amid happy squeals from Carmen and Kate and hearty here-heres from the men. "This is the kind of thing I have been praying for. Thank you for this miraculous story, Henry. It does lift my spirits."

"Glad to do it, Brother Buck!" the poet replied with a slick, smart smile. A perfect line of white teeth flashed below his midnight mustache. Then the monk took over the conversation.

"Now, you mentioned Sheridan in the Valley of Virginia, and I have news from that place as well." Buckley looked over at Long as he spoke. "I have been called to the Valley to investigate a series of murders related to General Sheridan's operations there."

"Don't say? Now that sounds like a good story," Timrod replied.

"Yes, a town of Mennonites was burned by rogue Union elements, I'm told, and some of those modest people have suffered mightily, though they are pacifists and abolitionists and have taken no hand in this war." Buckley spoke still to Timrod and the others, but found it difficult to keep his eyes from straying from Long. The Union man shifted his weight uneasily and looked away each time Buckley's gaze tried to engage him. "General Sherman himself has asked me to investigate the situation and my abbot has consented to the army's request. The general believes that in some small way I may be able to make informal inquiries among the people there, and as a Southerner may be more accepted than a Yankee provost or Pinkerton."

Then Buckley pointedly looked over at Tupper Long and rested an appraising gaze on the young man. He saw a young fellow who had been both on his high horse and down in the mouth since his discharge from the army. Maybe he could change that. "Mr. Long, the general asked me to give you this." The young monk drew a thin dispatch from his cassock and handed the white paper across the still existing prayer circle. Long took the once folded sheet, opened it and read.

"Sherman wants *me* to accompany you to Virginia and aid you in any way I can?" The former cavalryman fairly squawked the question like a rooster just dropped into a coup full of randy hens.

"He told me you are an able partner and believes you are trustworthy, brave and resourceful," Buckley answered with a kindly smile. "Will you go with me?"

Long's mouth hung open flabbergasted. An effort to close it went through a series of fits and starts before his red-haired jaws clamped shut enough to form words again. "But the old rattler cashiered me!" Buckley nodded sympathetically, knowingly.

"He said he was obliged to do that, but knows you are a good man, a worthy partner who can help me deal with Union authorities in the Old Dominion. He will provide you with an official warrant, officer's pay and both of us with safe transport, expense money and a letter to all Union military agencies asking them to assist us in the investigation. Will you help me? Will you go?"

Long clamped his mouth shut again, gulped air as if he had been holding his breath and said with a new power in his voice, "Yes, I shall, Brother." He threw his shoulders back and straightened his spine. It was the first time he had held his head high since being led from the courtroom by his former army mates. Buckley nodded with satisfaction. He saw it as a blessing that he could help provide this young man with a second chance.

It had taken some doing, but Sherman had finally seen the wisdom of sending a former army officer with a former Southern soldier into an area where both armies still operated. Long did not need to know this arrangement had been Buckley's idea and that the compliments the monk attributed to the commanding general had been part of Buckley's argument that Long be chosen for the job.

"I ask then that you go now to see about a train north, if you will," Buckley said.

"Of course." And Long, still in cavalry boots and blue kit, stomped enthusiastically out the door, across the broad veranda and jogged out into Blanding Street.

Chapter 73

Mother Lynch raised an amused eyebrow as she watched Long's unruly exit. "Now that's one happy Yankee," she chuckled. Little William Timrod had begun to fuss in his mother's arms and the nun turned to look up at the family still on the stairs. "Mr. and Mrs. Timrod, Come down. Let me show you the rooms we've set aside for you and your boy. We thought the English basement would give you the privacy a young family demands." She raised an arm, ushering the Timrods toward a rear doorway. She chattered on as the four of them left the room. "We've located a small crib for little Willie too, no doubt used by the Hamptons or Prestons for many years. Very good quality…"

"The Timrods have a beautiful little infant son," Buckley noted, turning to the only ones left of the group, Slim John and Carmen.

"Indeed they do," Carmen replied, looking up at her husband's face while absently touching her growing belly.

The moving operation continued heaving in and out of the house. Another Ursuline sister had gathered a small group of girls in the front parlor. The nun clap, clap, clapped the girls to attention as they formed two rows in front of an ornate marble fireplace mantel. Presently they began to sing.

"It is Compline, the evening prayer," Buckley noted. The students might have been the thrones and dominations of heaven, their young feminine voices ringing like perfectly tuned bells, echoing off the exquisite acoustics of wood-paneled walls and high-ceilinged millwork. A Gregorian chant in Latin spilled through open chestnut pocket doors filling the center hall.

Salve Regina, Mater Misericordia…

"It is the Salve," Buckley noted quietly. "Pray with me, in English." The Sweeneys bowed their heads. Everyone in the house had stopped in place and were praying silently or singing with the choir:

Hail, Holy Queen, mother of mercy,
Our life, our sweetness and our hope.
To you we do cry, poor banished children of Eve,
To you do we send up our sighs, mourning and weeping in this valley of tears.
Turn then, most gracious advocate, your eyes of mercy toward us;
After this our exile, show unto us the blessed fruit of your womb, Jesus.
O clement, O loving, O sweet Virgin Mary!
Amen.

The holy moment ended without further ceremony and as spontaneously as it had started; a simple Angelus, a brief respite in the midst of toil and chaos. The children, the nuns, the volunteer movers, picked up where they had left off, as did Brother Buckley.

"Now where were we?"

"The Timrods, their lovely child," Carmen answered.

"Ah, yes. It must be very difficult for them in the present circumstances." A musket volley of unknown cause boomed in the distance as if to accentuate the point Buckley was starting to make.

"Yes, I feel for the Timrods," Slim John replied, looking out the rear door to see if he could find the source of the gunfire. "Carmen and I wonder how *we* will raise our child in this kind of country."

"We worry how we will provide for the baby," Carmen added, taking Slim John's hand for reassurance.

"Or if I am up to the challenge at all," Slim John said glumly.

"Matthew 7:18," Buckley offered without hesitation. Slim John's face twisted in consternation. "A good tree cannot bring forth evil fruit…You are a good tree, Slim John Sweeney. I see before me a veritable modern day Joseph." The father-to-be waved his hands and shook his head in modesty.

"I shall try to be, Brother. But no, that's not me."

"If we have a son, we shall name the boy Joseph," Carmen said dreamily.

"Joseph John Sweeney," her husband stated with pride. "A friend of ours in Salisbury suggested it," he said, thinking fondly of Elizabeth Dunn.

"Ah, a lovely choice," Buckley said. He hobbled over to the foot of the circular staircase and plopped onto the second tread with an audible grunt. He allowed his blackthorn leg, looking like a gnarly mislaid broom stick, to lounge across the first step.

"Joseph was of course the father of Our Lord. His statue, standing over there is like most. It depicts him as a simple carpenter. He holds a plane and a saw. His images are not like the other saints, though. He is not praying, not venerating the cross or blessing the house as Saint Francis blesses the animals.

"No, Saint Joseph is a man of earthly action, a carpenter, but not so simple as we think. What does a carpenter do? He builds things, useful things. He makes things fit. He cuts materials carefully, not too deeply, not too short. Joseph the carpenter is a man of hard work, fine work. And yet he is skilled too; he is a craftsman, an artist. He craves the satisfaction of a tight joint. He constructs sturdy things; things that last; things which are creations of both his mind and his hands; things that can be used every day by everyday people. That's Joseph, that's a good father. Joseph built the family that nurtured the Savior of the World. And building a family: Isn't that what a good father does? With the mother's help, he builds a house, a home and a family. You can be that kind of father too, Slim John. That is what *this kind of country* needs. That is what your child will need."

"Thank you, Brother," a moist-eyed Slim John answered quietly. "I shall do my best." He held Carmen close. She leaned into him and reached to wipe a tear from his cheek.

"I know you and Carmen will be wonderful parents." Buckley sat up straight, balancing himself on his cane. "Now, I understand you are remaining here in Columbia for the time being."

"Yes, Brother. Travel seems an excessive risk right now."

"Indeed, but what of your compatriots from the train? Conroe, Captain Tilghman and Uma; where are they? What will they do next?" Slim John spread his hands and shrugged his shoulders.

"I haven't heard."

"Well, I'll tell you what I know. When last I saw of your sea captain friend, he was indeed with the African Uma. The captain asked me for clothes. The man Conroe was on the run, they said. The spy was not with them."

"I'm not surprised that Conroe lit out of town. But I find it odd that the slaver and the slave, well the former slave, have fallen in together."

"They have come to an understanding, I believe. Tilghman has agreed to give up the slave trade and Uma has agreed not to spatchcock him over a flaming pit!"

Chapter 74

South Carolina Rail Road Station, Gervais Street

An old black man lit the gas lights on the platform, moving down a long line of white passengers, heads bowed, backs bent, waiting for papers from the Union provost officer. The major sat imperiously at a railroad desk appropriated from the office inside. The official sported a wide white mustache and a pointed gray beard that resembled an aroused fox's tail. The man was flanked by an armed escort, four Union soldiers in full battle gear, rifles at the ready. He barked at a young woman who would not look at him. His thick Irish brogue rent the air like a cold horn at reveille.

Farther down the platform, the forlorn shadows of a raw February night danced like disembodied souls sentenced to limbo. Three Catholic priests, black round hats pressed to their chests, knelt in the dirt. More Union guards lined the tracks, protecting the train and watching the holy men praying over the coffin holding the relics of Saint Frumentia of Ethiopia.

"That Yankee major believed us? Can you see it?" Tilghman whispered out of the side of his unkempt beard. Uma snickered, an uncharacteristic reaction to his new business partner's incredulity.

"I think Brother Buckley's advice helped," Conroe whispered back without looking at the other man. "The Irishman seemed to know about Saint Benedict the Moor Mission in Savannah. And then he bought our tale that Uma here is Haitian, and made the connection with the mission's origins in the African community on Hispaniola. Who would make that up?" Conroe had to bite his tongue to keep from laughing out loud. He shook with effort, trying to stifle his titters. Uma picked up on his merriment and also started to chuckle, which he tried to disguise as a coughing fit.

"We're supposed to be praying here," Tilghman hissed sternly. "Praying over the relics of an African saint." The words spluttered out as he also lost his composure and began to giggle with the others. He covered his face with the *cappello* he clutched. A guard looked over at the men, one with his face buried in his hat and the others' heads hanging low. All three priests seemed to be shivering in the cold, the soldier thought.

Finally Tilghman got ahold of himself and raised up on one knee facing Conroe. "We should board. Savannah beckons. Buckley assured me that the monks there will help us. And the city has a good port so Uma and I can get back to the *Salem*. Oh, how I have missed her. And you may take your gold where you may, Conroe."

"Just so," Conroe answered. "Though the Union controls the place, I have contacts there still." The spy crossed himself and stood and the other men followed, planting their distinctive hats on their heads. Shortly a squad of black porters loaded the coffin and a few crates labeled Baltimore Can Company into the baggage car. The trio stood in the dark shadows behind the train and watched the men heave the precious cargo through the car's side loading door. Tilghman shook his head, unable still to understand Yankee gullibility.

"These Yankees," he sniffed. "Fooled again by black robes. Here we are slipping out of another city controlled by them; without a care in the world, with a pirate's treasure in gold no less."

"They *are* very trusting, I have found," the spy replied, eyeing the armed guards who surrounded the train yard. "I have gotten out of more than one scrape with disguise and deceit. In the right hands, a simple outfit and some well-delivered words are deadly weapons."

The crates of gold safely loaded, Conroe and his partners climbed aboard and found an empty compartment adjacent to the baggage car; the same seating arrangements they'd had on the Great Dismal Swamp Express in what seemed like a lifetime ago. The spy pulled open the car's flimsy door, and Tilghman and Uma took seats next to the window. The darkness outside made the window look like a rectangular black hole. Then Conroe lit the compartment's lamp which transformed the window into a dark mirror. That's when

Tilghman and Uma saw how ridiculous they looked in priestly garb.

"Father Aloysius Gonzaga McGillicuddy as I live and die!" Uma cried in a mock American voice as he pointed at Tilghman's reflection. The sailor burst into uncontrollable laughter, and both men almost fell out of their seats, heads thrown back, knees slapping, tears rolling. Conroe turned and saw the absurd tableau and collapsed on the floor, his loud guffaws sucking the energy to stand from his legs. Outside the train's whistle blew a low-pitched blast. "All aboard!" cried the conductor. Conroe, on his knees and doubled over with laughter, managed to slam the compartment door shut as the station bells sounded and the train pulled out.

Chapter 75

Washington City, March 4, 1865

The mud in Pennsylvania Avenue could have sucked the boots off a swollen corpse. Constant rains had left most of the capital city's streets thick soupy bogs. The Soldier made his way toward the boulevard that angles down from the Capitol building to the White House.

Along with thousands of others, he had attended Lincoln's second inauguration. His well-connected girlfriend had procured select seats where he had perched high on the East Portico of the Capitol. "If I had wished, I could have finished him then," The Soldier muttered to himself. His lean proportions formed the perfect human model for the finest formal suit that Washington's tailors could provide. He shined in this finery, from mirror-finish, leather boots to silken black top hat, to the silver handled cane he carried. Despite the morass of the street, he took long graceful strides, dodging the crowds leaving the inaugural festivities, picking his way around the steaming manure piles sinking into the cold mud of the road.

Standing at the head of the avenue, The Soldier searched for a cab. He twirled the cane and tugged at a brilliant red and blue cravat, his mannerisms overwrought, attention seeking, too proud. His sartorial splendor would not be sullied by the mud or the Republican hoi polloi. That's when he caught Lucy's eye. She had followed him, pressing her wiles upon him relentlessly. The forbidden fruit tempting Adam, that's what she was. But that was why he loved her.

He loved her despite the unfortunate fact that she was a born and bred Yankee. And now she sashayed across Third Street, a peach parasol shading her flawless, cream white face. The comely woman saw him and batted her bright blue eyes, the universal flirtation of the human female species. He stood there helpless as she approached him with the swinging rump she was infamous for, flouncing stylish mahogany ringlets like a girl much younger than her twenty-four years. Her full, curving figure belied that lack of maturity. She walked briskly across the street, but stopped abruptly in front of him and deftly put her free hand on a ripe round hip.

The Soldier pretended to be bored by her. "It's unseemly for a society belle to hail a gentleman in the street, my dear," he admonished. He could not suppress an adoring smile which did not match the sternness in his voice.

"*Are* you a gentleman?" the woman retorted, breaking into a fawning smile herself. The Soldier did not answer right away; he just looked into the eyes that had first sparked his infatuation with her. That's what his mother called it; another infatuation. But he knew Lucy was different.

"I'm more the gentleman than some of the company you keep," he snapped finally, jealously, an eyebrow raised indignantly. This drew a grudging chuckle from Lucy, who decided to change the subject. She knew her secret lover did not approve of her socializing with John Hay and Robert Lincoln. He'd recently caught her with Lincoln's closest deputies in the salons of The National Hotel where she lived now.

"What did you think of the president's speech?" she chirped, tossing her curling locks again. "With malice toward none; with charity for all," she quoted airily. "Beautiful, soaring oratory, is it not?"

"Well, Lucy it's not exactly Shakespeare," he answered condescendingly. Just then a cab clomped up and stopped at his signal. "Let me leave you with true poetry, my sweet," he said, drawing her close. "From the bard's *Hamlet:* 'Nymph, in thy orisons, be all my sins remembered.'" He breathed a heavy sensual sigh and gave her a longing eye. "And so, goodbye for now, my love. If we were not in the street, I'd kiss you."

Lucy gazed up at The Soldier, unable to speak, seemingly in rapture. "Sunday dinner at The National with your mother?" The woman simply nodded yes. The man expertly tossed his cane inside the cab, tipped his top hat and lithely hopped into the doorway of the carriage, hanging on with one white-gloved hand and waving goodbye with the other. "Until tomorrow then!" he called. "I'm off to work!"

"Ford's on Tenth," he told the driver before entering the already rolling cab. Minutes later, the carriage rolled up in front of a large brick building with six round-arched doorways along a whitewashed portico. Playbills for the night's show adorned every pillar of the façade. The Soldier exited the cab, paid the fare and stopped to read one of the posters. He theatrically twisted his long dark mustache while he read… and he smiled:

Ford's Theatre

Tenth Street, Above K

Saturday Evening, March 4, 1865

One Night Only

See the Shakespearean with No Peer

The Thespian 'A Tout Le Monde'

The Actor of the Ages

The Brightest Star of the Stage

John Wilkes Booth

Is

THE SOLDIER

51182143R00195

Made in the USA
Lexington, KY
14 April 2016